Praise for *The Cast*

★ 2018 IPPY Gold Medal Winner in Popular Fiction
★ 2018 International Book Awards: Finalist, Best New Fiction

"A dazzling debut that challenges the boundaries of longstanding friendships. You'll laugh, you'll cry, you'll relate. But, most of all, you'll wish it would never end."
—EMILY LIEBERT, *USA Today* bestselling author of *Some Women*

"This is my favorite novel of 2018. Your heart will grow after reading this story about the healing power of friendship."
—NORAH O'DONNELL, CBS This Morning Co-Host

"In *The Cast*, Blumenfeld deftly reminds us how friendship and love, when cultivated over decades, can transcend even the darkest moments. A heartfelt, moving page-turner."
—FIONA DAVIS, author of *The Address*

"In her captivating and wholly engrossing debut, Blumenfeld pulls the reader in from the very beginning. She deftly handles the perspective of multiple characters as well as writing about complicated issues with levity and grace. This well-told story is timely and relatable and leaves the reader wondering how she would handle similar situations."
—SUSIE ORMAN SCHNALL, author of *Subway Girls* and *The Balance Project*

"By page 25, I'd already laughed out loud—and cried too. Amy Blumenfeld has masterfully captured the depth and magic of decades-long friendships in a story that moves effortlessly between two life-changing events that occur 25 years apart. Each character is someone you'll recognize. Each step on their journey together is one you'll feel in your bones. Blumenfeld has a true gift for storytelling that leaves you hoping it never has to end."
—ELIZABETH ANNE SHAW, Editor in Chief, FamilyFun Magazine

"Amy Blumenfeld's *The Cast* is a heartfelt story about growing up, growing together, and sometimes growing apart amid life's gifts and grief. Ultimately, it is a novel about love and transformation. Readers will cheer and shed more than a few tears for these childhood friends, who come together for a reunion weekend against the backdrop of a dark history—one that resurfaces and tests their bonds."

—WENDY RUDERMAN, Pulitzer Prize-winning investigative reporter and co-author of *Busted: A Tale of Corruption and Betrayal in The City Of Brotherly Love*

"Brimming with tenderness, humor and heart, *The Cast* expertly explores how the experiences in childhood forever shape our adulthood. Blumenfeld has created richly drawn characters who are flawed and relatable and easy to root for despite their mistakes. This is a must-read!"

—Elyssa Friedland, author of *The Intermission*

The
Cast

A Novel

AMY BLUMENFELD

Published by SparkPress, a BookSparks imprint,
A division of SparkPoint Studio, LLC
Tempe, Arizona, USA, 85281
www.gosparkpress.com

Published 2018
Printed in the United States of America
ISBN: 978-1-943006-72-4 (pbk)
ISBN: 978-1-943006-71-7 (e-bk)

Library of Congress Control Number: 2018935993

Interior design by Tabitha Lahr

For
Mom, Dad & Josh
Dan & Mia
With love and gratitude

Part One

Chapter 1: Becca

First came the high-pitched squeak of the brakes, then a laborious chug. By the time the yellow school bus sidled up to the curb, I'd extricated myself from a crouched position on the sidewalk and ended my call. I tossed the cell phone into my canvas tote, along with the notes I'd frantically scribbled on the back of a grocery receipt, and made my way to the corner, smiling and waving at the tinted windows. For all she knew, I hadn't moved from that exact spot since drop-off at 8:35 that morning.

"Hiya, papaya!" I chirped. Emma looked down at her hot-pink sneakers and carefully descended the bus steps. She was balancing an art project in one hand and a damp-looking turquoise backpack on the opposite elbow. *Freeze this moment*, I instructed myself. I blinked away the wetness in my eyes and hoped she didn't notice through my sunglasses—cheap aviators that lacked UV protection but that I wore daily because she had picked them out for me at a street fair.

"We had Creamsicles for snack today," she announced.

"Yum! Good, right?" I took her backpack and flung it over my shoulder.

"Uh-huh. But I dripped some on my shirt. See?" She showed me the spot. "You think Grandpa can get it out?"

"Oh, he'll love that one!" Since his retirement from city government, my father had developed an affinity for the challenge and satisfaction of eradicating stubborn fabric stains. To my mother's delight, this pastime proved significantly more useful than other newly acquired interests, such as playing Bananagrams and binge-watching the History Channel.

"What's this?" I pointed to the painting Emma was holding.

"It's you, Daddy, and me on a beach. Do you like it?"

I admired the three stick figures holding hands beneath a rainbow. "I love it. This is definitely refrigerator-worthy."

She grinned and my heart ached as we passed the shop where we bought her first pair of shoes—a milestone I documented in a small, scalloped-edge scrapbook labeled "Emma's First . . ."

"Honey, I'm going to need you to play by yourself for a bit, okay? I have to make a call when we get home."

"Can I see one of the movies?" she asked eagerly. She tilted her head and smiled widely, revealing the space where she had just lost a bottom tooth. "Pleeease?"

Never in this era of high-definition DVDs would I have guessed that two VHS cassettes—our wedding video, and a home movie shot in my best friend's basement back in high school—would be riveting entertainment for a seven-year-old. And yet, given the choice, my child would undoubtedly turn down a Disney blockbuster to watch inebriated relatives dancing a hora, or a grainy old tape of my childhood friends making complete fools of themselves.

At home, I rummaged through the drawers of our entertainment console and, after bypassing *Annie* and Lindsay Lohan's version of *The Parent Trap*, came upon the old video from my friends. Emma settled herself on the living room couch and lit up as brightly as my neon-clad squad on screen. I closed the bedroom door, leaned back against my tufted headboard, and dialed my husband's office. Erasure's "Oh L'Amour" blasted down the hall, and I heard Emma jump onto the floor from the couch to mimic the dance.

"Hey, Bec," Nolan answered. He must have seen my name on the caller ID screen. "I've got Jordana on the other line. We were just talking about the reunion. I'm getting psyched! We're leaving on Friday, right?"

Oh my God! I thought. *The reunion at Jordana's!*

"Bec, we're leaving for Jordana's on Friday, right?" he repeated.

I ignored his question. Though I'd been looking forward to seeing everyone, after the phone call I'd received earlier, I had no desire to go. I just wanted to stay home with Emma.

"So, you have a minute?" I asked. *This is the point of no return,* I thought.

"Of course," he said, sounding unusually blasé. I could hear him tapping computer keys in the background.

We talked in quiet, solemn voices for the next fifteen minutes, until Emma called from the living room.

"Mommyyyy!" she shouted. "I'm huuunnngry. Can I have an Oreo and a . . ."

I sighed. "I've gotta go."

He exhaled slowly into the phone's receiver. "Do your parents know?" he asked.

"No," I said curtly. The mere mention of them turned my hands clammy. "We need our ducks in a row first. Same goes for Jordana, by the way. We're not ready to be cross-examined."

"Oh, shit," he groaned. "Jordana's still holding on my other line."

"I can't go to the reunion," I said. "I just can't imagine—"

"You *cannot* cancel. Jordana will have a fit if the guest of honor doesn't show up. We'll figure it out."

A lump formed in my throat. I couldn't tell whether the fact that Nolan chose to use "we," instead of "you," triggered it, or whether it was just the realization that we now had something to figure out.

"Mommyyyyy," Emma called again. "I'm huuunnngry."

"Go take care of her," Nolan said. "I'll be home within an hour."

"No, don't. It's only four o'clock. Get in as much face time at the office now as you can."

He was silent.

"Nol? You there?"

He cleared his throat. "Yeah, I'm here. Don't worry about work. They'll survive without me." My husband had never left early. Taking off before seven made him visibly uneasy.

After we hung up, I grabbed some Oreos and milk and sidled up next to Emma on the couch. I'd seen this tape countless times before, but never in twenty-five years had I experienced such a visceral reaction.

The sepia-tinged photograph displayed on the side table—the one of Mom and Dad dancing at Nolan's and my wedding—suddenly reminded me of the two of them on plastic hospital chairs, surreptitiously stealing glances my way every few minutes. The stack of coloring books on the leather ottoman beneath Emma's little feet was reminiscent of the gossip-laden teen entertainment magazines I used to keep on a rolling tray table. And the childhood versions of my friends' voices—Seth's prepubescent high pitch and the sweetness in the girls' timbre—took me back to my fifteen-year-old self. Though I was snuggling on the sofa with my daughter, every other part of my being was back in that room over two decades earlier, experiencing *Becca Night Live* for the very first time.

When they knocked on the door, I was awake, propped up on two pillows and flipping through the current issue of *People* magazine. My parents sat beside my bed, quietly reading hardcover books.

Seth was the first to enter my hospital room. His sterile blue gown was taut around the midsection and pooled at his sneakers like a dress in need of tailoring. A paper-thin shower cap sat perched atop his hair. Just below the elastic band, a capital letter *B* was shaved into the side of his buzz cut. My heartbeat quickened at the thought that pity was the reason he'd done it. When he extended a latex-gloved hand to my father, Dad jumped from his seat, vigorously grabbed Seth's shoulders, and pulled him to his chest for a bear hug.

"Oh my." Mom sighed and placed her hand over her heart as Jordana, Holly, and Lex filed in. I was pretty sure that behind her mask, Mom's mouth was contorting to stifle a cry. She rose to her feet and rested her tome about the Fitzgeralds and the Kennedys on the chair. Without saying a word, she kissed my girlfriends by pressing her mask to a small area of exposed skin on their foreheads. As she made her way down what looked like a receiving line at a hazmat convention, I watched my friends' eyes dart around the room. I could sense them taking inventory, trying to gauge whether this whole scene was better or worse than they'd anticipated.

"Okay, kids," Dad said, gathering his iced tea and wallet from the windowsill. "If you need anything, we'll be down the hall in the parents' lounge."

"There are some drinks in the mini-fridge behind Becca's bed," Mom said. She knelt down, opened the door, and gestured like Vanna White to our collection of snack-size juice cans—the ones that arrived on meal trays but that I rarely craved. "And if there's an emergency or if you have any questions, just press the red call button on the wall or run to the nurses' station. Got it?"

My friends nodded obediently.

"And . . . " Mom began again, before Dad cut her off.

"Come on, Arlene. They'll be just fine." He put his hand on the small of her back, inching her toward the door. He winked at me on the way out, the lines next to his eyes creasing. It was the same go-get-'em look he gave me every September when I headed out the door at the start of a new school year. Though his mask hid his wide smile, I could clearly envision it.

This was the first time I'd been alone in the room without adult supervision in seven weeks—weeks in which I had morphed from a teenager who hunted for lip gloss and dangly earrings at the dollar store with her girlfriends to a completely dependent, sponge-bathed bubble girl who often needed Mommy and Daddy to literally wipe her ass.

I glanced over at my friends, arms folded against their chests, standing in a line beside the wall of Scotch-taped get-well cards. *Are they disgusted by all the bags and tubes crowding my IV pole? Are they scared to come near me, afraid that even with their protective gear they might transmit germs and damage my compromised immune system? Does a tiny part of them worry I'm contagious—the way our cleaning lady did when she quit after learning I had Hodgkin's lymphoma?*

Once the thick wooden door closed, we stared silently through its small inlaid window and watched as my parents removed their gloves; untied each other's masks; ripped off their gowns, caps, and booties; and threw it all in the trash. Mom and Dad turned toward the glass to smile and wave one last time before they headed down the corridor.

I'd learned more about my parents in those weeks spent looking only at the area above their masks and below their cap line than I had in all the years of seeing their whole faces. There was so much you could intuit from just eyeballs and brows. I saw hope sparkle in Mom's baby blues if my daily blood counts were strong, droopy-eyed desperation when I was too weak to eat, squinting fear in Dad's chocolate-brown irises when I had an adverse reaction to a transfusion, and arched-brow elation every time I laughed. But most of all, I saw a tremendous partnership. They could communicate seamlessly without uttering a word. Though they were living a nightmare, they were in it together. They were a committed team with shared values, priorities, goals, and love—for each other and for me. I may have been only fifteen, but I knew that if I were lucky enough to survive, one day I wanted exactly what they had.

For a moment, the only sound in the room was the hum of my electronic IV machine. Suddenly, I felt homesick. I wasn't sure if it was a longing for my parents to return or if seeing my friends in this bizarre setting was a reminder of all that had changed. Either way, I felt like a little girl who wanted to hide in her mommy's lap.

"So? What do you think?" Seth asked, breaking the silence as he spun around on the heels of his Air Jordan high-tops. The surgical booties covering the rubber soles made him turn faster. When he came to a halt, he whipped off the shower cap and bent toward my pillow so the *B* was close to my face.

The girls rolled their eyes and moaned disapprovingly when he showed off his haircut. *Ahhh*, I thought, *there they are! I didn't recognize those gloomy girls!*

"Oh my God, Bec, can you believe what he did to his head?" Lex asked, as if she were embarrassed to be seen with him.

Lex often lacked a filter. I saw Seth deflate, and my heart hurt for him. He tended to let even the most innocuous statements marinate in his head and melt his confidence. "I absolutely love it," I said emphatically, as I ran my fingers over the *B*. I didn't let on that the look was better suited for a boy-band member than for a baby-faced ninth-grader whose mother still shopped for him in the Husky section.

There was no need for me to ask about Seth's motivation. He'd known for months that I dreaded hair loss more than death. We discussed the topic at length before I started treatment. I wasn't being superficial, or at least not entirely. I was a dancer and an athlete who could go from a ballerina bun to a swinging ponytail in seconds flat. I'd release the bobby pins from my updo, and, like a slow-motion shampoo commercial on television, my twisted hair would gracefully uncoil and fall perfectly down my back, resting just between my shoulder blades. No way was I a bald, bedridden kid. If I lost my long brown waves, I lost me. But then one night in the middle of June, while I was watching stupid pet tricks on *Late Night with David Letterman*, a nurse came in with a pair of scissors. For weeks, my strands had been thinning into an old-man comb-over, and she'd said repeatedly it was time to part with it (a pun she used more than once, which annoyed me to no end). I protested repeatedly. But that night, she held her ground. A few snips later, it was over and I was a bald, bedridden kid.

My first reaction was sensory: my head felt cooler and cleaner. I waved my right hand about an inch above my shoulder; the exact spot where I once reached to gather the hair into a ponytail. I poked my scalp, and my index finger quickly recoiled, as if it had touched a metal pan on a hot stove. Hopeful that the grotesque mental images I had of myself were worse than reality, I headed over to the medicine-cabinet mirror. Slowly, I moved to the left, and then to the right, mesmerized like a baby upon realizing the image reflected back was her own.

"I was too chicken to totally shave it," Seth said apologetically. "The *B* is for Becca, in case you're wondering. Solidarity, you know?" He made a fist in the air and then pounded his chubby barrel chest.

I knew how lucky I was to have a friend who was willing to look like an idiot on my behalf. Yet when I saw that *B*, I couldn't help but think about our old elementary school cafeteria. Every year on the Wednesday before Thanksgiving, students would gather to write cards or create an art project for children in need—kids who were homeless, or hungry, or sick and spending the holiday in the hospital. That *B*, I realized, was his art project. I had become the charity case.

Before I could respond, Lex hip-bumped Seth out of the way so she could grab his spot near the top of my bed. It was as if they were competing for my attention. As soon as he moved, she leaned her petite frame across the IV tubes on my blanket and peeled the latex glove from her hand. I was taken aback by the ease with which she embraced her proximity to "ickiness." This was not a girl who ever played in the mud. "What do you think of this color?" she asked, wiggling her fingers inches from my face.

"It's turquoise," I said, and looked at her quizzically. As a matter of philosophy, Lex wore only pink or red on her nails. She claimed it went better with her porcelain skin. She was right.

"'Robin's Egg,'" she corrected, and made quotation marks in the air. She had started doing that thing with her fingers at the beginning of eighth grade. "You like?"

"Yes, I like 'Robin's Egg.'" I chuckled, mimicking her air quotes. We locked eyes for a few seconds. But in that brief exchange, we acknowledged that there was no need to discuss her uncharacteristic color choice; we both knew she had picked turquoise because it was my favorite. "Thank you," I said softly. Lex had a harder exterior than the others, but her core was just as tender. She simply held those cards close to the vest.

"So, we brought you something!" Holly exclaimed, a little too exuberantly, as she dragged a chair across the floor. I was getting the sense that all this cheerfulness had been prearranged. As if they had agreed before walking in that conversational lulls were forbidden and it was their job to keep me entertained.

Holly parked the chair by my elbow. When she sat down, I could see wisps of her silky red hair peeking out of the sides of the cap. "Jord," she whispered forcefully. Jordana was perched atop the windowsill, where she was hugging her long, gazelle-like legs to her chest. She had clearly spaced out and missed her cue.

"Oh, right," Jordana muttered. She reached into her backpack and pulled out a black VHS cassette with *Becca Night Live* written carefully along the spine in her signature rainbow bubble letters. She passed the video to Holly, who handed it to me. Atop the cassette sleeve was a neon-pink square sticky note that read: "With Love, The Cast."

"What's this?" I asked. Jordana seemed a thousand miles away. I couldn't tell whether she was tired or simply out of her element—not that this room, or having cancer, for that matter, was my element, either.

Jordana shrugged nonchalantly. I wanted to put her out of her misery and tell her it was okay to leave. But I knew if I did, she would simply deny that anything was wrong and remain in a quasi-fetal position on the windowsill. Beneath the mask, she was probably making that reluctant grin of hers—that go-to look she did every time she was asked to read one of her beautifully crafted essays in class, or when the principal presented her with some award for academic achievement, which happened at least twice a year. It was the smile that revealed her timid side, the side that was scared shitless and knew that opening her mouth would cause her brave facade to come crashing down.

I loved the entire group, but Jordana was different. Her family became an extension of my own the day she moved across the street, when we were three years old. Lex, Seth, and Holly lived only a few blocks away. We were all in the same class until high school, but because Jordana's front door was literally twenty-five strides from mine (forty strides when we were younger), she was more like my sister than just a friend. I knew when someone was in her upstairs bathroom or doing laundry in the basement. I could smell her family's backyard barbecue in the summer and the smoky coziness of their fireplace in the winter. On the few occasions I threatened to run away from home—for the injustice of being denied ice cream before bed, or the time I claimed my "self-expression was getting muzzled" because I wasn't allowed to wear a bathing suit for fourth-grade picture day in November—my parents didn't balk. They knew that even if they were dispensable, I wouldn't last a day without Jordana. For most of junior high, the kids at school referred to us as Jordecca.

"We're not telling you what it is." Lex pointed her polished fingernail at me. "Just watch."

Holly popped the video into the VCR covered with partially peeled masking tape that read: "Pediatrics Dept.," and shut off the room's fluorescent ceiling light.

After a bit of static, the movie began with a forty-second still shot of the pilling mocha couch in Jordana's basement (the one in which we hid Halloween candy wrappers between the cushions when we were five, then completely forgot about them and remembered to retrieve them only when we were seven). They must have prematurely hit the record button, because the shot of the couch was uncomfortably long and I could hear Lex whispering directives in the background. But then, from stage right, Seth jumped into the center of the screen.

"*Live!*" he shouted, with his hands in the air.

"From Jordy's basement . . ." Holly came in from stage left, landing beside Seth.

"It's *Becca* . . ." Lex joined in, with a singsong voice.

"*Night Live!*" Jordana entered and crouched down on one knee, doing shimmying jazz hands.

For the next ninety minutes, we sat in my hospital room, snort-laughing at sketch after endearingly pitiful sketch. There was a group dance to the Electric Slide; a "Weekend Update" news analysis of ninth-grade gossip; a bodybuilding scene where Seth and Holly stuffed toilet paper into their sweatshirts like Hans and Franz; and a cooking segment that accidentally set off the fire alarm in Jordana's house, causing her father to run across the screen bare-chested and repeatedly scream, "What the fuck?"

The amount of effort they had expended on my behalf took me aback. Did they really think I was dying? "When did you do all this?" I asked.

"We shot most of it back in May when you left, but then we got busy with school and finals and stuff, so we finished it last weekend before Lex's date," Seth said matter-of-factly.

"Lex's *what?*" I rocketed into an upright position. This was major news, as none of us had ever been on a real date. I didn't know anyone was even interested in dating. Though we didn't publicize it, Jordana and I still played with dolls, for Chrissake!

"My date," she said, as if it were the most natural thing in the world. "Didn't I tell you? I thought I told everyone."

"Nope, no idea," I said, looking at Holly and Jordana for confirmation that this was a shocking headline. But it was clear this was news only to me—a realization that was more astonishing than Lex's announcement.

"It wasn't a big deal, Bec. I just went to Carvel with a guy from math class."

"No big deal? Please," Holly said, with palpable disbelief. "Let me tell you, Bec, it was like she was preparing for the Academy Awards. She changed her outfit seventeen times!"

"Yeah, well, it didn't matter anyway." Lex flitted her hand in front of her. "He was totally weird. It's not even worth discussing, 'cause that's not happening ever again."

I reclined onto my pillows. "Can you pass me that water on the rolling table, please?" I asked Holly. I felt a lump form in my throat as she handed over the plastic cup. Never before had I felt so on the periphery of this group.

I wondered if Lex had called about the date and my parents had forgotten to give me the message. I would've loved to hear the details—who he was, how he asked her out, what she wore, whether he kissed her. I glanced at the wall calendar opposite my bed. *What was I doing last Sunday?* I wondered. Oh, right. That was the afternoon Dad threw a container of Tylenol in a fit of rage. He knew I had tried repeatedly to swallow the tiny capsule. He knew my mouth was raw and sore. But right then, six weeks into my stay, something in him snapped. "You can handle chemo, radiation, multiple blood transfusions, and a fucking experimental bone-marrow transplant, and you can't swallow a goddamn Tylenol, Becca?" he bellowed, before storming out of the room and down the hall. There was no point in arguing. I could tell he'd reached his breaking point, and I knew that my normally calm father would return after he let off some steam. I simply took a deep breath like a patient parent who recognized her child needed space to work through his feelings.

I thought for a moment about the dichotomy between Lex's date and Dad's tantrum and wondered where I belonged. Was I the little girl for whom the closest thing to a date was getting Barbie ready for a night out with Ken? Or did life experience give me wisdom, maturity, and perspective far beyond my years, making it seem as if I were a fifty-year-old trapped in a teenager's body?

"You've got to see these closing credits! They're amazing," Lex said, as she stood up and rolled the monitor's stand closer to me. We had clearly moved on from the topic of her date. I turned my attention to the handwritten well wishes from teachers and classmates scrolling across the screen as Bette Midler's "Wind Beneath My Wings" played in the background. The whole thing would have been a complete tearjerker had they not accidentally recorded a toilet flush at the climax of the song.

When the screen faded to black, Seth flipped on the overhead lights and climbed onto the windowsill beside Jordana. My friends glanced at me, awaiting a response.

I searched my brain for the appropriate words. *Touching? The greatest gift I've ever received? It makes me feel loved and secure and like I have the best friends in the world, even if I do feel like a charity case?* I opted for keeping it simple. "It's incredible. I mean it. Thank you. How the hell did you do that?"

Four pairs of eyes crinkled with delight, even Jordana's.

"My dad won a Sony Handycam at his company's holiday party," Seth explained. "We set it up in Jordy's basement. As you know, her house is the cleanest—least amount of crap to have to move out of the way for set design." He leaned over and tenderly nudged Jordana's arm with his shoulder, clearly trying to elicit a small grin, but came up empty.

"We couldn't figure out the camera's edit function, so we just hoped the first take of every scene was good enough," Holly added. "Maybe when you get out of here we can make another video. All five of us. You know, the *entire* cast."

Holly always knew just what was needed to make someone feel better. It was her sixth sense. When we were little, she was the kid who'd momentarily leave a group of friends on the playground to extend a hand to the shy child sitting on the sidelines. Her radar must have been going off now, because, as much as I adored the tape, part of me was feeling marginalized, wondering if I'd ever be able to play again.

Just then, the door to my room opened and a nurse walked in. "I'm sorry, guys, but it's time to go. It's been two hours. Becca needs to rest."

In a single, fluid movement, Jordana ripped the shower cap off her hair, extended her lanky limbs, and jumped to the floor from the windowsill. Her silky blond mane swung from side to side.

"Mwah," she said, blowing an air kiss toward me with her hand. She already had one foot out the door.

Seth followed with a high-five and a promise to call. I knew he would, because he dialed my hospital room every day at 4:30 p.m. As he exited, I could hear him ask Jordana if she needed help untying the back of her sterile paper gown. I grinned. Despite the radical upheaval of my world, some things—like Seth's perpetual and unrequited fawning over Jordana—remained the same.

Not surprisingly, Lex made a dramatic exit. She placed a hand on her hip and sashayed her petite frame to the door. She stopped, pointed to me, and said, "You look mahvelous, dahling," imitating Billy Crystal on *Saturday Night Live*. I laughed. My reaction was genuine, but it was also what I knew she wanted. I could tell throughout the visit how hard she was trying to rise above her discomfort to make me smile.

Holly lingered. While everyone was disrobing outside the door, she leaned over my bed and whispered, "I miss you, Bec. Hurry up and get home. It's not the same without you." And then, like a doting mother, she lowered her mask and kissed my scalp with her bare lips. As she stepped away, I noticed Jordana watching us sullenly through the glass window.

In the weeks leading up to my hospitalization, I sensed something off in Jordana. If the five of us went out for pizza, she'd save me a seat beside her, as if sitting directly across the table weren't close enough. If I told a story to the group, she'd chime in with something along the lines of, "Oh right, you told me that the other day." These seemingly innocuous gestures staked her turf as the BFF with the inside scoop. I figured whatever was eating her would pass, but there it was again—right there at the hospital—in her silence, her distance, and her stare.

"So, how was the visit?" my parents asked when they returned to the room.

"Fine," I said.

"*Fine?* That's all we get?" Mom laughed and kissed my head.

My parents had grown so accustomed to knowing every-thing about me—my platelet count, my urine output, what I ate for breakfast—that our boundaries had blurred. Holding back and keeping a little something to myself didn't seem unreasonable. Not to mention, I didn't really know how I'd summarize it. On the one hand, this had been the first day in seven weeks that I had actu-ally felt like myself. Every fear I'd had about hair loss becoming a divide between my friends and me had completely vanished. It was almost anticlimactic. Their ability to take a look at the new me, process it, and carry on as if nothing had changed was exactly what I needed. Sure, Jordana wasn't herself, but the rest seemed to manage just fine.

On the other hand, I had never felt more out of the loop. Being excluded from Lex's news made me wonder what else I had missed. Did they assume I had no interest in a conversation about what to wear on a date because I was busy fighting a life-threat-ening illness? Did they think I'd be jealous or incapable of sharing her excitement? This disease had shaken nearly everything in my world to the core—my appearance, my burgeoning independence, my ability to simply walk outdoors. Would losing common ground with my friends be the next casualty?

I closed my eyes and pretended to fall asleep—the way I did whenever a social worker stopped by to chat, or when a circus clown visiting the pediatric ward knocked on my door. This time, however, I wasn't avoiding those well-intentioned professionals. No, this time, when I shut my eyes, all I saw were my friends.

I envisioned them schlepping into Manhattan from Queens that morning via the Q46 bus, then two subway lines operating on the excruciatingly slow weekend schedule, and braving a three-av-enue walk to the hospital in what I heard was quite the heat wave.

I looped the image of them donning those blue gowns, their eyes peeking over the masks and darting from wall to wall, ceiling to floor. To me, every inch of the ten-by-ten-foot sterile space was loaded. Even if we looked at the same objects, they wouldn't see what I saw.

To me, the cerulean-blue vinyl recliner in the corner by the window wasn't simply a chair; it was the bed my parents took turns sleeping on every night so that I was never alone. The algebra and biology textbooks piled high on the radiator weren't just study guides; they belonged to the residents and nurses who, for the entire month of June, spent their breaks helping me prepare for my New York State Regents Exams so I wouldn't fall behind at school. And that dent in the wall beside my bed? I created that the night I shook so violently from chemo that the footboard banged against the wall and chipped the paint. I remember Mom throwing her five-foot-two-inch frame atop my blankets, pinning down all eighty-seven pounds of me with the force of a professional wrestler, and in a single breath emitting the most desperate string of words I had ever heard: "Don't you dare leave me Goddammit Becca you stay with me do you understand don't you do this!"

I wanted so badly to tell her how I felt trapped in a foreign, defective shell. How the real me was right there, just beneath the shaky surface, ready to run and dance and be a kid. But I lacked the energy. I didn't have the words to explain the divide. Instead, I summoned every bit of strength, grabbed her hand, and whispered, "Ma, I'm here."

Despite my best efforts, I couldn't sleep. The warmth of the midafternoon sun streamed through the window, and when I opened my eyes I noticed Mom and Dad had assumed their positions beside my bed and were quietly reading, just as they had been that morning.

"No nap today?" Dad asked, looking at me over his glasses.

I shook my head.

"Well, I hear there's a new movie out and it's gotten rave reviews," he said, closing his book and carefully placing it on the windowsill. "Just so happens we were able to snag a copy." He smiled and waved the *Becca Night Live* cassette in his hand.

It was a good idea. I wanted Mom and Dad to see it. I wanted them to know I had others in my corner, and that they didn't have to carry the entire burden of buoying my spirits.

About a half-hour in, a nurse entered to check my vital signs.

"In all my years, I've never seen anything like this," she remarked, watching the movie, instead of the dial on my blood pressure cuff. "I wish I'd had a group like this when I was fifteen. I bet you'll be friends for life."

When she left the room, I shifted toward the wall so that my back faced my parents. I didn't want them to see me dab the tear pooling in my right eye.

Friends for life assumed so many things. Life, for one thing. But even if I survived, and even if this ugly, scary, acute stage didn't turn my friends away, I wondered if the ripple effects eventually could. Would this crazy experience be just another childhood memory we shared, like trick-or-treating on Halloween or trips to the beach? Or would my cancer become the game-changer—the pivotal event we could all point to as the cataclysmic moment when everything was permanently altered?

The sound of a turning key unlocking our apartment door jolted me out of my stupor, and I stopped the VHS tape.

"I'm home," Nolan called out. A second later, the door slammed shut.

"Daddy!" Emma hollered, and ran into the foyer. He dropped his black messenger-style work bag onto the floor, kicked off his shoes, and lifted her in the air above his head.

"I'm taking my girls out for dinner," he announced, flipping Emma upside down and tickling her belly. She squealed with delight. As he set her feet back onto the floor, his cell phone rang in the outer pocket of his bag. I caught him glancing at it and then looking away.

"Sugar and Plumm! Please! Sugar and Plumm!" She jumped up and down ecstatically. It was no surprise she'd selected our favorite local bistro, known for its decadent desserts.

"Sounds good to me! Now go get dressed," he said.

As Emma scurried off, Nolan's phone rang again, but this time he didn't even look at the bag. Instead, he gripped my face and leaned in so that our eyes were only inches apart.

"She can't know," he whispered firmly. "Not yet."

I nodded in agreement, and we both blinked away tears. A moment later, Emma skipped back into the hallway, wearing a sundress and glittery flip-flops and carrying a small zippered clutch—an Estée Lauder freebie my mother had received with the purchase of two lipsticks and passed along to her granddaughter for dress-up.

"Well, look at the lovely Ms. Scardino," Nolan said, admiring our daughter. Emma curtsied. "Sugar and Plumm, here we come!"

I grabbed my bag, and as we walked through the doorway, his phone rang again. "I'll get that for you," I said. Nolan's cell was practically an appendage. He never left home without it and never ignored a call.

"Don't bother," he said, and raced Emma down the corridor to the elevator bank.

Emma danced for the elevator's security camera as we rode down to the lobby and high-fived Eddie, our doorman, when we passed him at the front desk.

"Enjoy your evening, folks," he said, and playfully stuck his tongue out at Emma. She giggled, and the three of us waved good-bye, heading out onto the warm city streets as if this had been just another ordinary day.

Chapter 2: Nolan

The first time I saw the video was a few days after our college graduation. I didn't actually *watch* it; I merely became aware of its existence. I was helping Becca pack up her dorm room and noticed a cassette on her bookshelf, sandwiched between a high school yearbook and a Roget's thesaurus.

"What's this?" I asked, holding the tape in my hand. I was about to transfer it into a plastic carton with other books but stopped to inspect a slightly oxidized pink sticky note on the outer sleeve. The note's edges had begun to curl, and there was a tiny tear fastidiously repaired with glue beneath the words "With Love, The Cast."

Becca had been standing on her twin bed, simultaneously removing a wall poster of Vincent van Gogh's *Starry Night* and swaying to the Dave Matthews album we were playing on her portable CD player. When she pivoted toward me and noticed the videotape in my hand, she froze as if I had aimed a remote control in her direction and pressed pause.

After a few seconds, she said, "Oh, that's just something my friends made," and tucked a strand of loose hair behind her ear. "Would you mind sticking that on top of my backpack, instead of in the carton? I'm going to carry it with me. Don't want it to get lost."

Had she been one of my friends, I would have known whether to proceed with a joke or a follow-up question or simply leave it alone. But we'd met only a few days earlier and I didn't have a handle on her yet. Her evasiveness had piqued my curiosity, but I wasn't going to push. Slow and steady, I decided, would be my approach. There was something different about this girl.

Our introduction was improbable for a hundred different reasons. It was Senior Week at Columbia University—a series of celebrations in the days leading up to commencement—and I certainly didn't expect to meet my future wife during Game Show Night in the student center auditorium.

The five-hundred-seat theater was packed. After my buddies and I settled into the last available row, the curtains opened halfway to reveal three barstools and a screen partition. The house lights dimmed, and a spotlight shone on our school mascot—a six-foot, furry lion—frantically running through the aisles, searching for participants. Some students jumped or hooted to attract his attention; others sank in their seats and lowered baseball caps over their eyes. The lion pulled the first two contestants and then slowly roamed the auditorium for his final prey. As he neared the rear of the theater, he stopped, dramatically placed a paw over his brow, and did a gradual 360-degree turn to search the cheering crowd. When his spin came full circle, he planted his foot on the floor, extended his arm, and pointed down the row, directly at me. Flooded with adrenaline, I jogged up to the stage and took my place on the last stool, where I nodded to my buddies chanting my name.

"Welcome to the Dating Game!" the emcee announced, and a familiar tune began to play on the sound system overhead. I immediately flashed back to being a kid home from school on a snow day, watching daytime television in my parents' family room as the aroma of Mom's homemade minestrone soup filled the house. "Please give a warm welcome to our three lucky bachelors and our lovely bachelorette, Becca!"

"Hi, I . . ." was all I heard before high-pitched audio feedback reverberated through the room and everyone cringed.

"Um, hi," the girl on the other side of the screen repeated softly. Her voice didn't sound familiar. "This first question is for all three bachelors, but I'll start with Bachelor Number One. Which well-known—"

"We can't hear you!" several people shouted from the audience. "Speak up!"

She cleared her throat. I sensed she was nervous, and imagined an index card shaking in her hand.

"Okay," she continued. "Which well-known character—real or fictional—most closely resembles who you are, and why? Bachelor Number One?"

"Uh, hi. I have a question. Do you mean, like, physically resembles me or resembles my personality?"

"I'll leave that up to you," she replied, sounding more confident now. "Define it however you want."

"Hmm, okay. Well, I guess I'd say the Fonz, from *Happy Days*. Chicks dig me, I look good in leather, and I learned to ride a motorcycle before I could drive a car."

The crowd moaned.

What a loser, I thought. *"I look good in leather"? Who says that?*

"Interesting," she responded diplomatically, "Okay, Bachelor Number Two, same question."

"I'd have to say Ringo Starr," Number Two said, with a thick English accent. "I'm from outside London. I'm a drummah, I've been told on occasion that I have puppy-dog eyes, and I suppose I can be quite goofy."

"Nice," she said, sounding intrigued. I could almost feel her smile. "Bachelor Number Three, your turn."

I threw my shoulders back and sat up straight.

"First of all, hello. It's very nice to meet you," I said, and hoped my slight lisp wasn't apparent. "I would say I'm a combination of a few. Is that allowed?"

"Sure, that's all right," she said. "Go ahead."

I could tell she came from somewhere in the metropolitan area when she said "*awl* right." It was subtle, but her New York accent was unmistakable. As a Jersey boy, I felt at home with it.

"First, I'd say I'm a little Chevy Chase because I'm tall, with a similar build, and I tend to trip over myself and fall into things. Next, I'd say I'm a bit Alex P. Keaton, from *Family Ties*, because I was the only kid growing up who wanted to wear a clip-on necktie and a sport jacket on class picture day; plus, I liked being on student government. And third, I'd say there's definitely a part of me that's Harold, from *Harold and the Purple Crayon* . . . I don't know if you've ever read it, but it was my favorite book when I was little."

On one of our first dates, I learned that I'd sealed the deal with *Harold and the Purple Crayon*—a book about the power of imagination and the belief that anything is possible. She told me my answers had been "charming," and that she'd noticed people in the audience smile and sort of light up when I mentioned Harold.

After Becca announced the winner and bade farewell to the Fonz and Ringo, I emerged from behind the screen in my baseball cap, jeans, and red Lawrenceville T-shirt—which I'd bought in triplicate from my high school because the cut made my midsection appear more buff. I glanced over at the delicate, freckle-faced brunette wearing a miniskirt and pearls. She was attractive—not 007 James Bond–girl hot, like my last girlfriend, but very pretty, with a natural elegance. Had I not been standing on a stage in front of five hundred people, I would have offered to buy her a drink and found a quiet corner to talk. But, given the circumstances—and the fact that my buddies were standing on their seats, doing a lascivious, grinding dance while shouting my nickname, Dee-no (a derivative of my last name, Scardino)—I had to ham it up.

Not one to disappoint, I turned to the audience, dramatically dropped my jaw, and motioned with my thumb in her direction, as if to say, *Get a load of this! I hit the jackpot!* Then I lifted up her petite frame and carried her off the stage, to a soundtrack of hollers and whistles from the crowd. Thankfully, she didn't protest. In fact, she laughed and played along, which I found endearing. I don't know if it was the setting, if I admired her for having guts to get up in front of that crowd, if it was a look in her eye that made her seem real, or if I was just a sucker for a short skirt and pearls, but I was overcome with a sense of wanting to protect her. We exchanged numbers, and when I called a few days later, she mentioned that she'd just begun packing up her dorm room. I offered to come over and help, and we now think of that afternoon as our first date. We sat in shorts and T-shirts on the edge of her extra-long dorm mattress, sifting through her music collection and discussing the books we were packing into cartons. We ordered pizza from V & T's on Amsterdam Avenue, and by the end of the day I was smitten.

It wasn't until our third date—when we were beginning to think we had fallen for each other—that the video came up again in conversation. It was Fourth of July weekend, and the city felt like a ghost town. The weather was perfect: sunny, warm, low humidity, and ideal for the picnic I'd planned for us in Central Park. Becca and I were living just blocks away from each other in apartments on the Upper West Side of Manhattan and working as summer interns. She was shadowing a television producer at *Good Morning America,* and I was the head counselor at a YMCA day camp. I'd been offered a coveted research position at a big litigation firm but turned it down. My buddies thought I was insane for passing up such a plum résumé-builder, but I'd spent every summer of college working at large firms or in local government to boost my law school application. Now that I had been accepted to my top-choice school, I wanted to clear my head before I was enmeshed in torts and contracts for the rest of my life.

When I arrived at her apartment that afternoon, she looked particularly cute in denim overalls, a fitted white shirt, and a new haircut—that shoulder-length style that made all the girls I knew look like they had just walked out of a casting call for *Friends.*

"Hey," she said, welcoming me with a kiss. "Sorry, I need a couple more minutes. The phone's been nonstop this morning."

"Take your time; there's no rush." I placed a grocery bag filled with cheeses, olives, and a two-foot French baguette on the tiny kitchen counter. I knew nothing about gourmet food, so I had spent half an hour with a sommelier at a shop on Columbus Avenue, trying to pair the right wine with the cheeses.

As she headed into the bathroom, I took in her one-room studio, which was super-small but tastefully decorated in a style she described as "high-end IKEA with a splash of Pottery Barn." It definitely trumped the five-story walk-up I shared with a roommate and a bunch of mice. I gazed at the framed photographs of no one I knew lined up along the radiator cover and then noticed a video sticking out of the VCR tape deck. I picked up the cassette sleeve from the coffee table and realized it was the same one I'd asked about when we'd packed up her dorm.

"Okay, I'm ready. Let's go!" she said, bouncing out of the bathroom.

"Isn't this the video your friends made?" I asked, holding up the cardboard sleeve. "The one from your bookshelf?" Something about that tape still made me curious.

Becca looked toward the VCR, and when she opened her mouth to speak, the phone rang. She glanced at the caller ID and picked it up.

"Hey, Jord," she said. "Uh-huh. Yes, a picnic. Leaving as soon as I hang up with you." She paused, then said, "Really? I don't know. . . . Okay, fine."

Becca stretched the landline's coiled cord from the wall beside her bed to where I was sitting on the couch. "Call's for you." She smiled. "It's Jordana."

For me? I mouthed, taken aback. Becca had mentioned that an old friend of hers was going to be in my law school class, but I hadn't been expecting to speak with her now.

She nodded, pointing to a chiseled-cheeked, sylphlike blonde in one of the photos on her windowsill.

"Hi, Jordy!" I said, as if we were old pals. "How ya doin'? I feel like I know you! Becca's told me so much about you."

"Me too," Jordana said. Her voice had a soothing, full-bodied tone, like a yoga instructor's. "So, Becca tells me we're going to be in the same class."

"I know. You get your schedule yet?"

"No, not yet," she said. "Someone told me it should arrive in a couple of weeks."

"Yeah, I heard the same. You have big plans for today? Fireworks, parties, barbecue?" I was good at small talk, and I wanted to pack on the charm to impress Becca.

"Actually, this is the first time in a long time that I haven't spent it with Becca." She sighed. "But that's okay. I don't mind getting dumped for you."

"You want to join us?" I asked. Though I hoped she wouldn't accept, extending an invitation to our picnic seemed like the right thing to do. Plus, who was I to object to a two-to-one girl-to-guy ratio? I could think of worse predicaments.

"Thanks, but I made other plans. You guys have fun."

"Okay, then. Well, I'm looking forward to meeting you."

She paused for a moment. "Hey, Nolan?"

"Yeah?"

"Give her an extra hug today from me, okay? You get it, right?"

"Sure thing," I said, but I hadn't a clue what she was talking about. *Is it Becca's birthday? Is that why the phone's been ringing all morning and making her late?*

I hung up the receiver and pulled Becca in for a hug. "This is from Jordana," I said.

Then I cradled her in the crook of my elbow, dipped her toward the floor, and kissed her. "That"—I lowered my voice—"is from me. Happy birthday. Thanks for spending it with me."

"Um, Nolan?" She smirked, still lying in my dipped embrace. "My birthday's in October."

"I was just testing you," I deadpanned. I felt like a fool. "Then why did Jordana imply today was so special? She said you guys always spend the Fourth together, and she asked me to give you a hug. Am I missing something?"

"Come here," she said, leading me to the couch. "I wasn't going to do this so soon, but I guess it's as good a time as any." As we sat down, she grabbed the cassette sleeve.

"See this?" she asked, pointing to the sticky note. "My friends gave this to me exactly seven years ago."

"Well, I know it wasn't a birthday present," I joked.

She winked. "You're a quick study, Mr. Scardino. No, it wasn't my birthday. They made it for me because I'd been in the hospital for a while and they wanted to cheer me up."

"That's sweet. When my brother broke his toe skateboarding, all I got him was a Three Musketeers bar from the gift shop," I said. *I'm a babbling moron*, I thought. My palms got clammy. I wasn't sure if her telling me about the video was an invitation to probe or if I was supposed to respect her privacy and not ask any questions. But wouldn't avoiding her bait make me appear disinterested? I lifted the sticky note and looked at it. "So, your friends, are they the Cast?"

She smiled. "Yes. I mean, no one ever actually *uses* that name. It's just how they signed the note."

She went on to describe her friends, the various *Saturday Night Live*-style skits they'd created, and how they'd all watched the video together in her hospital room.

"Sounds like you have a pretty incredible group. I could tell from thirty seconds with Jordana how much she cares about you."

"Yes, I'm very lucky." She nodded. "Jordana's like a sister. She's very . . ." She seemed to be choosing her words carefully.

"What?" I asked, curious to see how she'd fill in the blank.

"Sometimes I think she'd put me in bubble wrap if she could. She's über-protective."

"Has she always been like that? I mean, it's flattering, but I'd think that could be kind of exhausting."

"Don't get me wrong, I love her—I absolutely do. I'd do anything for her. She's not just a friend; she's like a part of me. But I think when I was sick . . ." She paused for a split second and looked directly into my eyes. "I had cancer when I was younger, and I think it was hard on her. I mean, I *know* it was."

Becca wove this fact into the conversation so casually, I thought for a moment that I had misheard.

"Really? You had cancer?" I could feel my eyes widen. My grandmother had died of cancer. So had my friend's sister.

"Hodgkin's disease. It's a form of lymphoma."

I had sensed a subtle strength in Becca ever since the Dating Game. Knowing what she had overcome confirmed my intuition.

"Actually, a guy I went to boarding school with had lymphoma. I wasn't very close with him, but we lived on the same hall senior year. One night I happened to be in the bathroom when he was puking into a toilet. I wet some paper hand towels and offered to press them against his forehead. My mom did that for me whenever I puked as a kid, and it always made me feel better."

"That was sweet of you. I can't imagine anyone other than my parents wanting to hold my head when I threw up."

I started thinking about that guy, whose name escaped me. I could picture his narrow blue eyes, his tie-dyed shirts, and how he hung a map of the world upside down on his wall. It didn't occur to me back then, but I suddenly wondered if the South Pole near the ceiling was a metaphor for how his whole world had been turned upside down. I wondered if he had made it—if he was still alive.

"You know," I blurted out, along with a slight chuckle, still visualizing that map, "my roommate was friends with him, and one time he drove that kid to a sperm bank. He picked him up in his crappy old Dodge Dart and hid a *Playboy* in the glove compartment to give to him as a joke before he walked into the clinic."

Becca's cheeks turned bright pink.

It occurred to me that I was now having a discussion about fertility with a girl I really liked.

There was a lull. We both looked down at the parquet floor.

"Yeah, I'm not surprised that guy banked," she said. "I mean, you gotta figure, if they're going to try to save your life, they might as well try to preserve your ability to have children. They did that with me, too. I had an operation to shift my ovaries out of the line of radiation. I hope it worked. The technology keeps improving, but there are no guarantees that guy"—she cleared her throat—"or I will be able to have kids one day."

"So we'll adopt!" I blurted out like a reflex. It was a cross between a joke and the truth. I couldn't explain it, but part of me wanted to be with this girl no matter what.

Becca's wide grin turned into a soft chuckle. When she looked over at me, her eyes were glistening.

I tried to get back on more solid ground. "So, you're okay now, right? You feel okay? I mean, you *look* great," I said, putting my hand on her knee.

"Yes, thank God." She turned her head to the side and pretended to spit—a superstitious gesture both she and her mother continue to do. "I go for checkups and will for the rest of my life, but yeah, they say after five years you're cured, and it's been seven."

"It's gotta be the magical video, right?" I smiled.

"Gotta be." She laughed.

"Then I need to see it!" I kicked off my sneakers and placed my feet on her coffee table.

"What about our picnic?"

"We can go afterward. Unless you've got Bachelor Number

One coming over on his motorcycle to pick you up for dinner. I hear he looks great in leather."

"You're an ass." Laughing, she grabbed the remote, pressed play, and curled up beside me, her head against my chest.

Had it been a movie of my own friends acting like idiots, my cheeks would have ached from smiling. But because I didn't know these people, I found *Becca Night Live* more touching than comical. When I saw the handwritten messages on the closing credits, I grew somber. I couldn't believe that someone this young, healthy, and vibrant had almost died. I wished I had known her then. I wished I could have protected and guarded her. I wished I had been a member of that cast.

The picnic in Central Park never happened. We ended up watching the video, laughing, flirting, and eating manchego cheese and Greek olives on the floor of her apartment for the rest of the afternoon. Like the klutz I am, I managed to spill red wine all over her beige area rug. But, unlike my ex-girlfriend, who would have deemed that grounds for breaking up, Becca dismissed it. She grabbed a towel and a bottle of club soda from the fridge, and we got down on our hands and knees to blot out the stain. After sunset, we walked up to the roof of her building. I stood behind her, wrapping my arms around her denim overalls, and we lifted our eyes toward the Fourth of July fireworks exploding over the skyline. They sparkled against the blackness of night, and when they dissolved, the reds and blues merged into a vibrant violet hue.

"Wow, look at that," Becca said, pointing to the sky. "It's like Harold went to town with his purple crayon!" She slipped her fingers into mine and kissed my knuckles.

And that's when it hit me. My father would say it was a Sicilian thunderbolt, but I'd just call it clarity. Either way, I could see our future sketching out before us.

Almost two decades later, that area rug is still around (although it has been resized and reincarnated as the welcome mat for our apartment), her beloved denim overalls have found a home in our daughter's costume bin, and the *Becca Night Live* video (complete with the now-laminated pink sticky note) is the reason we will be the last remaining people on Earth to own a VCR.

The original cast is now grown up. Some have even become my own friends. A few months ago, when Jordana offered to host a "cast party" on the Fourth of July at her country home in honor of the twenty-fifth anniversary of Becca's kicking cancer, I thought it was a brilliant idea. Although my wife has always abhorred being the center of attention, she agreed to it for the sake of reuniting the group. After all, the last time the five of them were in a room together was at our wedding, nearly thirteen years ago.

Though work was extraordinarily stressful in the days leading up to the reunion, I wanted to create a special tribute. As husband of the guest of honor, I thought it was only right that I do a little something in addition to the expected toast. To me, the Fourth of July marked the night I fell in love with Becca on the roof of her apartment building. The fact that it happened to be the anniversary of her remission made it that much sweeter.

"What did you have in mind?" Jordana asked, when I called from my office on the Wednesday before the holiday weekend. I sensed the slightest hint of passive-aggressiveness in her voice when I raised the idea of a formal homage to Becca. As my unofficial sister-in-law and my former law school study partner, Jordana was almost as transparent to me as my own wife. And the tone of her question made it abundantly clear that she considered the details and planning of this weekend to be her baby.

"Don't worry, nothing big. We both know how she hates the spotlight. I just thought it might be nice to transfer the cassette to a DVD and make copies for everyone."

"Sorry, I made them months ago. They're already gift-wrapped," she said dismissively.

Of course she thought of it. Compared with Jordana, other type A's were slackers.

"Oh, okay. Well, I was also thinking of maybe making a video of my own. Maybe a tribute to Becca? What do you think?" Creative stuff wasn't my forte. Plus, even after all these years of being Becca's husband, I remained on the periphery of this group. For them, her illness was a crystal-clear, collective childhood memory. For me, the window into that part of my wife's life would always be foggy; no matter how hard I tried, I'd never be on the inside. They'd always know her in a way I never would or could.

"I guess," Jordana said halfheartedly. "I suppose you could—"

My second office phone line started ringing, but I chose to ignore it when I saw the managing partner's number pop up on the caller ID.

"Do you need to get that?" Jordana asked.

"Nope."

"Well, look at you, letting a work call go to voice mail! I'm impressed, Counselor. It's about time you relaxed a little. Are things slow at work?"

Fortunately, I didn't have to concoct a plausible explanation for the alleviation of my caseload, because as soon as the landline stopped ringing, my cell phone began to vibrate. It was Becca, which was odd, since it was four o'clock. We never spoke at this time of day. Normally, she'd be chatting with other moms at the bus stop or walking home with Emma, getting a synopsis of her day. "Jord, hold on—that's Bec on the other line."

"Becca? Now?" Jordana asked. She and my wife had committed each other's daily schedules to memory.

I put Jordana on hold and then heard the words I had been dreading ever since I'd fallen in love with Becca on that Fourth of July.

I never called Jordana back.

Later, as I recorded my video for the cast reunion, it wasn't just a heartfelt tribute; it was a mea culpa—a plea to regain my wife's trust, to be forgiven for hurting Becca in a way I had never imagined I could, and an appeal to be allowed back into her life.

Chapter 3: Jordana

The fact that Nolan placed me on hold and never clicked back to our conversation that afternoon wasn't surprising. He had a tendency to do that sort of thing, especially when Becca or his boss was on the other line. Like a well-intentioned but absent-minded professor, he'd get distracted, forget about the original caller, and then send an apologetic e-mail later in the day when he remembered. Sure enough, that evening I received a note:

> So sorry about cutting our discussion short. I'll figure something out for Becca's tribute. Anyway, quick question—would you be able to babysit Emma tomorrow? She doesn't have day camp and Bec and I have to do something. I seem to recall you saying you'd be taking off work to do last-minute preparations before the weekend. Any chance Emma can tag along with you? Thanks. —N

A smile spread across my face as soon as I read his message. I had been trying to find time to steal Emma away. I had tons of photos of Becca and Emma and thought a collage would be a meaningful present for Emma to give to her mom. Since the reunion would be an adults-only weekend, a collage also seemed like a nice way for some of the old friends who didn't know Emma to see the sweetness of Becca's relationship with her daughter. This babysitting request couldn't have worked out better. Plus, the fact that it came from Nolan, as opposed to Becca—the one who always arranged for anything related to Emma—could mean only one thing: Nolan had his own surprise in store. Becca and I tell each other everything, and she'd made no mention of any plans that day. I wondered if he would take her on a day trip to the beach, or perhaps a picnic in Central Park, like they were supposed to have on that July Fourth when they started dating. I was dying to know but decided not to ask, for fear I'd mess the whole thing up and let it slip. Instead, I happily agreed to spend the day with Emma and left it at that.

Nolan dropped Emma off at my apartment early Thursday morning on his way to the office, and I put her to work immediately.

"How about this one of Mommy and me on the swings?" Emma asked, sitting cross-legged among a sea of glossy four-by-six-inch prints on my living room floor.

"That's perfect! Put that in the 'keep' pile. I took that one of you guys at a playground in Riverside Park. I don't think you were more than two years old." I couldn't believe she was about to enter second grade.

"My hair was *so* short! I looked like a boy!" She scrunched up her nose and squinted her eyes, deepening the dimple in her upper cheek.

"Well, it did take a while for those gorgeous curls of yours to appear."

She had already moved on and gotten her fingerprints all over the next photo. "Was this when I was born?"

I reached for the picture, gently rubbed off the print marks with the edge of my shirt, and took a closer look. It was the one of Becca seated in an oversize rocking chair in a hospital nursery, feeding a tightly swaddled Emma her first bottle. I smiled, recalling what a joyous and emotional day that had been for the entire family. Every time I glance at that shot, I reprimand myself for not wearing waterproof mascara; I shed so many tears the day Emma was born that I looked like a raccoon.

"Yup. You were less than an hour old when I snapped this one."

"Aunt JoJo, you were there?" she asked. "You went to California to see me get born?"

"Psh! Are you kidding me, girlfriend? Have I ever skipped any of your dance performances or piano recitals? Did you really think I'd miss your big debut?"

She smiled. There was that dimple again.

"You rock," she said, and put her palm up for me to high-five. The smile stayed on her lips until she broke into song, decimating the lyrics of a Beyoncé melody and shaking her tush on my Persian rug.

I love my sons dearly, but Emma is the girl I never had. I feel tethered to her and want to protect her the same way I would if she were my own flesh and blood. Yes, she is the child of my best friend (which automatically makes her special), and yes, the fact that she happens to be an absolutely delicious kid by nature doesn't hurt. But it's more than that. I can relate to her because I *was* Emma. As an only child myself, I understand the bond she shares with her parents; I had, and still have, a similar one with my own mom and dad.

As with most kids, my greatest fear as a child was losing a parent, not just because I loved them intensely, but because without one of them, our family would diminish by a hefty 33.3 percent and that was one-third closer to being left alone.

But unlike Emma, I didn't grow up with a parent with a cancer history. Sure, Mom and Dad could have fallen ill at any point, but statistically they were at no greater risk than the general population. That can't be said of Becca. Of course, with a quarter century under her belt, she's had a damn good run. But I've been to the dark side with her and am well aware that any point the nightmare could creep into our lives, just as it did twenty-five years ago. I can't predict the future, but I can do my best to be a consistent, loving, and dependable presence in Emma's life and give Becca the peace of mind of knowing that, God forbid there should ever be a need, I'm here as her understudy.

Up until eighth grade, Becca and I shared everything: clothes, strep throat, cassette tapes, and earnings from our lemonade stand. Cancer was the first thing we didn't take turns using or divide evenly. To this day, I still wonder why she was hit while I was spared. It was unfair. I promised myself that if I couldn't shield her from pain, I'd do everything within my power to enhance her joy. And I have done my best to live up to that promise. I've celebrated every birthday, toasted every success, danced at her wedding, and held her hand across the armrest on our flight to California to witness Emma's birth through gestational surrogacy. Having a relationship with Becca's only child is part of my commitment. And this reunion weekend, the latest milestone, is yet another opportunity for me to show my dearest friend how much she is loved and how grateful I am to have her in my life.

Just as we were gluing down the final photographs of the collage, my phone rang. I glanced at the caller ID; it was Becca's mom.

"Hi, Arlene!"

"Hi, Jordy, how's girls' day going? You having fun?"

"Of course we are! In fact, we're just about finished with our art project."

"Wonderful! Then my timing is perfect. How's my Emma?"

"She's right here. You want to speak with her?"

"Yes, please. If it's not too much trouble."

I cleared my throat and channeled my best Mary Poppins/ Julie Andrews accent. "Well, Miss Emma is quite busy and may be in a meeting at this juncture, but if you would be a dear and hold the line, I will do my very best to try to find her. One moment, please . . ." Emma giggled.

"Oh, I do appreciate it. Thank you, dahling." Arlene played along, accent and all.

"Miss Scardino." I beckoned, still in character. "There is a call on the line for you. Some woman by the name of Grandma. Do you perchance know of anyone by that moniker?"

Emma cocked her head to the side. "I know Grandma, but who's Monica?" she whispered, perplexed.

"It's Grandma, you silly goose," I said, and handed her the phone.

As I cleaned up the glue, glitter, and markers, I overheard Emma telling Arlene about our day. How she'd had fun decorating the collage, how I'd let her make cookies while the paste dried, and how she didn't mind being inside because it was too hot even to go to the sprinklers in the park. Given that our previous girls' days had involved restaurants with singing waiters and trips to Broadway shows, I had been worried she might be bored, so hearing her positive review made me happy.

"Grandma wants to speak with you," Emma said, arm extended, receiver in hand.

"Hi," I said. "Sounds like you got the lowdown on our day."

"Yes, I may sign up for my own day with Aunt JoJo!" Arlene laughed. "Anyway, Bec called and said they won't be back until later this evening. Jerry and I are home and can watch Emma until they return. I'm sure you have lots to do for the weekend. Can I come over and pick her up?"

"Oh, did Becca say where they went? I'm so curious. I didn't want to ask, but I've been dying to know what they're up to."

"Me too, but no, she didn't say."

"Well, I guess we'll find out soon enough. Emma's just about finished with her project, and I have to pick up some stuff on the West Side, so let me bring her to you. I can get across town in twenty minutes."

"Perfect. Thank you," she said. "See you then."

When Nolan and Becca bought their apartment and declared they would stay in the city to raise Emma, thus opting out of the suburban exodus that had claimed so many of our peers, Arlene and Jerry sold their house in Queens and moved a few blocks away. Some people would cringe at the idea of their parents or in-laws living within spitting distance, but Arlene and Jerry were incredibly cool and respectful of boundaries. They had their own lives, filled with friends and theater subscriptions and lectures at the 92nd Street Y, but were now available at a moment's notice. It was a perfect setup and one I completely understood. Had I gone through what they had with Becca, I, too, would do everything in my power to be a part of the daily lives of my child and the miraculous grandchild I'd hoped for but never expected to have.

"Awesome day," I said to Emma on the sidewalk in front of Jerry and Arlene's building.

"Your mom is going to love your gift! I'll take a video on my phone of her reaction when she opens it this weekend and show it to you when we come home. Okay?"

"That sounds great!" Arlene said, patting Emma's ponytail. Emma nodded. "Thanks, Aunt JoJo."

"My pleasure. Love you, kiddo." I gave her a hug.

"I love you, too. Bye." She held Arlene's hand as they walked into the apartment building. When I turned and headed toward Columbus Avenue, I could hear Jerry bellow, "Hey, squirt!" from their lobby. I smiled to myself, envisioning the scene I'd witnessed countless times since Emma was able to walk. I knew in that moment that Jerry was crouching on his knees like a catcher behind home plate, and that his granddaughter was running full speed into his arms. Their routine always reminded me of the embrace Jerry gave Seth the day we visited Becca's hospital room all those years ago—that single, engulfing squeeze that conveyed unconditional love, gratitude, and a sense that this man took nothing for granted.

Despite the early evening hour, it remained as hot and humid as it had been at midday. It was, after all, summer in New York. My long hair was sticking to the back of my neck, so I sat down on a shaded bench to dig a clip out from my tote bag. I twisted the strands into a messy bun, which offered some relief. After a swig from my water canteen, I whipped out the yellow legal pad containing my six-page, color-coded to-do list for the upcoming weekend and reviewed the final items. The system—my method of organization—had been in place for years. It was as natural to me as breathing. Checking off those green (grocery items), blue (nonfood shopping), black (work stuff), purple (kid-and-family stuff), and red (miscellaneous) tasks has always given me a sense of accomplishment—something I never felt when tapping the delete button on a smartphone-generated list.

My remaining to-do's:

- Get kosher wine, cheese, and meat for Holly/Adam (green)
- Buy produce, preferably organic (green)
- Buy henna tattoo–making materials? Only if have time . . . (red)
- Pack Sal's clothes and my clothes (purple)

- Call garage attendant to pull car near lobby—have cash for tip (red)
- Ask doorman to help load car—have cash for tip (red)
- Get Lex from airport at noon (red)
- Head to country house (red)

Miraculously, I was able to get all the kosher items, as well as the henna materials, within two blocks of Arlene and Jerry's apartment. I was in great shape. Sal had already dropped off our boys at his parents' house for the weekend, so all that remained for the evening was to pack and get a good night's sleep.

I hailed a cab and minutes later was in front of the brass poles and hunter-green awning of my building on Fifth Avenue. As I waited in the lobby for an elevator, my cell phone whistled *yoo-hoo*. I realized I had missed several messages: five texts, one voice mail, and two e-mails of quasi-dirty jokes sent from my father, who passed along everything his bored retirement buddies forwarded to him.

Text #1, 5:25 p.m., from Lex:

> *Sooooo excited for the weekend. Been WAY too long. We're coming in on United #366 from O'Hare and should land at LaGuardia around noon. You picking us up or should we get a taxi from airport to your apt.? Either way totally fine. Can't wait to see you guys! Xoxo*

Text #2, 5:43p.m., from Holly:

> *Hello Jordana. Thank you again for your hospitality. Adam and I will meet you at the house right before Shabbas starts. Probably about 7:30 p.m.—ish. Need to make deliveries to a couple of overnight camps in the Catskills in the afternoon and will then head over to you. Please send address. Looking forward.*

Text #3, 6:59 p.m., from Seth:

> *hey, jord. psyched for weekend. how can I help?? need anything??*

Text #4, 7:01 p.m., from Becca:
Blank

The empty-speech-bubble text was unusual. A slip of the finger? I wondered. I dismissed it and checked my voice mail. There was a call from Becca around the same time as the text, and the only sound on the message was that of a phone receiver hanging up.

"That's odd," I said aloud when I got into the elevator. My arms needed a rest, so I dragged the packages into the car, pressed the button for my floor, and sent a quick text before the elevator doors shut.

> *Hi Bec! Saw you called. What's up? Had a great day with Emma. Hope you had fun too! Can't wait to hear about it!*

I figured she was probably getting Emma ready for bed and would call me back later. When we were little, we would get so pumped up for our birthday parties that we wouldn't be able to sleep. One of us would flick our bedroom lights on and off late into the evening before the celebration, hoping the other was watching from across the street, and then flicker back. The night before each of our weddings, we had a sleepover in the bride's childhood bedroom. The bride slept in her bed, the maid of honor just an arm's reach away beside her on a rollaway cot, just like the old days.

Yoo-hoo, my phone whistled again, as the elevator whizzed up.

Becca:
> *Hey, Jord. Something came up. Change of plans. Can't go tomorrow. Will definitely be there at some point over the weekend, just not sure yet when. Maybe Saturday? SO sorry. Love you.*

I reread the message. *What the fuck?* I thought. I crafted, edited, rewrote, and erased various responses. Then, as the elevator opened onto the fourteenth floor, it occurred to me that the text must be a joke. I pulled the packages onto the carpeted hallway and responded with a simple *LOL*.

A few minutes later, while I was rearranging my overstuffed refrigerator to accommodate the final items for the weekend, my phone whistled again.

Becca: *Not kidding. SO sorry.*
Me: *Call me! You okay?!*
Becca: *Can't now. Will call tomorrow. All should be fine.*

"All should be fine?" I reread aloud, utterly exasperated, as if the phone were another person in the room. I wondered if Becca had gotten a consulting gig that was too good to pass up. Though she'd mainly stayed home since Emma's birth, every now and then a call came in from a former colleague asking if she could pinch-hit and produce a story for the morning or evening news. But the thought of her holing up in an editing suite on this of all weekends was asinine and implausible.

Me: *"All should be fine"?! What's the "All"? Totally confused . . .*
She didn't respond.

I shoved the last triangle of Brie into a corner of the produce drawer and slammed the refrigerator. A fingerprint painting my sons had made for Sal on Father's Day fell off the stainless door and landed on the floor. I didn't even pick it up. I grabbed a wineglass from the cabinet and slammed that door, too. But because Sal had insisted on "soft close" cabinets when we'd renovated the apartment, the door shut unsatisfyingly, without a sound. I uncorked a new cabernet and settled onto a barstool at my marble-topped kitchen island. Suddenly, my eyes welled up with tears. I was the little girl whose birthday party had just been canceled. This was not a part of my color-coded weekend itinerary.

Why would Becca bail now? She knows how much effort I put into this! She's not a flake. She doesn't cancel plans unless there's a legitimate reason. My shoulders tensed. I could feel my heartbeat quicken and my underarms beginning to sweat. I pulled off my shirt and sat on the barstool, drinking alone in my bra, imagining every possible excuse she might offer.

As a forty-year-old public defender with a second full-time job mothering five-year-old twins, I knew quite well that things didn't always go according to plan. It wasn't the hiccup in the schedule that threw me; it was the sense of being disconnected from something important in Becca's life. I couldn't stand not knowing. Becca always explained. Whether she was running late to our yoga class because she couldn't put down a book or forgot to pick up the fruit salad she had promised to bring to a dinner party, she always told me the truth, even if it wasn't flattering. The last time she had been this opaque was when we were kids and she was sick, but even then, it wasn't intentional. No one knew what was wrong with her. She'd been losing weight and getting really tired and pale; we all thought it was a bad virus.

When I did learn Becca had cancer, I hadn't a clue what it meant. Back then, images of kids with the disease weren't ubiquitous. There were no Make-A-Wish Foundation ads. I don't recall ever seeing a television commercial with celebrities playing with bald children. I was unaware of how grave it was, and that death was a possibility. All I knew for certain was that my best friend had "the disease that makes hair fall out." That's how my parents explained it to me over bagels and lox one Sunday morning in our kitchen. Becca had missed a bunch of school days, and when I asked if they thought she would go back soon, they gave each other a knowing glance and then uttered those words. We didn't discuss it much after that. My parents and I have always been incredibly close and can have lengthy discussions about virtually anything. For some reason, however, this topic rendered them tight-lipped. Anytime Becca's illness came up, the conversation became clipped, succinct. Had I been an adult, or even in my upper teens, I might have felt more bothered and pressed them for additional information. But I was just a good kid who took what her parents said at face value. I didn't know enough about the disease to ask. All I knew was that my best friend wasn't at school, wasn't at our lunch table, wasn't on the bus, wasn't there at night. I hated being without her.

The day we visited her in the hospital was a nightmare. On the subway ride into the city, we decided we'd be upbeat and not talk about anything depressing. Our mission, we agreed, was simple: make her smile. Though Seth, Lex, and Holly were able to do the job, I couldn't get my act together. Seeing Becca attached to all those tubes, looking so pale and bald—my God, bald!—elicited feelings not only of pity, but of exclusion. I realized I was on the periphery of Becca's life, and the loss of that connection reverberated deeply, leaving me lonely and scared, as if a little part of Becca had already died. That was the day I realized my best friend had become part of a world to which I couldn't relate.

Sitting on the windowsill of Becca's hospital room, shrouded in a blue gown, cap, mask, gloves, and booties, I stewed with anger. I was pissed at the disease for hurting my friend. I was upset with my parents for withholding, or sugarcoating, the truth about her health: that her limbs had grown frail, her pasty face was puffed up from steroids, and a catheter emerged from her chest in the spot where her half of our "Best Friends" necklace used to rest. But more than anything else, I wanted to stand on that windowsill and scream down to the people walking along East 68th Street, *It's not fair!*

As I stared off into the subway-tile backsplash behind my kitchen sink, I swirled the stem of my wineglass a little too vigorously, splashing cabernet onto the white Carrara marble countertop.

"Shit!" I ran to grab a fistful of paper towels.

Moments later, Sal walked in from work.

"Heeey," he said slowly, taking in the scene of his teary, partially naked wife drinking alone. He placed his attaché case onto the kitchen counter, loosened his tie, and walked over to kiss my forehead. "You okay? What's going on?"

I looked at him the way our boys did when their lips quivered just before letting out a guttural wail. I did my best to keep it together but erupted in sarcasm instead. "Oh, Becca's just being a flake. She said she wasn't sure if she'd make it up tomorrow. She probably got a better offer from one of her new mom friends at Emma's school."

"That's interesting," he said.

I had fully expected Sal to snicker at my insecurity, roll his eyes, and insist I was being ridiculous. "Why is that *interesting*?"

"Well, Nolan just left me a voice mail about an hour ago saying he's not going to go with me tomorrow. We were supposed to take the train upstate together after work. Remember?"

"What?" I screamed. "He's bailing, too? Are you frickin' kidding me?" I tossed my wineglass into the sink, cracking the crystal lip.

Sal widened his eyes and raised his brows, which I interpreted as a subtle message that my decibel level and aggression might have been a bit over the top. I balled my hand into a fist as my mind raced for a way to figure out what was happening.

I grabbed my cell phone and sent a text message to Seth.

Seth—Need a favor. Looks like I have more stuff to do in the morning than I thought. Can you pick up Lex and her husband at airport tomorrow and drive them up to the house? United flight 366 lands at LaGuardia at noon. Let me know if that works. THANK YOU!

His response, two minutes later:

I've got a couple of early sessions with clients in the morning but can definitely pick them up. Not sure I'll recognize her, though— she still have those mile-high hairspray bangs?! Yowza! Give her my number and we'll figure out the rest.

Thank God for Seth, I thought. Now I had the morning free to deal with the Becca situation. I decided to text her again.

Me: *Still up?*
Becca: *Yup.*
Me: *Want to go for a quick walk tomorrow, 8 a.m.?*
Becca: *I have something at 9. Sorry.*

I wanted to respond, *Yeah, you were supposed to meet ME at 9 for the weekend I'm hosting in YOUR honor!* But instead I inhaled deeply through my nose and breathed out through my mouth—a technique I often used to retain composure in the courtroom. I couldn't start a fight with Becca. We prided ourselves on being the only girlfriends we knew who'd never fought over anything—not toys, or who got the bigger piece of cake, or who got the lead in the silly plays we'd created in my basement. I could have tiffs with others, but not with her, and I wasn't going to be the one to end our long-standing run of peace, even if she was the one creating the problem.

> Me: *Okay. Good night.*
> Becca: *You too. I'll let you know when I can come up.*
> Me: *All right . . .*

I knew ellipses could talk. They were the perfect punctuation mark to convey resignation, hesitation, or a disappointed sigh. My message could be interpreted as *Fine, you win*, or *I'm confused and not buying into this whole enigmatic act*. Either way, I knew Becca would hear me loud and clear. She could be cagey with others, but not with me.

I placed my phone in the docking station on my nightstand, neatly laid out my clothes for the next morning on the leather stool beside my vanity, and got ready for bed—a ritual that typically calmed me, simply by nature of being a routine. This night, however, it wasn't working. I still felt unsteady.

Sitting on the edge of my duvet, about to turn off the light switch, I was overcome by a need to recite a prayer, something I hadn't done since I was a little girl. I closed my eyes, breathed deeply, and was transported back to my childhood bedroom with the purple carpet and Kirk Cameron posters on the wall. I could feel the orthodontic retainer in my mouth, as well as the roominess of the hand-me-down nightgown I got from my cousin in Boston. I thought about my father—who, at this moment, was probably watching a late-night *Barney Miller* rerun—and how he used to tuck me snugly under my sheets, like an Egyptian mummy. He'd sit on the edge of my Wonder Woman comforter as we asked God to bless our family and friends with health, happiness, and peace.

"Good night, sweetheart. Sleep tight, and don't let the bedbugs bite. But if they do, beat them with a shoe until they're black and blue," my father would say. He would then pretend to shad-owbox with me but would kiss my head instead. It never failed to lift whatever worry I carried and ease me into a peaceful slumber. Now, though, I lay there wondering what was happening with my friend, conjuring up one horrible scenario after another, until finally, sometime around four o'clock Friday morning, I drifted off to sleep.

Chapter 4: Seth

I pulled into the far end of the Departures area at New York's LaGuardia Airport and nervously tapped on my steering wheel, hoping a cop wouldn't make me move. Illegally hanging out in the no-standing zone of Departures was significantly less chaotic than jockeying with the triple-parked cars in the Arrivals section and would make it much easier for Lex and her husband to spot me when they exited the terminal on the Friday of a holiday weekend.

As usual, I was early. I've always been a stickler for punctuality. Plus, I knew that if I arrived fifteen minutes before their flight was scheduled to land, I'd have just enough time to write up the progress reports for my morning clients.

While I used the armrest as a desk to write up my evaluations, someone started knocking on the trunk of my car. I squinted into the rearview mirror, expecting to see a traffic cop asking me to move. Instead was a skinny-jeaned brunette wearing a fitted white tank top and dark, oversize sunglasses, carrying a large leather bag with tassels hanging off the side. She looked like a model in a fancy luggage commercial.

"Hey," I yelled in warning, bursting out of the car to shoo the woman away. She may have been attractive, but she was still banging on my trunk.

"Hey yourself!" she said exuberantly, bouncing over to give me a hug.

Oh no—did I sleep with this girl? was my first thought.

"You were right," she said, after kissing my cheek. "This place is so much better than the zoo at Arrivals!"

"Leeeex?" I stepped back and slowly said her name in disbelief. My mental image of her involved stiff, gravity-defying bangs that stood at least two inches above her forehead.

"Seeeeth?" she said, mimicking me playfully.

Her smile was expansive—like, Julia Roberts expansive. It was similar to the wide-mouthed, toothy grin I remembered from childhood, but back then I found it dorky. Now it was stunning.

"Holy crap, Lex!" I exclaimed. "I didn't recognize . . . You look amazing!"

She lifted the sunglasses, nestled them atop her elegant, shoulder-length bob, and smiled. "Honestly, I would have walked right past you, too, if you hadn't told me to look for an illegally parked, shit-brown Mitsubishi."

I laughed.

"You know, Seth, we might have recognized each other if you had a Facebook account. I think you're the only person I know who's not on some form of social media."

"It's not for me. I like my privacy," I said dismissively. I reached for her small roller suitcase, as well as the bag on her shoulder, and loaded them into the backseat. "Where's your husband?"

She lowered the sunglasses back over her eyes. "Jack chose to stay home," she said flatly, as she sashayed over to the passenger side. That strut hadn't changed.

"Oh," I said. Her tone made me think this was not an amicable or joint decision. I racked my brain for a visual of her husband and came up with nothing, though I vaguely recalled that he was undeservedly cocky. "Does he have to work?"

"Golf, actually." She started inspecting her manicured nails—a childhood habit of hers that suddenly felt familiar to me again. "He didn't even bother to feign working. He just said there was a tournament at the country club that he couldn't miss because 'all the guys will be there.' You'd think he was a teenage boy trying to fit in with the cool kids, instead of a forty-five-year-old man with children of his own. He knew for months that this trip was on the calendar." She cleared her throat. "But anyway . . ."

I felt sorry for her. "Well, I'm glad you made it. It's good to see you. It's been a long time since the whole group was last together," I said, trying to find a more upbeat topic as I turned out of my illegal parking spot.

"You know, I don't think I've actually seen you since I moved to Chicago."

"When was that?" I pulled up to a red light.

"Right after my honeymoon, fifteen years ago."

"Seriously?" I turned toward her in surprise. "That long?"

"Yup." She nodded.

"Wow! And don't you have, like, seventeen kids or something?"

"Something like that." She laughed. "Actually, I've got three. Two boys and a little girl. The oldest is starting high school in the fall."

"*You* have a kid in high school?" Though it was almost inconceivable that a woman who could easily pass for twenty-five was actually the parent of a ninth-grader, the fact that she was the first one in our group to have children wasn't completely incongruous with Lex's personality. She had always been ahead of the curve—the first to go on a date, the first to try alcohol. As the youngest child of a large family, she yearned to catch up to her siblings. When she was only five years old, she asked our kindergarten teacher to call her by her given name, Alexandra, instead of her nickname, Lexi, because she wanted to sound more "manure and fassisticated." In fifth grade, there was a two-week period when she would answer only to Xandra, but no one bought in, so she settled on Lex and it stuck.

"This is the first time I've ever left my kids."

"Really?"

"It's true. I'm not one of these women who do girls' weekends or anything. I'd miss my babies too much." She patted her heart, and I noticed how her gigantic, diamond-encrusted wedding band protruded awkwardly, like a massive wart, from her delicate hand.

"But for Becca . . . " I said.

"Exactly. This trip was too special to pass up." She grew quiet. "It would have been nice for Jack to see everyone." Her tone had shifted, and I sensed something dark underneath what she was saying. It was too soon to pry, so I just kept my eyes on the road.

For a moment, all we could hear was the air-conditioning pumping through the vents.

"And how about you?" she asked enthusiastically, her wide grin reappearing, as if she'd had a shot of espresso. "How's your *job*? How are the *lay-dees*?"

"Job's great. Love it. Really love it, actually. Took me a little while to figure out the right path, but I got there. As for the ladies, well"—I chuckled—"I do okay."

"Are you kidding? Bec tells me you do *more* than okay." She winked knowingly.

I could feel my cheeks flush. "Actually, my girlfriend is going to join us tomorrow. She's got to work tonight, so she'll catch a bus in the morning."

"She's an actress, right?"

"Mmm, no, that was my previous girlfriend."

"But Becca just told me about her a few weeks ago."

I smiled. "What can I say? I'm making up for lost time."

"I'd just say you peaked a smidge later than others, that's all," she said generously.

"That's kind of you." I laughed.

"Come on, Seth, it's understandable. How could you *not* have been scarred by the whole weigh-in thing with your mom? It would have taken anyone years to recover from that."

I could feel my smile collapse as if someone had suddenly removed pins holding up the corners of my lips.

"You knew about that?" I said.

Her hand flew to her dropped jaw.

"Oh my God," she said. "Yes, everyone knew. You didn't know we knew?"

"Seriously? You *all* knew?"

"I mean, I knew whatever I heard from my mom," Lex said. "We felt so badly for you."

When I was growing up, my parents were extremely strict. The kitchen "closed" in our house at 7:59 every night, after which no one was permitted any snacks. Candy was forbidden, but I kept a stash hidden inside a hole I punched in my bedroom wall. One day when I was twelve, my mom found the hole, filled with Snickers wrappers, while cleaning my bedroom. After that, I couldn't play Atari for a month. My parents had struggled with their weight for years, and they feared my brother and I were genetically destined to follow in their footsteps. Even though I wasn't obese or even overweight—just a little pudgy—my mother insisted I "learn portion control from the experts." So, for most of junior high, she took me to her Weight Watchers meetings. It took me nearly a decade to get over my nightmares of women in 80s-style tracksuits pinching my cheeks, telling me to get my tush on the scale, and measuring me with their eyes. If I reached my goal at the weigh-ins each week, Mom would take me to Burger King for a Whopper. Even when I was a kid, the irony of being rewarded for dieting with fast food wasn't lost on me.

"Jesus, I can't believe that was public. I worked so hard to keep it a secret," I said, running my fingers through my hair. I was still mortified, even after all those years. "Anyway, I survived. It's all good."

"Clearly!" She posed her hands like a game-show hostess next to my biceps, as if they were the grand prize. "And it seems like the whole college-and-career debacle worked out for you, too. God knows our mothers were *en fuego* analyzing that one."

"How could I forget? Those conversations were the soundtrack of my early twenties," I said, and rolled my eyes. As a senior at the prestigious Bronx High School of Science, I received a coveted college scholarship to Princeton University. Unfortunately, I managed to lose that scholarship by the end of my first year because I had cut the majority of my classes to play poker with my dorm mates. By the end of sophomore year, I'd flunked out of school. Gossip-laden hypotheses abounded among the neighborhood yentas back in Queens about how this *shanda* (Yiddish for *disgrace*) could have occurred. The consensus was that I simply shut down in the face of stiff competition. That if I couldn't be the best, if I couldn't be number one, I didn't want to compete. At least, that was the theory my mother's friends went with during their stand-ing mah-jongg games in our living room on Thursdays between 11:00 a.m. and 2:00 p.m. I used to listen to the whole thing from my bedroom, and when I'd had enough, I'd cover my ears with my Walkman headphones.

"What really happened at Princeton? I never did get the scoop."

"Oh, I don't know," I said, and let out a long sigh. "Probably just your run-of-the-mill case of a kid getting his first taste of freedom."

Lex cocked her head and looked at me curiously. "Really? That's it?"

"Okay, maybe sprinkle in some cynicism and being pissed off that bad things happen to good people and deciding that killing yourself over academics is pointless if one day you'll wake up with a terminal disease, knocking on death's door." I looked over at Lex for a reaction. Her lips were slightly parted; she looked a bit shocked. "What? Too dark? Too deep?" I smiled.

"Mmm, just a bit. I was sort of expecting you to go with 'par-tied my ass off' or something along those lines."

"Oh, well, yes, I did that, too, but I figured I'd go a layer deeper, you know? Give you the psychological underpinnings of my carpe diem impetus to party."

Lex turned toward the passenger window and mumbled something I couldn't quite decipher, but I could make out the words "like my impetus to get married."

"I'm sorry—did you say something?" I pressed.

"Oh, nothing—just thinking aloud," she said, turning back to face me. "So, what did you end up doing when you moved home after Princeton? Did you just hang out in your bedroom, making crank calls telling people if they named thirty-one ice cream fla-vors in thirty-one seconds, they'd get a thirty-one-dollar coupon to Thirty-One Flavors?"

"Ah, yes," I said, letting out a long sigh. "The crank calls. So, is that the ingrained image you have of me from childhood—lying on the floor of my bedroom, dialing random numbers on a massive cordless phone and laughing hysterically?"

"Oh, Seth, don't worry—that's just one of *many* pathetic images I have of you." She laughed. "But in your defense, you had accomplices. The other girls and I were right there, egging you on. In fact, I was the one keeping track of the phone numbers you had already dialed so you wouldn't repeat any."

"That's true. I also recall one time when I got the cordless phone's gigantic retractable antenna stuck in your bangs, and how you kept kicking me because you'd used half a can of Aqua Net getting your hair into position and I'd messed it all up. Jordana came to my rescue."

"Yeah, you were always sort of wimpy that way. But the beating-up was deserved. I mean, if you had devoted an entire hour of your morning trying to look hot for Gavin O'Rourke and were planning to casually walk past him and his varsity baseball buddies outside the movie theater later that day, you, too, would be pretty pissed that your perfect, gravity-defying bangs were now limp and cockeyed," she said, adjusting her posture.

"Jeesh!" I said, grinning. "Still sensitive, are we?"

"All I'm saying is, back in high school, my hair routine was a top priority, and you ruined that day for me," she said, folding her arms and turning up her nose, before a giggle emerged, forcing her to break character.

Although I knew she was joking, I must have looked hurt. "Oh, I'm just teasing you, Seth," she said, and put her hand on my shoulder. "So, um, how did the workout stuff come about? You look absolutely amazing now. Did you start exercising when you were living at home?"

"Yeah. I guess when you spend six months sitting on your parents' Barcalounger, eating Doritos, you realize you're pretty much up shit's creek. So I got my ass off the pleather and rented an apartment with a guy who worked as a personal trainer. He made me go to the gym with him, and I started to really enjoy it. I decided to get certified as a trainer. I worked nights to pay the rent while I took physiology and biology classes at Queens College during the day. Training people was the first time I really felt inspired and excited. I loved the science of it and really enjoyed interacting with clients. I know it sounds cheesy, but I felt like I was able to help people make a positive change in their lives. Physical therapy became the obvious path."

"What is that saying, 'Man plans and God laughs'?" she said. "It's like you think you've got it all figured out, and then you wake up and realize maybe . . ." She turned and looked out her window.

"That maybe it wasn't the right path to begin with?" I said.

Lex turned to me and perched her sunglasses on top of her hair.

"Exactly," she said softly, raising a perfect eyebrow. "You know, I just saw this documentary called *Race to Nowhere*. It's about how we're putting so much pressure on kids to be 'successful,' but what does *success* even mean?"

"Mmm-hmm." I nodded.

"I mean, look at you," she continued. "You were Bronx Science valedictorian—"

"Salutatorian." I corrected her with a finger in the air. "That fucker Felix Kim beat me."

"Salutatorian, whatever." She rolled her eyes. "My point is, you had the brass ring within reach, but you blew it, or so everyone thought. But maybe you're having the last laugh. You got your shit together on your own time frame. I've only been with you for forty-five minutes, but you look amazing and you seem genuinely happy. And then there are people, like the ones who surround me every day, who do exactly what they're supposed to do—go to the right schools; get the big-name degrees; have multiple kids, the minivan, the dog, the family vacations; join the right clubs—and yet they feel suffocated the moment they wake up in the morning. It just makes you wonder."

"What does it make you wonder?" I asked.

"I don't know—maybe what the race is all about? Where are we running? What's the goal?"

Just then, her cell phone rang.

"Hi," she said, her tone suddenly becoming flat. "Yeah, the sunscreen is on the top shelf of the closet. It's there. Jesus, Jack. Just move things around. Try looking *behind* the beach bag. No? So maybe it's *in* the beach bag? Did you look in the bathroom? Okay. Good. Don't forget to spray their ears and the tops of their feet. Yeah, I'm with Seth. Seth Gottlieb. Remember? Yes. We're driving up now. Fine. Bye."

She hung up, lowered her sunglasses again, and looked out the window.

"Everything okay?" I asked.

She cleared her throat. "Just fine." She reached over and turned up the volume on the sound system with her French-manicured fingers. It was Billy Joel's "Miami 2017."

I sang aloud while drumming the beat on the steering wheel, and we both shouted and pumped our fists in the air when the lyrics referenced Queens. When the sirens played at the end of the song, I noticed that they seemed particularly realistic. In fact, when the song ended and the sirens kept going, we both looked into our side-view mirrors.

"Oh, shit!" I moaned. There was a police car directly behind me. I shut off the radio and glanced at the odometer, where the numbers were quickly diving down from the low seventies, then pulled over to the side of the Taconic State Parkway.

"License and registration, please," the officer said, leaning his face into my window and glancing around the car.

I handed over my license while Lex fished the registration out of the glove compartment.

"Do you know how fayst you were going, sir?" the officer asked.

"No, sir, I'm sorry, I don't."

"You happened to be going seventy-fayve miles an hour. The speed limit is fifty-fayve."

I struggled to place the officer's accent.

"Where ya goin' in such a rush?"

"We have a party," I said, remembering the advice a lawyer friend had given me, to answer only the question and offer nothing more.

"A party, eh—"

"I'm sorry to interrupt." Lex smiled, leaning over from the passenger seat. "By any chance, are you from the Chicago area?"

"Yes, ma'am. I am," he said, straightening his posture.

"Oh, I could tell by your accent," Lex said, wildly exaggerating the slight Midwestern inflection she'd picked up over her years spent living in Illinois. "I'm visiting the Big Apple from Chicawgo for the weekend to see friends. Where'd you grow up at?"

I was shocked. The Lex I remembered knew better than to end a sentence with a preposition.

"Glenview," he said, softening.

"Noo way!" she said, with a bit of flirtation. "My son is starting Glenbrook North High School in the fall. Did you go to North or South?"

"South."

"Oh, but I bet you went to Stanley Field Junior High, no?"

"Yes, ma'am."

"So, did you live south of Willow Road, near the Plaza Del Prado shopping center?"

"Exactly! Is the hot dog shack Dear Franks still there? I haven't been back in a while."

And with that, I knew I was home free. You can't bond over a hot dog shack and then hand over a ticket.

"No," Lex said. "They changed owners, and there's a new name, but it's still a hot dog place. Nothin' like good old Vienna beef, you know what I'm talking about?" She winked and flashed her gorgeous smile.

Cha-ching! The officer handed my license and registration back.

"Please be mindful of the speed limit and be safe this weekend, sir," he said. "And enjoy your party. Happy Independence Day."

"Oh, you have a happy July Fourth, too, sir!" Lex waved from her seat.

I rolled up the windows and stared at her in astonishment.

"What the fuck was that?" I said, grinning. "Where did you learn to talk like that?"

"I don't know what you're talking about," she said, thickening her accent even more. "I just think gettin' pulled over was bad karma and we don't need it. Say it with me, Seth: *baaayd karema.*"

"Baaayd kaaare-ma." I snorted, and she burst out laughing.

"That was Oscar-worthy, Lex."

"Oh my God, I don't remember the last time I laughed that hard," she said. "It's so good to be home."

I pulled back onto the highway. "Need I remind you that you're on the Taconic Parkway in Bumblefuck, New York?"

"No," she said. "This definitely feels like home."

I wondered what she meant by that. I parsed her words for the next two miles as I stared out at the rolling green mountains in the distance and she checked email on her phone. A sign for food broke my concentration and I declared that it was time for a pit stop. I pulled over to a restaurant on the side of the road with DINER spelled out in red capital letters over the roof. I parked and immediately unlocked the door to stretch my legs. Ever since I started working out, I haven't been able to take a long drive or a flight without the urge to flex and move—something I rarely craved back in my couch-potato days. I got out and did a few deep knee bends. When my cell phone dinged in the cup holder, Lex brought it out to me. "Text," she said.

She glanced at the phone, and her brow furrowed. I took it from her and saw the words she must have seen. They were from Nolan:

We need that surgical referral ASAP. Please send. Thanks.

Shit, I thought.

Lex stood with her hand on her hip, awaiting an explanation.

"It's Nolan," I finally said. "He fell off his bike training for the NYC triathlon and broke his collarbone."

"Yeah, I heard about that. Bec told me about his accident. She always said he was a klutz."

I was relieved that she seemed to buy the story. "He is, but I give him credit. He always gets back on the horse. That guy is determined and disciplined as hell. I see him a lot now. We've actually become pretty good friends. It's a side benefit of being a physical therapist, I guess—your klutzy friends are forced to spend time with you." I chuckled nervously.

"That's great," she said. "But wasn't the accident a while ago? Didn't he already have his shoulder repaired last fall?"

I had forgotten about Lex's stellar memory. When we were in junior high, rumor had it that she was partly to blame for the firing of our seventh-grade American history teacher because she corrected the content of his lectures so often.

I cleared my throat and held a fist to my mouth as if I were suppressing a tremendous belch. "Yeah, well, Nolan might want to get another opinion on his collarbone. It's still acting up a little." It was a stretch, but I needed a cover.

Again, Lex stared at me. I suspected she was deciding whether to drop it or inquire further. She was probably the kind of mom who didn't have to utter a word to make a kid confess wrongdoing. She would have made an effective boss if she'd worked in management after she'd gotten her business degree, instead of getting pregnant on her honeymoon and becoming a stay-at-home mom.

After an agonizing moment, the inquisitive look on her face softened. "Lunch?"

"Yes." I exhaled in relief.

We walked over to the diner, and I held the door open for her to walk in ahead of me.

"Uh, Lex?" I asked.

"Yes?"

"Just don't mention the surgery stuff this weekend, okay? It would be totally unprofessional for me to talk about it with anyone, even you."

"No praaablem," she said, in her exaggerated Midwestern twang, and then playfully snaked her arm around mine, resting her hand on my bicep. She leaned her head on my shoulder, and I caught a whiff of her hair as we walked to a table in the back of the restaurant. She smelled fresh and floral—intoxicating. I had to remind myself that this was the same girl who spread a rumor in first grade that I had cooties.

"Hey, Lex?"

"Yes?"

"I'm really glad you came home."

Chapter 5: Becca

I tapped open the Words with Friends app on my phone the moment I hit the chair. The waiting room was packed for a Thursday before a getaway weekend, and, given my determination to avoid small talk at all costs, I kept my head low and my eyes fixed on the game. Just as I was about to score seventy-five points on an optimally placed *Q*, Nolan walked in.

"Hey," he said quietly, taking a seat beside me on a beige couch. "I dropped Emma off at Jordana's. Not surprisingly, Jordy's got a whole day of activities planned for her, so we're covered."

"Okay, good." I pressed PLAY on *Quilts* and was pleased to see the word had given me a sizable lead against Emma's former nursery school teacher, whose addiction to word games rivaled my own. I then clicked on my news apps to skim through the day's headlines, and when that got stale, I put the phone away and scanned the room, despite the promise I had made to myself not to do so.

Ever since I had gone into remission in high school and had begun returning regularly for checkups, waiting rooms had been places where I could be a symbol of hope to others in the thick of a crisis. Once a year, I would lift my sleeve to display the patient ID wristband subtly broadcasting that I—the teenager with the long hair; the college kid wearing the Columbia University sweatshirt; the twentysomething young woman in the black business suit; the lady with the beautiful engagement ring; the mom with a photo of her daughter on her custom cell phone case—was a patient, too. I had been where they were, weathered a similar storm, and moved on. But this time felt different. I was returning not as a long-term survivor to impart wisdom, but as a patient in the eye of a new hurricane. I couldn't help but wonder if all this time I had just been a false advertisement.

"Scardino?" the receptionist called.

Nolan and I both looked up. "Yes?" we answered in unison.

"You can go in now. Room two, please."

As we settled into our positions in front of a mahogany desk, I pulled out the grocery store receipt with the notes I'd taken while sitting on the sidewalk at Emma's bus stop. I had been on autopilot as soon as I heard my doctor's voice on the phone and so intent on catching her every word that I had actually jotted down *you'd look amazing with implants!*

Though the news was jarring, the phone call I received on the street corner that day was not entirely shocking.

Mammograms and MRIs had been a part of my life since my mid-twenties, because the radiation that helped to annihilate the Hodgkin's put me at risk for breast cancer. It was sort of ironic to think that the medicine responsible for saving my life as a child could potentially kill me as an adult, but it was a price I happily paid. Over the years, I'd had a few suspicious mammograms followed by biopsies, but they had all turned out fine. I expected this to be the same.

"I'm sorry," I whispered, and reached for Nolan's hand as we waited for the doctor to enter the room. He had been reading her framed diplomas on the wall and turned to look at me as if I were crazy.

"For what?"

Though I knew none of this was my fault, I felt a need to apologize. I thought about how much Nolan had put up with already. Yes, I gave full disclosure right from the start of our relationship that the treatment I'd had could pose some long-term issues. But I couldn't help wondering if, had he known then what he knew now—all the hurdles we would face having a baby, or how, at age thirty-nine, his wife would be diagnosed with breast cancer—he would have reconsidered proposing to me. I was a risky stock. Yes, I looked pretty and polished, just like his friends' wives, but if you scratched beneath the surface, I was different. I wondered if, deep down, he felt like he'd gotten a lemon. I knew that marriage for everyone—with or without a cancer history—was a gamble. It was sort of like buying an airline ticket. You book a flight knowing there are inherent risks: mechanical delay, weather delay, overbooking, bumpy ride, fiery crash to the ground. But purchasing a ticket for a flight that has an increased likelihood of malfunctioning isn't something many people would willingly do. Nolan bought a ticket, got onboard, and buckled up, smiling the whole time. He chose to make *my* journey *our* journey. I was lucky he was mine.

"Just promise me you won't ever allow Emma to call anyone else Mom, okay?" I asked. I had fought long and hard for the title and was blessed a million times over to be the mother of this girl. The thought of another woman taking my place made my chest tighten. My face began to contort, and I knew I was on the precipice of an ugly cry.

"Oh, Bec! Stop!" he insisted, and pulled a tissue out of the box on the doctor's desk. When he dabbed it against my cheek, I broke.

"I want to be the only one she calls Mom." I sobbed like a child who didn't want to share her toys.

"Honey, stop. It's all going to be fine. I've got your back. I promise."

I knew he did. In fact, just that morning, without my saying a word, he had offered to drop Emma off at Jordana's and meet me at the surgeon's office. He knew I couldn't bear to watch my daughter walk away from me, grab the hand of another woman (albeit my best friend), and set off for a day of fun while I reprised the role of a patient. He also knew that I wanted to avoid Jordana. It wasn't that I didn't trust her. After all, I was in the delivery room when she birthed her twins; trust is hardly an issue once you've seen your friend's placenta. But I needed to be in control and have a plan before I shared my news and she started in with what would undoubtedly be a barrage of questions. Not to mention I knew there would be fear in her eyes, in the tone of her voice, in the way she clasped her hands and nervously ran her fingers through her hair. Every gesture and utterance would come from a place of pure love, but being the focus of her angst would be exhausting and suffocating. I couldn't cut her out entirely, but I could limit our communication to email and texts.

Just as I was checking my compact mirror for mascara smudges, the doctor entered.

"Becca, Nolan, it's good to meet you both," Dr. Baxter said warmly. A trio of gold bangle bracelets jiggled and chimed as she extended her arm for a handshake.

"Well, Becca, I've reviewed your records, which"—she raised her eyebrows—"are quite voluminous, and I'm impressed by how well you've stayed on top of the game in terms of long-term follow-up. I see pulmonary function reports, chest X-rays, bloodwork, MRIs, the whole gamut going back over two decades. Good for you. Not all patients are this compliant after so many years."

I smiled at the compliment. "I sort of feel like it's one of my jobs," I said.

"Well, you've done a good job. And it's because you've done such a good job that we've caught this. But, as you know, even with regular appointments and someone as responsible as you, these things can find a way to sneak in and rear their ugly head."

My stomach dropped. *Oh my God. How bad is it?*

"Normally with someone your age, we would recommend a lumpectomy, and then, based on the results from the biopsy, we would determine your course of treatment. Right now, we know you have a tumor the size of a small grape in your right breast." She reached for a notepad and sketched out two circles with a small, darkened oval on the inside corner of the right one. "What we don't know is whether the cells have spread to the surrounding tissue." She drew arrows shooting out in all directions from the darkened oval.

"What stage is she?" Nolan interjected.

"I can't say for certain. We won't know what we're dealing with until we see whether those cells invaded the lymph nodes. But if I were to guess, I'd say she's Stage Two."

"How do I get rid of this?" I asked.

"Well, Becca"—she put the pen down on the notepad and

looked at me with an expression that somehow conveyed fascination, admiration, and sympathy all at once—"you're in a different category than most other patients your age. Your chest and all the lymph nodes in the upper portion of your body were already treated with high doses of radiation to cure the Hodgkin's when you were a child. So radiation is not an option for you."

Oh my God. Don't say chemo. Please do not say the word chemo.

I suddenly had a vision of Emma and Nolan hovering over me in a hospital bed, the way my parents did when I was a child. I imagined Emma holding the basin at the ready in case I got sick. The image itself made me want to vomit. Years ago, my aversion to chemo had become so strong, I'd gotten nauseated at the mere sight of the nurse's scrubs and the scent of the gauze before the medication was administered. One time, I puked in the hospital elevator before we even reached the pediatric ward.

"Given your history," she continued, "there's a good chance this could recur in the same breast or the other one. So even though your left side is completely clear and, as far as we know, the right side has only a small affected area, I've consulted with some of my colleagues and I'd strongly recommend doing a bilateral mastectomy. This way, you won't have to worry about any sort of recurrence down the line. Does that make sense?" She cocked her head and looked at me kindly.

Where do I sign? I thought. *How could I pass up an opportunity to rid myself of anything that could pose an obstacle to being healthy and watching my daughter grow up?*

Though I knew I wouldn't totally be in the clear until after the surgery, when we would know whether the cells had spread, the thought that I could have this intrusion literally cut out of me and proactively shield myself from a potential threat down the line was enormously comforting. I actually exhaled.

"It absolutely makes sense," I said, and smiled. I felt the need to connect with her and differentiate myself from other young women, to show her I wasn't in any way undone by this news—that to me, this was a no-brainer.

"All right!" Nolan said enthusiastically, and rubbed his hands together. "Let's do it! That's one way to get a boob job, Bec!"

Though the doctor seemed unsure how to respond to Nolan, I laughed. He has always had an unpredictable way of reacting to things. A small scratch on a wood table can trigger a full-on freak-out, and his proclivity for ordering late-night infomercial exercise equipment has caused me at times to question his sanity. But in truly serious matters, he has always used humor to make me feel as if everything will be okay.

Sitting there in the doctor's office, I felt strong and secure. I was proud of myself for being vigilant about my care, and for having the clarity in a moment of crisis to confidently make a life-altering choice. I was grateful to be in the hands of this reputable surgeon, and at a hospital with a proven track record for saving my life. I had the unwavering support of a husband who kept me laughing even in my darkest moments, and if there was one lesson I learned from my experience as a kid, it was that laughter was powerful medicine. *Becca Night Live* and the cast got me through the first time; Nolan would be my supporting cast this time around.

"So, what's the next step?" Nolan asked.

"The next step would be for you to meet with our plastic surgeon. He's excellent and has a great deal of experience with young women. We operate on Tuesdays and tag-team the surgery. I start by removing the breasts, and then he inserts the implants. The whole thing takes a few hours. Of course, you could choose to forgo reconstruction. It's absolutely your choice. If that's the case, we have a very nice boutique downstairs with a variety of prosthetic options."

The word *prosthetic* made me wince. I didn't want a prosthetic. The fact that they had a set schedule of every Tuesday for doing the surgeries made the whole thing feel like a well-oiled machine, as if I were following an established path. Nolan and I looked at each other and seemed to communicate telepathically. We simultaneously turned back to Dr. Baxter. "We'd like to meet with the plastic surgeon," I said assuredly.

Ten minutes later, I was wearing a gown and sitting atop an exam table, reading the "Understanding Reconstructive Surgery" booklet the nurse handed to me when we walked in. As we waited for the doctor to arrive, Nolan checked his email and voice mail while I made notes, circled passages, and scribbled questions in the margins. In hindsight, that was my first red flag—I had a million questions, but Nolan seemed to have none.

Eventually, the plastic surgeon walked in and Nolan turned off his phone.

"Good morning. I'm Dr. Farrow, and this is my nurse practitioner, Anne. It's nice to meet you. Will you please remove your gown?" He was all business.

I glanced at Nolan, suddenly embarrassed. *Where do I plant my eyeballs while standing topless in front of my husband as another man manipulates my breasts?* I wondered.

"So, are we looking to match your current C cup?" the doctor asked. "Go smaller? Larger? What did you have in mind?"

"Definitely smaller," I said. I had never thought my chest size suited my petite frame. In fact, a guy friend in college actually nicknamed me the Letter P because my figure matched the outline of a *P*.

"Smaller? You sure?" Nolan asked.

I shot him a look, and he recoiled.

"Anne, would you hand me the B and C cup forms, please?" Dr. Farrow asked, holding out his hand toward the nurse but keeping his eyes focused on my chest. He held the forms up to my breasts for comparison. "This is not exact, but it should give you a rough idea of sizing."

I looked at my reflection in the wall mirror and tried to imagine the new look but couldn't. It wasn't that I lacked creative vision; it was that I had no interest.

"Now feel these," he said, placing another set of forms in my hands. "This one is silicone, and this is saline."

I had no idea what I was feeling for or how I was supposed to react. I passed them to Nolan so he could have a turn.

"Ooh, that's so weird," he said. I thought he might start to giggle. He had a tendency to do that in awkward situations.

Not knowing what else was expected of me, I began to ask Dr. Farrow the questions I had written in the margins of the handout. I morphed into reporter mode: focused, curious, unbiased, emotions in check—exactly the way I'd interviewed sources for the

Columbia Daily Spectator in college and then as a television producer for ABC News before Emma was born. I learned about the pros and cons of silicone versus saline implants. I was informed of the risks of infection, rejection, and potential leakage. I was told there would be not one but multiple procedures, and that my history of radiation could have created scar tissue that might cause some complications. Just like the mystery of whether the cancer spread to the nodes, they wouldn't know how extensive the scar tissue was until they got in there.

As the meeting wore on, the more difficult it was for me to remain detached. I suspected most of Farrow's patients found shopping for a set of new boobs to be the more uplifting (no pun intended) appointment of the day—the one that looked ahead to the future and helped women believe they were regaining control of their lives. For me, though, it was the opposite. I could feel my shoulders rise, my upper back hunch. *More surgeries, more recovery time, more appointments, more pain, more risk of infection, more time away from Emma . . .* The words ran on a loop in my mind. *And for what? Breasts?* I had been strong and secure in Baxter's office, but I could feel myself growing weak and uncertain in Farrow's.

"If you have no other questions," he said, "we should probably get you on the schedule."

I felt as if I were on a speeding subway. Everything was moving so quickly.

"I have one more question," I finally said. "Is it possible to do the mastectomy now and then do the reconstruction at a later date? Or does it all have to be done at the same time?"

"It's not *impossible*," Farrow said, "but the healing process is easier if you do it at the same time. I wouldn't recommend doing it separately. Now is the time."

"Have you had patients who have opted out of reconstruction?" I asked.

Nolan shifted in his seat and started twirling a pen with his fingers. It was something he tended to do when impatient.

"Well, yes, some women certainly choose to forgo reconstruction, but typically they are significantly older. I can't say I know of many, or any firsthand, who are on the younger side, like you."

There was a lull for a moment. Dr. Farrow removed his wire-rim glasses, buffed them with the edge of his white coat, and said, "You know, Rebecca, years ago, young women didn't have the options they have today. You're very lucky. We now have the ability to make patients look like themselves after such a radical and emotional surgery. You're not even forty. You have your whole life ahead of you. Don't you want to be made whole again?" He carefully placed the glasses back on his face.

Whole? I thought. It was an interesting word choice. *Would I somehow be incomplete if I didn't choose reconstruction?* I said nothing. I understood his point. There was no denying that the strides had been great, and the options presented were nothing short of a blessing for countless women. But at that moment, I just wasn't sure I was ready to be one of them.

When I thought about losing my breasts, I felt relief. I felt free. I felt liberated from fear. It never occurred to me that I would ever feel inadequate or stop resembling myself. I knew I would still be me, with or without breasts—just as I learned at age fifteen that I was still me, with or without hair. The only difference was that hair grew back and breasts didn't, and that with hair loss, there was no choice to be made. Thanks to reconstruction, I had the power to choose.

"Well, if you have no further questions, Anne will set you up with the paperwork and we can get you on the calendar. It was a pleasure meeting you," he said. He extended a hand to me and then to Nolan. "Feel free to call if you want to discuss anything further."

As soon as Dr. Farrow and Anne exited the room, Nolan seemed to come back to life. "So?" he asked. "Are you going to play it safe with a B cup, or are we going triple D?"

"Ha, you're funny." I slipped my blouse over my head.

"What? You want an A cup?"

"I don't know if I want any of it."

"Bec, you don't have a choice. You have to do this. You know that."

"I'm not talking about the mastectomy. I'm okay with that."

"Then what do you mean?"

"I mean *this*. I'm not sure about this whole implant thing. It's not really sitting right with me."

He was silent for a moment and then laughed nervously. "You're kidding."

I shook my head.

His face turned red. "You're *kidding* me," he said. He began to laugh, but not in the way he'd chuckle at a joke. This laugh seemed to be filled with resentment, and I could feel his anger begin to percolate. "I thought you were just curious when you asked that question about opting out. You were actually serious?"

I nodded. "Did you hear what he said about the risks and the multiple operations and not knowing how the scar tissue would impact the reconstruction?"

He stood up and began pacing the small exam room. "You know doctors tell patients all those risks because they have to. It's part of the whole deal. They need the disclaimer so you don't sue them if something goes wrong."

"Of course I know that. But honestly, I'm already sick of this. I'm sick of being a patient. I'm sick of hospitals and doctors and appointments and constantly looking over my shoulder. I'm one hundred percent comfortable with the mastectomy. It's what I have to do, and I have no qualms about it. But the thought of having multiple surgeries that introduce a risk of leakage and pain and possible rejection doesn't excite me. For what? Cosmetic purposes? I totally see the value for a lot of women. I really do. If I were thirty-nine and this were my first experience with cancer, hell yeah, I'm positive I would move forward with reconstruction, because I'd want to get back the body I had always known."

I paused to take a breath. Even Nolan's ears and neck were flushed. He looked at me as if I had six heads.

"I guess I'm coming from a different place," I continued. "I'm not saying this is a done deal. But it's very tempting just to have this shit cut out of me and move on. Why not minimize my time as a patient and maximize my time as a healthy person?"

Nolan grabbed a pen and threw it across the tile floor. "So that's it? I don't have a say? You've made your decision?" he bellowed.

"Jesus! Lower your voice! Of course you have a say. I'm just telling you what's going through my mind right now. This is a joint decision. We need to talk about it."

He took a deep breath and wiped sweat from his upper lip. I could tell he was trying to remain composed. "Listen, Becca, I love you and support you. Ultimately, it's your choice, but . . . I have an opinion."

"And let me guess. You want a brunette Dolly Parton." I smiled, trying to add levity and end this discussion. Anne would be returning to the room at any moment.

"No." He scowled. "I don't care if it's a B or an A or a freakin' mosquito bite, but I want my wife to have *something*."

"Why? What difference does it make? Come on—would you really love me any less if I had no boobs?" This was meant to be a rhetorical question, but he answered.

"No, I would still love you. But honestly"—he paused and then looked directly at me—"I'm not sure I would find you as attractive."

I didn't blink for a good thirty seconds. I just stared at him in silence as a wave of nausea came over me. Never in my life would I have expected Nolan to say those words. And what made it worse was that he had no remorse. He kept going in a completely measured tone.

"I understand you're scared. I get that you don't want pain. I'll be there by your side the whole way through, but you need to see the big picture here. It's most likely short-term pain for long-term gain."

"How do you know the pain will be short-lived? How do you know those implants will make me happy? What am I gaining long-term?"

"Oh my God!" His decibel level began to rise again. "It's not just about you! What about *me*? What about *Emma*? This affects us too, you know!"

There was no question the medical staff and other patients could hear us in the hallway outside the exam room. I blushed when family and friends serenaded me on my birthday in the privacy of my own home. Publicly airing dirty laundry made me extremely uncomfortable.

I gritted my teeth. "If I choose to forgo this part of the surgery, it will be because I am strong. Because I have inner strength—the same inner strength that enabled me to stare down kids in my high school who goggled at me with a scarf around my head."

"Oh, get over yourself with that bullshit, Becca."

I felt as if a tornado were beginning to stir and gain momentum inside my body. My stomach ached, my chest burned, my pulse quickened. I knew it was only a matter of time before I cried. "Who the fuck are you?" I whispered forcefully. "Where is my *husband*? Where is the guy who has always told me I'm just as beautiful on the inside as on the outside? Huh? Where's that guy?"

"That guy's sittin' right here, wondering how this is all gonna play out in his marriage. You've got to be kidding yourself if you don't think this is going to change us."

"First of all, no decision has been made. And second, Nol, it's *us*! You and me! The same two people. That part is not changing!"

He let out a long exhale and then looked down at the phone in his hand for a solid minute. He seemed frozen in place. I said nothing and hoped the storm had passed.

He shook his head and frowned. "I've got to tell you, Bec," he said matter-of-factly, "I'm not going to be that guy at the bar who all the other guys are whispering about and saying, 'Hey, did you hear? Scardino's wife has no tits.'"

My entire body tensed. The inner tornado was picking up speed; I could barely breathe. The fact that his imagination jumped to a scene of himself being mocked at a bar while he was still sitting in an exam room with me—his wife, who was confronting a cancer diagnosis and life-altering surgery—was nothing short of appalling. It was so self-absorbed, so egocentric, and so incredibly disappointing. Part of me wished I had a posse of friends and family standing beside me in that exam room to support me and make him realize how ridiculous he was being. The other part of me wanted to go home, get into bed, and hide under my comforter.

"Who's gonna know whether or not I have tits? And what do you mean you're 'not going to be that guy'? What are you saying? That you're gonna *divorce* me if I have no chest?"

He stared at the phone in his palm and wouldn't lift his eyes. *Oh my God*, I thought, *he didn't flinch when I said the word* divorce!

"I don't know," he finally said. "I don't know."

I had no idea who this man was. It occurred to me that I could lose my breasts and my husband in the same summer. I could hear my heartbeat in my ears.

I sat silently for a moment, taking in what had just transpired. I knew my next move was critical. I could apologize and make it all go away with a promise to have the reconstruction, or I could just say exactly what was on my mind, regardless of the repercussions.

"You're an asshole," I said. "A real asshole." I spoke so calmly and slowly so that the word was clearly enunciated. "I guess when the cards are down, your true colors come out, eh?"

"Screw you!" he said, and punched the air in front of him. "You don't know how good you have it. You have no idea how much shit I shield from you. I've taken on all your crap and never complained. Not once. I've been a fuckin' prince among men. All I'm asking is that my wife has breasts. Breasts! That she look like a normal woman. I don't think it's too much to ask."

There was a knock on the door. "It's Anne. May I come in?"

I cleared my throat and shot Nolan a get-yourself-together look, although I knew there was an excellent chance she'd heard every word we had flung at each other—a thought that made me cringe. "Yes," I said. "Come in." But all I could think was, *What could he possibly be shielding from me?*

Before she turned the knob, Nolan had swung his work bag across his chest and mouthed, "I'm out of here." As Anne entered the room with the paperwork for me to sign to confirm the surgery, he pushed past her and out the door without a word.

Twenty minutes later, I left the hospital. I checked my phone and saw a text from Jordana. It was a picture of her with Emma, with the caption *Em and JoJo having fun! Hope you are too!* I gave my phone the middle finger.

I tried calling Nolan. He didn't answer, and I hung up before leaving a message.

How can we possibly leave tomorrow for the reunion and survive the weekend, pretending everything is okay?

I felt like I might explode. I needed to talk. And yet I was too scared to verbalize or even believe what had just occurred. But I knew that once I was ready to put it into words and allow it to become real, there would be only one voice I could tolerate hearing.

Chapter 6: Holly

*T*he phone rang Friday morning the instant I put the gun in my hand. I had fantasized about this day for months, plotting my rebellion like a teenager conspiring to stay out past curfew. One hour was all I needed. I had promised myself I'd avoid all distractions, but when I saw Becca's number on my cell phone screen, I had to answer. Hers was the one call I'd never ignored.

I rested the registry gun on a store shelf next to the infant diaper display and lifted the phone from a crumb-encrusted pocket of my purse. "Well, if it isn't the guest of honor!" I exclaimed.

"Hey, Hol." It was only ten o'clock in the morning, but Becca sounded exhausted.

Suddenly, the loudspeaker in the store blasted in the background: "Lucinda to the stockroom. Lucinda to the stockroom."

"Where are you?" Becca asked.

I smiled. "Babies 'R' Us in Union Square."

"You actually started a registry?"

"Uh-huh. Can you believe it?"

"Wow. I didn't think you'd pull the trigger on this one. Did you buy a house, too?"

I laughed. Becca's affinity for puns rivaled that of an octogenarian English professor. She also knew about my guilty pleasure: online browsing. Virtual tours of suburban homes were my equivalent of porn, and while I spent much of my free time filling website shopping carts with strollers and high chairs, I never actually purchased anything.

"It's kind of pathetic how I'm getting a rush from this," I admitted. "If word gets out that I started a registry for my unborn child, it will be a total scandal. Trust me. The yentas will come out in full force, and frankly, I'm sick of being the talk of the town when it comes to babies."

For over a decade, Adam and I had been the couple everyone assumed would have a baby—except we never did. When we announced our long-awaited first pregnancy on my fortieth birthday, we were flooded with good wishes. But behind the smiles and hugs, I knew the women of my Orthodox community were doing the math and calculating that my child would be entering kindergarten the same year theirs would be graduating from high school.

I tried to disregard the pity in their eyes, because they were my friends. They were the ones who welcomed Adam and me into their world when we were twenty-two-year-old newlyweds. They became our neighbors and customers. Their patronage helped turn my business, Holly's Challahs—a small kosher bakery in Crown Heights, Brooklyn, that I started simply to pay the bills while Adam was in yeshiva—into one of the most successful kosher franchises in the country. Because of them, I went from being "the owner of that cute bake shop in Brooklyn" to being the CEO of one of the only US corporations to be led by an Orthodox Jewish woman. While the neighborhood ladies gathered in playgroups and dissected the virtues of various double-stroller models, I spent my time managing employees, speaking at national leadership conferences, and throwing one negative pregnancy test after another into the garbage. When I wasn't traveling, I'd bump into the women at the supermarket or see them at synagogue. Inevitably someone would ask, "So? What's new?" and then steal a glance at my midsection. On the rare occasion someone was tactless enough to ask why I was childless, I always smiled and responded that the bakery was my baby. No one knew that I stored IVF medication in the mini-fridge beneath my desk at work, or that whenever "Baby Got Back" played on my phone, it was my doctor's office calling to report another failed cycle. Other than confiding in Becca, I was very private about how

Adam and I ached for a child. We would have traded the bakery in a heartbeat for the chance to be called Mom and Dad.

During those years, I often found myself thinking back to that time in high school when Jordana, Lex, Seth, and I rode the subway home in silence after visiting Becca in the hospital. I had wondered why she of all people had been picked to suffer. When she finally recovered, I surmised that God must have had a plan—that everyone, no matter how good they were, experienced a certain amount of crap in life, and that Becca was simply getting her share over with early. I told myself that infertility was my "crap," and that I was in the midst of getting my turn over with. But with each passing year of unanswered prayers and dashed hopes, I grew increasingly bitter.

"Why?" I'd whimper, burying my face into my pillow at night. How could it be that Adam and I had made a conscious choice to lead a religious life—to keep kosher, to observe the Sabbath, to follow the laws of the Torah, to become active members of our Jewish community—and yet we were being denied the ability to fulfill the mitzvah to be fruitful and multiply?

Maybe it was the hormones, but when IVF finally worked and my pregnancy started to show, I became a flurry of contradictions: I was grateful my time had come but resentful it had taken so long. I thanked God daily for the blessing of a healthy pregnancy, but I questioned the existence of a higher power that could have allowed fifteen years of pain and sadness. Part of me was content to accept the theory that God had a plan and I was in no position to question it. I reminded myself that a rough patch shouldn't lead to the abandonment of faith and a culture. And yet something in me itched to break free. Impending motherhood triggered memories of my own childhood, and I suddenly found myself nostalgic for the decidedly un-Orthodox way I was brought up: Friday nights at the movies, Saturday morning cartoons followed by Little League softball, shrimp in lobster sauce from the local Chinese restaurant, and, most of all, public school.

All of the children in our community were enrolled in yeshivas. Forget public school—not one family I knew even sent their kids to a modern Orthodox yeshiva or a conservative Hebrew day school. Both of those were deemed too liberal and assimilated. For years, I assumed that Adam and I would just follow the pack. Why not? The intensive curriculum was a fabulous way to cement an understanding of our faith and culture from an early age. But as my due date approached and the reality of child rearing was upon me, I focused more on what my kid would be missing and less on what he or she would gain from the lifestyle that had enriched our lives for so many years. I was a proud product of the New York City public school system, where every classroom was a mini–United Nations. I celebrated Chinese New Year annually with my friend Jennifer Kim's family. Invitations to *quinceañeras* and first communions were pinned to the corkboard in my bedroom. Though I ultimately chose to immerse myself in a relatively insular community, I was rooted in multiculturalism and tolerance. How could I not want the same for my child?

You're on the cusp of motherhood! I told myself. *Figure it out! Which world is it going to be?*

Somehow, I was convinced that creating a baby registry would be my journey to the dark side—that little taste of rebellion I needed to get out of my system. Nowhere in the Torah did it expressly say, "Thou shall not create a baby registry," so I knew I wasn't breaking any laws, but it just wasn't customary in our superstitious circles. Sure, I could have easily shopped online, where there was no risk of getting caught, but I wanted a sensory experience, not a virtual one. I needed to smell the lotions, to run my fingers over the Pack 'n Play fabrics, to squeeze the bouncy seat cushions, to compare the cheerful melodies of crib mobiles. But more than anything, I yearned to hold that silly registry gun—to stand in the aisles of Babies "R" Us with my eight-months-pregnant belly and zap away at bar codes to my heart's content. My time had finally come, and dammit, I was ready to shop.

"Seriously," I now said to Becca, "is there really a difference between the sixteen brands of rectal thermometers I'm staring at? I mean, come on! Who are these so-called 'experts,' and how do they conduct the research? Do they stick babies on a table, line up the thermometers, and put different ones in their butts to see if they come out with the same number?"

Becca chuckled, but it was far from her typical cackle. Something about her response seemed forced and compulsory. Maybe she was tired, or anxious about being the center of attention. I recalled how overwhelmed she'd been on her wedding day, knowing that all eyes would be on her.

"So, when are you heading to the reunion?" she asked.

"I'll probably leave here in about an hour or so," I said. "Hey, I thought you were meeting Jordana and getting Lex at the airport. Shouldn't you guys be on your way by now?"

"Actually, that's why I'm calling. Slight change of plans. Seth is picking up Lex, and Jordana's already left. Any chance I can get a ride up with you?" she asked.

This was strange. Becca not with Jordana? There had been at least ten separate email chains in recent weeks about the logistics of the weekend. In every permutation, Becca was riding up in Jordana's car. In fact, Jordana had the itinerary down to the minute. It always surprised me how someone with such a bohemian facade could be the furthest thing from laid-back.

"Are you sure coming with me won't upset Jordana?" I asked, wondering if they'd had a spat. If so, I wanted to steer clear. Until I'd received Jordana's invitation to the reunion, I hadn't seen or spoken to her since Becca and Nolan's wedding. Starting in our senior year of high school, when she claimed I stole her boyfriend, any interaction Jordana and I had consisted of me walking on eggshells, trying to be extra nice, and Jordana avoiding eye contact. It was kind of her to invite Adam and me to honor Becca, and I didn't want to do anything to offend my host.

"Don't worry about Jordana," Becca said.

"Okay, meet me here and help me figure out the rectal thermometer situation; then we'll drive up together. It'll be fun. And besides, then you and I can get some QT in before Jordy takes over. You know she still resents me."

"Jordana and your husband were an item a hundred years ago." Becca sighed.

"Yes," I said, "and Jordana has ignored me ever since. We didn't plan it. We *got married*, for God's sake. It's not like it was a fling."

It was, in fact, quite the opposite. The summer before our senior year of high school, I hosted a house party while my parents were away on a cruise. Somehow, word spread and the small soiree turned into a John Hughes–esque teen extravaganza with over a hundred kids, three of whom sat on top of my neighbor's car and dented the roof. My parents learned of the party when they returned from their trip and opened an auto-repair bill that had arrived in the mail. Though I was a good kid and this was my one dalliance, my nonobservant but Zionist parents decided I needed some "straightening out" and sent me on a two-week teen tour of Israel. Jordana's boyfriend of two years, Adam, happened to be on the same excursion. We went to separate schools, and Jordana was our only common friend. I don't know whether it was the distance from home, or the fact that it was our first taste of independence, or because it was the culmination of a fabulous vacation, but Adam and I kissed on our last day in Israel.

All the way across the sea, we contemplated how to tell Jordana. In the end, we never had to. She was standing at the International Arrivals terminal at JFK at 5:00 a.m. with a neon-yellow WELCOME HOME, ADAM poster when she saw him lean toward my ear and whisper something that made me grin as we rolled our luggage through the automatic doors. From that one gesture, she knew. She dropped the sign, ran out of the building, and never forgave either one of us.

Though our families and friends wrote it off as a phase, Adam and I returned home from Israel inspired to become more religious. Neither of us could identify a single event from our trip that had been the turning point. It wasn't the morning we hiked up an ancient desert fortress at sunrise or the afternoon we lit a memorial candle together at the Holocaust museum. It wasn't the fact that we learned Jewish history by standing in the exact locations described in the Torah or that, just hours later, we planted our own trees in the soil near those very spots. And it wasn't the Friday afternoon when deliciously exotic aromas guided us through a crowded Jerusalem marketplace or the Sabbath eve when we shoved tiny handwritten prayers into the crevices of the Western Wall as the Old City glistened in amber and gold. No, it wasn't just one of those experiences that changed us; it was all of them combined.

And so, from the moment he walked off the plane, Adam wore a black felt yarmulke. And while it took a few weeks for me to part ways with my beloved cutoff jean shorts and tank tops, I eventually adopted modest attire, wearing long skirts and three-quarter-length sleeves. Before long, we were praying three times a day, studying with a rabbi, eating kosher food, and asking our parents to use separate cookware for meat and dairy meals. It all just kind of happened, quickly and naturally, the way things tend to unfold when they feel preordained.

Becca yanked me back to the present moment. "Jordana invited you this weekend, didn't she? She wouldn't have done that if she didn't want you there."

I sighed. "Yeah, I suppose it was an olive branch. I'll see you soon."

Half an hour later, Becca arrived, lugging a quilted paisley weekend bag over her shoulder. She wore army-green cargo shorts, a plain white tee, a delicate gold necklace, and beige leather ankle-strap sandals. She looked like a walking advertisement for Banana Republic.

"Look at you!" she said, as she headed down the toy aisle.

Becca gently rubbed my belly with both of her palms. This was the first time she had seen me in person since I'd started showing. We lived a borough apart, but our busy schedules made get-togethers tough to book.

"Crazy, huh?" I smiled and rested my hands atop hers. I took a mental snapshot, hoping always to remember the moment when my best friend—the one in whom I'd confided throughout my struggle, the one who I prayed would live long enough that we could be mommies together—saw me pregnant for the first time.

"I'm so happy for you," Becca said, as she hugged me. "It's your turn. You're going to be the best mom."

Is she tearing up? I was taken aback. She wasn't the weepy, sentimental sort. For the third time that day, I felt as if something was off.

"Thanks," I said. "You know you're my inspiration, right?

I want to be the kind of mom you are to Emma: fun and cool. The way she looks up to you—"

"Please," Becca interrupted. She caressed the sapphire solitaire around her neck, Emma's birthstone. She subtly bit her lower lip, forming the same expression she made in sixth grade when Anthony Edings accidentally slammed a soccer ball into her shins and she didn't want to cry.

There was definitely something going on. I could feel it in my bones. I stared at her for a second, trying to gauge whether she was ready to talk, but I got the sense that she wasn't quite there yet. "What's the deal with *this* contraption?" I asked, pointing to a large circular toy at the end of the aisle.

"I call it the Circle of Neglect," an unfamiliar female voice said from behind me.

Becca and I turned to see a very fit, young pregnant woman in black spandex pants and a high blond ponytail. She was pushing a shopping cart with a toddler throwing Cheerios from the small seat beside the handlebar.

"Let me tell you, that activity center is a godsend," the woman said with an air of authority as she pried the Cheerios from her son's clenched fist. "I just stick him in the seat and turn on the music, and he spins around and plays. Gives me at least thirty minutes of downtime."

"We had one for Emma a few years ago, but it was much more basic," Becca said.

The woman smiled and nodded toward my abdomen. "When are you due?"

"August. How about you?"

"Our girl's supposed to arrive on Labor Day. You know what you're having?"

"No, it's a surprise," I said.

"Well, whatever it is, good luck!" she said, and pushed her cart away.

"So, what's the under-over on that hot mama?" I whispered to Becca. "I'd say she's somewhere around twenty-four. And did you see the way she got the Cheerios out of that kid's death-grip fist? That's skill."

Becca shrugged. "You'll figure out the Cheerio death grip for yourself. And so what if she's young? You're a hot mama, too," she said reassuringly.

"I've gained thirty pounds, my boobs are like watermelons, and my dainty feet now require extra-wide shoes. The only thing about me that hasn't changed is my red hair. Even my freckles seemed to have expanded!"

"But you're glowing. You really are. You look beautiful."

Just as I was about to thank her, Becca's phone rang. She glanced at the screen and then ignored it.

"I forgot to ask you," I said, running my fingers over the stroller blankets, "if you're driving up with me, how's Nolan getting upstate?"

When Becca didn't respond, I looked up and saw her frozen in place, staring into the distance like a deer in headlights.

"Hey, you okay?"

"Yeah," she said unconvincingly. "Why?"

"Because you didn't answer me."

"What did you ask?"

"I just asked how Nolan is getting upstate."

"Oh, sorry," she said. "I don't know."

"What do you mean, you don't know?"

"I mean exactly that," Becca said, her tone now biting. I wondered if I had offended her in some way.

Her phone rang, and, once again, she checked the caller ID and didn't pick up.

"Is that Nolan?" I asked gently.

"Actually, no," she said, "it's Jordana. I'll be right back. I've got to go to the bathroom."

That was when I knew something was very wrong. I could count on one hand the number of times my germaphobe best friend had ever used a public restroom. I continued to zap items without much enthusiasm until she came back. Her mouth formed a forced smile, but her eyes knew better and refused to cooperate.

"What's wrong?" I asked, putting my hand on her forearm.

"It'll be fine," she said.

"*What* will be fine?" Now I was really worried.

"Nothing. Let's finish your registry." She waved a hand as if to shoo away my question.

The dark bags beneath her eyes made her sockets appear cavernous, and the sparkle that normally shone from her hazel irises had dimmed. She looked spent. Suddenly, I didn't care about shopping.

"Forget the stupid registry," I said.

Becca shook her head as if to say no, but then her face contorted and her hands flew to her mouth to muzzle her sobs.

"Oh, honey," I whispered. I quickly threw the gun into my purse to free my hands. My belly was too big for a proper embrace, so I wrapped an arm around her back and pulled her toward me. She buried her head in my neck, and we remained fixed in that side hug long enough for her tears to saturate my shirt.

"Let's get out of here. I'll drive, you talk, okay?" I said when she caught her breath. I wiped a tear rolling down her cheek with my thumb.

"I can't go," she said, sounding utterly defeated. "I have too much to figure out at home."

"What's going on? Is Emma all right? Are your parents okay?"

"Yes, everyone's fine." Becca sniffled. She looked as if she were about to open up, but then caught herself. "I just need some time alone to clear my head and think. As much as I love everyone, I'm just not up to schmoozing."

"I don't know what's going on, but Lex is flying in from halfway across the country, and Jordana has devoted six months to planning this shindig. You can't flake out in the eleventh hour because you're not in the mood."

She folded her arms in protest. I tried to think of a way to get her in the car.

"Listen," I said. "The trip is only a couple of hours, but for an eight-months-pregnant lady with sciatica and a constant need to pee, that's like an eternity. I'm going to have to stop along the way and may get tired. It's probably not a good idea for me to be alone. I might need you to take the wheel."

Becca processed my request for a moment. "Fine." She revealed the slightest hint of a smile. I linked my arm through hers, and together we exited through the automatic doors.

For the next ninety minutes, Becca essentially interviewed me while I drove. As a journalist, she'd spent years perfecting the art of getting people to talk. She knew how to strategically frame questions and when a sympathetic glance, instead of a verbal prompt, would yield maximum loquacity. That's how she was able to spend the majority of our trip shining the spotlight on me. She inquired about my pregnancy, about Adam, and about how we planned to balance caring for the baby and the bakery. All of this was a cover for not talking about whatever was bothering her. But even though I was on to her diversion tricks, I let it happen. Sometimes the best thing about old friendships is knowing when not to push.

But when we reached a rest stop on the highway, I pulled the car into the lot and looked at her, waiting. I knew she needed to talk and that this would be our last moment alone before Jordana and the others gathered around her.

"What?" she asked.

I raised my eyebrows and said nothing. I didn't even blink. She was cornered, and she knew it.

She took a deep breath. "So, you know how I go every year for my follow-up appointments with my Hodgkin's doctor?" she finally said. She fiddled with a ponytail holder on her wrist.

"Uh-huh," I said.

"They do a lot of different tests because they don't know the long-term impact of the treatment I had years ago, because it was all high-dose and experimental."

I nodded. I didn't like where this was going.

"Well, for the last twenty-five years, my heart, lungs, boobs, bloodwork—everything—has always been clean. But this past week, they found something. It's in the early stages, and I'm going to be *fine*. It just needs to come out. So I'm having a double mastectomy in two weeks. That's all."

I stared at her from across the front seat, questions flooding my mind. "If it's that small, why do you need surgery?" I asked. "Why can't you just watch and wait, or do a less aggressive treatment?"

She shook her head. "I'm high-risk because of my history. The chances of this coming back are too great to wait it out. I'm not like someone getting diagnosed for the first time. I'm in a different category. The less aggressive approach would be radiation, and I don't qualify because I already had radiation to my chest. In fact, that's what they think triggered this."

I reached for her arm. "I can't believe you have to go through this shit again. I'm so sorry."

"This is nothing like what I had when I was a kid. This is a blip. Do you hear me? A blip," she said, with a reassuring smile. "Honestly, it will be a relief not to have to worry about when the other shoe will drop. Because it's dropping right now. And I'm taking care of it."

I stared out the windshield for a moment and ran my palms over my belly. I thought about Becca's parents. I worried constantly about the health of my unborn child; I couldn't imagine what it must be like for them to watch their daughter fight for her life not once, but twice.

"I'll be okay," she said when I dabbed the corner of my eye. "If this is the price I pay for twenty-five good years, I'll take it."

"How did your parents take the news?" I asked.

"They don't know," she said softly. "I haven't told them yet. I'm not ready for that conversation. They're so happy right now in retirement and grandparenthood, I don't want to ruin it. If I can put off worrying them a little while longer, then why not?"

I understood. "How did Jordana react?" I asked, knowing how hard it would have been for Becca to tell her.

"She doesn't know yet, either."

"What?" I said. "Seriously? How are you going to get through this weekend?"

"I have no idea." She sighed and tilted her head back onto the headrest.

"Well, it goes without saying, I want to help however I can. I'm here for you, although I know you'll be in great hands with Nolan. I'm sure he'll be waiting on you hand and foot."

Becca cleared her throat. "Yeah, well," she scoffed, "I'm not so sure about the Nolan part."

Chapter 7: Nolan

A sleepless night on the living room couch was no reason to break routine. So, as I did every Friday morning at seven o'clock, I met Seth at his physical therapy clinic in midtown for my regular session.

"You excited for this weekend?" I asked Seth, whose sculpted legs were planted beside my face as I lay back on a weightlifting bench. I was happy to focus on fifty-pound barbells, instead of my fight with Becca.

"Yeah," he said, "My girlfriend's coming up on Saturday night, so you'll get to meet her."

"Which one is this?" I asked. "The actress?" I couldn't keep track of his women.

"No, the Pilates instructor," he said matter-of-factly. "I broke up with the actress a couple of weeks ago."

"Right," I said. Seth identified his girlfriends by their jobs, not their names. This was one of the many things I'd learned about him over the past year and, oddly, one of the reasons I liked him so much. He wasn't trying to pretend to be anyone other than who he was.

These physical therapy sessions, and the friendship they spawned, were undoubtedly the silver lining to my klutziness. My newfound bromance with Seth was certainly the upside to falling off my bicycle and breaking my collarbone during my third triathlon. Whether we discussed politics or *Star Wars* trivia, Seth's flavor-of-the-month girlfriend, or Emma's dance recital, our bond deepened with each appointment. For years I had viewed him as Becca's friend, but now he was mine, too. "It's a new relationship with Pilates Girl, but I figured I'd bring her to Jordana's. I didn't want to be the extra wheel, given that the rest of you guys are couples."

The moment he mentioned couples, I felt compelled to tell him what had happened. I suddenly wanted it out in the open, out of my head. *Here's my entrée,* I thought. "Well, if I don't meet her this weekend," I puffed, "I can always meet her here in the city."

"She's gonna show up, dude," he insisted, and rested his meaty hands on the indent of his waistline. "She likes me. She's not gonna flake. I even got her a ticket to the concert Saturday night."

"No, I meant if for some reason *I'm* not at the reunion this weekend, I can meet her another time."

Seth laughed. "You're funny. Keep your back straight and tighten your core."

"No, I'm serious," I said, panting between repetitions.

"Oh, please! I know Bec doesn't like being the center of attention, but come on, she's the guest of honor. You know sometimes she needs a little push to get out of her shell, and then she's fine," Seth said, as if he knew my wife better than I.

Maybe he does know her better, I thought. *Maybe I don't really know her.*

I sat up and wiped my face with a towel. "Hey, can you keep something between us?"

"Sure," he replied, as he laid out a floor mat and elastic bands in preparation for my next strength-training exercise. I was glad he wasn't looking at me.

"No joke. You can't tell anyone," I said.

He stood up from the mat and focused his attention on my face, instead of the equipment. I squirmed.

"I promise," he said. "What's up?"

I took a deep breath. *Maybe we didn't see the right doctor yesterday,* I thought. *Maybe another surgeon would put her at ease about the reconstruction.* "I think I need another surgical referral from you. For a second opinion."

"I thought you liked the guy who fixed your shoulder," Seth said. "What's wrong with Dr. Schwartz?"

"Oh, no, no, Schwartz was great, my shoulder's great," I said. "I'm not talking about orthopedic surgeons."

"Then what kind of surgeon? What's wrong?" he asked, his tone shifting.

Should I tell him about the fight Becca and I had at the doctor's office? I wondered. *Should I mention how, at 2:00 a.m., I stood in the doorway of Emma's bedroom, crying as I watched her snuggle her teddy bear, because the happy family I thought we had cemented in place was cracking?* I grabbed my water bottle and took a swig.

"I don't know," I finally said, my voice trembling. "I was just curious if you have any general or, uh, plastic surgeons you like." I took another sip from the water bottle.

"Plastic?" Seth asked, clearly surprised.

I nodded.

He smiled. "Hey hey, so you're finally getting that enlargement!"

I offered only a partial grin in response. I wasn't in the mood for our typical sophomoric ribbing.

"Sorry, I couldn't resist," Seth apologized, his hands in the air. "Bad joke. Listen, plastic surgeons tend to specialize in parts of the body. Do you want a general surgeon or someone with a specialty?"

I stared at him blankly, mute for several seconds. To publicly utter the answer to his question would make this all too real.

"No problem—I don't need to know," he said kindly, surely sensing my discomfort. "I'm going to do a little research, and I'll text you by the end of the day. And if you need more or want to talk, I'm here. Okay?"

I nodded appreciatively. I knew a second opinion was a long shot, but figured it couldn't hurt to call for an appointment after the weekend.

As I stood on the floor mat and began performing another set of exercises, I could hear Seth counting the repetitions and felt my body respond appropriately to his instructions, but my thoughts had drifted. Lifting the weights reminded me of the way I scooped Becca's ballerina-like body into the air the day we met. I wondered if I would always be able to do that—just pick her up and carry her away, no matter what the situation, like Superman rescuing Lois Lane. *If only it were that easy,* I thought. I wanted to be her hero, to fix this and make it all go away, but I didn't know how. For the first time in my life, my purple crayon was missing.

After my workout, I dressed and went to the office. I sat at my desk on the forty-first floor, overlooking the Chrysler Building, ignoring all communication from my wife, who had left five voice mails, two emails, and innumerable text messages regarding my whereabouts and intentions for the weekend. There were also a few calls from Sal, asking if I was still planning to meet him at Penn Station for the two o'clock train. I never responded. Instead, I spent forty-five minutes sitting on the windowsill, nursing an iced coffee and dreaming up elaborate stories about the people I saw in the windows across from my own on Lexington Avenue, just like Emma did every time she visited my office. When that got stale, I logged on to Facebook and squandered two consecutive hours examining other people's photographs. I learned that my child-hood neighbor's son had an Elmo cake for his first birthday, that my college roommate celebrated his tenth wedding anniversary on a Caribbean cruise, and that my cousin got a new puppy—a Labradoodle named Poozie.

The law firm, with its carpeted, wood-paneled hallways, felt like a ghost town before the holiday weekend. I was utterly sapped of motivation, so, in a sense, it was not wholly unfortunate that my workload had been temporarily reassigned. Just days before Becca's diagnosis, I had been called into the managing partner's office for a meeting—something that had happened countless times throughout my career at Gordon, Michaelson & Stewart, LLP. This time, however, the head of risk management and the firm's general counsel were present and awaiting my arrival.

"Take a seat, son," Mr. Gordon said kindly, gesturing to the leather couch by the corner windows. "I'll get right to the point. I received a call from a fact-checker at a magazine asking to verify some information in one of their upcoming articles. It's a trade pub-lication, one of the most widely circulated in the beverage industry. A freelance business reporter somehow obtained information about the Thibault deal—information to which only the top brass at the Thibault Corporation and our firm are privy. And, as you know, we are still in active negotiations. The deal is far from done."

"How'd that happen?" I asked, exasperated.

Ilene Weston, the head of risk management, took a sip of ice water and glared at me over the rim as she drank.

"Well," Mr. Gordon continued, "naturally, the magazine would not reveal its source. And, needless to say, Thibault is ballistic. They blame us for the leak. Of course, I denied any involvement and explained that integrity, trust, and the privacy of our clients are the utmost priority of our firm. And then . . ." He looked at Ilene and seemed to pass an invisible baton to her with his eyes.

"And then," she said, picking up where he'd left off, "we Googled the reporter's name. One click led to another, and we saw this posted on Facebook." She opened up her laptop and turned the screen toward me.

I squinted at a picture of me at a bar about a month earlier, grabbing drinks with some old high school buddies.

"Do you know this man?" she asked, pointing to a guy tagged as Tennessee Morse.

"No. I met him for the first time that night. He knew one of my friends, but we didn't speak, other than a brief introduction. Why do you ask?"

"Tennessee Morse is the reporter. Is it possible, while you were socializing that evening, that you could have discussed the Thibault deal?"

My mind raced to recall the events of that night: A dive bar. Midtown. Thursday night in late May. Two beers, at most. Drunk? No. Buzzed? Perhaps. We were throwing darts and shooting the breeze. Did I talk about my job? We all did. These were old friends. No one was a lawyer. No one was in the beverage industry. The fact that I was working on a deal that would nominally change the ingredients and packaging of a soft-drink line hardly qualified as juicy gossip. Though my friends respectfully feigned interest in how I spent the majority of my waking hours, none of them actually gave a shit that a popular soda company had decided to go green and use naturally sourced materials.

Unfortunately, I never considered the ears or occupation of Tennessee Morse, the quiet guy nursing a gin and tonic on a nearby barstool.

My jaw dropped and the blood drained from my face when I realized the potential consequences of my loose lips. Not only had I put my firm's stellar reputation and long-standing relationship with this client at risk, but the financial repercussions for all parties were significant. Everyone in the room was waiting, I assumed, for an admission.

Mr. Gordon put his hand on my shoulder. "Listen, son," he interjected, usurping the lull like a good lawyer so I wouldn't confess or perjure myself, "I've reshuffled case assignments until we get this all sorted out. You're off the deal, for the time being."

This soft-spoken six-foot-five man had been my mentor since we'd met at a Columbia Law networking event when I was still a student. We had stayed in touch, and he had offered me a job after graduation. He was the gentle giant for whom I had endured countless all-nighters double-checking my work so that I'd never let him down. Disappointing him with such a careless, stupid gaffe triggered a stabbing sensation inside my gut. It was as if I had let down my own father.

I walked out of his office, and for the first time in my life, I worried about the stability of my employment.

I never told Becca about any of it. I'd been planning to, of course, but when her diagnosis piggybacked on my news, I decided to keep the work drama to myself. She didn't need another stressor. I could handle it all. *This will blow over,* I told myself. And yet, despite being in the best shape of my life, I'd never felt heavier.

Leaning back on my ergonomic desk chair, I stared at Emma's crayon drawings Scotch-taped to the wall beside my computer screen. I would have given anything to be home with her, snuggling on the couch and watching reruns of *Cake Boss,* our favorite television program. Both Emma and I marveled at the elaborate designs the decorators could create—cakes with flashing lights, hydraulics, moveable cranes, running water, even fire. But what we appreciated as much as the edible art was watching the antics and personalities of the host's big New Jersey Italian family.

It reminded me of my own big New Jersey Italian family—a bois-terous group whose constant chaos mesmerized Emma because it was a wholly different family dynamic than her own. Sitting in my parents' kitchen was like having a front-row seat at the circus. And at this moment, all I wanted was to sit beneath the big top and enjoy the show.

Though Becca and I were close with both sides of our family, my side was more of an occasional treat, while hers was a daily fixture. Becca's parents knew when she had a dentist appointment, and that Fridays were my physical therapy mornings with Seth. They posted Emma's after-school activities on their wall calendar and remembered the names and hobbies of her friends. If they had extra produce from their CSA share, they would let themselves into our apartment and stuff a bag of organic vegetables into our fridge as a surprise gift.

It's not that my mom wouldn't do the same—she was equally loving and ignorant of boundaries. It was simply a matter of geog-raphy and circumstance. The Millers lived three blocks away and didn't want to miss a moment with the grandchild they'd never expected to have. Emma was the grand prize after the hell they went through when Becca was sick, and they'd be damned if any-thing got in the way of their silver lining. My parents, on the other hand, lived an hour away, had a packed social calendar, and didn't like to drive in the city. The onus fell on us to visit, which we gladly did on birthdays and holidays.

I leaned back in my leather desk chair and looked at a photo-graph on my bookshelf. It was of the three of us from a trip to the Jersey Shore boardwalk the previous summer. Emma was sitting on my shoulders, her little legs dangling over my chest and her chin rest-ing atop my bald spot, making our heads look like a double-scoop ice cream cone. Becca stood beside me, natural and relaxed with her beachy hair and aviator sunglasses, wearing the baby-blue halter sundress that made her look like a petite supermodel. I grabbed the picture and held it inches from my face, as if the close proximity to my thoughts would make it possible to telepathically fix things.

I wished I could pick up Emma but knew that was a terrible idea. She was staying with Becca's folks, and I could already hear my mother-in-law's voice: *What do you mean, you're not upstate with Becca? Don't you know Jordy made this whole spiel for her? Are you feeling okay? Where are you taking my Emma?"*

As much as I resented the inability to gain access to my daughter without creating a tsunami of panic and confusion, it wasn't worth the drama. I also realized that I couldn't stay home. With in-laws practically around the corner, I could run into them and Emma in the neighborhood. Plus, the fact that they occasionally used the key to our apartment if they wanted to borrow something or if they were babysitting and Emma left a beloved toy at home meant that holing up as a prisoner wasn't an option, either. I had no choice—I needed to leave the city. I didn't know if it was the back-to-back iced coffees I'd consumed throughout the day, or the realization that it was lunchtime on the Friday of July Fourth weekend and I was sitting in my office with nothing to do, but suddenly I had an urge to flee.

I grabbed my cell phone, swung my gym bag over my shoulder, and speed-walked across town to Penn Station. I tried to hail a cab, but all were either off-duty or occupied. There was no way I had the patience to wait for a crosstown bus, and a sweltering subway platform was the last place I wanted to be in the July heat. Tackling the one-mile distance on foot was the only way to go.

When I arrived at Penn Station, I shifted my weight from leg to leg as I studied the train schedules on the wall. It was as if my body were telling me I had to be in a perpetual state of motion. I had ants in my pants, as Becca often said. But unlike my usual ants, which motivated and directed me, these ants needed a GPS. I didn't know where to go.

As I stood amid swarms of people shoving past on their way to escape the city, I closed my eyes and channeled my old friend Harold. I tuned out the sound of the muffled voice on the Penn Station loudspeaker, ignored the malodorous combination of stale doughnuts and urine, and visualized Harold holding his purple crayon before a blank easel. It took a moment, but soon I saw a stick-figure version of myself standing beside two rectangular roadside signs with little wooden stakes in the ground—each on a divergent path. Both signs read HOME.

"What the hell, Harold?" I said aloud, my eyes still shut. I had been hoping for a clearer directive: Amtrak to Becca upstate, or New Jersey Transit to my parents. *Which one is home?*

I thought for a moment, and then it clicked: there was no doubt I should go "home" to my wife, even if it wasn't our own home. I should be with Becca at the reunion, despite all that had transpired between us over the last twenty-four hours. *We committed to Jordana's reunion, and that's where I should be. My wife is my home.*

The electronic ticket machines were down, so the lines at the counters were lengthy. I glanced nervously at my watch and wondered if I would miss the train. The next one to Jordana's house wouldn't be for another two hours. As I inched closer to the counter, I overheard a young family talking excitedly about their trip to the Jersey Shore. It reminded me of the picture on my office bookshelf. Although it was only in my mind's eye, the beautiful image of Becca on the boardwalk in that form-fitting blue dress once again made my chest tighten and my muscles tense in anger and resentment. *If she has her way and forgoes this surgery, she'll never look that beautiful again.*

"Sir, did you hear me?" the woman behind the ticket counter asked.

"Excuse me?" I replied. My mind was still clinging to that blue dress.

"Sir, *how may I help you?*"

"I'd like a one-way ticket, please."

"To *where?*" the woman sneered.

All I could think about was that happy family en route to the beach, and how my own family was a mess.

"Sir," the cashier growled, "if you don't know where you want to go, please step aside."

"New Jersey transit," I spit out. "Montclair–Boonton line."

Ninety minutes later, I arrived at Holiday Lane just in time for dinner. As I walked up the circular driveway to the sprawling beige stucco split-level ranch, the aroma of fresh tomatoes and garlic from the kitchen greeted me. I could hear my nieces and nephews splashing in the pool, their vociferous squeals emanating from the backyard like a top-of-the-line stereo system. As I opened the double wooden doors, adult voices bellowed from the kitchen, one thick New Jersey accent booming over another in an effort to be heard. I dropped my bag on the foyer's tiled floor and kicked off my work shoes, the same way I used to remove my backpack and sneakers upon returning home from elementary school. I casually sauntered into the kitchen, pulled the cell phone out of my back pocket, and placed it on the counter, before hopping up onto the flecked granite. I sat there smiling for a good thirty seconds until my mother looked up from her cutting board and screamed, *"Dio mio!* Oh my God!" and continued in warp-speed Italian as she quickly untied her apron and flung herself upon me. Anyone watching this might have presumed she hadn't seen me in years, when in truth we had gotten together for dinner just a few weeks earlier to celebrate her seventy-fifth birthday.

"Hey, hey!" my two older brothers said in unison as they walked over to greet me.

"What's up, Lance Armstrong? You injured again, or is there no marathon today?" my oldest brother, Emilio, asked.

"You know, I heard the health insurance companies got one of those 'America's Most Wanted' pictures of you in their offices—they're all freakin' scared of you," my other brother, Antonio, chimed in.

Before I could respond, my father—who was wearing his favorite linen shirt, with palm trees all over it—had placed his hands on my face and kissed each of my cheeks. *"Bello mio!"* He beamed with a grip as tight as Mama's embrace.

I had been in the house a total of five minutes, and already I felt nourished. Even the brotherly joshing felt good. The hero's welcome reminded me of the times I would return home on break from boarding school—when I'd strip out of my preppy L. L. Bean fleece, loafers, and chinos in the train station bathroom and throw on track pants, sneakers, and a New York Jets jersey before reuniting with my family. Growing up, I was always trying to fit in. I idolized Emilio and Antonio, who were sixteen months apart from each other but nearly a decade older than I. Even our names were indicative of the massive disparity between us. My brothers were born shortly after my parents immigrated to the United States and were given authentic Italian monikers in honor of relatives back in Sicily. I, on the other hand, was named after Nolan McMenamin, our Irish next-door neighbor in New Jersey and the first man my parents ever knew to own a Cadillac. When they learned that he'd attended boarding school as a teenager, they insisted I apply to his alma mater. The following fall, I became the only member of our family to receive a private education.

"Where are Becca and Emma? They still in the car? Gian-Carlo, go and help the girls in the car!" Mama directed Dad, who immediately ran to the front door at her command.

"No, Dad, come back. It's just me," I said, stopping him. "Emma's at her friend's house for the night, and Bec has a girls' weekend out of town with some of her friends."

Unlike the Millers, who knew their granddaughter refused to sleep at her friends' homes and that their daughter abhorred being away from her family, my parents were an easy sell. They were unaware of the finer brushstrokes of Becca's and Emma's personalities.

"Dude, you're a bachelor for the weekend and you came *here*? What the hell's wrong with you? I could think of a million other places I'd be right now if my wife and kids had plans," Emilio said, with a head shake. He shoved an entire piece of bruschetta into his mouth.

I laughed.

"Seriously, did me and E not teach you *anything*?" Antonio turned to Emilio and asked, "Where'd we go wrong?"

I pulled up a chair at the kitchen table and let myself believe that the comfort of the scene meant I was doing the right thing. Absent my brothers' beer guts and receding hairlines, it could easily have been the 1980s, with the three boys in the same spots. I looked out the window to the backyard.

"Who's that?" I asked, nodding toward a svelte brunette standing beside my parents' pool. I knew my nieces had matured but couldn't imagine that any of them had changed that drastically since my last visit.

Seated across the table, my brothers turned their thick necks at the same time, as if they were mirror images of each other.

"Oh, that's Emilio Jr.'s latest," Emilio said with pride. "My kid's a freakin' stud. Did you see the tits on that girl? *Jeeeesus.* What I wouldn't do to die and come back as my own son. You know what I mean?"

I tensed.

"What? Did we offend you, Mr. Prim and Proper?" Emilio said, noticing my discomfort.

"Once a freakin' tight-ass, always a freakin' tight-ass," Antonio chimed in.

I checked my watch. It had been only fifteen minutes, and already the near-chemical transformation into my childhood role as the tortured, stuffy straight arrow had begun. I felt as if they might shove me inside a kitchen cabinet at any given moment, just like when we were kids.

"*Patatino,* come here, please. I need your help," Mama called from the counter. She was always saving me from them. I was a grown man, but would forever be, as my pet name suggested, her little potato.

I rose from my seat and walked over to where she was slicing prosciutto. She put the knife down on the cutting board, wiped her hands on the apron around her waist, folded her arms, and stared at me.

"You always tell me the truth. What's going on?" she whispered, but her voice was demanding, hard. "I didn't mean to snoop. It was just there," she said, pointing at a spot on the granite.

"What are you talking about?" I was thoroughly confused.

"Your phone. I didn't mean to snoop. It was just there," she said, pointing to a spot on the granite. "I saw the texts. There are a lot of them."

Before responding, I scrolled through the messages I had missed.

From Becca—2:41 p.m.:
Where in the hell are you?!

From Seth—2:55 p.m.:
hey, just sent you an email with a list of surgeons. didn't want to hand it to you in front of everyone. what's your eta? you coming?

From Becca—3:15 p.m.:
Nol, you're making me nervous. We'll figure everything out. Just tell me where you are and that you're OK.

"Oh, don't worry, Ma," I said, still glancing down at the phone. "Everything's fine." I hated lying to her.

Mama grabbed my hand and led me out of the kitchen and into her carpeted bedroom, locking the door behind us.

"What's going on?" She directed me to sit beside her on the burgundy velvet love seat across from the canopy bed she shared with my father.

I stared out the window through the taffeta draperies, the ones with the small tassels I used to put on my head and pretend was a toupee—and tried to concoct a response. But when she lovingly placed her hand on my cheek and turned my face so that we could look each other in the eye, I broke. It was impossible to hold my head upright—it seemed to drop like a weight into her lap.

"Oh, Patatino," she said softly. "Mama's here. I'm gonna fix everything."

She rocked me back and forth until my tears graduated to sporadic sniffles. I exhaled and sat up. It was the first time I'd felt like myself in days.

We watched in silence as the sun lowered behind the backyard pool. I knew she wanted an explanation, but all I could get out was an embittered "She's *incredibly* selfish."

"Who? Becca?" Mama asked. "You had a fight?"

"You could say that."

"I don't understand."

"Becca has breast cancer and . . ."

Mama gasped. One hand flew over her mouth; the other clutched my knee.

"She needs a mastectomy," I continued.

"*Dio mio!*" she whispered, and then fell silent for several seconds to process the news. "She'll be okay, right? A mastectomy is smart. She'll get the implants, and it will all be fine. They do amazing things now. You'd be so shocked if I told you how many people have them. You know my friend Rose? She has. And Barbara? She has, too. I tell you, doctors now, they can go bigger, smaller, whatever you like. They can take skin from other parts of your body to make them. They can even tattoo de nipples."

Am I seriously having a conversation about breasts with my mother? Visions of what Rose and Barbara's nipples might look like flashed across my mind. I thought I'd gag.

"What?" she asked, clearly registering my discomfort.

I unbuttoned my shirt and pulled up the collar of my white tee like a towel to wipe the perspiration off my forehead. "I don't think she wants it," I said into the cotton fabric.

"You don't think she wants what?"

"The reconstruction. The implants. Any of it." I lowered the T-shirt but let it hover over my mouth like a mask for a moment, just as I did with my security blanket as a boy.

"She has to have the surgery to get healthy!"

"No, Ma. The mastectomies are not the issue. It's the follow-up part. I think she just wants to cut out the problem and move on."

"Oh," Mama said thoughtfully. "Hmm. Okay."

"Okay? That's it? *Okay?*" I was exasperated. How could she not see this the way I did?

"Yes," she said calmly. "*Okay.* It's her choice." Mama wiped her palms together to punctuate her statement—*that's done.*

I stood up and began to pace the floor. "Listen, I'm not trying to tell her what she can or cannot do. But what if she looks in the mirror and has regrets? What if people make jokes or Emilio and Antonio says something stupid about my wife being a man? Have you listened to your sons speak?" My voice grew louder and sharper. "I'd be handing them a lifetime supply of mockery on a silver platter!"

My fists clenched. I dug them into my pants pockets to avoid punching the wall.

"This is private business between a man and his wife. No one needs to know. Including your brothers. I won't tell anyone. Did you tell Becca how you feel?"

I nodded.

"Oh, no!" Mama winced. "What she say?"

"She told me that only someone who was *supremely self-absorbed* would find out his wife had cancer and then immediately worry what his idiot brothers thought about it. Then she got all philosophical and said something like, 'The true test of someone's character is not making Phi Beta Kappa or winning a popularity contest, but how he conducts himself in a crisis.' Seriously? She's gonna lecture me like I'm a child?"

I whipped my hands out of my pockets and smacked my palms against the floral wallpaper. "Fuck, that hurt!" I screamed.

We were quiet for a moment.

"So this is why you came home, eh? To run away from all of this?"

I shrugged my shoulders tepidly.

"What? There's more?"

"No, no, it's nothing, Ma," I said, unconvincingly.

She folded her arms across her chest and stared at me, waiting.

"Work's not so great lately," I finally said. I didn't have the heart to reveal that both my personal and my professional worlds were in shambles.

"You want to leave your firm?" she asked, as a smile spread across her face. "Come work for the family! Finally!"

From the moment I decided to take the law school entrance exams, my parents had fantasized about the day they could retire and I would take over the business end of my father's menswear franchise. My brothers were great with the customers, but my parents wanted me running the back office and overseeing the company. To their dismay, it never appealed. In fact, to me, it was a last-resort scenario.

"Maybe now's the right time, no? Just say you'll think about it. Okay?" She clasped her hands together as if she were about to recite her nightly prayers.

I nodded politely to appease her.

"So, where *are* Becca and Emma?" Mama asked, returning to the original crisis.

"Emma's in the city with Arlene and Jerry, and Becca's at our friends' country house for the weekend."

Mama nodded. "And you're supposed to be there, too, eh?"

"Yes," I said sheepishly.

"Then go," she said with certainty.

"I can't, Ma," I said, collapsing onto her bed. "I'm too tired. From here it will be at least a three-hour drive. I just want to sleep."

"So sleep. But when you wake up in the morning, you're gonna take my new Cadillac," she insisted, and walked over to a white leather tote bag on her dresser to fish out a set of keys. "You'll love it! GPS, sunroof, satellite radio, and nice, soft beige leather seats."

"Ma, really, I don't want—"

She lifted an index finger in front of my face to shush me before she continued. "I listened to you; now you listen to me. She's your wife. She needs you. You need her. I got a minestrone soup frozen in the extra refrigerator in the garage. It's her favorite."

"Ma, it's the Fourth of July. No one wants soup!" My temples were beginning to throb.

She straightened her posture, pursed her lips, and raised one eyebrow; it was the look that never failed to silence all four men in her house.

"Okay, fine, I'll go in the morning," I lied, and wondered where I could disappear in her luxury sedan over the next two days.

"That's my boy," she said sweetly, and grasped my hand. "Come on, the family's waiting. I have trays for you to bring outside. Let's go eat."

Chapter 8: Jordana

"It's nearly noon on Friday, and I don't know where the hell Becca is!" I shouted from behind the wheel of my SUV, as if I were talking directly to my husband's face, instead of to a Bluetooth speaker on the dashboard. "It's ruined! The whole damn weekend is ruined!"

"It's not ruined, and I'm sure she's fine," Sal said calmly. "Just focus on the road. You can control only what you can control."

"Come on, Sal, admit it. This is *totally* strange," I said, lowering my decibel level.

"It is what it is. You've contacted her. I've reached out to Nolan. We can't do anything else."

I took a deep breath and marveled at Sal's ability to remain calm. No matter what the crisis, he could handle it, and that in turn empowered me to at least attempt to do the same. I might have a closet full of breezy bohemian apparel, but my husband, in his stiff, custom-made designer business suits, was the naturally unflappable one. In fact, Sal's cool composition had been evident since birth and was the reason his parents had chosen to name him Salil, the Hindi word for water. Just like water, they believed, he had a serene presence. They were right.

I clenched the steering wheel in frustration for the entirety of my ride upstate. Though Becca's behavior was atypical, a last-minute ditching by Nolan was not shocking. There was a reason he had been the youngest employee in the history of Gordon, Michaelson & Stewart, LLP, to make partner: until Emma was born, he practically lived in that office. His dedication and diligence were admirable, but at times they clouded his judgment. I'll never forget how he invited people to a small surprise party in their apartment for Becca's twenty-ninth birthday. Only hours before the guests were scheduled to arrive, he called me to say a deal had "exploded" and that he was running late—could I save him and get everything ready? I said yes, of course, but all I could think about that night—aside from being grateful I had steered clear of a job in corporate law—was how unfazed Becca seemed that her husband missed the first half of the celebration. I wondered if there had been other disappointments to which she had grown numb.

Two hours after the start of my journey, I turned off the highway and made the mile-long drive from the main country road up the mountain to our gray-shingled Cape. I slowly inched toward the front porch along the rustic dirt-and-pebble path we called a driveway and parked beside the geraniums Sal and the kids had planted in the spring. Seeing the flowers reminded me of my twins, whom I already missed, although I knew Sal's parents were spoiling them on Long Island. I had never stayed at the country house without the boys, and the absence of their backseat bickering on the car ride up felt unnatural—almost as unnatural and unsettled as I felt about Becca.

Within twenty minutes of my arrival, I had unloaded the car, refrigerated the food, chilled the wine, opened the curtains, removed the dust bunnies from under the couch, fluffed the pillows, and arranged a vegetable platter with hummus dip on the kitchen island. *What difference does it make if I have an immaculate home if the guest of honor is a no-show?* I thought. Just as I was about to hop into the shower to get ready, I heard the sound of tires slowly crunching over the dirt road leading up to the house. I glanced at my watch. There was at least another hour before anyone was supposed to arrive.

Through the front window, I could see an unmarked white van pulling up to the porch, and I remembered a conversation Sal and I had not long after the geranium planting. We'd seen wasps by the back deck and wondered if there was a nest nearby. *Maybe Sal finally called the pest control guy*, I thought.

"Oh, hey," I said, projecting my voice from the open front door and waving to the van's driver, who was invisible behind the tinted windows. "You can pull around back if you like. It's easier to get to the deck that way."

Between the early July heat and infinite chores, I was drenched with sweat. As I fanned myself with the collar of my favorite Dave Matthews concert tee—the faded and nearly sheer one I had worn since college—I noticed that the driver didn't intend to move his van. He stepped out onto the dirt driveway, wearing polished black dress shoes. The open van door and darkened window blocked the upper portion of his body. I squinted at the shoe. It was an unexpected choice for an exterminator on duty.

"Hey, um, I'm sorry, but are you here for the wasps?" I asked, walking toward the van.

"WASPs? Wow! I'm not even out of the car, and we're already having a discussion about religion and ethnicity," the man said. His voice was familiar, but I couldn't quite place it.

I continued to squint, resting my hand against my eyebrows to block the midday sun, and then the van door slammed and everything became clear.

"Holy shit!" I cried. "Adam!"

"Jordy!" he said, with the exact tone and eye twinkle I spent my entire senior year of high school trying to block from memory. It was that innate sparkle that had first attracted me to Adam. He was a talented artist with an encyclopedic knowledge of music and film who played intramural ice hockey and requested a subscription to the *New York Times* as his fifteenth-birthday present. We started off as friends, but then one day, in the middle of tenth grade, he said he would marry me if I could correctly identify the European singer we were listening to on the radio. I could visualize the artist, and the woman's name was on the tip of my tongue, but when I blanked, I was genuinely disappointed in myself. Not because Björk's name escaped me, or because I was thinking about marriage, but because I felt I had blown an opportunity to become his girlfriend. It wasn't long after that, however, that we did start dating.

Other than a thick five o'clock shadow, the addition of funky horn-rimmed glasses, and a splash of salt and pepper on his side-burns, Adam hadn't aged a bit. He still had the same slight but athletic physique and cool-guy vibe—as if Zac Efron had dyed his hair black, shrunk a few inches, and become an observant Jew.

Though I was mortified by my body odor, I walked over to give him a hug. As I extended my arms and leaned in for a welcoming embrace, he recoiled. *No fucking way*, I thought, stunned. I was a forty-year-old, happily married mother of two with a life I loved and career I was proud of—and yet, with a single gesture, I was instantly reduced to my scorned teenage self, standing at JFK's International Arrivals terminal, getting rejected, once again, by Adam. He'd been gone only two weeks on a teen tour of Israel, but he'd left as my boyfriend and come back as Holly's.

"Sorry," he said apologetically, adjusting the black velvet yarmulke atop his lightly gelled hair. "I, um . . . it's just a religious thing. Don't take offense. I can't touch any woman other than my wife."

"Oh? Oh! No offense taken at all," I said awkwardly.

"Let me tell you, getting the middle seat between two women on an airplane is hell for me," he said with a smile. It seemed to be a joke he had told before, to put others, like me, at ease. I offered up a grin but then caught him glancing a second too long at my breasts, before he quickly averted his eyes. He was clearly embarrassed.

I instinctively folded my arms across my chest and wished I'd put on a bra that morning.

"Man, this house, wow! It's incredible! And that view!" he said, as he rolled the cuffs of his white shirt up to his forearms and placed his hands on his hips.

The view truly was extraordinary. A few years earlier, when Sal and I purchased five densely wooded acres near the New York–Massachusetts border to build a cozy weekend cottage, we had no idea that clearing away some trees would lend itself to such breathtaking views of the Berkshire and Catskill mountains. I had to admit, it was the type of year-round scenery that would make a movie producer salivate—snowcapped peaks in winter; wide-open, pink-sky sunsets in summer; and rolling hills of golden, green, and crimson foliage as far as the eye could see throughout fall and spring.

"Where is everyone?" Adam asked.

"Actually, you're the first to arrive," I said.

"Oh, I'm too early! I'm sorry," he said. He quickened the pace of his speech and started gesticulating with his hands, a nervous tendency I recalled. "I had to make these bakery deliveries to sleep-away camps in the area, and it turns out your house is a lot closer to them than I thought. Listen, I can drive around and come back. Do you need me to run some errands? You want milk, eggs, paper towels? You name it, I'll get it. I've got GPS; just give me an address. There's gotta be a supermarket or something nearby, right?"

"Don't worry. It's all good. Grab your bags and come inside. You must be famished. I've got a refrigerator filled with kosher food for you and Holly."

He smiled. "You were always so thoughtful," he said, and picked up two large duffel bags and a body-length pregnancy pillow. "Thank you."

"You can drop your stuff in the guest bedroom next to the bathroom. It has the largest bed, so I figured it would be the most comfortable for Holly," I said, before disappearing into my own room to change shirts and spackle on deodorant.

When I returned—wearing supportive undergarments and an opaque T-shirt—I found him sitting on a wicker barstool at the kitchen island, holding a carrot from the vegetable-hummus platter and mumbling some Hebrew words to himself. I recognized them as the blessing over food I learned in Hebrew school as a child.

Adam smiled at me from across the marble counter.

"Listen, Jord," he said, his tone unexpectedly intimate, "I just want to say, before everyone gets here, that it was very cool of you to include us this weekend."

"Sure! We're all here for Becca. It wouldn't be the same without Holly, and you too, of course," I said cheerfully. I was trying.

"No, seriously, we haven't seen you in years. It was very gracious of you. I know Holly would not have wanted to miss this."

Just then, my cell phone whistled, announcing an incoming text message. I practically leaped to grab it, hoping it would be Becca. It was.

Hey! I'm coming up today after all! Sorry for the confusion. I hitched a ride with Holly. We'll be there soon.

I was relieved to hear she was en route, but it stung deeply to learn she had flaked on our plans to hang out with Holly. I stared at my cell phone and furrowed my brow. "Did you know Becca was driving up here with Holly?" I asked Adam.

"Who?" he asked, feigning confusion.

"Your wife, wise-ass." I smiled and rolled my eyes. I felt like we were fifteen and flirting again. He still managed to give me butterflies.

"Yeah, I think it was a last-minute thing, 'cause I didn't know about it. Holly just called before I got to your house to say they were on their way up together. I think they went shopping or something. I figured you already knew."

"It's news to me," I said, and shrugged. I couldn't believe I was the last to know. Like an uncontrollable involuntary twitch, my trial-lawyer mind began to rapidly fire off questions like a machine gun: *Why didn't Becca simply tell me she was going shopping with Holly? What did she need at the last minute that warranted canceling our plans? Why did Nolan leave a message for Sal the night before, saying he and Becca might not make it up at all? Is Nolan now coming, too?*

"You want a beer?" I asked, pulling two bottles from the fridge. I decided the dinner preparations could wait.

"Sure," he said, and checked the label.

"It's kosher. Don't worry. I did my research."

I watched as he looked for the small insignia of approval from a rabbinic authority that the ingredients were up to standards. He smiled broadly. "Wow. Thanks, J." The uptick of my pulse upon hearing his former nickname for me was pathetic, even though I knew he had no idea how quickly my heart was beating.

"Are these yours?" Adam asked, with a hint of surprise, as he picked up a photograph of my kids.

"Yes, those are my sons, AJ and Matthew."

"They are absolutely stunning!" He stared at the picture and then up at me. "They're the South Asian version of you."

I felt my cheeks flush. "Thank you. Yeah, they clearly got Lefkowitz hair and the Singh complexion."

I took a swig of beer and stared at him. *I am alone in my house with Adam. Adam!* It was completely surreal—I actually pinched the inside of my bicep when I folded my arms. I had dreamed about this moment for years after our breakup. Decades later, here we were, both happily married and moved on, but the chemistry was still palpable. I wondered if he could feel it, too. "Come with me. I want to show you something," I said, giving him an unnecessarily flirtatious wink.

I led him down to the basement, and when we reached the bottom of the stairs and turned the corner, he gasped. "Holy crap!"

I smiled in satisfaction. I still knew how to thrill him.

He was pointing at my sons' drum set. "That's a DW Collector's Series twelve-piece set with Zildjian K custom twenty-two-inch cymbals," he cried. He then dramatically reached his hands to the sky and tilted his head backward, as if he were praising God. "And it has the *champagne sparkle finish!*"

I laughed.

"That's my *dream* set!" he said, "Everything is better in champagne sparkle, but this particular set in champagne sparkle is extraordinary."

Adam had always been a frustrated musician. He had absolutely no natural rhythm, yet in high school he mimicked the gestures and swagger of rockers in the hopes that he could pass for one. He played in a garage band that was so bad, even his mother couldn't fake compliments, but they managed to book gigs because all the guys were cute like Adam and never let ineptitude dismantle their confidence.

"One of my sons wanted lessons," I explained. "We told him he couldn't do it in our apartment because it would be too loud for the neighbors, so we promised he could play up here in the woods. We figured it might help scare away the bears."

Adam remained transfixed. I doubted he'd even heard me.

"May I?" he asked, eagerly pointing to the drum stool. He downed his final drop of beer and set the empty bottle on the windowsill.

"Of course! Actually, if you like, I can put on some music and you can jam. Okay?"

"Yeah! Bring it!" Adam said, as his fingers caressed the rim of the snare drum and gently flicked the symbols.

I tapped on an iPad installed in the basement's wall, and a moment later the Red Hot Chili Peppers was blasting from built-in speakers in the ceiling. When we had constructed the house, two years earlier, I had objected to Sal's turning our original vision for a simple log cabin into a state-of-the-art urban oasis in the country. And while I was certain that easily finding my high school boyfriend's favorite band was *not* what my husband had in mind when he touted the convenience of having the latest technology at our fingertips, I could now see the benefits of certain amenities.

Adam grabbed the drumsticks and began banging away to the band's classic "Give It Away." Though his beat couldn't have been further off, I held my beer in the air, belted out the lyrics, and shimmied around as if I were one of his groupies.

Shortly after I climbed atop our heavy-duty Ping Pong table, the music suddenly stopped, leaving Adam's cymbal thrashing the only sound in the room. I suspected there was something wrong with the iPad, but when I turned toward the wall behind me, I found Becca and Holly standing there, mouths agape. They had turned the music off.

Touché, Holly, I thought. *It took only twenty-something years.* I may have been forty, but I still longed to heal the wound of having been jilted. I still yearned to have that fifteen-year-old boy love me back. I wasn't going to ruin anyone's marriage—mine or theirs—but I certainly enjoyed this glorious moment.

Adam looked over at his wife, a pregnant deer in headlights, and the drumsticks slipped from his fingers.

I jumped off the Ping-Pong table, spilling beer onto the beige Berber rug as I landed.

"We're heeere," Becca announced in a slow, reluctant singsong.

"Hol!" Adam said, hopping off the drum stool and briskly walking over to greet his wife like an obedient puppy. Had he possessed a tail, it would have been tucked between his legs.

In a split second, there I was, back at JFK airport at 5:00 a.m., getting dumped, once again, for Holly. I suddenly felt foolish and juvenile. "Hi, guys!" I said, and hugged my guests. "Holly! It's splendid to see you after all these years!" *"Splendid"? Where the hell did that come from?* I couldn't remember the last time I had used that word in a sentence. I suddenly felt nervous in my own home.

Both women smiled. I knew Becca's was forced, but it had been eons since I'd spent time with Holly, so I couldn't tell if hers was genuine.

"It's good to see you, too," she said, and immediately handed me a small, rectangular box with a red bow on top. "I know I mentioned it in an email, but really, it was so nice of you to include us. Thank you."

"Oh, you didn't need to bring anything."

"It was the least I could do," she said, and gently put her hand on my arm. "It's just a few treats from the bakery."

"Wonderful!" I squealed, a bit too loudly. Becca shot me a look that said, *You all right?*

Though a part of me would always hate Holly for stealing Adam and for being Becca's backup best friend, I had to admit, it was surprisingly nice to see her. I had heard updates from Becca over the years about her success, but I had always been numb to the reports. Seeing her in person and hearing her voice again somehow softened me, and I was suddenly flooded with happy memories, not sour ones. What came to mind was not her betrayal or the passive competition I had always sensed between us, but playing with our Cabbage Patch Kids in her childhood bedroom and sitting next to her on the school bus, sniffing her red hair to see if it smelled sweet like Strawberry Shortcake's auburn tresses.

"Adam, can I speak with you for a sec?" Holly asked, pointing toward the sectional couch at the far end of the room. "Just want to get business talk out of the way so it's not on my mind," she explained, turning back to me with a smile.

"Oh, no problem. I have some things to do upstairs anyhow."
Like shower, I thought.

I looked at Becca and motioned with my head, as if to say,
Follow me up the steps.

"I've got to pee," Becca said, and bolted to the bathroom.

When I got upstairs, I could faintly hear Holly and Adam's
conversation through the floor vent. I stepped closer to the grates
to listen.

Unlike my prewar Manhattan apartment, where the rock-
solid walls made each room feel like a soundproof recording studio,
the bones of our country home were a bit calcium-deficient. Aesthetically, the house possessed the same clean lines yet unstuffy feel
as our Upper East Side home. Both residences had the same crisp
white kitchen cabinets and the same silver-plated picture frames
that I bought in bulk from Bed Bath & Beyond. They even shared
identical built-in white bookshelves that ran the length of the living
room wall and were stuffed with paperbacks and an eclectic mix of
colorful pottery. But somehow, despite my consistent style, the two-
year-old wood-frame Cape felt hollow compared with the hearty
construction of a Fifth Avenue classic six.

"Are you kidding me?" Holly whisper-shouted at him. I
imagined him cowering. "Did you even make the bakery deliveries, or did you just drive directly to Jordana's so you could watch
your old girlfriend practically pole-dance on a Ping-Pong table
before I got here?"

"Come on, you know that's ridicu—"

"Oh, really?" She cut him off. "I don't remember the last time
I saw you drink a beer or play the drums!"

"Well," he said gently, "first of all, to answer your question, yes,
I made the bakery deliveries. Second, in terms of the beer, I drank it
because she went out of her way to find a kosher brand, and I didn't
want to offend my host. I didn't think it was polite to tell her that I
prefer scotch. As for the drums, you haven't heard me play because—
and this may be news to you—*we don't own a drum set*! Should I go on?"

"Please do," Holly said. "And by the way, I'd be happy to buy
you a drum set and a Ping-Pong table if you'd move to a house in
the 'burbs. I'm just saying . . ."

Adam ignored her last comment. "I have said this before, and I'll say it again." His tone remained calm but firm. "I love you. I will always love you. I had no regrets then, I have no regrets now, and I will never regret choosing you over Jordana. She's a wonderful person, but it ends there. I *never loved her.* Never."

I felt breathless upon learning that the first boy ever to have professed his love for me—the one whose last name I used to affectionately doodle over and over as my own—had regarded me as nothing more than "a wonderful person." *Fuck him! And fuck her!*

Holly sighed. "Okay. Fine. I just had to get it off my chest. I'm over it. I actually have more pressing stuff to discuss with you." She sounded completely different, as if she had hit a reset button replacing her *Fatal Attraction* tone with one of concern.

For a few minutes, I heard nothing. They were no longer shouting, which was just as well because even if I had heard the sounds of their words, I would not have been able to process the meanings. I was fixated on the fact that he never loved me, despite the countless letters he'd written that proved otherwise. Standing there at the kitchen island, gripping the airtight cap of the expensive barbecue sauce I had ordered from an online kosher gourmet shop specifically for them, I fantasized that I had kept all those love letters and could shove them in their faces as evidence. I felt so betrayed and belittled knowing my love had been unrequited. It was the same sense of rejection I'd felt upon learning Becca had chosen to go shopping with Holly instead of driving up with me for the weekend I was creating in her honor. *Could Holly squeeze me out of Becca's life the way she squeezed me out of Adam's?* I wondered.

I must have taken my frustration out on the barbecue sauce, because, after several failed attempts at unscrewing the lid, the jar slid from my hands, shattered glass everywhere, and splattered marinade all over my white backsplash.

"Dammit!" I muttered. "You're acting like a child, not a forty-year-old woman, Jordana! Stop being so insecure." I didn't want anyone to hear me. But instead of immediately cleaning up the mess, which I would normally have done, I washed only my hands and then crouched down on the floor beside the air duct. When all I could make out were whispers, I tightened the messy bun atop my head, shut my eyes in concentration, and pressed my ear against the vent. Despite my best efforts, their hushed tones remained inaudible. I opened my eyes, and standing beside my face was a pair of bare feet—each toenail painted a different color and covered with sparkles. I knew immediately that the feet belonged to Becca—not only because of the high arches from her years of ballet, but because, other than I, she was the only person I knew who'd publicly display a pedicure given by a child.

"What on earth are you doing?" Becca asked, as she stared down at me.

"Oh, hey," I said nonchalantly, as if attaching one's ear to an air duct was perfectly normal. "I broke the barbecue sauce and was just picking up some of the glass."

"With your eyes shut?" Becca stared at me skeptically. "Come on, you're a better defense lawyer than *that*."

Sighing, I stood up and massaged the vertical lines the metal grates had made on my cheek. I felt like an idiot.

"You were totally eavesdropping!" Becca poked my shoulder. "Admit it!"

"Fine! Guilty!" I said, rolling my eyes en route to the sink.

"So, what did you hear?" Becca asked.

"I couldn't make out much." I didn't need to delve into some trivial conversation of how Adam had never loved me. Yeah, it was hurtful, but it didn't sting nearly as much as knowing I was out of the loop of Becca's life. I craved an understanding of what was going on with her and Nolan.

Becca looked around and surveyed the kitchen. "How can I help? Give me a job."

"There's another jar of marinade in the pantry. Can you open it and pour it over the chicken wings? I'm clearly inept," I said, gesturing to the shattered jar in the sink as proof.

While Becca prepared the meat, I picked up shards of glass that had sprayed across my counter and pine floor. What started out as a conversational lull had now matured into an uncomfortable silence.

"So, what's the deal?" I said at last.

"The deal with what?" Becca asked.

"Bec . . ." was all I said, but the voice inside my head screamed, *Don't play coy with me!*

Becca walked over to the sink to rinse barbecue sauce off her hands.

Fine, I thought. *I'll fold.* "I just need to know that everything's okay. I was worried when you suddenly changed our plans. And then Sal got a message from Nolan saying he might not even come up this weekend. What's *that* about?"

"Listen, it's a lot to get into," she said, drying her hands and looking out at the mountains through the window above the sink. "Here's the deal. I went to the—"

Just then, Adam opened the basement door and walked into the kitchen. "Hey. Hope I'm not interrupting anything," he said with a smile.

Becca and I both jumped, as if we had been jolted out of a deep sleep. *Motherfucker!* I thought. *I was finally getting somewhere.*

Though I could barely make eye contact with Adam, given how mortified I was by my new insight, I did glance his way long enough to notice the leather-bound book in his hand.

"Jordana," he said politely, "I was wondering . . . would you mind if I went out on the deck for a bit? I need to daven before Shabbos starts."

I had not heard the word *daven*, the Yiddish word for *pray*, in years. Neither had I heard *Shabbos*—the more traditional pronunciation of *Shabbat* or *Sabbath*. I loved the sound of both; they reminded me of sitting at my grandparents' dining room table, slurping matzo ball soup over a white lace tablecloth.

"Of course. Go right ahead," I said, mutating back into happy hostess. I reminded myself that my high school heartbreak was ancient history. I needed to move on, act like an adult, be gracious to the people I'd invited into my home, and try to ignore the tensing muscles between my neck and shoulders. "I'll be out on the deck in a few minutes to start the barbecue. Make yourself comfortable."

Becca and I watched through the kitchen window as Adam opened his prayer book and began *shukkling*—standing with his feet in a fixed position, subtly rocking his body forward and backward to enhance concentration.

"I'm gonna go see how Holly's doing," Becca said. I wondered if she was trying to escape the conversation we had started. Before I could pick up where we'd left off, she had exited the room.

I stared at the horizon out the kitchen window, thinking about Becca and how screwed-up this dream weekend was turning out to be, but then the sight of Adam praying caught my eye again and I was transfixed. There was something incredibly intriguing about someone who could jam to the Red Hot Chili Peppers one minute and wholly immerse himself in prayer with such profound devotion the next.

I wondered what he was saying. It had been so long since I'd heard anyone speak Hebrew. My parents were both raised in observant homes but chose not keep up the traditions. Instead of going to synagogue on the high holidays, we went apple-picking. Rather than lighting candles on Friday nights to welcome the Sabbath, we ordered in pizza. It wasn't that my parents were atheists or disliked the customs; they were simply tired from working all day and didn't care to put in the effort to make a formal Sabbath dinner or a Passover seder. To them, it was enough to be culturally Jewish—to use Yiddish-isms like *schmutz* and *oy vey* and eat gefilte fish year-round. While they did send me to Sunday school at the local synagogue, I was enrolled because it was the thing to do, not because it was particularly important to my parents. Yet, despite a relatively secular upbringing, I was quite spiritual. Faith and culture had always fascinated me. While I did not convert to Hinduism when Sal and I married—there was something I couldn't abandon about my Jewish upbringing—I was very excited to adopt his family's rich Indian and Hindu traditions as my own and to blend them with Judaism in my children's lives.

I slowly slid open the glass doors and tiptoed onto the deck so as not to distract Adam, who was standing several feet away. As I quietly arranged the disposable aluminum pans of marinated raw meat along the side of the grill, I noticed Holly step onto the deck, make a beeline for her husband, and quickly whisper something in his ear while he was praying. He nodded in recognition, though his body didn't break the *shukkling* stride.

Before stepping back inside the house, Holly turned to me and asked, "Do you need any help setting up?"

"No, go relax. I've got it," I said softly.

Seconds later, as I placed the chicken on the grill, I heard Adam passionately recite several Hebrew words aloud. Most were unrecognizable, but a few sounded familiar, like *Mi Sheberach*, which I knew was a prayer for healing. Immediately following the prayer, I heard him say *"Rivkah avigail bat Sarah"*—Becca's Hebrew name. From the time of Becca's diagnosis until a year after her remission, my parents recited the *Mi Sheberach*, along with Becca's Hebrew name, to pray for her return to health. Given my parents' general indifference toward Jewish customs, their unwavering dedication to reciting this particular prayer for Becca always surprised me. When I finally asked my father about it, he said simply, "There are no atheists in a foxhole."

A shiver went up my spine. Adam and Holly knew something I didn't. Something about Becca and her health. I now knew why Becca was behaving so strangely. The thought that something might be wrong with her—again, after all these years—made me dizzy. And it was compounded by the fact that she had let them in, but not me.

I walked back into the house and downed a tall glass of water. I knew I couldn't make Becca talk to me, certainly not in front of all these people, so I decided to busy myself with preparing dinner. I set the table. I folded napkins. I pulled out tinfoil, covered the food, and placed the serving platters along the island—appetizers on the left, entrées on the right. I wrote the names of the dishes in cursive on tiny linen place cards and put them behind the platters—the same way buffets were presented at the corporate cocktail events I attended with Sal. There was something calming about creating order out of chaos.

The house was eerily silent. Alone in the kitchen, I dimmed the lights in the cavernous great room and poured a glass of cabernet. Through the back window, I could see that Adam had finished his prayers and was strolling around the property with Holly and Becca. I glanced at my watch, over to my perfectly set table, which would have made Martha Stewart proud, and then at a photograph of my children on the mantel. A wave of homesickness overcame me. I felt abandoned, uneasy, and scared—like a little girl who wanted nothing more than to cuddle with her parents after a nightmare. I yearned for normalcy, for routine, and to go back to my apartment in the city with Sal and the boys.

Minutes later, Seth, Lex, and Sal arrived, and Adam, Holly, and Becca returned inside. The house filled with the sounds of laughter and squeals—the music of old friends reuniting. I summoned the strength to fill drink requests and busied myself with unnecessary kitchen tasks, like taking out the garbage and wiping down the already-glistening countertops. The last thing I wanted to do was stand up in front of everyone and deliver the heartfelt toast I'd crafted about lifelong friendship.

"Hey," Sal said softly, walking over and kissing me on the head as I folded the dish towels. "It looks great in here! Have you heard anything from Nolan?"

I shook my head and looked at the dinner table. Nolan's absence was grossly apparent, particularly now that everyone else had arrived. While my guests chatted around the island, Sal and I quickly removed Nolan's place setting and chair from the table. I feared the empty seat would highlight what needn't be a focal point.

As everyone nibbled on appetizers and caught up, I ducked into my bedroom to call Nolan. Not surprisingly, he didn't pick up. I didn't leave a message.

I stepped into the bathroom and splashed some water on my face. "Just keep it together," I said to my reflection in the mirror.

When I headed back to the kitchen, I saw Holly reaching for a matchbook. Although this had not been billed as a Sabbath dinner, I had purchased kosher wine, challah, and special candles because I knew Holly would want to light them to welcome the Sabbath at sundown. I had fond memories of watching my grandmother light candles on holidays and was looking forward to seeing the tradition carried out in my own home, even if I wasn't the one to do it.

After everyone gathered around the table, Holly lit the two white candlesticks and waved her hands three times over the flames, before covering her eyes and reciting the blessing.

"Wow, I haven't seen someone do this in years," Seth commented under his breath to no one in particular. He had renounced religion within hours of returning home from our hospital visit with

Becca back in ninth grade and never looked back. He wouldn't even attend his parents' Passover seders.

Just like my grandmother, Holly continued to keep her hands over her eyes until she had completed her silent prayers. We all stood quietly behind our chairs and watched. I suspected they were all as mesmerized as I was by the breakneck speed at which Holly moved her lips. I could hear her inhale through her nostrils and exhale out unidentifiable words that blended together to form a *swish-swish-swish* sound. At one point, her mouth curled and a single tear came streaming down her left cheek. She sniffled, and everyone looked around uncomfortably. Adam put his hand on the small of her back, but the gesture didn't interrupt her concentration. It was as if this happened all the time and was part of their routine. *Is Holly praying for her unborn child or reciting a* Mi Sheberach *with Becca's name, like Adam did?* I wondered.

Eventually, her hushed tones became more audible and I heard Holly mutter the same prayer for healing that Adam had said on the deck. This time, I was sure of it, because when Becca's Hebrew name was detectable amid the *swish-swish-swish*, I wasn't the only one to flinch. Though Sal was oblivious, the rest of us had spent our childhood carpooling to Hebrew school three days a week. If there was a single takeaway, it was recognition of each other's Hebrew names.

Lex's hands shot over and squeezed Seth's arm, as if she were holding on to him for dear life. *Weird*, I thought, of the lingering, intimate gesture. *They haven't seen each other in years.* I shifted my glance to Becca, who was staring at the candle's flames. She looked up, our eyes locked, and then she lowered her gaze to her plate, as if to say, *You got me.*

I felt winded. Something was very wrong with Becca. I knew it as surely as if she had told me herself.

Holly removed her hands from her eyes, wiped away the tears that had made their way to her chin, clasped her hands together, and said, "Amen!"

"Excuse me," Becca whispered politely, grabbing her cell phone from the kitchen island and walking out of the room.

Everyone looked around the table with identical expressions of shock.

"I'll go," said Holly.

"No," I said sharply, stepping ahead of her. Had she not been pregnant, I might have shoved her. "I've got this." She could have Adam, but I'd never let her take Becca.

Chapter 9: Becca

As we all stood around the knotty-pine farm table, watching Holly recite the prayers over the Sabbath candles, all I could think about was my daughter. Being away from Emma made my heart ache. Had it been a typical Friday evening, Nolan, Emma, and I would have been playing Uno, baking brownies, or curling up on the living room couch to watch a movie. Instead, I was stuck in the middle of nowhere, missing my daughter and wondering where in the world my husband was—when suddenly I heard Holly say my Hebrew name. Like an inattentive student jolted out of a haze by a teacher, I was thrust back to the present.

I looked up at Holly and saw a tear trickling down her cheek. A moment later, I felt an onslaught of penetrating stares. I glanced up at Jordana. When our eyes locked, my stomach lurched.

I headed to the bathroom to compose myself. I knew the time had come to tell Jordana, and I dreaded it the way I dreaded having to tell my child.

As soon as I caught sight of the subway-tiled walls, my mind immediately flashed to my own bathroom and how the cold, sterile environment seemed bizarrely appropriate for the conversation I was about to have. After all, my most intimate talks with Emma have taken place while she was on the toilet and I was seated on the stepstool beside her dangling feet.

The most recent one took place when she was six. She was sitting naked on the toilet, and as I drew her bath, she asked *the* question. It came out of nowhere; we hadn't had a conversation in recent weeks about her birth story. Nevertheless, she wanted to know, right then and there, at six thirty on a Tuesday night, exactly *how* my belly broke.

When Emma was born, Nolan and I agreed never to sugar-coat how she entered this world. She is the product of my egg, his sperm, and the womb of a West Coast angel who affectionately referred to her uterus as the Penthouse Suite. I had told Emma that my belly was "broken." After all, I reasoned, it's not a bad lesson to learn that beauty can emerge from imperfection. We couldn't have been more grateful or proud, and wanted Emma to feel the same. Hiding it during her childhood but divulging the truth later on didn't seem right. Why lie?

As she got a little older, the explanation blossomed into a baking analogy. Nolan and I became the ingredients, our surrogate the oven, and Emma the delicious cake. This elementary version of the events satiated her curiosity. But soon she craved more—more details about our carrier, about the experience. Did we feel her kick in utero? Yes, when we flew out for some of Elizabeth's ultrasounds. Why couldn't we use a surrogate here in New York? Gestational surrogacy wasn't legal in New York State. Did Elizabeth have her own children? Yes, a boy and a girl. Had Elizabeth been a surrogate before? Yes, twice.

For reasons I never understood, all of these conversations took place in the restroom—during a bath, while brushing teeth, or as a procrastination technique to avoid flossing.

Emma's question that night when she was six, though, was different than the others that came before it. Those were about the surrogacy process; this was about the catalyst—about what caused her birth story to be so different than that of her friends and cousins. Her question deserved a thoughtful response, and I was guided by our cardinal rule not to lie. So, once again, I ventured down the path of diluted truth. But how do you explain to a six-year-old, without scaring the absolute shit out of her, that you had cancer when you were a kid? Would divulging this fact make her wonder if I'd get sick again? That maybe Mommy wasn't as healthy as she looked? That, God forbid a billion times, it could happen to her one day, too?

I leaned over the bathtub, turned off the running water, and assumed my position on her stepstool.

Me: "Well, honey, my belly broke because I didn't feel well and needed some really strong medicine. That medicine made me all better, but it made it hard for me to carry a baby."

Emma: "Was it pink medicine, like when I have an ear infection?"

Me: "No, it was different. I didn't swallow it. It was like a laser. I lay on a table, and the doctors zapped me in different spots."

I lifted my shirt to show her the tiny tattooed dots along my torso that targeted lymph nodes from my neck to my thighs. I then pointed directly to one on my abdomen.

Me: "That's the one that hit the spot where babies grow."

Emma: "But the laser didn't hurt your cake ingredients, right? That's why I look like you."

Me: "That's right! Isn't that amazing? My ingredients were protected. I had an operation to move the ovaries— sort of like the carton holding my eggs—over just a little bit inside my belly so the laser couldn't hit them. I had smart doctors. They were thinking ahead."

Emma: "What was the name of your cold? Was it an ear infection? A stomachache?"

Me, as cool and calmly as I could manage: "Cancer."

Emma: "Oh."

Silence.

Me: "Ready for your bath?"

Emma: "Don't old people die from cancer?"

A teacher at her school had recently passed away from the disease, so she was familiar with the word and its impact. Even little kids can get what it means when someone is there one day and gone the next.

Me: "Sometimes people die from it, but lots of people are able to get healthy again and live a long time. Just like me."

Emma: "Mommy, you're not old. How did you get cancer?"

Me: "Anyone can get it. But listen—it is not very common. Most people *do not* get it."

Emma: "How old were you?"

Me: "I was a teenager. But I took my medicine, and then I was healthy again."

Emma: "How did you know you had it?"

Me: "I was really tired a lot. I had a cough and a fever. I went to the doctor, and they did some tests and told me."

Emma: "Can I catch it?"

Me: "No."

Emma: "Will you get it again? Promise me you won't get it again!"

I held her arms and looked directly into her eyes.

Me: "Listen to me very carefully, Munchkin. That was a long time ago. I'm strong, I'm healthy, and I'm staying right here. With you."

Emma: "Mommy, *promise* me you won't get it again."

I thought of the peace of mind that promise could give her. I wanted to tell her I was vigilant about my follow-up care for that exact reason—so I could be around to be her mom. I would never tell her that I could relapse, or that I was at higher risk for a secondary cancer, or any of the other things long-term survivors of childhood cancer think about. No. She would never know that my worst nightmare was dying young and leaving her. In that moment, all my six-year-old wanted was a promise that I'd be fine. I had no idea if it was a promise I could keep, but I gave myself permission to make it. My two cancer-free decades were proof enough that I was in the clear.

> Me: "I promise. I'm not going anywhere."

I gave her a hug and kiss.

> Emma: "Mommy?"

She looked intensely into my eyes.

> Me: "Yes?"
> Emma: "I love you."
> Me: "I love you, too, more than anything in the world. You are my greatest gift."
> Emma: "Mommy?"
> Me: "Yes, sweetheart?"
> Emma: "Can I have Cheez-Its for snack tomorrow?"

This was the conversation that was now stuck in my head. It replayed in my mind like the continuously looping Christmas Day yule log that aired on all the local television stations when I was a kid, making the day off from school a buzzkill for all the non-Christian kids in the neighborhood, because unless your parents shelled out dough for cable—and none of ours did—you had nothing to watch on TV.

My brain's frequency was frozen on that scene in the bathroom with Emma when I heard footsteps marching down the hallway from the great room. I could tell by the clunk of her Birkenstocks that it was Jordana. The thought of sharing the truth with her made my chest pound, the same way it did when I thought about telling my parents or Emma. I sat down on the closed lid of the toilet.

Knock. Knock. "It's me," Jordana said, as she turned the knob and swiftly entered. She shut the door, flipped the lock, and leaned her back against the handle as if she were standing guard to block an oncoming stampede.

"All right, what's the deal?" she said, staring down at me.

I laid out the facts: Early-stage breast cancer. Most likely a long-term side effect of the radiation. Caught during an annual checkup. Most likely just surgery, but won't know for sure if it spread or if I'll need chemo until they get the post-operation biopsy results.

Jordana listened intently and nodded but remained silent. I had expected a cross-examination and tears. Though she was physically present, she seemed to have disappeared. The buzz of the lightbulb in the wall sconce was the only sound in that bathroom.

Eventually, the life returned to her eyes. "Okay," she said resolutely.

"Okay?" I asked. *That's it?*

"Yes, *okay*, we'll get through this," she said, sounding bizarrely upbeat. "This is the shoe, right? It's dropping. Believe it or not, I've been preparing myself for years for this day. We've always known this was a possibility, right? Well, it's here and I'm ready. Just tell me what you need. I'll do whatever it takes. I'll quit my job, I'll take Emma, just say the word."

I flinched when she said "take Emma." Although I knew she meant "babysit," a small part of me heard a willing understudy for my role as her mother. *Has Jordana already contemplated a scenario in which I die? Does she have a color-coded plan for how she'll raise my daughter?*

"I have just one question," she continued. The assuredness she had displayed a moment earlier had quickly dissolved into vulnerability. "Why didn't you tell me?"

"I haven't even told my parents." I sighed. "Honestly, the thought of telling them, Emma, and you"—I clutched my stomach—"completely turns my insides."

"Why? Why is it any different than telling a friend—you know, like, say, oh, Holly? I mean, *she* clearly knew."

Seriously? You're fishing for compliments? Are we still in high school?

"Jord, come on. I truly love you all, but *you're* my family. You know that. Plus, I didn't want to ruin the weekend—you worked so hard planning this amazing reunion."

"How could you tell her before me?" she asked. For a split second, I saw her lip quiver and her eyes glisten.

Though I didn't say a word, I must have appeared annoyed, because the exasperated look on her face softened and I felt her make a conscious choice to shift gears, package up her pain, and shelve it for later.

"I'm sorry. You could never ruin anything, Bec. Listen, I'm going to go back out there. It's sort of rude of me to invite people into my home and then ignore them. Right now, just try to relax and enjoy. After the weekend, you and I will sit down and map out a plan. Everything will be fine," she said, her take-charge voice returning. But what I saw beneath her grit was sadness and fear.

I was surprised that the topic of Nolan's absence never came up. Like Emma, who could seamlessly ask for Cheez-Its as a follow-up to "Mommy, promise me you won't die," Jordana had always been good at sweeping the messy stuff away and moving on, particularly for the sake of a drama-free social gathering. But unlike my child, who was not mature enough to know, Jordana was well aware that promises couldn't always be kept. I made a mental note not to be shocked by an unhinging at some point.

When we returned to the table, everyone was making small talk to avoid the tension. Eventually, when they ran out of compliments about the food, Lex dove in.

"So, Bec, what's going on?" she asked gently. "Look, it's just us. What's the deal?"

I exhaled. It was time for this to be out in the open. "I'm sorry, guys. I wanted this to be a happy, easy weekend. I appreciate the effort all of you made to be here. It really is amazing and very touching. And Jordana did so much work and such a beautiful job, I didn't want to spoil anything. I mean, look at this spread," I said, pointing to the abundance of food beautifully displayed on her collection of craft-fair ceramic serving platters.

I was filibustering, and I knew it. They all put their forks down and stared at me, waiting.

I told them about the diagnosis and surgery.

"Oh my God, I'm so sorry," Lex said, her hand over her

heart. "So, is Nolan working this weekend to get things off his plate in time for your operation?"

"That's a generous assumption, Lex," I said. "The truth is, I don't know where Nolan is. I thought he would be here by now."

I had just extended an invitation for inquiry, and my heartbeat quickened in acknowledgment.

"I'm confused," Lex said.

"As am I." I slipped off my shoes and crisscrossed my legs on the seat of the chair.

"I'm gonna fetch some more wine from the basement. Excuse me," Sal said.

"I'll help you," Adam offered, rising in his seat.

I looked around at my old friends and continued. "So, over the last two days, he has basically disappeared. Physically, emotionally, in every way—gone. We had a blowout fight in the plastic surgeon's office." I could feel a lump form in my throat as I recalled the way in which Nolan barely flinched when I sarcastically threw out the word *divorce* in the exam room.

"What?" Lex shrieked.

I noticed Seth shift uncomfortably beside her.

"It's true," I nodded. "He was barely fazed when I told him about the diagnosis. Would I have liked him to be a little scared and concerned? Yeah, probably—I mean, it is, after all, a life-threatening disease—but I wrote it off as Nolan's eternal optimism, which I have always loved, so part of me appreciated it. But then we met with the plastic surgeon to discuss reconstruction, and the shit hit the fan."

"What do you mean?" Lex asked.

"I mean, reconstruction is presented as the thing you do after a mastectomy, especially if you're young. It's like one-stop shopping at these clinics. Before I knew it, they were taking pictures of me naked at all angles and asking if I wanted to replicate the breasts I had, or go bigger or smaller. They even scheduled the operation right then and there. It was like this train that just kept moving and moving and all I wanted was to jump off. I kept thinking: more operations, more pain, more risks of infection, more days to keep me away from Emma. And for what? Breasts? I never cared about having boobs to begin with! Do I even want this surgery?"

"Anyone need some water?" Seth asked softly, rising in his seat.

"I'm sorry," I said. "Is this too much information for you?"

Seth smiled. "Bec, please. I'm just a little parched. You think I'm going to shut down a conversation about breasts? Really? How long have you known me?"

We all laughed. Acting the clown had always been Seth's role, and he seemed to be reprising the part.

"What happened after the plastic surgeon booked the operation?" Lex asked.

"At the end of the meeting, the doctor left the exam room and Nolan said something like, 'Well, this is one way to get a boob job!' And I said, 'I don't know if I want it.' That's when he blew up."

"Blew up?" Lex asked.

"Yeah. He said I was insane. He called me selfish. He started ranting about how I would look like a 'freak.' There was no way the people in the hall didn't hear."

"Jackass!" Lex seethed, and muttered something under her breath about her husband.

I noticed Seth was biting his nails—a childhood habit of his I had long ago forgotten but immediately recalled. A vision of Seth sitting on a metal folding chair during our eighth-grade graduation dance quickly flashed before me. While the rest of us stood in the middle of the junior high school gym, awkwardly swaying and wrapping our arms around our dates, Seth just nibbled at his cuticles and stared at the floor as the DJ's pulsing strobe light illuminated him sitting alone against the wall.

"Honestly, I'm more distraught about Nolan than I am about this diagnosis or surgery." I felt myself unraveling. It felt good to vent. "I get that he's entitled to be upset and have a reaction, but this is sort of extreme, if you ask me. How could I have been so blind? I thought he was this amazing guy everyone loved for a reason. I mean, he takes my ninety-year-old grandfather as his date to corporate work events when he knows Poppy will like the guest speaker. That's the father figure I want for my child and the man I want as my husband. I can do without the asshole version."

I looked across the table at Jordana, the only one who was expressionless and mute.

"Don't make this choice for anyone but you," Lex said. "My only question is—and mind you, I will fully support you no matter what you decide—have you really weighed both sides of this?"

"What do you mean?" I asked.

Lex turned to Seth. "Are you sure you're okay with this conversation?" she inquired, lightly touching his bicep again with her fingertips and leaving them there for what struck me as a long time. There was something very comfortable and easy about their interaction that I hadn't noticed before.

"Yes, it's okay," he insisted, biting away at his cuticle.

"Well," Lex continued, "Bec, how will you feel when you look at yourself in the mirror and there's just a big scar across your flat chest? Personally, I don't know if I could handle that."

"That's a good question," I said, as I envisioned myself standing in front of the full-length mirror that leaned against the wall in our bedroom. "I suspect there will be days when I feel confident and days when I look at myself and think I'm some kind of botched science experiment. But, honestly, my money's on the good days. It's like when I was a kid and I stared down people on the street who gawked at my bald head. You've just gotta own it. I'm still me. I am who I am—hair or no hair, breasts or no breasts."

"God bless. You're strong, Bec," Lex said, straightening her back and adjusting the black sunglasses still perched on her hair like a headband. "I'd be screaming and throwing shit against the wall."

"I'm coming to all of this from a different place," I explained. "I'm not like other women, who are experiencing this disease for the first time as an adult. If I had no history, I'd probably just go ahead with the reconstruction. But I've been around the block, and I'm tired of feeling like a professional patient. I'm done. I don't want multiple surgeries. I don't want even the slightest, most minuscule risk of infection. I don't want to wonder if my scar tissue from the radiation I had as a kid will make breast reconstruction more complicated or painful and cause me to visit the doctor repeatedly. Just cut the disease out of me and let me live my life. I don't mean to be blithe, but that's how I feel. As for not looking like a normal woman, I don't care. I'm the same person either way."

Everyone was quiet.

"He doesn't deserve you," Lex said. "You have incredible strength. That man should count his lucky stars he found a woman like you." She took the edge of her linen napkin and dabbed the corners of her eyes.

We were all quiet for a moment. I looked over at Jordana. She was staring into her plate. I felt awful I'd ruined the weekend, but it was a relief to have said everything out loud.

"Do you know what Nolan told me?" I said, swirling a carrot stick in the hummus on my plate so I wouldn't have to meet anyone's gaze.

"What?" Holly asked.

"He said I'd be a fucked-up female role model for Emma." Tears pooled in my eyes at the mention of my girl's name.

"No, he *didn't!*" Lex exclaimed, slamming her hand down on the table, making the silverware jump. "Shut the fuck up!"

Jordana exhaled loudly and started stacking the plates and walking them over to the sink.

Finally! I thought. *A reaction!* Her silence and obvious unease throughout the meal reminded me of the day they all visited the hospital to deliver the *Becca Night Live* videotape—the day she practically sprinted to the door when the nurse told her it was time to leave.

"The thing is, what if he's right?" I said, regaining my composure. "But if I get the implants, am I telling my daughter you can be a 'woman' only if you have boobs? And if I *don't* have the reconstruction, is she gonna be disgusted or embarrassed because I don't look like her friends' moms? Or will she feel guilty one day for having boobs because I don't?"

The only sound in the room was the clink of dishes and utensils as Jordana cleared the table with the grace of a Stormtrooper.

"Who knows what will be, but give yourself a little credit, Bec," Holly said, breaking the uncomfortable silence. "Look at how you've explained surrogacy to her. The kid is in her single digits and already has a solid understanding of third-party reproduction. But, more important, she's proud! You taught her to see the beauty in it. She takes her cues from you, and she can learn to own this, too. If you're good with it, she'll be good with it. Whatever you choose, you'll find a way to instill pride and explain it to her, just like you did with her birth."

Seth cleared his throat. "Either way," he said, "you still have a great ass. I'll whip Nol into shape and make him an ass guy."

Lex laughed and sat up a little straighter.

I knew he was joking, but in that moment, I wasn't in the mood. "I'm not sure it will make a difference. I feel like I'll lose my husband and my chest in the same summer."

"Then fuck it," Lex cried out. "You don't need him. You will resent him forever. You will destroy your marriage if you do it for him and not for you. *Trust* me."

Seth's brow furrowed, and he shot a quizzical look at Lex, before turning back to me. "Nolan would *never* force your hand, Bec. He adores you. He's not shallow. You know that."

"The Nolan I know isn't the Nolan I've seen over the past days. This guy is practically mute. He won't even look at me. Put it this way: Would the Nolan you know not show up for a reunion weekend in celebration of his wife?"

"I think he's in shock," Seth said. "I think he's scared. Nolan's a can-do guy. Give him a problem, and he'll do whatever it takes to solve it. I'm not a shrink, but maybe he's realizing he can't fix this. Maybe convincing you to do the reconstruction is like him trying to control this situation. Maybe you guys should talk to someone, like a couples' counselor. I don't know, though. What do I know about relationships?"

I noticed Lex take a swig of wine.

Jordana walked over to the head of the table, wrung her hands on a dish towel as if she were about to asphyxiate it, and fixed her gaze on the wall in the distance. She seemed to be revving up to something profound. We all turned to her, awaiting whatever it was she was about to opine.

Finally, she shifted her eyes to our faces and proclaimed in a calm, controlled, yet authoritative voice: "You all just need to check your privilege."

"*What?*" we said, as a single, confounded chorus.

Oh boy, here we go, I thought.

"Is this one of your trendy, politically correct, social justice–y catchphrases?" Seth asked playfully.

Jordana glared at him. She was in no mood for ribbing.

"Sorry," Seth mumbled, lowering his chin shamefully toward his chest.

"Every day at work, I check my privilege," Jordana said passionately, gently pounding her chest with the crumpled dish towel as if she were making a dramatic closing argument in the courtroom. "I remind myself that as someone who is well educated, financially secure, and surrounded by friends and family who are similarly blessed, I must put aside my advantages in order to gain a better understanding of my clients' realities. I know that, no matter how hard I try, it's impossible for me to truly comprehend what it's like to walk in their shoes. Most of the time, they are victims of circumstance. They face uphill battles because of the color of their skin or where they live or how they dress, and I try to remember that at all times, even if they talk down to me or disrespect me despite my help. It can be hard, but you know what do I do? *Check. My. Privilege.* I remind myself to look at all angles and think about where they're coming from before I speak or make a move."

"Where is she going with this?" Lex groused, leaning into Seth's shoulder.

Jordana noticed but chose to continue speaking.

"My point is that it's the same thing with Nolan. I want to throttle him, don't get me wrong. But we all need to recognize that for him, it's just different. He wasn't there. He doesn't have the same *privilege* we have. Not to say seeing Becca sick when we were kids was a privilege, but you get my point. He doesn't have the same insight the rest of us have." She turned to look at me. "He didn't see the fifteen gazillion bags of blood and medicine hanging from your IV pole in the hospital, or how you passed out that time in your bedroom at home when I came over to drop off your algebra homework. Do you remember that? I ran downstairs to your mom and told her to call an ambulance. I thought you'd died."

"I forgot about that," I said softly, a pang of guilt washing over me. I wondered if I had unintentionally soured all of their childhoods by wrecking their innocence. Would my health now sour my marriage, too?

Holly shifted in her chair. "Do you remember how you made me a 'VIP' bat mitzvah party at your house because you were too sick the day of my real party? We played limbo using a closet rod and did the electric slide in your parents' living room. My brother came over with mix tapes to be the DJ."

I smiled, recalling that day. "Remember the sign-in board I made?"

"You were the only one to sign it!" Holly laughed.

Jordana cleared her throat. "Maybe it's the defense lawyer in me," she said, jumping back in, "but I'm thinking everyone should ease up on the Nolan bashing and give the guy some time to grieve."

"*Grieve?*" Lex said. "She's not *dying!*"

"I know. I don't mean *grieve* as in death; I mean he needs to mourn a loss."

"*Mourn a loss?*" Lex was exasperated. "What's wrong with you?"

If it were socially acceptable to slap a guest across the face, Jordana might have taken a swing at Lex. Instead, she simply rolled her eyes.

"All I'm saying is, he's facing a major change affecting the love of his life," Jordana said. "I mean, none of you is married to Becca. None of you has that intimacy. None of you is affected as deeply and daily as he is. I know there's a lot of love at this table, but, realistically, you'll all go back to your lives at the end of this weekend and life will march on. But she's his family. She's his person. So maybe all of you should cut him some slack and accept that it's simply different . . ." Her voice trailed off, before she added, "for *him.*"

If I hadn't known better, I'd have thought she was talking about herself.

"I don't know, Jord. I kinda think if it acts like a jerk and sounds like a jerk and disappears like a jerk, it's probably a jerk, no matter how many times you 'check your privilege,'" Lex said, forming air quotes with her fingers, the way she did when we were kids.

At that moment, Sal and Adam returned to the room, wine bottles in hand.

"Can we change the topic, please?" I asked. The tension in the room was making my chest tighten.

"Actually, my sciatica is killing me. I think I'm going to lie down," Holly said resting both hands on her back. Minutes later, she and Adam had disappeared into their bedroom.

Lex and Seth offered to help Jordana load the dishwasher, but she insisted she and Sal had a "system" and that they should grab a bottle of wine, go outside, and enjoy the beautiful country night. They followed her advice and took their glasses out to the Adirondack chairs on the front porch. I was about to offer to help package up the leftovers and place them in the fridge, when my cell phone buzzed with a new message. It was a video my mother had sent to both Nolan's phone and mine.

The clanging of dishes and running tap water from the sink made it impossible to hear, so I walked down the hall to my guest room and pressed PLAY.

"Hi, Mommy and Daddy," Emma said softly. She was lying on my parents' duvet, wearing the pajamas with watermelons I'd bought her. "I just wanted to say good night, and that I miss you, and that I love you, and . . ." Emma's voice began to tremble.

"It's okay, honey," I heard my mother say sweetly in the background. "Mommy and Daddy love you very much and are going to be home on Sunday. I promise. Don't cry, sweetheart. Mommy and Daddy always come home."

Emma forced a smile and looked as if she were summoning all of her strength to appear brave. "Mommy and Daddy"—she spoke our monikers as if they were one name—"I love you and I miss you. I hope you are having a good time with your friends, and that you come home as soon as you can on Sunday. Good night." She blew a kiss, and the video ended.

I exploded into tears. I buried my face in the quilted pillow sham to muffle my cries. I would have given anything to be curled up in bed, snuggling beside her. Though it seemed like self-inflicted torture, I had to watch the video again. Just as it ended, another came in. This one was from Nolan.

He appears! I gasped and immediately pressed PLAY.

"Hi, sweetie pie!" he cooed. He was holding the phone close

to his face. "I love you and miss you, too. Looks like you're having a great time with Grandma and Grandpa! That makes me happy. Have a good night. I'll see you on Sunday. I love you soooooooo much."

Where is he? I played the video a second time. When he blew a kiss to Emma, he pulled the phone back a bit and I caught a glimpse of something green on the wall. I played it again and again. It looked like a woman wearing something green. *Is it a photo? Why does that look so familiar?* And then it hit me. *Oh my God! It's the poster of Kathy Ireland in the green bikini that he's had tacked to his childhood-bedroom wall since sixth grade!*

A torrent of adrenaline shot through me. I couldn't tell whether it was anger, resentment, shock, or devastation, but my body practically ejected itself from the bed and shot into the bathroom to prepare itself for whatever would come next. I brushed my teeth so vigorously, my gums bled. I splashed water on my face with such ferocity, I soaked the collar of my shirt. After I spackled on enough makeup to cover my splotchy cheeks, I perfected my best happy face in the mirror and hatched a plan. I'd record a quick video wishing Emma good night and tell her how much I loved and missed her. I'd send it off and then call Nolan. We needed to speak—have a real conversation, instead of exchanging bedtime videos intended for our child.

After texting Emma's video to my mom, I dialed Nolan's number. No answer. I waited a few minutes and tried again. Direct to voice mail, no ring. *He turned off the damn phone to avoid me. What kind of man does that?* Any guilt I had about having betrayed him at dinner had now vanished.

I could no longer sit still. I had to leave the bedroom and get some air. When I walked outside, Seth and Lex were slouched in the Adirondack chairs, holding wineglasses and engaged in an intense conversation. I felt as if approaching then would be an intrusion but reminded myself that it was just Seth and Lex. What could I be breaking up?

"Hi, guys," I said stepping onto the porch. "Seth, you've got to help me out. Do you know where Nolan went after his appointment with you this morning?"

"I'm pretty sure he went to work," Seth said.

"Did he seem like himself? I mean, did he say anything odd?" I wondered if I sounded as frenetic as I felt.

Seth shot Lex a quick glance, before looking back at me—and suddenly I understood: they knew something about Nolan that I didn't.

"He definitely seemed more stressed than usual," Seth said. "He didn't exactly say why, but now that I know what's going on with you, it makes total sense."

Seth was lying. I debated whether to command him to tell me the truth or to leave it alone. I desperately wanted to know what Nolan and Seth had discussed that morning, and yet, by asking, I'd be putting Seth in the middle of our marital drama—a predicament I didn't want and he didn't deserve. I said good night and returned to the house. But as I shut the door and started down the hall toward my guest room, I heard Seth and Lex's hushed tones through an open screen window. I stopped to listen.

"Stay out of it," she warned him. "Don't get involved. Ultimately, you're her friend, not his."

"Of course Becca comes first, but the guy seemed so sad. How can I just turn my back when a buddy asks for a favor?"

"It's easy. If the favor could potentially create more stress for Becca, then you just say no," she cautioned again.

I stood frozen by that screen window. It took every ounce of restraint I had not to walk back outside and pump them for information, but I resisted and retreated to my room. I changed into pajamas, turned down the quilt, and slid between the crisp cotton sheets. The space from one corner to the other seemed vast and lonely. *So this is what it would be like*, I thought. Unlike the rare occasion when Nolan traveled for work and I enjoyed having the whole mattress to myself, along with control of the television remote, this felt different. When you've had the worst fight of your marriage and can't track down your husband, 800-thread-count Egyptian-cotton linens and unlimited movie channels somehow lose their appeal.

I tossed and turned. I repositioned pillows. *What were Seth and Lex talking about?* I wondered. I got out of bed, pulled a sweatshirt

over my tank top, and headed back to the front porch. I opened
the door, expecting to see them in the same spots on the chairs, but
they were gone. I heard whispers coming from the driveway. The
country night was pitch black, and it was difficult to see even a few
feet ahead. I walked to the edge of the front steps and with my eyes
continued to follow the voices down the pebbled driveway until I
noticed the distinct glow of a cell phone coming from the bed of
Sal's beaten-up old pickup truck and illuminating Lex and Seth's
faces. I watched as she tilted her head back, smiled, and flipped her
hair. I noticed how he stretched out an arm and laid it across the
rim of the truck behind her back. If I hadn't known better, I would
have sworn they were two flirtatious sleepaway-camp counselors
stealing a private moment in the middle of the night while their
campers slept soundly in cabins.

I tried to listen in but couldn't make out the words. I turned
and tiptoed back to my room, concluding that it would be unfair
to entangle them in my marital mess any more than I already had.
After all, I thought, *they seem to be quite capable of getting entangled in a
marital mess of their own. Maybe we'll all end up single again.*

Chapter 10: Seth

It was a magnificent July night. The cool country air smelled like fresh pine, and I hadn't seen a sky so clear and full of stars since the summer my mother sent me to fat camp in Pennsylvania. Sitting in an Adirondack chair on Jordana's front porch with a glass of wine in my hand and an old friend by my side would have been absolute perfection, had it not been what it was—a reprieve from the conversation at dinner.

"Some night, eh?" I said, when Lex and I stepped outside, away from the group.

"Not at all what I anticipated." She sighed, settling into her chair.

"I don't think it's what any of us anticipated." I took a sip of wine and thought about Lex's impassioned defense of Becca at the meal. Before I could edit myself, the words tripped out of my mouth. "So, *you* were pretty fired up in there."

She straightened and turned to face me. "Well, how can you *not* be angry? It sounds like Nolan's been a total ass! Do you disagree? I mean, I know you two are buddies, but come on, Seth!"

"I wasn't really talking about Nolan or Becca. I was just saying you spoke with, I don't know, authority. Or wisdom? Like you had some sort of insight that the rest of us didn't." Maybe it was the moonlit ambience or the alcohol or both, but I felt emboldened to learn more about the girl I had eaten Play-Doh with in kindergarten and consoled in eleventh grade when she hit the curb parallel-parking and automatically flunked her first driver's test.

"Believe me, I had no inside scoop on Becca's news," Lex said, reaching for the glass she'd placed beside her chair.

"What I'm trying to say is that you advised her with a *trust me, girlfriend, been there, done that* vibe." I snapped twice in the air and bopped my head from side to side, the way we did when we were kids. I hadn't made that gesture in years. There was something about hanging out with this group again that altered my chemistry. My inhibitions felt unshackled; my speech loosened. "I was just wondering if everything is okay with *you*."

Lex looked at me over her glass as she swirled the wine in it. Based on her squinted gaze, she seemed to be debating what information to share and what to keep private. I hoped I hadn't overstepped any boundaries.

After a lengthy sip, she finally spoke. "Do you think you'd be as successful as you are now if you hadn't gone through all that crap when you were younger?"

I looked at her quizzically, unsure where she was going with this.

"You know," she said, "getting kicked out of school and flailing around all those years? You ever wonder if it all happened for a reason?"

Wait, I thought, my old insecurities kicking in, *so, does she consider me a success or a slacker?* "I don't really think about it much. Why do you ask?"

She shrugged. "I don't know. It's been on my mind a lot."

"My getting kicked out of Princeton has been on your mind?"

"No, you doof. About all the curveballs I'm seeing lately." She leaned her head back onto the chair and looked into the distance. "I wonder if there's a grand plan, some divine construct that we all just need to sit back and ride out, or if it's ultimately up to us to catch those curveballs and take control of our own destiny." She turned back toward me.

"Lex, did you . . ." I suggestively raised my eyebrows and pinched my fingers to my lips as if I were smoking a joint.

"No! Stop it! I'm serious!" She smacked me playfully on the arm. Her gigantic diamond ring actually hurt upon contact.

When we were kids, Lex was the life of the party and the loudest of the bunch. I remembered her reading *Seventeen* magazine or *Sweet Valley High* books under her desk and claiming not to care about school, despite making the honor roll every semester. She was the kid who didn't study but aced the final, the one teachers swore was daydreaming but had the most insightful comments to share when called upon. Of our group of friends, she and I were the only two selected to take the admissions test for the Bronx High School of Science. When we were accepted, she claimed the hour-long commute each way would cramp her social life and didn't enroll. My mother and the rest of the neighborhood yentas went on for weeks about how her parents were insane for allowing "such a bright young lady" to prioritize loitering outside the local pizzeria to flirt with cute boys on the baseball team and forfeit a coveted spot at one of the nation's top schools. Mom said Lex "hid her light under a bushel." Back then, I didn't understand what that meant, but now those words were ringing in my ears. Lex was funnier, deeper, and more complex than I had remembered.

"I have to say," Lex went on, "it was very hard to listen to Becca and not get *passionate*, to use your words. It's not just the illness that's upsetting; it's all this unnecessary drama. That's what pisses me off. She should be free of that so that she can focus her energy on being healthy. She has to make the choice for herself. I'd hate for her to think that if she and Nolan don't see eye to eye and she gives in and chooses to do what *he* wants with *her* body, it will guarantee happily ever after. It won't. *That*, I can promise."

How can she promise? What's with this authoritative tone?

My phone buzzed with an incoming text. It was Nolan:

Hey, man. Sorry didn't make it up tonight. Got your email earlier—thanks for the list of docs. I looked them over and have a favor to ask. Would you mind calling and getting me an appointment ASAP with the second doc on the list? Thanks, buddy. I know I can count on you. —N

"Shit," I muttered.

"What?" Lex asked.

I handed her my phone. She read the screen.

"Fuck no!" she cried, passing it back to me. "He's got some chutzpah, putting you in the middle."

Just then, the front door creaked open. I turned around, and there was Becca, standing on the porch. She inquired about Nolan's behavior and his whereabouts after our physical therapy appointment that morning.

"He definitely seemed more stressed than usual," I offered. "He didn't exactly say why, but now that I know what's happening, it makes total sense."

Seeming satisfied with my response, Becca hugged us both good night, then retreated inside.

"This sucks, on so many levels," I said, and stood up to stretch my arms, before crouching to do a few deep knee bends.

"Wanna go for a walk?" I asked.

"Sure." Lex took a final swig of her drink and set the glass beneath her chair.

We stepped off the porch and, with our cell phones illuminating the way, started down the pebbled path. We stopped at the base of the driveway.

"Holy cow! Is this the Beast?'" she asked, giggling when we came upon Sal's disheveled secondhand pickup truck. "Jordana told me about this when he got it. Her description is spot-on!"

"It must be," I said, circling and inspecting the truck with my flashlight. "It's exactly how she described it: rusty, corroded hubcaps, chipped paint job, broken front grill, a virtually useless two-wheel drive, 1980s styling . . . This thing is fantastic! Totally inconsistent with his high-tech house and Brooks Brothers shirts, but if he thinks this makes him a legit country boy, more power to him."

I heard a clank and looked up. Lex was standing on the bed of the truck. "What do you think?" she asked, posing with a hand on her jutted hip. "I have to admit, it's kind of cool! Actually, my kids would love this! Come check it out!"

"Maybe you should follow Sal's lead and scour the used-truck ads. Would your husband spring for one?" I couldn't remember his name.

"Jack? Pfft!" She waved her hand dismissively in front of her face. "If everyone at the club did it, then for sure he'd buy one. He marches to the beat of others' drummers, not his own. Ask him his favorite color, he'll take an office poll and get back to you."

"Ouch." A slight electricity came over me when I sensed tension in their union—a sense of possibility. I noted it and then pushed it down.

"Maybe *that's* the 'wisdom' or 'insight' you detected in me at dinner," she said, as she sat down and reclined so that she could look up at the sky.

I hoisted myself onto the truck bed to join her. Lying beside her on that uneven and slightly corroded metal surface, I could smell her delicate floral scent. I could see the beauty mark in the soft crease of her neck. I tried valiantly to avert my eyes from the inch of exposed abdominal skin where the hem of her tank top lifted above the waist of her jeans. She looked sexy and surprisingly taut for a woman who'd birthed three children. Twenty-five years ago, I would have stuck my finger down my throat and mock-gagged at the thought of this moment. Instead, there I was, shifting my position so I could surreptitiously sniff my armpit, praying I didn't have body odor and trying to recall whether I had spritzed cologne on that morning. I didn't think I had. *Chill out! It's just Lex!* I reminded myself. And yet there I was, wishing we had a blanket so we could stay there all night.

"We were in love," she said. "All I wanted was to plan a wedding, get pregnant, and make dinner for Jack when he got home from work. I guess watching *Leave It to Beaver* reruns as a kid must have seeped into my subconscious. I drank the Kool-Aid; I believed in the happily ever after shtick. But then about a year and a half ago—"

Just when it was getting juicy, Lex's phone buzzed. She looked at the caller ID.

"Hello, this is Lex," she said, sitting up. "Oh, hi, Stephanie! I didn't recognize your number. Great! Yes, uh-huh, absolutely! We can do that. Uh-huh, yes, we just got them back in stock. You've made a great choice—as you know, it's one of our hottest items. . . . You know the drill. Just send me an email with your color preferences, the recipient's address and the baby's name, and I'll send it out. Oh, you too, hon. Thank *you*! Have a great weekend."

She lay back down next to me. "Work call," she said apologetically.

"On a Friday night? July Fourth weekend?"

She shrugged. "I recently started this mom-and-newborn-gear company online, and I have to say, it's doing well, a lot better than I ever expected. We do diaper bags, workout clothes, personalized stationery, jewelry, welcome-home baskets—that kind of thing. I don't normally get calls this late or on a holiday weekend, but it happens. That woman is a repeat customer and totally nuts, but I love her. She's got tons of friends and orders a gift the second she finds out one of them has given birth. She makes Jordana look laid-back."

"That's fantastic. Good for you!" I said. I wanted to be supportive but was eager to return to our conversation. I cleared my throat. "So, uh, you were saying something about a year and a half ago . . ."

"Right. Well, talk about curveballs and destiny." Her biting tone returned. "The party line is that I started the business because my three kids were getting older, the little one was in school all day, and there was only so much tennis a girl could play . . ."

"And the non–party line?"

She took a breath. "The non–party line is that about a year and a half ago, I realized that I wanted—actually, *needed*—to have my own income. I wanted something for me—my own business, my own baby, if you will."

"So, a lightning bolt just struck you?"

"I wanted another baby," she said abruptly.

"Oh." I wasn't sure how I was supposed to react.

"Jack gave me a flat-out no and said three kids was 'more than enough.' He wants to retire as soon as possible and not have to work another eighteen years to support a child."

"I'm sorry," I said. I assumed that was the correct response.

"Thanks, but the part that really stung was when he turned it around and said I was impossible to please. He was like, 'I love you, Lex. I've given you everything you've ever asked for: a huge engagement ring, a big house in your top-choice suburb, we joined a country club because you wanted it, I even picked up golf and joined a fantasy football league with your friends' husbands because you insisted *these* were the people I needed to befriend. You've orchestrated our life, and here I am, enjoying it, taking ownership of it, working hard to pay for all of it, and you say I'm embracing it too much? I can't win!'"

I cringed. "And what did you say?"

"What is there to say? He's right." She sighed. "I have pretty much cherry-picked the stuff in his world, and he's gone along with it. But at some point, I'm not sure exactly when—maybe when he was traveling for work, or playing golf, or grabbing a drink at the club—we grew apart. And the parties and social stuff I'd always prioritized and even gave up Bronx Science for when we were kids—our mothers were right, by the way; I should have gone—are no longer as important to me. I've outgrown the need to constantly see and be seen, and now he's the one who's miserable missing an event."

I started nibbling nervously on my thumbnail. I didn't know what to make of the fact that I was pleased to hear about the stress in her marriage. I also didn't know what to make of my excitement in hearing that she yearned for another baby her husband didn't want to give her. I felt evil taking pleasure in her pain. "So, the business? How'd you start it?"

"Well, I knew I didn't want to bring a child into the world without the support of its father, so I dropped the baby thing and we never spoke about it again. But I promised myself that I'd give birth to something in a different way. Helping other moms felt right. So I started making and selling little bibs and burp cloths to friends, and it took off. I added more products, and word spread, and now it's a real business."

"And this fulfills you? It replaces the desire for another kid one day?"

"I wouldn't go that far. I mean, I'd never say never to another child. I love being a mom. But for the first time in my life, I feel that I could be self-sufficient. And I'm being challenged in a way I wasn't before. I know I'm not an idiot, but I really didn't believe I could pull it off. I've never experienced that sense of independence.

So, yes, this is satisfying. It's not a baby, and it's nothing remotely close to the empire Holly has created with her bakery, but it will do, for now."

I dissected her words. "For now?" I asked. "What does that mean?" I knew I was prying, but as the sole boy in a group of girls, I'd been the nonthreatening, asexual guy-friend sounding board for Becca, Jordana, Holly, and Lex. I was simply reviving my role.

"Jack and I have a partnership, essentially, if you can call it that. There's a shorthand between us because we've been together for so long. Most days we can navigate the ship smoothly. I know how he likes his laundry folded. He knows how I take my coffee. I drive his mother to the grocery store on Wednesdays after I drop him off at the 7:44 a.m. train. In that sense, it's effortless. You'd look at us and never know how far we've strayed from what we were. We wear the right clothes to the cocktail parties. He buys me beautiful jewelry for every birthday and anniversary. We know how to smile for the cameras at the school plays, which, by the way, you would see if you had Instagram or Facebook. But do we talk to each other the moment the valet closes our car door and we head home after a dinner party? No. I don't remember the last time the two of us were alone and laughed."

"That stinks. I'm sorry." I really was. A lack of humor was a deal-breaker for me.

"I'd have said you were insane if you'd told me years ago that my marriage would be one of convenience."

"So, what are you going to do?"

"Probably nothing. It would take a lot for me to ruin a stable home and traditional family life for my kids. I'm resigned to the situation. I've come to accept that this is my fate. And please—it's not like I'm abused or anything horrible like that. He's not evil. He'd make someone who wanted the things I thought I wanted very happy. I just feel stifled. That's all." She grew quiet. "Actually, you know what I think about a lot?"

"What?"

"I think about what it must have felt like for Becca to lie in that isolation room for two months. I know there were days when she was too exhausted to do anything, but I vividly recall a conversation we had over the phone one day when she was starting to feel better and how she told me that she was itching to pull out the IV tubes and run in that schoolyard across the street from the hospital. That's sort of how I feel, Seth. I mean I know being a sick child trapped in the hospital is wholly different from being an intellectually uninspired suburban mom, but I'm more than ready for my next chapter. That being said, my kids are my priority. As long as I'm surrounded by them, I know I'll be okay."

Lex doesn't deserve a loveless marriage. I get that she's staying in it for the kids, but did she learn nothing about how short life is when we all watched Becca suffer, and again now?

"Well, if you ever need anything . . . " I said genuinely. "Just someone to vent to . . ."

"Thank you," she said, placing her manicured hand on my forearm. Her fingertips electrified my skin. "Actually, come to think of it, I do need something. Would you take a look at my business plan? I mean, now that you've got your own company, maybe you could tell me if I'm doing things right. You'd think, given my degree in marketing, I'd have a clue, but I'm eons out of practice. I asked Jack for his opinion—the guy's got an MBA from Wharton, after all—but he keeps saying he'll read it and never does. I suspect that's because he considers my job less of a business and more of a 'pastime to avoid watching Bravo TV all day long,' as he once so eloquently put it."

"Yowza!" I exclaimed. *"Yowza"? I never say that. Where did that come from?* I then turned my palm face-up and said, "Hand it over." For the next twenty minutes, we lay on the bed of Sal's truck, reading the business plan off her phone. I offered some suggestions, which she took immediately. Just as we were finishing up, Nolan called.

I froze. Should I go with a friendly "Hey, bud" greeting? Or a concerned "How are you holding up?" greeting? Or an angry "Get your ass up here" greeting? I wasn't sure which tone to set or where my loyalty lay—with Nolan or Becca—and I was acutely aware that Lex was watching.

I opted to go neutral. "Hello?" I picked up, feigning surprise, as if I didn't have caller ID.

"Hey, Seth, it's Nolan."

"Nolan who?" I couldn't resist. The familiar sound of his subtle lisp made it difficult to stay mad at him.

"Ha ha, very funny. Did you get my text?"

"Uh, which one?" I knew exactly what he was referring to but needed to buy some time.

"The one about setting up the appointment? I know these doctors are in demand and you need to book these things weeks in advance, but could you expedite the process, the way you did with my shoulder surgery?"

Lex was sitting right next to me and could hear everything. "Tell him no!" she mouthed, shaking her finger at me. I grabbed her hand and pulled it down. When I did, neither one of us pulled away. *I'm not moving a centimeter,* I thought. *She's going to have to be the one to pull away first.*

"Yeah, I got the text," I said, trying to refocus. *Our hands have been touching for at least thirty seconds . . .* "Listen, lots of doctors and their staff are away over the holiday weekend. It's a busy time. I can't do anything tonight."

"I get that," Nolan said. "But maybe if you leave a message this weekend and then call again first thing Monday morning?" He sounded desperate.

"Yeah, maybe Monday or even Sun—" I said, but cut myself off when I felt Lex squeeze my hand.

"Becca needs us," she whispered.

I nodded in acknowledgment.

"Listen, I know you're probably at work, but honestly, man, the corporate mergers can wait, especially on a holiday weekend. You really should be up here already."

"Yeah, about that . . . Not sure what my plan is right now."

"Dude, she *needs* you."

"Wait, what?" he said. "What did Becca say?"

"We're her old friends," I said. "She told us, okay? Just come up here. It will be all right." I looked at Lex for support. Our hands were still touching. "You'll be stronger together than apart," I said.

A smile crept across Lex's face. She still didn't let go of my hand.

Nolan hung up without a goodbye, and we sat there, staring down at the blank screen of my phone, still touching. It was titillating and uncomfortable and scary, all at once.

"I feel like I failed a mission," I said, to cut the tension.

"Relax," she said, giving my hand a gentle squeeze. "You did the best you could. You can't change an asshole."

"He's really not an asshole. I promise."

"Tomato, *tomahto*."

"I know you don't know him very well, but take my word, he's really a good guy. I don't think the last twenty-four hours are an accurate representation of his character or his love for . . ." I stopped speaking when I noticed a shadow on the front porch. Lex turned to see the object of my attention. When we saw the shadow transform into the silhouette of a woman, we disconnected our hands. It was like the parting of the sea. *I hope that's not Becca listening in*, I thought.

There was a crackling of pebbles as the woman approached. She moved slowly and deliberately. When I shined my light her way, I was relieved to see it was Holly.

"Hey!" Lex greeted her. "I thought you went to bed. Isn't the pregnant lady supposed to be sleeping?"

"Oh, this pregnant lady can't sleep." She groaned and waddled closer to the truck. "So, uh, whatcha doin' up there?" She sounded a bit winded.

"What? You don't spend your Friday nights hanging out on the beds of rusty pickup trucks?" I asked.

Holly laughed. "I must say, I *can* see the temptation with those charming corroded edges and bird-poop stains. You must be loving this, Lex!"

"I'm more daring than you think." Lex smiled at Holly but shifted her eyes toward me. *Is she flirting with me? What's that supposed to mean?*

Holly lifted her right knee onto the bed, but it failed to reach. She tried her left leg, but that didn't work, either. She attempted backing into a seated position, but even when she stood on tiptoe, it was a lost cause.

She laughed. "This truly may be one of the most embarrassing moments of my life. I think we need some sort of pulley system if I'm going to join you."

"Wait a sec," I said, jumping off the truck and running over to the garden by the front porch. "Try this." I flipped over an empty flowerpot to use as a stepstool.

"Genius." She smiled, stepping onto the metal bed and cozying up beside Lex. They linked their arms, and Lex leaned her head onto Holly's shoulder.

"How *is* the pregnancy going?" Lex asked.

"Other than my inability to gracefully hop onto a pickup truck, it's going well," she said. "I mean, I could share details about acid reflux, hemorrhoids, and sciatica, but I suspect Seth has reached his threshold for conversations about women's bodies for one night."

The three of us were quiet for a moment.

"I can't stop thinking about her," Holly said somberly. "Has anyone heard from Nolan? Do we know if he's coming?"

"Actually, he just called me. I'm not sure what he's doing. He didn't say."

"This is absolutely ridiculous." Holly shook her head in disappointment.

"Well, you know how I feel," Lex said acerbically. "He's a dipshit, if you ask me."

I glanced at my phone, hoping Nolan would call back or text after hanging up earlier. *Come on, man!* I thought. *Show 'em you're just a good guy going through a hard time and that they should cut you some slack. You're not making this easy for me!*

"I hear you loud and clear, Lex, but I think for Becca's sake, we need to hold back on any negativity. It's not going to help her," Holly said. "We need a plan. Show her we've got her back. Focus on the positive and try to make this weekend as much fun and distracting as possible. Whatever it takes, we're here for her, even if her choice, or the decision-making process, or Nolan, or any part of this makes us angry or uncomfortable. We've got to set aside our personal stuff to minimize her stress and keep her afloat."

"Yeah, I agree," Lex jumped in. "We've got to keep her busy and get her mind off this. But I can't promise I'll be able to keep my trap shut when it comes to Nolan."

I checked my phone again. Nothing. *Dammit*, I thought.

"Look, guys," I said, "I think our mission is clear. For whatever it's worth, we've got experience. We've rallied before, and we can do it again."

"Nolan wasn't there the first time, and I guess we don't need him now, either," Lex added.

Holly nodded in agreement and rubbed her abdomen. "Okay, time to pee. Who's gonna help me up?"

Lex and I jumped to our feet and carefully eased her off the truck. As soon as Holly was steady on the ground, she palmed the bottom of her protruding belly as if she were lifting a basketball off her bladder and began to toddle across the pebbles. "Good night, guys! Love you both!" she chirped on her way into the house.

"Love you, too," we called back and watched through the screened window of the great room as she made her way down the hallway.

Lex and I smiled awkwardly at each other. A breeze rustled through the colossal trees surrounding us, and a chorus of chirping crickets filled the property, as if Sal had blasted a recording of insects through his outdoor speaker system.

"I had a *really* nice day with you, Seth," Lex said thoughtfully. "I had forgotten how much I've always enjoyed your company."

My *company?* I thought. I had never known she distinguished my company from that of anyone else in the group.

"Me too," I said. I was glad it was dark outside, and that she couldn't see me blush. Had she been any one of the countless girls I had dated over the last decade, I would have pulled her close and done whatever it took to get her into bed. Instead, I stuck my hands in my pockets and kicked a few pebbles, feeling like an insecure seventh grader standing beside his first crush.

"Well, it's getting late," she said. "I should probably call my kids and wish them good night. It's an hour earlier in Chicago."

"Yeah, cool beans," I said. *"Cool beans"? Seriously? What is this, 1991?*

Lex giggled. "I don't think I've heard that expression in twenty years!"

"Me neither," I said sheepishly. "Not really sure where that came from."

"You've always made me laugh, Seth." She smiled and kissed my cheek, before turning toward the front door. I stood by the truck, admiring her graceful stride. Unlike Holly's cacophonous crunch, Lex's feet seemed to skim across the pebbles without a sound.

"Wanna run the lake tomorrow morning?" she called out from the porch. "Jordana says it's about four miles around and really beautiful."

"Definitely!" I said, feeling a rush of adrenaline.

"Great! It's a date!" she said, then closed the door.

Get it together! I thought, as I sauntered toward the house. *It's Lex, for crying out loud! She's married, with three kids, and you're an ass.*

I scooped up the wineglass I'd left on the porch and gulped the remainder of the cabernet before walking inside. I placed the glass in the kitchen sink. As I headed toward the staircase, I noticed the flickering blue light of a television illuminating a bedroom near the kitchen.

The door was slightly ajar. I poked my head inside and saw Becca in her pajamas, lying atop the quilt and staring gloomily at a muted TV. Amid the room's angled cathedral ceiling and California king bed, she reminded me of a sad Alice in Wonderland, dwarfed by her surroundings.

"Hey," I said. "Whatcha doin'?"

"Just flipping through the channels," she replied. "I can't sleep."

"Mind if I join you?" I couldn't walk away and leave her to wallow in depressing local news.

"Sure." She shrugged like an apathetic teenager. It wasn't the most welcoming invitation, but I accepted nonetheless.

I was tempted to ask if she had heard from Nolan, but I could intuit the answer just by looking at her. *Maybe the others were right about him*, I thought. *After all, I would never have uttered the words Becca said he shouted at her in that doctor's office.*

I kicked off my shoes, reclined on the tufted velvet chaise in the corner of the room, and watched the channels flip past.

"Wait a minute," I said, "Go back. I just saw Christie Brinkley in a swimming pool."

"Really?" she asked, a bit of verve returning to her. I could tell she knew exactly what that meant. *National Lampoon's Vacation* had been a staple of our childhood. My father recorded it on our living room VCR when it played on local television one holiday weekend. Despite the abundance of commercials and the fact that it had been cleansed of its raunchier content, the movie never failed to make me laugh. That was the cassette I would bring over to Becca's house on the days when she was too tired to play Parcheesi but still yearned for company. We'd sit in her parents' den—I reclining on the frayed tweed La-Z-Boy, Becca sprawled out on the brown corduroy sofa with a needlepoint throw pillow beneath her head—mouthing along with Chevy Chase and Beverly D'Angelo for the entirety of the film. When we eventually rented the original, rated-R version from Blockbuster, we enjoyed it, but we agreed that my father's grainy VHS cassette with the Crazy Eddie commercials was far superior.

For the next hour, we lay in our spots, reciting the movie verbatim, just like we did as kids. There was no need for conversation; we were just two friends hanging out, enjoying the distraction from our lives. And that was enough.

Chapter 11: Holly

I woke Saturday morning when Adam slipped out of bed. I watched as he draped an ivory linen prayer shawl over his head, opened his prayer book, turned east toward the window, and began reciting his morning invocations. As the sun rose over the hilltops and cast its light upon a corner of our guestroom, I rolled onto my side and tried to go back to sleep.

Sometime during my first trimester, when exhaustion had become the only gear in which I operated, I decided that sleep should take precedence over going to synagogue on my only day off from the bakery. The Sabbath was a day of rest, I reasoned, and I would wholeheartedly obey that commandment.

This morning was no different. But between my racing mind and my inability to find a comfortable sleeping position, catching some shuteye was as likely as the women in my community throwing me a baby shower. I decided to get out of bed and head into the kitchen for a glass of juice. That's when I saw Lex at the counter, decked out in form-fitting black and fuchsia Lululemon spandex, with a perfect ponytail and her giant sunglasses perched on top. She looked like a celebrity preparing to jog past paparazzi.

"Good morning, hot mama!" I said. I felt homely beside her in my terry robe. I couldn't recall the last time I had gone for a run or worn spandex as an outer layer. "Where are you off to?"

"Seth and I are going to do a loop around the lake. Jordana

says it's beautiful and just across the street from the base of the mountain."

I heard a cell phone ring down the hall. *Can't be mine*, I thought. It was Saturday morning, and I never used the phone on the Sabbath.

"All right! Let's do this! Who's ready for a power run?" Seth clapped his hands like a track coach as his neon sneakers pounded the treads of the wooden staircase down from the second floor. "You ready to go, Lex?"

"Am *I* ready? No, Seth, the question is, are *you* ready?" Lex asked. She turned and winked at me.

He smirked. "Check out the trash-talking Midwesterner. I guess you can take the girl out of Queens, but you can't take Queens out of the girl."

"I'm full of surprises, Mr. Gottlieb," Lex said, hip-bumping him out of her way, before bolting out the front door for a head start.

If she weren't married and he weren't Seth, they'd actually make a cute couple, I thought.

I started to pick at some of the leftover challah from the night before, when I heard the cell phone down the hall again. A moment later, Adam came ambling out of our bedroom.

"Hey, Hol, can I see you for a sec?" he said, nodding toward our bedroom. "I need to speak with you."

Adam never interrupted his prayers, and it was only 7:30 a.m.—way too soon for him to have finished the morning Shachris service.

I followed him. "What's wrong?" I asked, as he closed the door behind me.

"You forgot to turn off your phone before Shabbos," he said.

"I'm really sorry," I said. "I must have forgotten to—"

He cut me off. "*Everyone* knows we don't answer the phone on Shabbos, so I thought maybe, you know, God forbid . . ."

"Well? Who was it?" I demanded. I didn't want to look at the phone and break the Sabbath rule right in front of him.

"Babies 'R' Us called," he said. "They want their gun back."

"What?" I didn't think I had heard him correctly.

"Babies 'R' Us is missing a registry gun, and they tracked it back to you. I insisted they had the wrong phone number and that my wife would never steal anything, let alone create a baby registry, so I hung up. But when I put the phone back in your purse, I found this." He dangled the zapper in front of my face as proof.

Oh my God! I thought, staring at the evidence. *I must have thrown the gun into my purse when Becca got upset!*

I felt awful for not having told Adam about the registry, and awful for having stolen someone else's property.

"I can explain," I said to Adam, whose disappointed eyes stung more than if he had erupted in anger.

He put up his finger to shush me. "Not now. I want to finish Shachris. We'll talk about this later."

"Please, let me explain," I begged, but he was already wrapping himself back in his prayer shawl and flipping to the page where he had left off.

I exited the room and headed down the hall with the gun in one hand and the cell phone in the other. When I reached the kitchen, I saw Becca sitting alone at the island, sipping herbal tea and dabbing at her eyes.

"Are you all right?" I asked.

She flashed a smile that collapsed as quickly as it formed. "I'm fine," she said unconvincingly.

I remembered the vow Lex, Seth, and I made the night before: *distract her, lift her spirits.*

"Where is everyone?" I asked.

"Seth and Lex are jogging, Jordana went to run an errand, and I think Sal is still sleeping. Can't tell you where Nolan is. . . ."

I showed her the registry gun. "Look what I've got," I said.

"Why do you have *that?*" Then her eyes widened. "Oh, shit!"

I nodded and bit my lip.

"You just found it?" she asked.

"Adam did. They tracked me down. I need to return it. Do you think there's a Babies 'R' Us nearby?"

Becca looked up store locations on her phone. "Here," she said pointing to the screen. "There's one twelve miles away. If you give me the keys to your car, I'll take it back. I know you can't drive on Shabbos."

I hadn't ridden in a car on the Sabbath since Adam and I had returned home from our Israel trip in high school. But the thought of Becca's driving twenty-four miles alone in the middle of nowhere was unacceptable.

If I were to get in the car with her, I rationalized, *I wouldn't be breaking the rules of Shabbos for a frivolous reason. I would be supporting a friend in crisis—a friend who would otherwise be hanging around Jordana's house, staring at a clock and waiting for her absentee husband to arrive. It would be a good deed, an act of loving kindness to distract her. I wouldn't buy anything at the store; I would simply return what I should never have taken in the first place.* The car, I convinced myself, was merely a vessel—a conduit to cleansing myself of the sin of theft, as well as a means to help a friend in need.

"Give me three minutes," I said. "I'm coming with you."

Becca looked dumbfounded. "Really? Have you lost your mind? They've got a million of these stupid guns. I'm sure they'll understand if you bring it back on Monday! And honestly, I'm happy to make the drive myself. Maybe the open road and some music will help clear my mind."

I ignored her and returned to my bedroom to get changed. I pulled an ankle-length denim skirt and long-sleeved cardigan sweater set from the duffel bag on the floor beside the dresser. "I'm going out," I whispered to Adam, who was mid-prayer, his eyes fixed on the pages of his book and his lips in perpetual motion. I slipped on my black opaque stockings and a pair of Mary Janes, wrapped a blue-and-silver-flecked scarf around my hair, reached for my sunglasses on the nightstand, and grabbed the gun.

"I'm ready!" I announced, waddling back into the kitchen.

"Are you sure?" Becca asked.

"I'm a grown woman, and I want to. It's my choice. Let's go!" I really did feel very much at peace, and even slightly empowered, like I was seizing a rare opportunity to make a difference in Becca's life. There is so little to do when a friend is ill. Opportunities to really help don't always present themselves. Sometimes you need to create them.

Becca held the passenger door of my car open as if she were my chauffeur. I stepped in, sank into the caramel-colored leather, and gazed at the treetops through the sunroof on our descent down the mountain. *Don't feel guilty for taking pleasure in the experience,* I reminded myself. *This is a mitzvah ride.*

During the twenty-minute drive from Jordana's house to Lenox, Massachusetts, I couldn't help but marvel at the region's beauty. Hidden among the tall, lush trees that blanketed the winding roads, I spotted modern hilltop homes with huge picture windows, as well as quaint historic houses with rickety rocking chairs on the front porch. There were open fields with farm animals and scarecrows, shingles hung from mailboxes advertising glass-blowing or antique quilts, and even a small town with a banner announcing its annual zucchini festival. I didn't know a zucchini festival was a "thing."

"So, you think there's any symbolism in the fact that this road is named Church Street?" I asked, as we drove through the charming town of Lenox and watched as women in strappy sundresses and flip-flops strolled lazily past art galleries with avant-garde sculptures and beautiful boutiques with hand-knit clothing in the windows. "Because, personally, I think it's a sign, given this is the first time I'm breaking Shabbos in twenty years."

Becca laughed.

She's laughing, I thought. *Mission accomplished.*

"You know you didn't need to sin on my behalf," Becca said.

"I'll atone for it later." I pretended to beat my chest in repentance.

"Seriously, won't Adam be upset?"

"Sometimes you just gotta do what you gotta do. Life changes, and you redraw the lines a little."

"What do you mean?" she asked.

"I'm more open-minded now. Maybe the line I was willing to draw when I was twenty-five is different than the one I want to draw now."

"Redraw the lines, huh?" Becca said. "How do I do that?"

"I think you know," I said. "Bec, you're the most authentic person I've ever met. Other than that crappy fake purse you bought on the street corner—McPolo or something?"

"That was a great bag!"

I rolled my eyes. "Anyway, my point is, you've always been real and honest. You wore that scarf on your head in high school and didn't give a hoot if the kids stared. When you guys were dating, you were up front with Nolan about your medical history and about how you could relapse or have a hard time having kids, and guess what? He wasn't fazed. He wanted to marry you anyway. You turned heartache into a beautiful success story with Emma; she understands about her birth and has explained it to her friends. There's a theme here, and it's authenticity. So whatever you choose to do about the surgery, be true to yourself and let the cards fall where they may."

"How can it work out if Nolan won't even tell me where he is or what he's thinking?" she asked, and then curved into the parking lot of Babies "R" Us. As we entered the store that Shabbos morning, I thought about how smudged my own lines had become. There I was, finally on the cusp of motherhood—a time when I was supposed to be settled, stable, and ready to be my child's role model—and yet, for the first time in over two decades, I was coloring outside the lines.

You talk a big game, kid, I thought. *Here you are, touting the virtues of authenticity to Becca, when you're an impostor!* The voice of our rabbi back home rang in my ears: *If you choose to look the part of an Orthodox Jew, you need to act the part of an Orthodox Jew. You are a representative of our faith and our community, and when you dress in this fashion, you accept certain responsibilities.* I wondered what our rabbi would say if he saw me walking around a national chain store on Shabbos morning with my long skirt and covered hair. Was I helping a friend in need or deserving of a scarlet letter for breaking the rules and being a disgrace to my community?

Returning the gun was wholly uneventful. There were no lines, no documents to sign, and I was absolved of my crime in ninety seconds.

"Wanna browse?" I asked, remembering my mission to keep Becca busy. "I won't buy anything today, but you wouldn't have to twist my arm to check out the layette section."

"Okay," she said, giving me a quizzical look. It was the same look my parents displayed when, at age seventeen, I asked them to toss their cookware, torch the inside of their oven to burn away the residue from the non-kosher chickens they bought at the local supermarket, and buy two brand-new sets of utensils, pots, pans, and dishes—one set for meat meals, one set for dairy meals. Just like Mom and Dad, who complied with my request, albeit with furrowed brows and how-long-is-this-gonna-last skepticism, Becca agreed to ogle the onesies with me. But just as we started down the clothing aisle, her phone rang. It was Jordana.

"Where are you?" I could hear her voice through Becca's cell. "I went to pick up some coffee, and by the time I got home, you were gone. No one's here except Sal. What's going on?"

Becca motioned for me to follow her toward the exit. I waddled behind like an obedient duckling.

"Sorry," she said, fishing my car keys from her purse. "We had to run an errand. Long story. We'll be back in twenty minutes."

Poor Jordana, I thought. *She put so much effort into this weekend, and nothing has gone smoothly.*

We settled into my car and turned back onto the main country road. "You know," Becca said as she slowed at a traffic light, "you can do it, too."

"Do what?"

"Make a new drawing of yourself."

"I'm not having a midlife crisis—at least not *yet*." I laughed.

"I'm just saying, you give good advice. Maybe you should listen to yourself sometimes."

I leaned my head back against the headrest and stared at the clouds through the sunroof.

"I just don't want to mess up motherhood, you know?" I said. "I've waited so long for this, Bec. I just want to get it right, and I don't know what *right* is. And what if my right is different than Adam's right? I'm a month away from delivery. I want this all settled before the baby comes. Do we stay the traditional course, which Adam and I have been on for the past twenty-something years, or can I blur the lines a little and incorporate some of the things I loved from my childhood, even if those things are inconsistent with Orthodoxy?"

"Like what?"

"Like eating out at a restaurant. Right now, we eat only at strictly kosher places. I doubt Adam would do it, but I'd consider going to a regular restaurant and ordering a salad or pasta. But once you try it, you're labeled. It's one thing to pick that path if only *you* are affected. It's a whole other ballgame to put your innocent child in that position, and they get excluded from playdates and birthday parties because of the choices you made."

"Which feels more authentic to you?" Becca asked.

I suspected I knew the answer, but, just like Becca in her situation, I wasn't yet ready to verbalize it.

"Listen," I said, turning to look at her, "I'll be your gut-checker if you'll be mine. Two rules. One: brutal honesty. Two: no judgment. Deal?"

"Deal," she said. We started up the mile-long mountain road toward Jordana's place. When we finally pulled into the driveway and neared the house, I noticed a white Cadillac parked beside the front porch.

"Whose car is *that*?" I asked, leaning forward in my seat to read the New Jersey vanity plate: SCARDINO.

Becca had a stunned expression. "That," she said, "is my mother-in-law's."

Chapter 12: Nolan

"It's all packed," my mother whispered, gently nudging me awake.

I rolled over and turned my back to her in protest, just as I had as a child every Monday morning before school.

"Come, Patatino, get outta bed," she prodded. "It's time to make up with your wife. So you had a fight. Okay, fine. It happens. Now you go fix it. I just took my soup out of the freezer and put it in the car. I double-plastic-baggied it in case it defrosts before you get there. I don't want no water ring all over my new beige leather seats."

"Ma." I groaned and rubbed my eyes. "She's not gonna want minestrone for breakfast."

"*Stunad!*" Mama muttered, and playfully smacked my head. "Just give her the peace offering and tell her you're sorry."

But I'm not sorry, I wanted to say. *I've been honest. Why should I apologize for speaking my mind?*

Despite the hour and my exhaustion, I remained a dutiful son who obeyed his mother's command. I showered, dressed, accepted the keys to her Cadillac, and backed out of the driveway at exactly six thirty. But as I pulled around the corner and onto the main road, I knew I wasn't yet ready to see Becca. I needed more time to myself. More of an opportunity to process everything in solitude, but where could I go? I had outstayed my welcome with my parents, my own home was not an option, and I would have preferred a root canal to shacking up alone in a hotel on the anniversary of falling in love with my wife.

I drove past the entrance to the highway and pulled into the parking lot of a Dunkin' Donuts to pick up breakfast and devise a plan. Before exiting the car, I grabbed my wallet and phone and noticed a new message in my inbox from Ilene Weston.

Nolan,

Just wanted to give you a status update. My risk and compliance team, as well as the general counsel and managing partners, will be having a conference call in the next 24 hours to discuss the Thibault deal. You should be aware that Thibault has made passing references to a lawsuit against the firm.

I'll be in touch soon.

Ilene Weston
Chief, Risk Management
Gordon, Michaelson & Stewart, LLP

Dear Ilene,

Thanks for the update. Please continue to keep me posted. Have a great weekend.

Nolan

A lawsuit? Oh my God! But I quickly reassured myself: *Simple. Direct. No need to apologize or elaborate.* I clicked out of my email, exited the car, and headed into Dunkin' Donuts. While a young, uniformed cashier with horrific acne filled my order, I nervously strummed my fingers on a Formica counter and stared up at the flat-screen TV above the sugar-packet console.

Escape! A throaty woman's voice beckoned on the commercial as images of cocktails and casinos flashed across the screen.

"You ever been?" the cashier asked, nodding toward the monitor. He plunked a Styrofoam cup of coffee down in front of me.

"Atlantic City? No, not in years," I said dismissively. "Last time I was in AC was my brother's bachelor party, and now his youngest kid's graduating high school."

"Well, then I guess you're overdue for a trip," he said, as I paid the bill. "Enjoy your holiday, sir."

By the time I reached the car, I knew exactly where I'd be spending the rest of the weekend. I peeled out of the parking lot and merged onto the Garden State Parkway South toward Atlantic City—the perfect destination for two days' worth of distractions.

I cracked the sunroof, flipped through my mother's preprogrammed radio stations—a cornucopia of soft rock, smooth jazz, and Radio Italy Live, where practically every song had someone crooning about *amore*—and took in the early-morning open road. *This* is what I need, I thought, as I set the cruise control to sixty-five miles per hour.

Twenty minutes into my ride, just as I was passing the exit for Newark Airport, my phone rang. The number on the screen was my in-laws' apartment.

They must have spoken with Becca about our fight and are calling to disown me.

"Hello?" I said flatly, as I held the phone to my ear. I hadn't bothered to program my number into the Cadillac's Bluetooth system.

"Good morning, Daddy!" Emma said. My heart melted, as always, at the sound of her high-pitched voice and the way she enunciated the *dd* in *Daddy*. "We're having chocolate chip pancakes for breakfast. Do you want me to save some? You and Mommy can have them as a snack when you come home tomorrow? I told Grandma you like breakfast for dinner sometimes, so she said I could call and ask if we should make extras for you."

"Oh, sweetheart, I would *love* that! Thank you so much!" I said enthusiastically, hoping she wouldn't detect any tension in my voice.

"Okay. Can you put Mommy on the phone? I want to ask her if she wants me to add sprinkles and marshmallows to her pancakes."

My stomach churned as I crafted a response. "Mommy's with her friends right now, sweetheart. You can call her cell phone if you like."

"Grandma thought it was too early to call; she thought I would wake you up! I knew I was right!" After her exclamation, I heard her shout out to my mother-in-law, "See, Grandma, I told you I wouldn't wake them! Mommy's with her friends."

"They got up and out before seven a.m.?" I heard Arlene say in the background.

Here we go, I thought.

"Emma, honey, listen," I said, "I'm just out picking up something to eat. You can try Mommy and ask her about the pancakes. I'm sure she would love to hear from you."

"Okay, Daddy," she said, and hung up before I had a chance to say goodbye.

Though I hadn't told an outright lie (I *had* stopped at Dunkin Donuts, and Becca *was* with her friends), what I had said to my daughter was not entirely truthful, either. *She deserves better than this,* I scolded myself. *This child oozes goodness and sweetness and innocence; she deserves more. She deserves stability.*

I pulled into a roadside gas station and filled up. I couldn't even look at my reflection in the Cadillac's tinted windows as I leaned against the door and held the pump in the tank.

My job is intact, I'm a valued employee, and there will be no lawsuit, I reassured myself, as the gas glugged into the car. *Seth will come through with the second opinion for Becca, and that will make all the difference. She was just in shock when we spoke with the first plastic surgeon. She'll definitely be more clearheaded by next week and will realize that I'm right.* I took a deep breath and thought about Emma. *Everything will be just fine. Just keep your family together.* I started up the car and pulled back onto the highway. This time, however, I headed north, to the Berkshires.

Three hours later, I pulled into Jordana's driveway. I grabbed the plastic container of soup—which was still frozen—walked up to the front porch, and knocked on the door.

"Come in! It's unlocked," I heard Jordana call out.

When I pushed through the door, I saw Seth and Lex seated on the kitchen island stools, drinking out of mugs. Jordana was arranging food on a platter. None of them was looking up when I stepped inside.

"Good morning," I said. All three rotated toward me. For a moment, they seemed frozen. But after a beat, Jordana wiped her hands on a dish towel and ran over to greet me.

"I knew you'd make it," she said, reaching up to hug me. "We missed you. So glad you're here. Didn't I tell you he'd make it?" she said, turning back to Seth and Lex with *I told you so* written all over her face. They remained on the stools and stared coolly at me.

Seth wouldn't stand or greet me. He just sat there, looking me over as he sipped from his mug. I immediately felt the sting. I knew my absence had let them down, but I didn't regret it—I'd needed that time to myself. Yes, I was late, but I'd shown up and I was determined to have a smooth weekend.

"Come on in," Jordana said, grabbing my hand and leading me toward the others. "No bags?"

"No, no bags. But I have this. It needs to go in the fridge. It's soup. Don't ask," I said, and handed over the Tupperware.

"Hey, man, where ya been?" Seth finally said.

I went over to their stools to melt the ice. I patted Seth on the back and then leaned in to kiss Lex. "Good to see you, Lex. It's been years! You look wonderful." She did. With their workout clothes, running shoes, and still-perspiring faces, they had clearly just come in from a morning run. Despite her matted ponytail, Lex was glistening and gorgeous.

Lex didn't respond to my compliment. She flashed a quick smile that immediately dissolved into a snobbish stare that Becca once described as Lex's resting bitch face. "Trust me, she's an awesome person inside," I recalled my wife telling me the first time she introduced me to Lex. "She sometimes comes across as a little cold and judgmental, but there's a golden heart in there. Just give her a chance."

After a slow, condescending once-over, Lex averted her eyes. *Okay, so this is how it's going to be,* I thought.

"Would you look at that!" Jordana suddenly piped up and pointed toward the driveway through the front window. "Perfect timing. Becca's back!"

I wondered if my arrival would elate her or infuriate her. "Where'd she go?" I asked.

"If you'd been here, you wouldn't have to ask," Lex muttered under her breath. She stepped off the stool and brushed past me on her way to the door.

I stood nervously on the porch, leaning against one of the supporting wooden beams, and watched as Jordana, Seth, and Lex swarmed around my wife like bees to a hive. They surrounded her as she exited the driver's seat of a car I didn't recognize. When Holly emerged from the passenger side, she joined the others. They were protecting Becca from the enemy, and that enemy, I realized, was me.

Jordana ran up to the porch, grabbed my hand, and led me down the path. "Look who I found," she announced. She staked her ground between us while Lex, Seth, and Holly stood right behind Becca, ready to sting the moment she issued the signal.

There was something very *West Side Story* about the whole scene, as if we were two gangs battling for control of their turf. It was an obvious showdown over who knew Becca best and who loved her more.

"Hey, you're here," Becca said. She smiled, and I wanted to scoop her up and carry her away in my arms, the way I did in the Dating Game back in college.

Out of the corner of my eye, I noticed Lex fold her arms across her chest and could hear her quietly harrumph. She probably perceived Becca's welcoming tone as weakness.

"Of course I'm here, I wouldn't have missed it," I said, as if she were crazy for thinking otherwise. I walked over to hug her. She rested the side of her face against my chest, and I lowered my head so my cheek touched her hair. I wrapped my arms around her shoulders and pulled her close, feeling her breasts press up against me and breathing in her familiar, clean scent—a subtle mix of Dove soap and Tide laundry detergent. Though I knew our tension was unresolved, in that moment, I felt a peaceful sense of homecoming.

All of a sudden, we heard someone call out "Holly" from the base of the driveway. There was Adam, panting as he walked slowly up to the top. "I've been looking everywhere." *Pant.* "I walked all around the property." *Pant.* "I went down to the lake." *Pant. Pant.* He wiped his brow, leaned forward, rested his hands on his knees, and caught his breath. "Where have you been?"

Holly shot a quick look at my wife. Becca responded with the same *you can do it* nod she often gives Emma when she's afraid to try something new.

"I'm fine," Holly said. She started wobbling over to her husband, who looked genuinely scared.

"Let's go inside," Jordana said to Seth and Lex, clearly trying to give both couples some privacy. Seth and Lex followed her in. A minute later, Adam and Holly had disappeared down the driveway and Becca and I were alone.

"You smell like Emilio's boys" was the first thing Becca said to me. "Like you bathed in Drakkar Noir and are about to go clubbing."

I laughed. "It's body wash. It was the only stuff my parents had in the guest bathroom."

She folded her arms across her chest, the same way Lex had earlier.

"I went to my parents' for the night," I said.

"I know. I saw Kathy Ireland in the background on your video to Emma."

"Ah, nice job, Columbo," I said.

"I guess I needed some space."

She looked hurt. "You needed space from me?"

"From you, from everything," I said breezily.

Think of Emma. Remember your mission: keep the family together, I told myself.

"Come," I said, putting my arm around her shoulder. "Let's go for a walk." For the next half-hour, we toured the property and skirted anything of import. We stood silently for several minutes to observe a hummingbird on a birdfeeder. We commented on how sweet the country air smelled. We talked about how Emma would love the colorful flowers in Jordana's backyard and promised to pick some to take home to her. We admired Sal's vegetable garden—which was the size of our living room—and I vowed to tease Sal that he must be compensating for something by growing such massive zucchini.

We walked on eggshells, as if we'd been set up on a blind date. There were a million questions to ask, but neither of us seemed poised for interrogation. Eventually, we headed back up to the front lawn and collapsed into the hammock.

"Ahh." I exhaled when we finally settled into a comfortable position. "I think my ass is scraping the ground."

"Other than the fact that you smell like a Russian nightclub, I'm good," she said, reclining beside me.

We had run out of small talk. I grabbed her hand. Our fingers interlaced, and I gave our united knuckles a long kiss.

"We'll figure it out, Bec," I whispered. "You know, the last time we lay in a hammock like this was at that resort in California the weekend before Emma was born."

"That feels like a lifetime ago."

"Seven years. Remember how nervous you were that you'd lose the papers proving Elizabeth was our surrogate—that the baby was ours, not hers?"

"Yeah. I brought those manila files everywhere with me that weekend. I put them in the beach bag, took them to the restaurants in my purse . . ."

"But I was the one who was a complete wreck the day she was born," I admitted. "I was pacing and didn't shut up."

"You weren't a wreck," Becca said. "You were just giddy. And the video camera was glued to your hand. You recorded random people in the hospital walking to get coffee, the magazines on a coffee table, our family taking pictures of you videotaping them . . ."

We laughed and then both grew quiet. My mind traveled back to that magnificent day. I thought about the DVD of Emma's birth and how it opens with me having a conversation with Becca's parents in a hotel suite. Her dad occupies a wing chair while her mom sits demurely on a couch. An empty car seat and stroller rest against a window in the background, warming in the California sun. Her parents appear to be engrossed in their books until I announce that the camera is on, and then they suddenly jolt to life.

My remarks from behind the Sony Handycam are peppered with that laugh I get when I'm über-excited about something. It's the same giggle I emit when I'm nervous, the one that was sprinkled into my marriage proposal to Becca (and I quote): "Hee-hee . . . Will you, hee-hee, marry me? Hee-hee . . . Hee-hee . . ."

The energy and joy in the room are palpable—especially because it's early, 7:00 a.m., and everyone appears caffeinated, even though they have yet to partake of the all-inclusive continental breakfast in the hotel lobby.

"Okay, so, what's today?" I ask Becca's father at the start of the DVD.

"Here we are in beautiful California, awaiting the arrival of our first grandchild, your first child," he says in his thick Brooklyn accent, leaning back on the burgundy wing chair and resting the book in his lap. "Is it a boy? Is it a girl? Will it be healthy? Who does it look like?"

"I've been up since three thirty this morning," her mother whispers, leaning into the camera lens as if she is sharing an intimate secret with the viewer.

Her dad continues speaking, growing more dramatic with each word. "We have all descended upon California for the arrival of this baby. Our hopes, our dreams, our fantasies—we're all starting to imagine and project onto you, child! Get out now! Run! Go!"

Every time I watch this video, I can't help but think, *They really deserve this.* Her parents probably never thought that day would come. After all they went through with Becca's illness— after the inconceivably difficult choices they were forced to make, after the fear, the pain, the prayer—there we were at an extended-stay hotel where the manager must have gotten a seriously steep discount on Native American–themed polyester fabric, and life couldn't have been sweeter.

Now, seven years later, I turned to Becca on the hammock.

"Remember when the OR nurse burst through the doors and pulled down her mask?" I asked. "Do you remember what she said?"

"Congratulations! You have a daughter!" we said in unison.

"I'll never forget it." I gave her a squeeze. *This is why I came up to Jordana's. This is what matters.*

"Me neither, and you know what else I won't forget?" she said, her eyes suddenly wet. "Seeing our whole family crowd together by the big glass nursery window as they watched us hold Emma for the first time."

An image flashed across my mind: my in-laws looking down at Becca as she sat in a rocking chair, looking down at her newborn in her arms.

"Remember saying goodbye to Elizabeth?" I asked.

"That was rough," Becca groaned. "I mean, how do you say thank you to someone like that? How do you walk away in your skinny jeans with your beautiful infant and leave the woman who delivered your child to recover alone on a maternity ward filled with new moms?"

"I know. I mean, we fulfilled our end of the contract, but still . . ."

"Remember the plant we bought at the hospital gift shop?" Becca asked.

"I do. I remember how you came up with the concept of wanting to give her the gift of a living thing. We did our best; it was a tough situation."

I recalled how Elizabeth lay in a hospital bed, attached to an IV, recuperating from the caesarean section. "Well, thanks so much for everything!" flew out of Becca's mouth as she handed her a foil-bottomed pot of leaves. The phrase seemed inappropriate, vapid. Nodding, Elizabeth said, "No problem. Just doing my job."

"But what was I *supposed* to say?" Becca asked, just as she did that day when we left the hospital. "It's not like there's a Hallmark card section for Woman Who Gives Birth to Your Biological Baby."

"Like everything else, we made it work." I kissed the top of her head. For a fleeting moment, I thought this might be the right time to tell her about everything going on with my job. Keeping it from her was killing me, but, given the stress we were already under, I decided to shut my mouth and cling to this happy scene.

I closed my eyes and inhaled deeply. "The country air is nice," I said.

Silence. The laborious blind-date conversation had returned.

"I'm kind of thirsty. I'm gonna get something inside," she eventually said, swinging her feet over the side of the hammock. It was as if she had gotten bored speaking with me at a party and was making an excuse to walk away. This set off a slight panic in me.

"I'll come with you," I said. I hadn't driven three hours to sit in a hammock alone.

As we headed down the path to the house, the front door swung open and Seth stood in the frame, his hands on his hips.

"Hey," I called out, with a friendly wave. He nodded in acknowledgment but didn't smile, and his eyes remained fixed on Becca. With the biceps poking out of his T-shirt and his no-nonsense demeanor, he resembled a stocky nightclub bouncer.

"You okay, Bec?" he asked, like a big brother checking up on his little sis. I wondered if he'd been watching us.

"Yep, just need a drink," she said, scooting past him into the house.

Seth was about to follow her inside, but I stopped him. "Hey, can I speak to you for a sec?" I motioned to the Adirondack chairs on the front porch.

He looked bothered, as if I were putting him out, but he closed the front door and took a seat.

"Any progress on that doctor appointment?" I asked.

He snickered, shook his head, and rubbed his chin.

"What?" I asked. "What's so funny?"

"Talk about a man on a mission. Wow, nothing stops you once you set your mind to something, does it?" he asked. He was controlled, but I sensed a palpable underlying fury in him. "Listen," he went on, "I agreed to help out with a second opinion before I knew what was going on between you and Bec. I gave you the doctors' names and the numbers. If *you* want an appointment, you'll need to make it yourself. If you *and* Becca want an appointment, I'll be happy to call in a favor and expedite it. Otherwise, please keep me out of this."

Ah, so you're actually her friend, not mine. "Understood" was all I said. I'd have to convince Becca on my own that a second plastic surgeon's opinion was necessary.

Seth stood up, leaned his back against the front door, and peered at me as if he were about to say something, but then shook his head.

"What?" I asked.

"Look," he said, crossing his arms. "I'm not going to pretend to understand women, or marriage, or even how to have a real relationship. As you know, I'm hardly an expert in that department—the longest run I've ever had was a few months. But what I can tell you is what it's like to live with regret. I know what it's like to have the brass ring and then lose it because you acted like a schmuck. Not a day goes by that I don't wonder what my life would have been like had I not been such a monumental fuckup at Princeton. Yeah, you could say I eventually got my act together, but let me tell you, I still wake up every morning pissed at myself and thinking about what could have been."

Seth never spoke about what had happened at Princeton. I had heard stories from Becca's parents about how his poker habit "royally flushed his life down the toilet," but I had never gotten the details directly from Seth. I wondered if this self-loathing had anything to do with his string of failed relationships.

"All I'm saying is," he continued, "screw the bravado, man. Don't gamble with Becca. If I had a shot with a woman half as special as any of the ones in this house, you bet your ass I'd do whatever it took to keep her. Pick your battles. Is this really the one you want to go down swinging on? Because if you're not careful, you could lose it all. You're not an idiot. Don't act like one."

"With all due respect, man, you're not a part of my marriage," I said calmly.

"With all due respect, man," he fired back, mimicking my tone but at high volume, "you pulled me into this when you asked me to hook you up with a surgeon. You never told me what it was for. Had I known how Becca felt, I would never have gotten involved, but now that I am, I gotta be honest: I've seen a lot of tits in my time. And you know what? I'd trade them all for a family like yours."

His condescension was perturbing. "I'm not planning to *gamble* away or *lose* my wife the way you screwed up your future because of Princeton. In fact, I'm trying to do just the opposite. I'm trying to hold on and preserve her as she is. I don't want her to change."

He flung his hands in the air to show he was ridding himself of any entanglements and then reached for the doorknob. "We done here?" he asked bitingly, his thick eyebrows arching like humpback caterpillars.

We done here? Those three little words stung. *Does he mean our friendship or the conversation?* I felt immobile.

And then, as if his acerbity weren't clear enough, he added a postscript to punctuate it: "On my roster, she comes first, man.

Not you." With that, he opened the front door and entered the house. Had he been standing on a stage, that would have been the moment he dropped the microphone.

I waited outside, seemingly in his dust, feeling as if I had just lost a schoolyard battle with my buddy. By walking ahead of me and leaving the door ajar, he seemed to be passively telling me to choose my path: stand alone on the outskirts or join the inner circle with the rest of them.

Minutes later, when I arrived inside, Jordana appeared to be in the eye of a multitasking storm. I slid onto a barstool beside my wife.

"Yes, ma'am," Jordana said into the cordless landline receiver she was balancing between her ear and shoulder while transferring food from the refrigerator to the counter. "I'm just confirming that there will be nine tickets for tonight's performance on hold at the Tanglewood box office."

Nine? I thought, and then recalled Seth's having mentioned something about his new girlfriend meeting up with us.

"Wonderful," Jordana said cheerfully into the phone, as she closed the refrigerator door with her knee. "Yes, I'll spell it. *L-e-f-k-o-w-i-t-z*, hyphen, *S-i-n-g-h*. Yes, that's the name on the credit card." She sniffed a container of potato salad, made a face, and threw it in the garbage.

"Thank you very much. See you then," she said, as she reached across the sink for the paper towel roll, tore off some sheets, and cleaned up some spilled coleslaw, before returning the phone to its docking station.

"Well, that was impressive," I remarked. I recalled how, back in law school, Jordana had managed to balance being on law review, working an internship, and making photocopies of her copious class notes for our entire study group.

"I'm gonna go get showered and dressed for the concert," Jordana said, walking out of the kitchen, leaving us alone at our barstools.

I placed my palm on Becca's back and felt her instinctively recoil. I offered a half-smile to show her I was trying my best. She placed her hand on my knee, but her fingers were tense.

We smiled politely for a moment.

"So," I said. "Come here often?"

I sensed my flirtation had lost its charm and was beginning to irritate her.

I peered at her face for a minute, waiting, hoping she'd tell me she had come around. Maybe she would admit her reaction at the doctor's office had been irrational.

"What?" she asked.

I continued to stare, growing increasingly mystified. *Just say the words! Admit you overreacted, and we can try to enjoy the rest of the weekend!*

"What?" she asked again. The corners of her mouth collapsed into a frown.

I could feel the tensing of muscles between my shoulders. "Nothing," I finally said. If we couldn't resolve our problems quickly, I just wanted to Band-Aid them until we got home. I gave her hand a soft, reassuring squeeze.

"I'm gonna go get ready for Tanglewood," she announced, hopping off the barstool. Her forced smile was equal parts resignation and disappointment.

I watched as she walked down the hall and into the bedroom. Then, as soon as she was out of sight, I whipped out my phone to check for an update from the firm. Nothing. Not a single email, text, or call. I marveled at how they managed to ping me at all hours of the day and night when a client was in need, but when my own ass was on the line? Radio silence. I leaned forward onto the kitchen island and buried my head in my hands.

"How did I end up here?" I whispered into my palms.

Just then, I felt a hand on my back. I lifted my head, and there was Jordana beside me.

"Hey, you all right?" she asked.

"Oh, fine." I smiled. "Just got a lot on my mind, that's all."

"No shit."

I closed my eyes and rubbed my temples. "You got some aspirin?"

She walked over to a kitchen cabinet and retrieved a bottle of Advil.

"I'm sorry, Nol," she said, handing me two pills and a glass of water. "This all just sucks."

My phone dinged, alerting me to a new message. In a Pavlovian response, my arm instinctively reached for it, but I knocked over the glass of water and saturated the phone.

"Dammit!" I screamed, and pounded my fist onto the counter.

Jordana immediately scooped up the phone, removed the case, and started patting it dry with a dish towel.

"It's okay, don't worry, I've done this before," she reassured me as she filled a plastic Ziploc bag with rice. "My boys dumped mine in the bathtub one time. Sal did exactly what I'm doing now, and the phone survived."

I began pacing beside the kitchen island, my arms over my head, pulling at my hair. "I need that phone to work, Jord."

"Hey, chill out, Mr. Fancy-Pants Corporate Lawyer. Gordon, Michaelson, and Stewart will not fall apart if you're off the radar for a little while."

"Actually, they may be better off," I muttered.

"What do you mean?"

I told her everything.

Chapter 13: Jordana

*T*he early-evening summer sun shone brightly as I turned my SUV onto the sprawling grassy field at Tanglewood. I followed the waving hands of men in hunter-green shirts directing me to a spot. Minutes later, our group had joined the herd of sandal-footed, wine and cheese–schlepping fans, many of whom flocked to the Berkshires simply for James Taylor's annual July Fourth performance. The place was a mecca for aging hippies, urbanites weekending from Boston and New York, college hipsters, and young families carrying infants in papoose slings. One after another, we traveled across the open field, down the tree-lined road, and through the main gates. The picnic tables, rolling mountains, and uniformed staff made it feel as if we had entered a high-end overnight camp.

I picked up our tickets at the box office but left two at the window for Holly and Adam, who would be arriving after the Sabbath ended at sundown—perfect timing, I assured them, for when JT would actually take the stage.

I led our group to my favorite spot on the grass. It wasn't too far a hike to the bathrooms or concession stands, but not too close, either. Seats within the amphitheater were prime, but to me the beauty of Tanglewood was being sardined on the lawn among strangers, listening to music, and picnicking with loved ones while inhaling the scents of whatever substances wafted by.

"Here we are!" I announced, while Sal and I lowered an over-size blanket onto the grass in a single, fluid movement.

The guys anchored folding chairs onto the blanket's corners while the girls took out the yellow gingham plastic picnicware I had purchased for the occasion and arranged a makeshift buffet atop the beverage cooler.

"I'd like to make a toast," I announced, pouring wine into six clear plastic cups. "I'm sure you will find this incredibly sappy, but I just wanted to express my appreciation, you know, given that we're here at a *James Taylor* concert and all. So, in the spirit of—"

"C'mon! Just do it, Jord!" Sal interrupted, egging me on. "Enough with the introduction. Just jump in!"

"Okay! All right! Here I go," I smiled broadly, cleared my throat, and held a glass of pinot grigio in the air. *Finally*, I thought, *something is going according to plan.*

"I just wanted to say *hello, old friends!* Thank you for coming to visit on these *country roads. How sweet it is* to see *your smiling face, on the Fourth of July.* I know we are creating *golden moments* together. *I will follow* you all through *fire and rain*, from *Belfast to Boston* and even to *Mexico. That's why I'm here: you've got a friend.* I want to *shower the people* who are *forever my love.* Thank you all for coming. That's it. Good night!"

I smiled and winced, bracing myself for a barrage of moaning and eye rolling at my mélange of James Taylor songs, which I had composed earlier that week during some downtime at work. Writing it felt like assembling one of those posters the girls and I used to make when we were kids—clipping random words from fashion magazines and pasting them into a colorful collage with varying fonts. This was far from one of my finer poetic creations, but levity was the goal and I believed I had accomplished my mission.

Everyone applauded, and then Seth raised his glass in the air. "That was great, Jord, but here's to not quitting your day job." He winked my way.

"Oh, stop! I loved it! Don't listen to Seth," Lex said, elbowing him in the ribs, before tilting back her head to finish off her wine. She grabbed an open bottle from atop the cooler and refilled her cup nearly to the rim.

"I'd like to make a toast, too," Becca chimed in. "To Jordana, for hosting, organizing, being our chef and an all-around-incredible friend. We all really do feel the love and effort you put into this weekend. Thank you."

I swelled with joy. It wasn't the kudos I craved; it was the fulfillment of knowing my hard work was not for naught. To see Becca enjoy and appreciate the weekend was all I'd ever wanted.

"Hear, hear!" Nolan raised his glass high in the air. It seemed to me that ever since he arrived, he'd been trying too hard to meld into the group, as if he wanted to erase his playing hooky on Friday from our memories.

Well into her second cup of wine, Lex turned to Nolan and planted her index finger in his chest.

"Yes. You. Are," she said, poking him three times, like an exclamation point after each tipsily drawled word.

Nolan looked at her quizzically. "Huh?"

"You were late to the party, my friend, but yes, you are finally *here, here!*" Lex was clearly an alcoholic featherweight.

"*Lex!*" Becca said, widening her eyes.

"What?" Lex asked. "I'm just saying what's on everyone's mind, that's all."

I grabbed the side of my Indian-print maxi-dress and crinkled the material by my thigh into a tight ball. I instantly regretted the preconcert cocktails I'd served my guests back at the house. I hadn't realized how poorly Lex handled liquor.

"Brie, anyone?" was all I could think to say, and I lifted a plate of cheese and crackers from the top of the cooler.

"I don't get it. What did I say?" Nolan quietly asked Becca, but since everyone was standing in a tight oval, it was impossible not to hear him.

"That's right, you *don't* get it." Lex inserted herself again, this time at a slightly higher decibel level than normal. "Bec, you don't have to put up with his shit. You're better than that."

Nolan simply remained still, staring at his wife, who was now ashen. For someone like Becca, who detested being the center of attention, this was an absolute nightmare.

"That's enough, Lex," I said firmly.

"There you go again, Jordy. What is it with you always defending the underdog?" Lex slurred.

Seth cleared his throat and whispered something in her ear.

"Fine," Lex said reluctantly, like an unruly teen being reined in by a parent. She handed her nearly empty wineglass to Seth and turned her back to Nolan.

"Pardon me," Nolan said, bowing slightly to the group like a geisha. "I'm just going to go get some air." He looked wounded as he walked away.

"Nolan, wait," I called out, but he was already at least five picnic baskets away from us. The drum and guitar introduction to James Taylor's "Your Smiling Face" began to play, and the crowd burst into applause.

"Oh, he's a big boy. He'll be fiiine," Lex said loudly, with an exaggerated swat of her hand in the air. "But if you want, Sethhhhh and I are happy to stay here while you chase after him . . . Ha, did you hear me say *Sethhhhh*? It's like I have a lisp! Like Nolan's. *Sethhhhh* and I will hold down the fart. I mean fort! Ha! I said *fart*, *Sethhhhh*!"

She's completely shitfaced, I thought, grabbing a water bottle from the cooler and handing it to Lex.

"Why are you backing him?" Becca asked. She was sitting a few feet away on a patch of grass, her back against the trunk of a willow tree.

"I'm not taking his side." I crouched down next to her. "I'm always on your side, no matter what."

She raised her eyebrows, as if to say, *Really? Doesn't seem that way.*

"Look," I said, "I agree he should have shown up last night, but it just seems like everyone has been ganging up on him. I guess my only point is that there are two sides to every story." I thought back to the stricken look on Nolan's face when he told me about the Thibault deal: how he knew he'd messed up, how sorry he was, and how that witch in the compliance department practically had his severance package ready to go. Add that to my inside scoop on how fear of losing your partner could fuck with your head, and, once again, I felt compelled to defend him.

"How are there two sides to the fact that he's trying to control me?"

"Everything that comes out of my mouth today sounds wrong," I said, but she offered no sympathy. "Here's my point. You need to let Nolan work through his feelings. I know it's not fair to you, and that the timing of this tantrum—or whatever you call it—definitely sucks, but he needs to get it out before he can clear his head."

"If he really loved me," Becca said, "he'd get his act together."

"It's not always that easy. Do you know how many conversations I've had with Sal—when we were dating and still, to this very day—about when you were sick? Not just about the details of the hair loss or your medicine or any of that . . ." I looked up at her face. "Becca, I thought you were going to die! Die! In ninth grade!"

She was silent. I looked over at the audience and noticed Seth and Lex jumping and hooting, "JT!" If I hadn't known better, I could have sworn they were two college kids on summer break.

I glanced down at the grass. "And even when you went into remission and things got back to normal, it was never the same. *I* was never the same. Even now, all these years later, I worry every time my kids get a fever that maybe it isn't just a virus—that a cough or afternoon nap could be masking something more. Their pediatrician hates me, you know—thinks I'm insane."

I could see Becca's eyes had pooled.

"My point is, there was a ripple effect. You weren't the only one who suffered."

"I know," she finally said. "But I don't see how this relates to—"

"Did I ever tell you I wrote a psych paper in college about the healthy siblings of ill children?" I asked, cutting her off. "There's a body of research *just* about those kids."

She nodded.

"Holly may have brought you algebra homework a couple of times, and Lex came over to paint your nails once in a while, but I was there nearly every day. Homework, then *Love Connection* with Chuck Woolery or a marathon Monopoly game. Remember?"

"I remember," she said, and dabbed at her eyes with the edge of her shirtsleeve.

I kept going. "I never told you," I continued, "but after most of those visits, I'd go home and fall apart. Sometimes I'd lash out at my parents; sometimes I'd write these long, melodramatic diary entries."

"You never told me," she said, sniffling.

"And then when I visited and saw you bald and scary skinny and I couldn't touch you? Forget it. After that, I started checking things a hundred times before leaving my house. The lights. The alarm clock. The lock on the front door. I created routines to keep you alive. To make sure I didn't catch it. I even made a pact with God that I'd give up Kit-Kats if it guaranteed your health."

"*That's* why you stopped eating them? You used to love those! I never knew why you cut them out."

I shrugged. "I know I'm technically just a friend, but part of me feels like I'm one of those life partners who have been in a relationship for forty years and get denied hospital visitation rights because legally, they're title-less."

I inhaled deeply and continued. "Bec, I'm getting away from my point here, which is that Nolan's scared. He's a good guy who's just afraid of change. I can see it. And I have to say, I can sympathize. I'm not saying what he has done and said isn't hurtful or shitty. I'm just saying hang in there. I really believe he will rise to the occasion. And you've got me to vent to in the meantime. Even if you piss me off with your cryptic texts . . ."

"I'm sorry," she said. "I didn't know how to tell you. You worked so hard, I just didn't want to spoil the weekend. Plus, it was all so fresh and—"

"This, my friends, is called true love!" I heard a familiar voice say. I looked up, and there was Holly. "This lawn is like an obstacle course! I must have stepped over two hundred pairs of legs."

Becca and I stood up to welcome her. Adam had already made himself at home on the folding chair beside Sal. Though it was still odd seeing my husband and former flame together, I was pleased that they got along well.

Just then, a big boom sounded over the mountains in the distance, and red, white, and blue lights showered down through the night sky as James Taylor performed "On the Fourth of July."

Becca, Holly, and I turned to one another with knowing glances. I grabbed a blanket and folding chair and set them up beside the tree. Becca and I gently helped Holly into the chair, and then the two of us lay on the ground beside her, gazing up at the fireworks. We remained that way for several minutes without saying a word.

"A quarter century," Holly finally said softly.

"I was thinking the same thing," I remarked.

"Do you remember what we were doing twenty-five years ago?" Holly asked.

"Vividly," I chuckled. "I spent the entire day watching my mother terrorize the Merry Maids of Bayside while they disinfected Becca's parents' house from top to bottom."

Becca laughed. "I remember hearing about that."

"It's true!" Holly laughed. "Jordana's mom morphed into a dictator right before my eyes—a freakin' tyrant looking over their feather dusters to make sure every inch of that house was clean enough for your immune system."

"I remember sitting on your stoop after the Merry Maids left, waiting for you to come home," I said. "I was counting down the minutes on the Swatch watch you got me for my tenth birthday."

"Oh my God, that trip home was exhausting. I get dizzy just thinking about it." Becca put her hand on her forehead. "Between walking out of that hospital room for the first time in months, getting fresh air, and sitting in stop-and-go rush-hour traffic on the Fourth of July, I was completely wiped out."

"Do you remember your first request when you got to the house?" I asked, as a champagne cork flew by. I could hear the group on the other side of the tree making toasts.

"The couch," Becca said with certainty. "I just wanted the couch."

"Yes, you made a beeline for the couch, but do you remember what you asked me to get you? The only thing you wanted was ice water in a long-stemmed, thin-lipped glass. You directed me to the cabinet in the dining room where your mother kept the tall crystal goblets with the flowers etched on the side—the ones she inherited from her grandmother that you used to sneak out for our tea parties when we were little."

"How do you remember that?"

"I'll never forget it," I said matter-of-factly. "I figured you would have wanted a home-cooked meal or something special, but all you craved was ice water! So I filled it up and handed it over, and you closed your eyes and relished it like you'd been in a desert for forty years. I think you even licked the condensation on the side of the glass."

"I had daydreams about those freakin' glasses," Becca said.

"Hey, you guys need anything?" Seth asked. "I'm going to the snack stand."

"No, thanks," we all said.

Someone stumbled over my feet.

"Hi girls!" Lex cried, as she crawled unsteadily, like a baby, up Becca's extended legs and snuggled beside them. "Awwww, I love you guys! I'm soooo glad we're doing this!"

"We love you, too, Lex," Becca said, as she, Holly, and I shot wide-eyed looks at one another.

James Taylor played "Shower the People," and several couples nearby stood up and started dancing barefoot on the grass. A woman about twenty feet away ethereally twirled a hula hoop over her head and around her body like a 1960s flower child on LSD. I looked over at our crew and noticed how Becca was stroking Lex's head. Lex grew quiet and calm. I wondered if she had drifted off to sleep.

"Do you remember the blue scarf, Bec?" Lex finally piped up, her words muffled because her face was resting against Becca's rib cage.

Becca smiled. "I do. It was beautiful."

"It was silk, with a sort of Mondrian color-block pattern," Lex said, her fingers drawing the squares in the air. "I went to Macy's with my mother and didn't know what to get you as a homecoming gift. They were having a Fourth of July sale, and I saw the scarf and I thought it was chic—like, Jackie O. chic. I figured if you had to wear something on your head, you might as well look elegant."

"I remember when you gave it to me," Becca said.

"The night you came home. We were on the brown couch in your parents' den, watching the fireworks on TV," Lex said with a smile.

The crowd at Tanglewood began to suddenly cheer as the band started up "How Sweet It Is (to Be Loved by You)."

"Come on, girls—get up!" Lex declared, and jumped to her feet, pulling the rest of us along with her.

"I shut my eyes at night, wondering what am I gonna do without you in my life," Lex shouted, wrapping her arm around Becca's waist.

"Wrong words, Lex!" Holly and I declared, and laughed.

"Hey, I want in on this, too!" Seth yelled, as he deftly navigated the lawn's intricate maze of coolers and chairs on his way back from the concession stand.

He started singing and joined our kick line, linking up on the end beside Lex.

This was the evening I had envisioned. With the fireworks, the friends, the music, I finally felt a semblance of fulfillment. It wasn't exactly how I had thought it would play out, but when I looked over and saw all of us standing in a line, arms overlapping each other's lower backs, I wished I had a camera to capture the moment. And then I noticed Lex's hand slip down into the back pocket of Seth's jeans, cupping and squeezing his butt. I squinted, unsure if my eyes had deceived me.

"Bec!" I whispered loudly into her ear, and gestured with a head nod toward Seth's rear end.

Becca turned and then whipped back to me, a look of horror on her face. "Holy shit!"

Unable to look away, we shifted our eyes back and watched as Seth surreptitiously glanced down at Lex beside him. He looked transfixed, as if he were about to lean in for a kiss. Instead, the two of them just stared at each other, volleying the words *by you* back and forth at the end of James Taylor's "How Sweet It Is . . ." They were oblivious to the fact that Holly had traded our kick line for a folding chair and that Becca and I had started a running commentary on the sidelines like Statler and Waldorf—the two crotchety old men sitting in the balcony on *The Muppet Show*.

"I guess the bottle of water you gave Lex didn't help," Becca muttered.

"Should we remind her that she is married—with three kids—and that this is Seth?" I remarked angrily. "I mean, if you're gonna go down Adultery Road, would you really cheat with *Seth*? Plus, wasn't *I* his childhood crush? Not that I would ever want Seth—I mean, *please*—but when did he ever show an interest in *her*? *I* was the one he asked to his prom, not Lex!" I flashed back to that night at the Plaza Hotel and the look of astonishment on his classmates' faces when we walked into the ballroom. They hadn't believed him when he'd said his date would be a leggy blonde from another school. As soon as I realized my presence had exponentially raised his cool factor, I led him onto the dance floor and wrapped my arms around his neck, and we swayed to Eric Clapton's "Wonderful Tonight." When the song ended and a large contingent of Bronx Science's senior class was still gawking, I kissed Seth's cheek and he dipped me, for maximum effect. No one needed to know we were just old friends putting on a show.

Becca remained fixated on the scene before us. "Lex has a family! What's she doing?"

"Should we stop them?" I asked, vacillating between whether to avert my eyes or interfere like a chaperone. I was still a bit shell-shocked that, in the course of my life, I'd occupied the top spot in the heart of not one but two of my male guests that weekend, and that in both instances, two of the women I was hosting had usurped me. What were the odds?

Just then, we heard a female voice bark Seth's name as if it were a question.

"*Seth?*" the woman boomed from behind us. Becca and I jumped, spun around, and found a bronzed, statuesque, and incredibly toned woman with one hand on the waist of her cutoff denim shorts, and the other hand holding back the wide brim of her floppy straw hat.

"Yvonne!" Seth exclaimed. He immediately plucked Lex's hand from his back pocket as if it were a hot coal briquette burning a hole in his ass.

Oh, Jesus, I thought, and covered my gaping mouth with my hand. *This must be Seth's girlfriend.* Seth had mentioned he was dating a fitness instructor, and she certainly looked the part. I could easily envision her leading an Upper East Side spin class and chastising her clients for being wimpy.

Then, with a shit-eating grin, Nolan strolled up, carrying a pink leopard-print duffel bag. "So," he began, "while I was out on my walk, I found this very distressed young woman waiting at the security gate all by herself. Apparently, her *boyfriend* instructed her to call him when she arrived at Tanglewood. He promised he'd meet her at the entrance with her ticket. Poor thing had been out there stranded since the beginning of the show, leaving him repeated phone messages."

Seth buried his head in his hands. "I'm so sorry!" he said emphatically. "I totally screwed up!" He seemed paralyzed as the two women eyed each other. Yvonne gave Lex a cursory glance. Lex, on the other hand, took her time. She deliberately checked out Yvonne's tanned, sculpted calves and chiseled face, and those taut butt cheeks that dipped ever so slightly beneath the white fringe of her Daisy Dukes.

Nolan stuck out his palm. "Give me the ticket, Seth," he said. "I sweet-talked the security guard into allowing her in. I told him I would be back in five minutes with her ticket."

"No," Yvonne said, her eyes on Seth but her hand suddenly on Nolan's shoulder. "Don't bother. I never should have come."

I could only imagine that if *I* had worked most of the day, trekked three hours on a bus from the city, and then stood with my duffel bag at the entrance of Tanglewood, waiting forty-five minutes for my boyfriend to pick up his damn phone, then, I, too, would be exasperated to find him pawing another woman. I'd definitely want him to grovel and beg for forgiveness.

"I'm sorry," Seth said. Though he had stepped closer to her, I couldn't detect a trace of remorse.

Yvonne just stared at him, waiting.

Seth made a fist and held it to his lips. He cleared his throat, straightened his posture, and said politely, "May I walk you out?"

No! He did not just dismiss her like that, did he? I thought. I looked over at Lex, who was beaming unapologetically.

"I don't need you to walk me out," Yvonne scoffed. "Thank you for helping me at the gate and for carrying my bag, Nolan. Seth, take a good look at your friend over here. This is what a true gentleman looks like."

"Ha! If you only knew!" Lex shouted.

Nolan handed Yvonne her duffel bag.

Yvonne reached over and tapped Becca's arm. "You've got a good one here," she said, motioning toward Nolan. "As you can see, there aren't many of them left."

None of us spoke. Our group just stood there, barefoot on the grass, watching Yvonne and her suspended buttocks sashay away as James Taylor crooned "Fire and Rain."

Once her floppy hat had disappeared into the crowd, Seth grabbed a beer and downed it so quickly that I actually wondered if it was a deliberate gesture made to highlight his alignment with the inebriated Lex. As the rest of us started to fold up the blankets and seal the containers of food, a cell phone rang. It was Lex's, and she sat down on the lid of a cooler to take the call.

"Hi, *sweeeetheart*," she answered in her mommy voice. Her enunciation was clear, but the delivery of her words was slower than normal. "Oh, I miss you, too. Yes, I know, it's very loud here. I'm at a concert. James Taylor. No, not Taylor Swift. *James* Taylor." Lex snatched a nearby bottle of water and gulped half of it down. "Of course I can buy you a souvenir. Okay, I love you, honey. Sweet dreams. See you tomorrow night."

Lex hung up and chugged the rest of the water. When she finished that one, she guzzled another and swallowed an aspirin. Based on her actions, I surmised that the conversation with her daughter had literally been a wake-up call.

"I'm going to go check out the gift shop, if anyone cares to join me," Lex announced, as she lifted the leather strap of her cross-body purse over her head.

"I'll go!" I blurted out, hoping to beat Seth to the punch. As host, I felt responsible for all of the events that took place over the weekend—even the ones beyond my control, like the repercussions of Lex's behavior.

Unfortunately, Seth had already started walking away with Lex. I stood there, a Tupperware lid in my hand, and watched as he playfully hip-bumped her to James Taylor's "Mexico" and then disappeared into the night.

Sal sidled up, kissed my head, and said softly, "It's not your job."

"I know." I sighed. It was as if he could read my mind, and I was flooded with a sense of good fortune. I turned to face my husband, reached up and wrapped my arms around his neck, the Tupperware lid still in my hand. "I love you," I said, and kissed his mouth. The thought of doing anything to jeopardize our marriage was unfathomable. Sure, we had our spats, but typically they were over benign matters, like the necessity of installing an iPad in a wall. We'd been lucky, and I knew it.

"We should probably wrap this up," I said, waving the Tupperware lid in my hand. "I think it's safe to say it has been a memorable night."

Sal smiled. Together we lifted the blankets from the grass, folded them up, and packed them away.

Chapter 14: Seth

*H*ad Lex been one of the many women I met as a single guy in New York City, I would have known exactly how to play the game. I would have transformed my attraction into something tangible—a first kiss, an official date. There would be no need to second-guess her tendency to touch my arm when we spoke, or wonder why she held her gaze a split second too long when she smiled at me, or question her intentions when she slid her hand down the back pocket of my jeans at Tanglewood. None of it would have been a mystery. But with Lex, everything was gray.

"I'll come with you" were the words that ignited an internal ricochet of nervous excitement when we returned to Jordana's house and Lex followed me down to the basement and out the glass doors to the backyard. Everyone else had claimed to be exhausted, but after the Yvonne fiasco, I was too wired to turn in.

As we walked out onto the slate patio, she said, "Wow, I didn't realize they had a fire pit! How cool is that?"

"Don't get your hopes up. I'm not exactly an Eagle Scout," I said, heading over to a large, lattice-framed shed to look for supplies.

She didn't miss a beat. "Maybe if you had stayed at sleepaway camp a little longer you would have learned how to make a fire," she said, and settled onto a cushioned sectional couch beside the fire pit.

I tried to think of a comeback but came up empty. "Are you kidding me?" I finally said, as I returned with a box of matches and a single wooden log. "You knew about that, too?"

Lex covered her smile with her palm. "Well, if it makes you feel better, I never got the real scoop about camp. I just heard you were asked to go home for a few days."

After several failed attempts to light some twigs, I finally ignited a weak fire. "You wanna know what happened?" I asked, sitting down beside her. She immediately turned onto her back and lay across the cushions, resting her bare feet on my lap. My heartbeat quickened. Her burgundy toenails and smooth skin were practically calling out for a massage, but instead I interlaced my fingers and placed them in a safety zone behind my head. "So, three weeks into overnight camp, my parents came for Visiting Day and I begged them to bring me home. All the athletic boys in my unit were bullying me mercilessly. Mom insisted I stay until the end of the season because she had paid the tuition in full and it was nonrefundable. I figured my only way out was to get in trouble. So the next morning I drank three glasses of orange juice in the mess hall, snuck outside, climbed a tree, and hid on a branch where no one could see me. When my bunk met up under that tree after breakfast, I pissed that juice down on top of them like rain on their heads."

"No you didn't!" Lex's eyes bulged. "You're making that up! You'd *never* do that!"

"Hey, what can I say?" I responded with a cunning smile. "I was home by five o'clock. Did what I had to do."

"You're evil!" she said, and laughed.

"Shrewd, resourceful, wily, clever, determined—take your pick," I said, winking at her. "Never evil."

She lay back on the couch and put her feet on my lap again. I could tell she had sobered up since the concert; maybe her quiet gaze just meant she was tired.

"Seth?" she asked, breaking the silence. "What's it like to follow a different path?"

"You mean in life?"

"Yes."

"I don't know. My path's not different to me."

She smiled. "True."

"What are you getting at?" I asked.

"I was just thinking about how you got kicked out of camp. And kicked out of college. But if you hadn't flunked out of Princeton, moved home, and become roommates with a gym rat, you never would have become a trainer and a physical therapist."

"What's your point?" I was still sensitive about my failures.

"My point is that sometimes the right thing doesn't always present itself in the most traditional or obvious ways. Sometimes you just have to wing it." A smile inched across her face as she looked up at me.

"Yeah." I grinned. "Sorta see what happens . . ."

"One step at a time," she said, tilting her head coquettishly on the pillow.

I noticed how her hair lay softly against her shoulders. I tried to remember the flat-chested, freckled, eleven-year-old version of Lex but couldn't pull up that memory. She was here. She was grown-up. She was stunning.

"You never know where things can lead," I added. The hem of her sundress draped across her shins and onto my lap. I wanted to touch her legs.

"And somehow, if it's meant to be, it works out in the end," Lex said. Her tone was more intense, and her blue eyes, glowing from the soft light of my pathetic fire, remained fixed on mine.

I knew that if she weren't married, this would be the moment I'd make a move. Instead, I swallowed and broke her gaze.

"Hey, your flame's burning out," she said.

"Huh?" I asked, still mid-trance.

She motioned toward the fire pit.

"Ah, yes, such is the fate of a summer-camp dropout." I sighed and removed her feet from my lap. "I'm gonna get a log from the shed and see if they've got some lighter fluid, or possibly a blow torch. I would never have survived as a caveman."

I grabbed another box of matches and reached for a piece of firewood from the back wall of the shed. Just as I turned around to return to the patio, the corner of the log I was holding collided with her forehead.

"Ow!" she cried out.

"Jesus! Lex! What are you . . . I'm so sorry!" I exclaimed. "I didn't know you were right behind me! Are you okay?" I dropped the log on the ground and placed the matches back on a shelf.

"Yeah, I think so," she said, rubbing her head.

"Do you need ice? Aspirin?"

"No, no. I'll be okay. But, um, it feels a little tender," she said, and pointed to a spot over her left eyebrow. "Can you see if I have a splinter?"

"Go over here. The light is better," I said, directing her to sit atop a foot-high pile of fertilizer bags stacked beneath a patio sconce. I crouched down onto my knees so that we were at eye level and leaned in just inches away from her face. I glided my finger across the reddened area above her brow. Though I was focused on the task, I could feel her eyes searching my face. "I don't feel anything," I said, as I inspected the spot for damage.

Her eyes welled up with tears. "But I do," she whispered.

"Oh, Lex." My stomach turned. I felt terrible for hurting her. "Don't worry. I'll go find a flashlight and tweezers. I'll get the splinter out. I promise."

As I stood up to head inside, she grabbed my hand and gently guided me back down to the floor of the shed.

I resumed the position on my knees, facing her. "What is it?" I asked softly.

She started bawling.

I was utterly confused. *Does she want me to get the tweezers or not?*

"I wish, I wish . . ." she continued, practically hyperventilating between words.

"It's okay, honey. Just breathe," I said, wiping away her tears with my thumbs and unintentionally creating skid marks of black mascara across her beautifully sculpted cheekbones. I was surprised a splinter could be that painful to a woman who had given birth to three children. "Whatever it is, Lex, it's okay. I'm here. I'll help you. Tell me what you need."

With bloodshot eyes, she looked at me, her mouth quivering. Her lips formed a word but emitted no sound.

"I'm sorry, I can't hear you. Can you say it again? What do

you need?" I asked, placing my hands on her bare shoulders beside the spaghetti straps of her dress. I was beginning to suspect something was very wrong.

"You," she said softly.

"What about me?" I asked, furrowing my brow.

Lex, typically confident and cool, offered a fragile, vulnerable smile.

"I think I need *you*," she whispered, and wiped her dripping nostrils with the back of her hand, like a little girl.

Had we not been the only two people in the shed, I surely would have looked around, wondering if she were speaking to someone else. In my mind's eye, I was still the fat, funny kid with whom she swapped chocolate for licorice when we went trick-or-treating.

My heart raced. My hands remained frozen in place and my lips mere inches from hers. A minute earlier, the physical distance between us had seemed innocuous. But now the chemistry had changed. My fingers released their grip and repositioned themselves on her face, as if they had a mind of their own. I could feel her breath—a warm cocktail of alcohol and Mentos—and watched as she closed her eyes. I glanced down at her mouth; her full bottom lip was ripe and beckoning me closer. Her manicured nails slipped onto my scalp and ran through my hair. Still on my knees, she pulled me close and our lips touched.

When I cut class to play poker in college, I knew it was wrong. I was fully cognizant that nothing good would come of my delinquency, yet I wouldn't stop myself. I had been a good kid for so long that a perverse adrenaline rush accompanied seeing how far I could push the envelope; how much I could get away with, regardless of cost, which I suspected would be tremendous.

As I kissed Lex and gently touched her in a way that was wholly different from when we played schoolyard tag as kids, I knew I was doing something immoral, but I couldn't stop myself. The thrill was similar to the one I experienced at Princeton, but this time, there was no sense of doom and inevitable destruction. What I did in college was an act of rebellion—a mutiny against injustice, parental expectations, and years of pressure. But this?

This was no act of defiance. This suddenly felt like an acceptance of destiny—albeit a complicated one.

I loved the way she smelled. Though I couldn't place the notes, it was sexy, like fresh wood mixed with vanilla. I inhaled her as I kissed the crevices of her neck.

"Seriously, when did you get so hot?" she whispered. Suddenly I felt something pull my hair. I reached up to the spot and realized a few strands were snagged on her ring.

I slowly removed her hands from my head and held them in my own. "Maybe it's a sign," I said, motioning toward the gigantic diamond. I kissed the tops of her fingers before releasing my grip.

She placed my hands on her heart and began to speak.

My palm is on her boobs, my palm is on her boobs was all that went through my head. After a moment, however, I tuned back in.

"I don't remember the last time I felt this alive," she said. "This has been the best weekend in . . . I can't tell you how long. I haven't been this happy in years. Years! And I know it's in part because we are *all* together, but I have to tell you, the best surprise has been reconnecting with you, Seth. I love . . . being with you."

She looked up at the ceiling as if she were trying to stop the pools of tears in her eyes from overflowing.

I blushed. She was still clamping my palm onto her chest, and I wanted it to stay there forever. I wanted to stay with *her* forever. Yes, she was beautiful, but it was more than that. She was like that sabra plant we learned about years ago in Hebrew school: prickly and tough on the outside, soft and sweet on the inside. I wanted to tell her how I felt. I closed my eyes and tried to organize my thoughts. I wanted to explain how I had been attracted to plenty of women before but had never felt anything remotely close to the way I did with her. I wanted her to know that I felt my best with this group—and my *very* best with her. I wanted to tell her how I thought I was falling in love, if it was possible to fall in love with a childhood playmate you haven't seen in over a decade but have just spent a really great thirty-six hours with. I had been so preoccupied by choosing the right words, however, that I failed to realize that two excruciatingly long minutes had passed without my saying a single one. I opened my mouth to speak, but she released her grip and relinquished my hand.

"I'm sorry, did I . . ." She pointed back and forth between us. "Am I making this uncomfortable?" she asked, suddenly self-conscious. "Oh no, I'm so embarrassed!"

"No! Not at all," I insisted. Only then did I realize how my lengthy silence must have confused her.

"I'm making a complete fool of myself. I shouldn't have said anything," she said. Her voice shook as she gracefully tucked a lock of hair behind her ears. I found her utterly enchanting.

"Lex," I began, before she cut me off.

"Don't say it!" She put her hand in front of my face. "It's okay if you're not feeling it. You don't have to say it."

"Lex!" I said more emphatically, then looked nervously down at the floor. The words *composted manure* written across the fertilizer bag on which she was sitting caught my eye and distracted me. It occurred to me that we had begun this new chapter in our relationship on a literal pile of shit. I suddenly wondered if the universe was trying to tell us something. I was determined not to make Lex the next major screw-up in my life. I wanted her—*oh, man, did I want this woman*—but only when it was right. In that instant, I ditched my plan to profess my love and quickly shifted gears.

"You have no idea how much I want this. Really. *No* idea. But you've got a husband and kids. I mean, we just bought them T-shirts at Tanglewood's gift shop." I looked her in the eyes. "Lex, I'm not going to be *that* guy. I'm not going to destroy your marriage."

She nodded, stared off into the lattice, and then burst into tears. "But it's already a mess," she sobbed. I pulled her close and held her until she calmed.

"You're still wearing a ring. You still live in the same house. You still share a bed."

"He hasn't touched me in almost two years," she whispered, and cocked her head like a shy child, before another round of tears trickled down her face. She held up two fingers to illustrate her point.

I found it incomprehensible for a man to live with this woman and not touch her.

"That doesn't mean the marriage is irreparable," I said gently, while a voice inside my head implored me to shut up. "Have you talked to anyone? Have you tried to make it work?" The voice returned. *You schmuck. Don't blow it! It's like you're genetically predisposed to ruin any great opportunity that comes your way!*

"It is irreparable if you don't want to fix it," she said, and then seemed to catch herself, falling silent for a minute or two. "Wow, I don't think I've ever said that out loud before. I don't think I ever felt it so strongly—that I don't want to fix it."

Neither one of us uttered a word.

She repositioned herself and crisscrossed her legs.

"I guess I stuck to the traditional recipe, you know?" she said, dabbing a tear at the outer corner of her eye. "I did what I thought I was supposed to do. I married after college, had kids about ten minutes later, got a house that actually had a white picket fence . . . Don't get me wrong. I don't regret any of it, because, had I not married Jack, I would never have had these particular children, with whom I am completely in love."

"I feel a *but* coming," I said.

"But," she began, with a laugh that rapidly disintegrated into another cry, "other than being their mom, I'm miserable! Until this weekend, I don't think I really realized how bad it's become. But since the moment you picked me up in that shit-brown car of yours, I've felt like the best version of me. Grounded. Authentic. Real. If I could bottle the way you make me feel and take it home to experience it every day for the rest of my life, I would."

"So would I," I said. I felt the words fly out of my mouth. My palms began to sweat.

"I mean, my God, look at Bec . . ."

"What do you mean?"

"Get real. She could—" She stopped herself. "I mean, how many—" She stopped herself again.

I knew where she was going, but I refused to finish the sentence: *How many lives does any of us have?* Or: *How many times can one person cheat death?*

"All I'm saying is, how much time does any of us really have? We may as well be happy for as much of it as we can."

One strap of her dress dangled off her shoulder, all the way down to her bicep. Her gaze remained fixed on my face. Her body language could not have been less subtle.

I could tell she was waiting for me to make a move. It was as if I were twelve years old again, locked in a closet with Lauren Applebaum during a game of Truth or Dare at her junior high graduation party and scared shitless to lean in for my first kiss.

Everything in me wanted to ravish her, but my body stayed fixed. Lex pulled the wilting strap of her dress back up onto her shoulder. She seemed disappointed and self-conscious. I cleared my throat but remained immobile. She folded her arms across her chest.

"Hey," I said, gently brushing away some stray hairs covering her eyes. "You are gorgeous. Inside and out. You're a riot and brilliant and a sweetheart, and exactly what I want and need. You're the brass ring. You hear me? The brass fuckin' ring. But if we're gonna do this, I want to do it right. I've screwed up enough opportunities in my lifetime; I'm not going to make you the next casualty. Figure out whatever you need to figure out. And when you do, I'll be here." I touched her chin and kissed her forehead, then stood up. "It's late. I'm gonna head inside. Plus, staying out here any longer may be physically torturous for me."

She rose to her feet from the fertilizer bag and dabbed another tear from her eye. "Okay. I think I'm just going to hang out for a few minutes by myself. Just me, the stars, and an empty fire pit."

I stepped forward and enveloped her in a long, full-body squeeze. We stood that way quietly for nearly a minute, until I whispered, "Damn, you smell good."

Neither of us would release from the embrace. She gradually inched her hand down the small of my back and into the rear pocket of my jeans, just as she had at the concert. My fingers—once again declaring independence from my conscience—reciprocated the gesture and found a resting spot on the outer curve of her butt. A moment later, we were kissing beside a wall of hanging gardening tools. I noticed the spades, brooms, and shovels surrounding us like art in a museum and swiftly flipped Lex around away from the sharp objects. But in the heat of the moment I neglected to take note of the rake tooth hooked onto the belt loop of her dress.

"Seth!" she screamed, her hands flying behind to cover her ass and right hamstring, which were now exposed, thanks to a huge gash across her sundress.

"I am so, so, so sorry, Lex," I said, and bent down to help her lift the dangling piece of cotton fabric. I couldn't believe that in the course of a single hour I had whacked her in the head with a slab of wood and ripped off her clothes with a garden instrument. It wasn't kinky; it was klutzy and embarrassing.

With her smudged makeup and shredded garments, Lex peered at me as I crouched in front of her, and she burst out laughing.

I gazed up and smiled. "I know what you're thinking. You're amazed at the lengths I'll go to get your clothes off. . . ."

She was howling and could barely catch her breath. "If this is how . . ." *Inhale.* "You treat women . . ." *Inhale.* "I now know why . . ." *Inhale.* "You're still single!"

I was glad to see she had a sense of humor about it all. "Listen, do you want me to get you anything to cover it up? A sweatshirt or blanket?"

Her eyes darted around the shed for an adequate cover-up, but the only thing that came close was an enormous orange plastic tarp concealing a pile of firewood. She looked back at my face and then lowered her eyes to my chest, where they rested for a moment. "How 'bout the shirt off your back?" she asked softly, and bit her lip in a way that was both seductive and endearingly vulnerable all at once.

I smiled, granted her request, wrapped the shirt behind her backside, and pulled her toward me.

Chapter 15: Becca

When Nolan and I heard footsteps creaking up the basement staircase, we opened the door, and there on the last tread before the kitchen were Seth and Lex, wrapped in an embrace, his bare chest and her perfectly taut, lace-thonged butt displayed before us. She immediately spun around, our jaws dropped, and the four of us just stood, aghast, staring at one another.

For a solid thirty seconds, no one moved or uttered a word.

"Minestrone?" I asked, breaking the silence and awkwardly extending the half-eaten bowl of soup in my hands.

What are they thinking? This is incest! Once I fully registered that their inebriated flirtation at Tanglewood had actually come to fruition, I was overcome with fear. Fear of how this would change our group's dynamic. Fear of how this could upend Lex's entire life. And, selfishly, I feared this was a foreshadowing of my own fate. *If I'm not careful, my marriage could fall apart, too.*

Lex looked at me (as well as my soup) with absolute horror, and then, like a shot from a cannon, secured Seth's shirt around her waist as a cover-up and bolted off to her bedroom.

"Well, it's getting late," Seth said, as he stepped into the kitchen, "I'm gonna call it a night." It was as if he thought he could get away with murder.

While my mind scrambled to find the right words, Nolan folded his arms across his chest and blocked Seth's path. "What are you doing, bud? Lex is married!"

"Like you're one to talk about *marriage*," Seth bit back, and pointed an index finger in Nolan's face. The intensity in his eyes scared me. "Did you really think riding up here in your shiny Cadillac made you some kind of prince on a white horse? I got news for you, *bud* . . ." The way Seth said *bud* made my muscles tense. "You're no Husband of the Year."

Nolan glowered, slack-jawed, at Seth. Their faces were just inches apart, like flared-nostril featherweights in a boxing ring, preparing for a showdown. I knew Nolan's frozen stance meant he was crafting some sort of humorous retort to keep the peace, but with my pulse throbbing as it was, I couldn't wait for his wit.

"Okay, guys, that's enough," I cautioned, and placed my soup on the counter. I walked over to position myself between them, but it was too late.

An elongated, guttural grunt emerged from my husband like a precursor to an explosion. He lifted a knee to his waistline and then, with all his might, slammed his shoe downward. Clearly, Seth's foot was the intended target, but, not surprisingly, Nolan missed and smacked the floor instead.

This pitiful attempt at a fight elicited a snigger and disapproving head shake from Seth. "Nice try. You learn those moves in prep school? Let me show you how it's done in Queens." He then balled his hand into a fist and threw a punch at Nolan's stomach but stopped short of impact. Nolan, braced for a beating, looked confused. "Don't fuck with us," Seth growled, his fist still in position. He stared confidently up at my considerably taller but less muscular husband and then walked away, giving Nolan a final, sideways glance that I interpreted as, *I'm watching you.*

Nolan did not look at Seth or at me. His gaze was fixed straight ahead like a soldier's.

As Seth climbed the fourteen creaky stairs to the second floor and blew me a kiss good night, I wondered what I would say to Nolan. After all, which words do you use when one of your best friends calls your husband an asshole and 90 percent of you concurs?

At that moment, however, all I could think about was the dissenting 10 percent—that voice, which sounded a lot like Jordana's, whispering in the back of my mind, *You're not the only one hit by this diagnosis.* I was overcome with a need to repair whatever I could so I'd never find myself in a troubled marriage like Lex's.

I reached for Nolan's hand, and he pulled away angrily. "Nol, please," I said gently, and tried again. This time, he followed me to the couch by the fireplace. "Listen," I started, looking him directly in the eyes, but I wasn't sure what to say next. Between the fight with Seth and my diagnosis, I was overcome with a sense of guilt. As if I were a bad investment Nolan had made back in college and he was now getting a shitty return. I knew that neither the cancer I had as a child nor the one I faced as an adult was in any way my fault, and yet I felt as if I had somehow pulled a curtain over his eyes and duped him into believing he had married someone normal. He could have had anyone, but he chose me. This handsome, smart, kind man took a chance on a pediatric-cancer survivor and never looked back—not in law school, when he skipped a ski trip with his buddies because my crap immune system turned a case of sniffles into pneumonia; not six weeks after our wedding, when a suspicious mammogram ended up being a false alarm; and not on our third wedding anniversary, when we decided to deplete our savings so that we could pay a more fertile woman to birth our biological child. *He has never given up on me. He has never made me feel weak or inept or anything short of beautiful and limitless. Why should I give up on him during his moment of weakness? Is it really so terrible that he doesn't want his wife's appearance to change?*

I took a deep breath. "I'll book the entire surgery for the end of the month," I said, stroking his hand. As my chest tightened and my gut turned at the sound of my promise, a mammoth smile spread across his face.

"Oh, Bec," he sighed, and then hugged me so tightly I coughed.

"I need to schedule the mastectomy anyway," I said over his shoulder. "I can always cancel the reconstruction at the last second, right? At least we'll have something on the calendar while I do my research. I'll read everything I can get my hands on. I'll talk to women who have done the reconstruction, and I'll try to find some who have passed on the reconstruction. I promise I'll keep an open mind."

This is an olive branch, I thought. *I'm doing right by my husband and my marriage.*

Nolan gripped my biceps and held me at arm's length in front of him. "I knew you would come around! I knew you were too smart to give up the chance to look like a woman."

I could almost hear the screeching of the brakes in my ears. "I'm sorry? What did you say?" I asked in disbelief. *I must have misheard,* I assured myself.

He said the words again, just as earnestly: "I knew you were too smart to give up the chance to look like a woman."

My face grew numb. Any goodwill I had possessed at the start of our conversation vanished. I jerked my hands away from his. "Why are you making this so difficult for me?" I cried. "Can't you see I'm trying here? I want to make this work."

"But—" He tried to interject, but I wouldn't let him.

"Are you listening to yourself? I can't believe this is *you*! You keep attacking me! You're punishing me for this situation that isn't my fault. I didn't choose this! I love you, and I love our family, and I just want to live without risk and pain and operations and hospitals. I just want to move on and continue living our lives. Don't you get that? Where the hell *are* you in there?" I asked.

I was raised to believe that people who truly love each other don't walk away or get embarrassed. They stay. They buoy. They help you straighten your own back and lift your own chin in a moment of weakness. I witnessed this tenfold during my illness, and I knew then that would be my model for love. I thought my husband understood. I thought we were on the same page. But all I could feel at that moment was negativity, disapproval, and pessimism grabbing like poisonous tentacles. The thought that he of all people could strip me of my confidence infuriated me even more. My husband had transformed from my other half into someone I barely recognized.

"Do you honestly think I won't be a woman if I pass on the reconstruction? Or that I'd be *stupid*"—I made air quotes with my fingers—"not to have it?"

"You're not stupid. That's not what I meant."

"Bullshit," I seethed.

"No, really," he protested, and mumbled something about how his big mouth was ruining every part of his life. "What I meant was that you are too smart to base this huge, life-changing decision on one doctor's appointment. You still have time to learn more. Let's get a second opinion."

I slumped lethargically onto the sofa cushion. Yes, I agreed we needed to gather more information. But this was no longer about the surgery; it was about his response.

A door unlocked down the hall, and I could hear someone shuffling toward the kitchen. The interruption wasn't unwelcome. I was spent and just wanted peace.

"I thought I heard voices out here," Holly said, as she opened a cabinet, pulled out a glass, and pushed it into the water dispenser on the refrigerator door.

I raised my eyebrows and looked at Nolan as if to say, *I think this discussion is over.* I walked over to Holly. "Can't sleep?" I asked.

She smiled and took a swig from her glass. "Sleeplessness is sort of my general state of existence these days," she said, and tucked a few loose strands of auburn hair beneath the edge of her headscarf.

I looked at Holly, in her long-sleeved, neck-to-ankle bathrobe and the blue cloth wrapped around her scalp, and wondered if she was uncomfortable. Had I been eight months pregnant on a hot July night, I probably would have stumbled barefoot into the kitchen, braless, in an oversize college T-shirt, my hair a mess. I knew Holly could walk around with her long hair flowing freely when she was alone with Adam, or even privately with me, but she was required to cover up in the presence of the rest of the world. I wondered if she felt stifled, or if she still welcomed the customs the way she had in the past. Never once, in the twenty-something years she had lived this way, had she complained. And yet I couldn't help but wonder if this was what she had been referring to that morning at Babies "R" Us. Was she yearning to break free from all these rules?

"I'm gonna turn in for the night—it's too late for me," I said, and gave her a kiss on the cheek.

"Love you," she said softly, and squinted her eyes, as if to ask, *Everything okay?* I responded with a shrug, which I hoped she would interpret correctly as, *No change; it is what it is.*

"I'll be in soon, hon," Nolan called out, in the same way he did almost every night at home when I retreated to our bedroom to read and left him sprawled out on the living room couch, watching Jimmy Fallon.

"Okay," I called back, as if everything were normal. It was the easiest road to take; I didn't want to fight, but I didn't have it in me to offer up a good-night kiss.

I changed into the coral tank top and matching cotton pajama pants that Emma had given me for my birthday and stepped into the bathroom to wash up. I opened the mirrored medicine cabinet to retrieve some toothpaste, and, upon shutting the door, I noticed how the bottom of the mirror cut off my reflection just a few inches below my collarbone, so that I couldn't see my chest. Up on my tiptoes, I could see my sagging, braless boobs, but if my feet remained flat on the marble-tiled floor, it appeared as if the smoothness of my décolletage simply continued southward. I arched my feet into the relevé position I used to do in ballet class as a girl, so that my chest was now in view, and smashed my boobs down like thick pancakes with my hands. I tried to envision what it would be like to see my entire torso as one long, smooth plane. I turned to the right and then to the left, but gained no insight other than that I looked like an inept mammogram tech. I collapsed my arches and dabbed some Colgate onto my toothbrush.

Twenty-seven more days until the end of the month, I thought while I rinsed. I played out the various permutations in my mind while I flossed: husband and boobs; husband and no boobs; no husband and no boobs. I dug dental floss deep into my gums for a pinch of reality.

I shut the bathroom light and climbed into bed. Tucked beneath the pale gray-and-white patchwork quilt, I stared up at the vaulted ceiling and listened to the central air push through the vent. The breeze blew against the mattress, and the linens felt cool against my skin. Had Nolan been next to me, and had this been a typical night at home, I would undoubtedly have slid my feet beneath his calves to warm them. He had always been my comfort zone—emotionally and physically.

Twenty-seven days, and my life will change forever, I thought. It was similar to the sensation that had percolated inside me for the entirety of our pregnancy with Emma—when I had embraced the powerlessness of having another woman carry and deliver my baby.

As I pulled Jordana's quilt around me, I thought back to all those instances when I had no control—like the end of the first trimester, when Elizabeth called to say she had booked herself on a Mexican cruise. Of course we knew she was entitled to a vacation, but, given our against-all-odds pregnancy, we never would have gone so far from home had I been the one carrying. Then there was the time Nolan and I flew to California for the sole purpose of sitting in a darkened ultrasound room and experiencing the joy of seeing our baby appear on the monitor. But when we checked in at the reception desk, Elizabeth decided that she preferred to have a private consult and Nolan and I realized we had flown three thousand miles to sit in a waiting room. And then, of course, there was the pièce de résistance, when she called to say she was tired of being pregnant and wanted to move up our scheduled C-section and deliver early.

"You can't do that," I said, laughing. I really thought she was joking.

"Actually, I can," she said. "The doctor will do it at thirty-seven weeks as long as the baby's lungs are mature. So I'll need an amnio to test the lungs."

"An amnio? *Now?*" I asked, exasperated. "But you're in the home stretch and the baby's healthy. What's another week or so? Why introduce a risk when we've come this far?"

I called doctors. Nolan called lawyers. Sympathetic as they were to our situation, everyone agreed Elizabeth, not our baby, was the patient. As long as the doctor was willing and the baby's lungs were indeed mature, thirty-seven weeks was permissible.

I felt sick to my stomach the day we left New York for the amnio. I packed our suitcase, along with a duffel bag full of gender-neutral baby clothes prewashed in Dreft, booked a room at an extended-stay hotel near the hospital because I had no idea how long we would be living on the West Coast, interviewed pediatricians with rights to the hospital where Elizabeth would be delivering in California, as well as New York–based pediatricians for when we returned home, and looked into renting an RV to drive across the country, in case we were told we were free to leave but that air travel was too risky for a newborn.

I've done all I can, I remember telling myself throughout the process. *All I can do now is remain cautiously optimistic.*

Those words swirled in my mind as I drifted off to sleep. The bed felt empty and the sheets were cold as my foot drifted fruitlessly to the other side of the mattress in search of warmth.

Chapter 16: Nolan

*A*fter Becca went to bed, I assumed Holly would follow suit and that I would lie on the suede couch in Jordana's great room for the remainder of the night, strategizing about how to repair the shit storm of my marriage and my career. Instead, Holly opened a kitchen drawer, pulled out a pair of scissors, and snipped the strings off one of the bakery boxes she'd brought up from her store.

"It's a new recipe," she said, carefully lifting a chocolate babka out from the cardboard packaging and lowering it onto a paper towel atop the kitchen island. "Tell me what you think."

This was a deliberate invitation—no doubt about it. I wasn't interested in desserts, and I dreaded what Holly really wanted from me. After all, I'd received a monumental amount of stink-eye from Lex, and Seth had practically thrown a punch at me minutes earlier. I wondered if it was now Holly's turn to chastise me. Seeing no way around it, I walked over to the island and broke a piece off the flaky loaf to take my lumps like a man.

"This is delicious! You made this?" I asked in amazement, licking the sweet golden crumbs from my fingers.

"So, I take it this is a positive review?"

"Uh-huh," I said, and shoved a second helping into my mouth, savoring the taste of chopped pecans embedded in chocolate.

"Well, if you like that, I have some other new recipes I brought to test out on everyone at brunch tomorrow. You want to be the first?"

"Bring it on!" I said. For twenty minutes, I waited for Holly to start lecturing or interrogating me as she plied me with a smorgasbord of baked goods. Tarts, pies, cookies, and breads were lined up on the counter, each one more mouthwatering than the next. I stood there, nibbling away, wondering when she would start in on me—but she never did.

"Thank you," I said, wiping my lips. Though I suspected she interpreted this as gratitude for her pastries, I hoped she could sense my appreciation for her mercy as well.

"Thank *you*! You're my guinea pig," she said cheerfully, and then suddenly winced and leaned against the edge of the granite counter.

"Are you okay?" I asked, stepping toward her. She nodded as she exhaled slowly through her mouth. "Here," I said, running to the dining area and dragging a chair to the center of the kitchen. I held her elbow, eased her into a seated position, and then grabbed a throw pillow from the living room sofa to place behind her back. I could feel the sweat begin to bead on my forehead as I handed her a glass of water. I didn't want anything going awry on my watch. "You want me to wake Adam?" I asked, dabbing sweat from my upper lip. "I should probably wake him, right? He'd want to know. I mean, I'd want to know. I'm gonna wake him. Okay?" I was babbling nervously.

"It's okay, really. Let him sleep," she whispered, as she stroked her belly. "I'm still a few weeks away from delivery. Don't worry. They're just Braxton-Hicks—practice contractions. They'll pass in a minute or two."

The pain seemed to be subsiding as quickly as it had come on. "So, uh, how's the bakery biz?" I asked.

"Forget about me, Nolan," she said. "How are *you* doing?"

Shit. "Oh, I'm fine," I said. I leaned back against the counter and folded my arms across my chest.

She raised her eyebrows and looked up at me from her chair.

"Listen, go lie down. Take care of yourself. You have enough going on right now; you don't need to stay up and try to make me feel better."

"But I want to," she said kindly. "Becca's my friend, but you're my friend, too."

For a solid minute, we sat in silence as I gathered my thoughts. Part of me yearned to remain quiet and keep the anger, confusion, and fear to myself. I didn't want to talk about my problems. On the other hand, never had I felt such a sense of impending eruption.

"I feel like everything I do and say is wrong, even if I don't intend it to be," I finally said. "Like no matter what, I come off sounding like an asshole."

"You're not an asshole," she said.

"I feel like I am. Becca deserves to have people support and empower her, not confuse and frustrate her. She's like a freakin' rock, resilient as hell. And I'm the jerk who's bringing her down, unintentionally fucking with her mind and weakening her at a time when she needs to stay strong—and all because I won't lie. I have to tell her how I truly feel. But what do you do when honesty and supporting the person you love contradict each other?"

"Have you told her all of this?"

"We're too far gone. The damage is done. Honestly, at this point I think she deserves someone way better than me."

"So, what's holding you back?" Holly asked.

"Holding me back from what?"

"From being that person. The one you think is *better* than you?"

I shrugged. "From the moment we met, I have been loyal, devoted, and committed to this relationship. Honesty has been our bedrock. I'm not going to change that now. How can I not be truthful about my feelings to the person I love the most, especially during a moment of crisis? I don't know if this proves that I'm shallow, or an ass, or what—all I know is that I thought I could handle this, but now I'm not so sure. She deserves someone who can. She deserves a better"—I cleared my throat—"a better man."

A wave of nausea came over me as I realized that I'd failed to be the man my wife needed and merited.

"Nolan," Holly said, "through all of this fertility crap Adam and I have been dealing with, *you two* were my inspiration. When we had no control over all those failed IVF treatments, do you know what I thought of?"

I shook my head.

"I thought of Becca in that hospital room when we were kids, fighting such a valiant battle; you and Emma were her ultimate prizes."

"Thank you. I appreciate that, but—"

"You know what else I thought about?" she asked, cutting me off. "I thought about how the two of you weathered that surrogacy process, and all the stresses that came with it, with such grace. You kept your priorities in focus and made it through. Stronger for it, I might add."

"I know, but honestly, this feels different. I don't know how to handle this," I said, feeling my throat tighten.

"Why?" she asked, adjusting her position in the chair.

My eyes stung, and I glared at the counter. I noticed a water ring and began rubbing it out with my thumb.

"Why is this different?" she asked again.

"Because," I said, "I'm fucking scared!"

I looked up to gauge her reaction, and she nodded sympathetically.

"I don't know how to do this . . . this illness thing," I said. "I naively assumed it was all in the past. I swear, I believed all those caveats about long-term repercussions were the equivalent of fine-print legal warnings that you acknowledge but know are improbable. I was sure that part of her life was over—like cancer was Act One and I arrived at intermission, in time for the uplifting Act Two. But what if there is no happy ending?" My voice cracked. "What if she *dies*? Holly, what am I going to do if she *dies*? How am I going to raise Emma as a single dad?"

"She's going to be okay."

"You don't know that," I said reproachfully. Tears stung my eyes. I tried to blink them away, but they spilled onto my cheek. I ripped a paper towel off the roll beside the sink and dried them.

"No, I don't," she said somberly. "It's a legitimate concern. I think about it, too. We all do. I mean, look at us: Seth, Lex, Jordana, and me. We're up here on *this* particular weekend, of *this* particular year, for a reason. You think I'd schlep my pregnant, hemorrhoidal *tuchas* up here for anyone else? It's because the four of us were collateral damage then and still are now. In some way, shrapnel from the explosion of Becca's illness hit all of us. Hard. It was horrible. Seeing her that sick robbed each of us of our childhood innocence. There was no blissful ignorance after we presented her with that tape in the hospital. We thought it was our goodbye, and that we were sending her along to the next life with a smile on her face. The concept of 'young and immortal' completely flew out the window for us. We were all permanently scarred. Honestly, I don't think Jordana has ever recovered."

I looked away. It was hard to listen to this. Of course I had heard the stories over the years, and they'd always saddened me. I couldn't be more proud of my wife's strength and fortitude, but I often cringed when anyone reminisced about that time. Envisioning the hospital room and picturing her friends and family at her bedside made me feel useless and peripheral, despite my status as her husband.

And then, improbably, Holly said, "Welcome."

"Welcome? To what?"

"The Cast. The story line may be different, but it doesn't change the fact that you are also a victim of what happened all those years ago. You got hit, too. Think of it this way: you're just one of those stars who arrived in a later season. It's like we're the originals—Gilda, Jane, Lorraine, and Bill Murray—and you're, I don't know, Steve Martin? Mike Myers?"

I chuckled. "Jimmy Fallon?"

"Perfect. Jimmy Fallon it is," Holly said. "The point is that you're not alone, Nolan. We're always going to be here. Season after season. We're like the cast that never retires."

"Great!" I moaned sarcastically, and rolled my eyes.

"All right. I'm gonna try to get some sleep. Doubt it will work, but I'm gonna try." She reached for the edge of the counter and pulled herself to her feet.

After Holly waddled down the hall and closed her bedroom door, I wiped up the crumbs we had sprinkled across the island and washed the empty soup bowls Becca and I had left in the sink.

When I returned the soup spoons to their proper spots, I accidentally opened a kitchen drawer that did not contain utensils.

As it shut in slow, "soft-close" motion, I noticed an old VHS tape, a DVD, and an envelope with Becca's name, held together by a rubber band.

Though I knew no one was awake, I looked over my shoulder as I carefully removed the items from the drawer. Both the VHS tape and the DVD were labeled with the initials *BNL*. The envelope with her name across the front was sealed, but I knew it was from Jordana, since her return address was embossed on the stationery. Normally, I wouldn't invade Jordana's privacy, but I felt compelled to snoop.

I cracked the bedroom door where Becca was sleeping, grabbed my messenger bag, and crept back to the great room to unpack my laptop on the coffee table in front of the fireplace. I inserted the DVD, plugged in my earbuds, propped myself up on the throw pillows, and lay back with the computer on my belly.

As soon as the DVD began, with its vintage picture quality and elongated shot of a pilling couch in a wood-paneled basement, I knew immediately that this was a copy of the original *Becca Night Live* that Jordana had told me she'd made in advance of the reunion.

I had seen *Becca Night Live* only once—that July Fourth in her studio apartment when we had just started dating. My takeaway back then was that it was just a bunch of silly skits performed by some goofball friends who were undoubtedly devoted to, and beloved by, her. But now I knew the people those kids had grown into. Now, the sight of a pudgy, adolescent Seth stuffing his gray sweatshirt with toilet paper rolls for muscles was side-splitting, as was the discovery that he had been one of those kids whose saliva gathered in little pools at the corners of this mouth when he spoke. And watching Lex sing Cyndi Lauper's "Girls Just Want to Have Fun," bedecked in hot-pink lace, bangs sprayed several inches above her forehead, was not only entertaining but enlightening— her edge and sass were detectable even then.

When the novelty of witnessing everyone circa early 1990s wore off, I began to see new subtleties. I noticed Jordana sulking in the corner unless she thought she was on camera, in which case she suddenly turned on and lit up with an ersatz grin. I saw Lex clearly take on the role of the upbeat leader wanting to direct and organize. And then there was Holly, smiling warmly throughout the ninety-minute production, her sweetness as palpable as it was now.

When Becca shared the video with me in college, I viewed it as a relic from my girlfriend's past. It was touching, but only marginally more meaningful than if she had shown me her childhood soccer trophies or pictures from a junior high school yearbook. But knowing what I knew now—how draining and scary it had been for her friends to deliver that tape to her hospital room, how transformative and indelible the experience of buoying her spirits had been for all of them—I saw that the video was much more than a bunch of kids goofing around with a Sony Handycam.

I watched the whole thing, including every last handwritten credit that scrolled by. At the very end, someone put the cap on the lens but neglected to turn off the camera. I could hear The Cast shuffle away, and then, once they were out of earshot, the sound of a man's voice became clear. I turned up the volume and felt certain it was Mr. Lefkowitz.

"I can't bear to watch them filming down there," he said.

"I've cried nearly every day since that child was diagnosed," I heard Mrs. Lefkowitz say. "I don't know how Arlene and Jerry do it."

And that's how the video ended. I shut the laptop, placed the DVD, cassette, and envelope back in the kitchen drawer, and checked on Becca in the bedroom. It was 3:00 a.m. She was sound asleep. I crawled into bed and spooned against my wife's back.

"I love you," I whispered into her hair, the way we often did with Emma when she was curled up with her blanket and we wanted to breathe her in but not wake her. And, just like her daughter, Becca remained still. Though I had seen her sleep soundly countless times, in that moment I was overcome with a profound and unsettling sense of loneliness. I missed my wife desperately. I missed us.

How did her family do it? I wondered, thinking back to Mrs. Lefkowitz's voice at the end of the tape. In all the years I had known my in-laws, we had never discussed their experience. I never asked, and they never volunteered. The topic of Becca's illness was hardly taboo, but when it was raised, it was usually as a reference point—an era in their family's history known as When Becca Was Sick.

Too wired to sleep, I crept out of bed and retreated to the living room couch. I grabbed a newspaper from the stack in the wicker basket beside the suede sofa and opened up to the "Hunt" column in the *New York Times* Real Estate section. Like addicts, week after week Becca and I turned excitedly to it to see how people navigated their search for the ideal home. Would a gorgeous facade reveal a total shithole? Would prospective buyers jump on a sun-flooded, "mint-condition" apartment despite the four-floor walk-up and vents that wafted in Chinese takeout from the restaurant downstairs? It didn't make a difference whose quest was featured; it was the process of getting to the finish line that fascinated us. It was a quintessential study in human nature and decision making. Anyone could dream, but no one got it all. There was always a compromise, a perpetual give and take. And it was interesting to see where and how people drew their lines.

About a paragraph into a story about a couple getting priced out of Brooklyn and settling for a more affordable space on the West Side, I could no longer concentrate. The apartment was next to our favorite playground, and it reminded me of Emma. I wished my phone were working so I could pull up some of our home movies. Those videos were priceless and always ignited a flutter in my heart, a tear in my eye, or a snort of laughter. Just a couple of minutes could cure any ailment. And then it occurred to me. All this time I had been searching for an intervention—a purple road map from Harold, or restorative nourishment from my mother. But maybe I didn't need any of that. Maybe Holly was right—it was my season to join The Cast.

Chapter 17: Holly

"Adam," I said, with as much control as I could muster while digging my nails into the side of the mattress. *In through the nose, out through the mouth*, I reminded myself. I looked at the digital clock on the nightstand. It was 5:00 a.m. *Just breathe.* "Adam," I said again, more loudly this time. "Wake up!"

My husband's head shot off the pillow like a bullet, lifting his torso ninety degrees into a seated position.

"What? What is it?" he gasped, vigorously rubbing the sleep from his eyes. "Is it the baby? Is it time?" he asked, panic spreading across his face. Adam had always been a fairly laid-back guy—a biblical scholar and frustrated drummer who was perfectly content with a day job as the delivery guy for his wife's bakery. But when I became pregnant, a switch flipped. At first I found his new, protective nature charming. But as the due date approached and his anxiety grew, he became almost overbearing. He jumped out of bed and changed his clothes so quickly, I would have guessed he'd run practice drills.

"I don't know if this is labor, but we should get to a hospital to make sure," I said slowly, hoping my enunciation would allay his tattered nerves. I refrained from explaining that a trip to the ER had been the recommendation of my ob-gyn, whom I'd just called because I was experiencing some mild but unusual cramping. I thought for sure the doctor would downplay it. But then he asked me when I had last felt the baby move. I said I couldn't recall. I told him that I'd been distracted in the Berkshires and not as observant as usual. The double entendre of that statement hit me as soon as it left my mouth.

After tenderly easing me onto my feet, Adam threw my purse over his shoulder, grabbed his wallet, keys, and Tehillim (book of psalms), and guided me out of the bedroom, his hand on my lower back. We walked through the quiet great room, dimly lit by the early stages of sunrise, as well as by tiny pendant lights dangling over the kitchen island. As our footsteps sounded across the plank floors, Jordana spun around at the kitchen sink.

"Hey, what are you guys doing up so early?" she asked, wiping her hands on her sweatpants. She had already set the table for brunch and was in the middle of arranging a fruit platter. "Is everything okay?"

"It's probably just gas," I said, forcing a smile and trying to avoid drama. But while I spoke, I was clutching my belly. Everything in me wanted to hold on to this pregnancy and suppress the nightmare of a stillbirth—a scenario that had taken my mind hostage since that phone call thirty minutes earlier.

"You're not going home, are you?" Jordana asked endearingly, her hand on her chest.

"No," I said. "We're just going to the nearest hospital."

Jordana didn't even let my words settle before she reacted. "I'm driving you," she said, already sliding into her Birkenstocks. "The closest hospital is easily a half-hour away. Let's go."

"No, Jordana. Thank you, but you have all these guests. Please. Stay here and—" A mild cramp hit. I winced and squeezed Adam's forearm.

"We need to leave right now," Adam said urgently. "Yes, please, J, will you drive us?"

Even in pain, I was a wee bit peeved by his use of *J*, but I was also enormously grateful he'd said yes.

Jordana plucked her keys from a dish by the front door. The three of us piled into her Range Rover. I sat in the fully reclined front passenger seat, Adam in the back, hovering above my face like a drone. He'd stroke my hair and I'd swat him away, too uncomfortable to be touched. He'd apologize, I'd apologize. He'd touch me again, I'd swat his hand away, again. This cycle continued for the thirty-minute ride until we pulled up to the Berkshire Medical Center.

"My wife's in labor!" Adam announced, as he burst through the ER's electric doors. I trailed a few steps behind, leaning on Jordana for support. "She's thirty-six weeks and needs to be seen immediately."

Who is that? I thought, as I took in the tornado that had once resembled my husband. He spoke so quickly and so authoritatively, I barely recognized him.

"Well, there's an expectant dad," Jordana snickered.

A woman in green scrubs jumped out from behind the reception desk with a wheelchair, and a moment later I was seated and being rolled down a long hallway, Adam and Jordana trotting along beside me. When we arrived at a private triage room, Jordana put her hand on my shoulder. "I'll be out here if you need me," she said with a kind smile.

I waved in thanks as the door closed behind us. A nurse eased me out of the wheelchair and handed over a gown. I undressed, Adam helped me onto to the exam table, and I lay back atop the crinkly white paper as he settled onto a rolling stool. The only sound in the room was the scratch of his pen against the clipboard as he filled out insurance forms. I turned toward the wall and bit my lip. Tears trickled down my face and landed on the table's exposed vinyl padding. It had been only seven minutes since the nurse had left the room, but it seemed like seven years until there was another knock on the door.

"Come in," Adam said, and a youthful, copper-toned blond woman in a perfectly pressed white coat walked into the room.

"Hello there. I'm Kira Sharofsky . . . uh, excuse me, *Dr.* Kira Sharofsky," she said, running her finger over the MD on her badge. *Ah, it's July,* I thought, recalling that the universal start of the hospital residency year was July 1. *Damn, I hope she knows what she's doing.*

"So, Holly. I'm told you've been having some pains. Can you describe what's going on?"

"Well, I got up to pee around four thirty this morning, which is common, but this time I had some cramping, which is not," I babbled. "I figured, *Hey, I'm not home, I'm moving around a lot, I'm eating slightly different foods—maybe my body's reacting to being on vacation* . . . I mean, if you can even call it that, 'cause let me tell you, this hasn't exactly been a stress-free getaway, but better safe than sorry, right? So I paged my doctor and thought for sure he'd just tell me it's nothing, but instead he asked when the last time was that I felt the baby move, and"—I burst into tears—" I couldn't remember! For months I recorded every flutter, but I was so distracted this weekend, I forgot to pay attention! The one time . . ." I sobbed and turned to Adam. "I'm so sorry!"

Adam had lost all color in his face, and the poor newbie resident appeared shell-shocked.

"Well then," she said, handing me a tissue. "We'll do a check of the baby's heart rate ASAP. Once that's squared away, we'll try and figure out the cramping issue. I'm gonna go grab the heart rate monitor from down the hall. Be right back." I nodded, and out of the corner of my eye, I saw Adam reach for his book of psalms from my purse.

Please, God, let this child be healthy; let me be healthy, I thought, as the door closed behind the doctor.

This scenario—me on an exam table, Adam seated beside me, doing the only useful thing he knew to do: pray—was all too familiar. With over a decade of failed infertility treatments under our belts, the exam rooms, the doctors, the crinkly white paper, and even the scent of the antibacterial soaps were all fraught with disappointment and failure. After eight and a half months of positive, happy visits and feeling like a normal pregnant woman, I thought those days of fear were behind me. But there I was, back at the start of what felt like the ultimate marathon, as if the past eight months of joy had been merely a dream.

"Adam," I whispered, my arm shaking as I extended it to him. He grabbed it and rolled toward me on the stool. "Is this my fault?" I asked, my voice cracking.

He rose and kissed my forehead repeatedly, hovering over me like he had in the car, but this time, I welcomed it. "It's not your fault," he said softly. "First of all, we don't even know what we're dealing with here. But even if something is not right, how could it possibly be your fault?"

"I went to Babies 'R' Us," I sobbed again. "On Shabbos! I thought I was doing a good thing by being with Becca and supporting her. But maybe I—"

"Stop. You didn't create this scare. You did what you felt you needed to do in the moment. You were a good friend. Okay, so you broke Shabbos one time in what, two decades? And it was not for some frivolous reason; it was for someone who is sick."

I felt a cramp on my side after he said the word *sick*.

"We are human beings, Hol. We're not infallible. You tested the waters. You made a mistake. Okay! So you won't do it again."

I took a deep breath. "But what if it wasn't a mistake?"

Adam shook his head in confusion. "I'm sorry, I don't follow—"

"Knock, knock. I'm back," Dr. Sharofsky said. She was holding up an external fetal monitor like a prize. "Would you mind lifting up your gown, please?"

I closed my eyes as she squirted gel onto the probe. I couldn't bear to watch. I knew that the mental calisthenics involved in trying to decode a medical professional's flat facial expression while performing an exam could be more detrimental to my psyche than the result itself.

I could feel Adam come near and his fingers stroking my hair as Dr. Sharofsky glided the probe across my abdomen. His breath was warm against my ear where he whispered, "I love you," over and over, as an endless sentence, until it resembled the continuous *swish-swish-swish* sound of his prayers. And then suddenly he stopped and pulled away.

My eyes shot open. Adam was standing beside Dr. Sharofsky, looking down at the fetal monitor, which, I now noticed, was beeping steadily and strongly.

"Awesome sauce," Dr. Sharofsky muttered with detectable relief, as if she were reassuring herself it would all be okay. She held up the screen with a flashing heart as proof.

"*Baruch Hashem!*" Adam cried out, thanking God in Hebrew.

She cocked her head, looking befuddled by Adam's declaration, and then performed a quick internal exam to see if I was dilated, which, thankfully, I was not.

"This is all great news, but I'd still like to monitor you for a wee bit longer just to be on the safe side, given the cramping you experienced. As you know, your age makes you a high-risk pregnancy. And given the stress you say you've had over the last few days, plus the heat outside, you may be more strained and less hydrated than usual. I'd like to run an IV to kick up your fluids, and then, as long as you're stable, we'll get you outta here. 'Kay?"

I nodded and averted my eyes as she inserted a needle into my arm and hooked me up to a bag of clear liquid. As soon as she was finished and had exited the room, Adam and I looked at each other and both exhaled. "I guess I'm already a bad mom. My child is literally attached to me, and I didn't bother to check in and see if it was moving!"

Adam laughed. "I have absolutely no doubt you will be the best mother in the world. I've known that since the day we met."

"I don't know about that. I still have so many questions."

"No one has all the answers. We'll figure it out as we go."

"You can't do that with everything. Some things need to be ironed out in advance."

"What needs ironing?"

I sighed. *Are we really going to have this conversation now?* I thought. "Well, education, for one. Should we send the kid to yeshiva, like all the kids where we live? Or something a little more contemporary, like a day school or a modern Orthodox yeshiva? I know public school is probably off the table, but I loved PS 188 as a kid. There was nothing wrong with the way you and I were raised. We turned out just fine. Should I keep going?"

I didn't wait for his response. I knew I was rambling, just the way I had with Dr. Sharofsky when we'd arrived, but every unresolved issue that had been chipping away at my conscience and nudging for a resolution came pouring out of me on that exam table.

"And how about summer camp? Will we enroll in Jewish summer camp or try a nondenominational camp to get a more multicultural experience if he or she is in a yeshiva for ten months

of the year? And then what about eating out of the house? Ever
since we came back from Israel, we have eaten only at kosher
restaurants. I know it seems totally foreign at this point, especially
given the fact that I'm the poster woman for maintaining a kosher
diet while being a successful international executive, but what if we
start eating vegetarian meals at mainstream public restaurants? Do
we want our kid to grow up eating only at kosher establishments?
And if that's the case, should we move? Because then we'll sort of
be pariahs in Crown Heights, right? I mean, maybe we should look
at houses on Long Island—somewhere a little more modern but
still religious. But, forget education, housing, and *kashrut*—we hav-
en't even figured out how we want to *name* the baby! Do you want
to name the baby according to my family's tradition of naming
after the dead or your family's custom of naming after the living?"

Adam smiled, grabbed a tissue from the dispenser on the
wall, and gently wiped the snot running from my nostrils.

"Do you remember the night we first kissed, in Tel Aviv?" he
said, his face just inches from mine. His voice downshifted into that
slow, mellifluous tone that never ceased to captivate me.

"Adam, I'm serious! These are real issues we need to talk
about. This is not the time to reminisce about—"

"Holly, look at me," he said, his timbre intimate and sexy.
"Do you remember what I said to you after that kiss when we sat
together on the plane and flew back to New York?"

I nodded.

"I told you that the trees we planted in the Jewish National
Fund forest weren't the only roots we planted on our tour. Even
though we were thousands of feet above the ground, I had a feeling you and I were planting our own roots. Do you remember me
saying that?"

I nodded again.

"Over the last twenty-something years, our roots have grown
in ways I think neither one of us ever expected. Right?"

"Mmm-hmm . . ."

"We've changed the way we dress. The way we eat. The way
we live. You're a role model not only to observant Jewish women,
but to all women around the world, and I'm still your delivery boy."

I smiled.

"Our lives are completely different than they were when we started on this journey," he continued. "So if the branches of our tree twist and turn a little more and new buds form, I'm okay making adjustments, as long as we grow together. This is the tree of our life."

I reached for his hand.

"We'll figure it all out. I promise. You're the most important thing in the world to me. We need to be honest and do what feels right—that's what I whispered in your ear when we came home from Israel. It's what I'm promising again now."

Just then, we heard a light tapping on the exam room door.

"Yes?" Adam called out.

Jordana poked her head around the edge of the frame. "Hey," she said softly. "They told me it was okay to come back here. You up for a visitor?"

"Of course," I said. "Please."

She pulled up a chair and squeezed my foot. "How are you feeling?"

"Okay. Better. Heard a heartbeat, thank God. No verdict on the cause of the cramping, though. They're still watching me."

"All right. Better safe than sorry," she said. "I know so many women who have gone to the hospital, only to be sent home. My friend Andrea was sitting in the audience at her husband's business school graduation when she thought her water broke. He took off the cap and gown, and they went to the hospital—but it turns out he missed his commencement because Andrea peed in her pants."

"Yikes," I said.

"And I also have a friend who was convinced she was having gas pains, and the baby ended up falling into her pajama bottoms."

"No way," Adam exclaimed.

"Yup, it's true. She just sat there in her apartment with the baby attached to her until the paramedics got there. Anyway, my point is, I'm glad we came."

"Me too," I said. "Listen, don't feel like you need to wait around for us to be released. I know you have a brunch to host. We can take a taxi back to your house."

"Are you kidding me? You're giving me a rare opportunity to bask in the glory of being anal and organized! The table is set. The food is prepared. All I have to do is take the platters out of the refrigerator. Plus, it's only seven fifteen! Everyone is still sleeping. We'll be back before they wake up; they won't even know we were gone."

The way she regaled us with stories of her friends' deliveries in an attempt to offer peace of mind reminded me of her charm. It made me miss our friendship. I wondered if now, twenty-plus years after I stole her first love, we could officially move on.

"Thank you for coming, Jordana," I said, and took her hand in mine. "I appreciate it."

She seemed startled for a moment, and turned to look at Adam and then back at me. But when we both smiled, she did, too.

For the next hour, Adam and I heard tales about Jordana's job at the Legal Aid Society; about her sons, AJ and Matthew; and about the rewarding work she had done with the Innocence Project, where she had worked as part of a legal team to help exonerate a man who had been imprisoned for decades. Over the years, we had received the major Jordana headlines from Becca, but it was good to get the details straight from the source.

"You know, there's one thing I'd always wondered about you," I said. "How did you end up a defense attorney? I could see prosecution or juvenile justice, but criminal defense?"

She laughed. "Sixth grade. You were there. The moment of origin was when Ms. Kelly accused me of cheating off David Lieberman during an exam. I sneezed and turned my head so snot wouldn't splatter all over the test, but because I'd perfected the silent sneeze, Ms. Kelly just saw my head facing David's desk. I was sent to the principal's office to plead my case. I won, and from then on I was hooked on defending the underdog."

"Really? So your life's course was charted with a single accusation. One moment changed everything."

"I guess so," she said, and smiled.

"That happened to me when we came home from our trip to Israel. It was just one second, but I knew what Adam whispered in my ear would alter our lives forever."

Jordana gasped, and her face fell from a pleasant and hopeful demeanor to one of shock and hurt. Her porcelain skin turned fuchsia, and Adam's eyebrows arched in surprise. It took me a few seconds to register what had happened. In the ease of the moment, I had forgotten to whom I was speaking. Our conversation with Jordana was so effortless and smooth, I was no longer on guard and had not edited out the history of our love triangle.

"Oh my gosh." I leaned my head back onto the thin exam-table pillow. "I'm so sorry, Jordana. I didn't mean to bring that up. That was so stupid and insensitive of me. I'm so embarrassed. I didn't think. Please accept my apology. If I could rewind and take that back, I would."

Adam's face, buried inside the pages of his book of psalms, reddened as well. I was on my own with this one.

"Well," Jordana said with a chuckle, "I guess now we're even."

"What do you mean?"

"Remember when you and Adam showed up late to Becca's twenty-first birthday party and announced your engagement?"

I laughed. "Of course."

"Remember what I did?"

"No . . ."

"Are you kidding? You *don't* remember? To this very day, every time I replay that scene in my head, my face flushes in embarrassment. It's one of the moments in my life that I would do over if I could."

"It couldn't have been that bad if I don't remember."

"You were standing with a whole bunch of Adam's friends—the ones I used to hang out with when we dated. I walked over to congratulate you, and they all fell silent. All eyes were on me, watching to see what I would say. It was awful. I was so self-conscious, but I wanted to do the right thing and wish you both well before I left the party. But somehow I froze and my mind blanked. So I grabbed your left hand, and, in the most annoyingly nasal imitation of my mother's New York accent, I said, 'Sooo, let me see the ring . . .' I told you it was beautiful, to wear it in good health, that Adam was a great guy and I wished you a love that continued to be sui generis. I meant every word. But when I smiled and waved goodbye to everyone, no one smiled or waved back to me.

I could feel them staring as I walked away, like I was this pathetic, Latin-obsessed freak who couldn't resist a mental snapshot of the ring that might have been hers."

"Oh, Jordana, I'm so sorry! I remember you being gracious, but that whole night was such a blur for me. I honestly don't recall any of those details."

At some point during my conversation with Jordana, Adam had repositioned his chair away from us so that he faced a corner of the room. Given his *shukkling* and *swish-swish*ing prayer sounds, he had successfully managed to stay quiet and isolate himself.

"If it's any consolation," I added, "I never liked those friends of his anyway. We haven't seen them since our wedding."

"Can we make a deal?" she said. "I'll absolve you if you absolve me."

"Deal!" I said. "Although I think I got the better end of that, since I have no recollection of any wrongdoing. By the way, what is sui generis? I've never heard that before."

"It means one of a kind. Unique. Special." Jordana looked at the tile floor for a second, and then back to me with a smile. "You guys were a sui generis couple from day one."

I was about to tell Jordana how I'd missed our friendship and how glad I was to be airing out our years of tension, but then Dr. Sharofsky returned to the room.

"How you feeling, Holly?" Dr. Sharofsky asked.

"Much better, thank you."

"Wonderful. Then I'll set you free and get the discharge papers ready. But promise me you'll keep drinking water. You need to stay hydrated, and I'd like you to check in with your ob-gyn when you get home this week. All right?"

"Will do."

Jordana stood as soon as the doctor exited. "I'll go get the car while you guys sign the discharge forms. I'll meet you in front."

Adam and I signed the paperwork and walked out of the room. As soon as we got in the car and I was attempting to get the seat belt around my midsection, Jordana's phone rang.

"Lex! Hey, what are you doing up so early?" she said. There was a moment of uncomfortable silence; then Jordana said, "Are you sure? Okay. Yes. Fine. No, no—they're both with me. We'll be there soon."

"Everything okay?" I asked after she hung up.

"Lex is leaving," Jordana said, and let out a long sigh. "She rebooked herself on an earlier flight back to Chicago."

Chapter 18: Jordana

By the time we returned from the emergency room, it was nine o'clock and Sal was standing alone at the kitchen island, arranging a lovely breakfast buffet. He had already dotted the perimeter of the cream cheese tray with sliced cucumbers, organized the utensils in an aesthetically pleasing diagonal pattern, and picked some catmint flowers from the garden and placed them in a vase as a centerpiece. He had even remembered to go down to the spare fridge in the garage and bring up the smoked-fish platters I had ordered from Barney Greengrass on the Upper West Side as a surprise for Becca.

"Oh, honey, thank you!" I said. I'd texted him to ask if he could get the food on the table in time for Lex's unexpected early departure.

Sal stole a piece of whitefish from the platter and rolled his eyes in ecstasy after dropping it into his mouth. "Listen," he said, licking his fingers clean, before wrapping them around my waist, "this is nothing. You're the one who has taken care of everything this weekend. I know it hasn't gone exactly according to plan, but still, it's just beautiful."

"I'd kiss you, but you have herring breath like my grandfather," I said. He exhaled heavily over my nose as payback.

I looked across the great room and noticed the *New York Times* strewn across the coffee table beside the sofa. When I walked over to tidy up, I saw Nolan curled up in the cushions, drooling onto one of my throw pillows.

Did Becca kick him out of bed? I hated to rouse him from what appeared to be a peaceful slumber, but the thought of his waking to a crowd encircling the couch made me cringe.

"Rise and shine; it's time to get up," I whispered, touching his shoulder as if I were waking my seven-year-old sons for school. Nolan's body remained still, but his eyes popped open and dashed around to survey his surroundings.

"Oh, shit," he grumbled. "I'm sorry. What time is it?"

"Nine."

"Okay. I'm rising and shining." He yawned and slowly sat up. "You need help with anything?"

"Nope, it's all under control."

"Of course it is," I heard him mutter, as he rubbed his eyes.

"Just get dressed before everyone comes in, okay?"

"Yes, ma'am." He saluted and rose to his feet. He began to walk away but after a few steps pivoted back to face me. "Jord?"

"Yeah?"

His eyes were fixed on the area rug by the couch. "You think," he whispered, "you know . . . they could actually, like, *fire* me?"

I puffed out my cheeks. *Absolutely*, I thought but didn't have the heart to verbalize. "Oh, Nol," I sighed. "What do I know? I'm not a corporate person. I've been a public defender my whole career. I have no idea how firm politics work."

"Yeah, that's sort of what I figured you'd say." In all the years I'd known him, never had he appeared so sullen.

Just as I was about to ask if he had plans to tell Becca about his work crisis, she walked into the kitchen.

"Nope! We're all good, Nol, but thanks for offering to help set up brunch! Now, go get dressed!" I declared way too loudly, and gave him a gentle nudge for good measure. I'd never been a good actress. I detested the weightiness of overcompensation.

Nolan blew his wife a kiss and scooted off down the hall. Her brow furrowed curiously, and I knew I needed a distraction before her mental calisthenics took over. I quickly walked over to the kitchen island and gracefully positioned my arms beside the fish platters like Vanna White on *Wheel of Fortune*. "Ta-da!" I sang, and shimmied my hands.

"You brought *Barney*!" she exclaimed. I knew Barney Greengrass was Becca's absolute favorite. With its no-frills fluorescent lighting, vinyl chairs, and uneven table legs, the century-old eatery reminded her of her grandparents, who practically subsisted on lox and sable and whose kitchen was nearly identical to the restaurant's decor. Plus, it had been the site of Becca's, Nolan's, Sal's, and my first double date, which was why I thought a little bit of Barney would add an extra-special touch to the weekend's final meal. She walked over and gave me a hug. "You're the best. And"—she began to sniff my clothes—"you smell . . ." Her face scrunched up. "Why do you smell like a doctor's office?"

I smiled. "Your nose really is incredible." Becca's sense of smell was on par with that of a police dog working in a narcotics unit. It was one of the long-term side effects of her chemo treatments as a kid and significantly more useful than the heightened sensitivity to cold in her extremities. "I was in the hospital this morning with Adam and Holly. Everything is fine; it was false labor. She and the baby are totally fine. I waited with them while she got checked out. Anyway"—I lowered my tone—"you're not going to believe what happened." I couldn't wait to tell her about my reconciliation with Holly, but just as I was about to dish, everyone started shuffling into the kitchen.

Seth, Adam, Holly, and Nolan filled their plates and found spots around the dining table, Seth and Nolan selecting seats at opposite ends. There was an undeniable chill between them, and I had noticed an avoidance of eye contact and of morning pleasantries while maneuvering around the buffet. At nine thirty, exactly thirty minutes before I knew she needed to leave, Lex finally entered the great room, her luggage in tow. She set the roller bag upright by the front door, and it promptly tipped over.

Seth leaped from his chair. "Hey, you need a hand?" he asked.

"No, thanks, I've got it," she said, righting the suitcase.

"Then let me make you a plate," he said, heading toward the stack of dishes on the counter.

"That's okay, I can do it," she said dismissively, and raised her hand to stop him.

Their interaction played out like the breakfast version of dinner theater, complete with a rapt audience seated at the farm table. Though I couldn't avert my eyes, watching them act like bickering lovers made me squirm. When I turned to grab a glass of juice, I noticed Nolan subtly shaking his head disapprovingly.

"So," Lex sighed, addressing the group at the table. "Looks like I'm gonna need to take an earlier flight today. I'm sorry, guys." She made an exaggerated frown. "Lots of stuff going on with the kids. I need to be with my family."

My eyes instinctively volleyed to Seth, who appeared crestfallen. "What time's the flight?" he asked.

"Two o'clock from LaGuardia."

Seth looked at his watch. "You'll need to leave *really* soon!" he said, his eyebrows arched in surprise.

"I know," she said coolly. "I called a car service."

Something about this dynamic reminded me of the college "walk of shame." I couldn't make sense of it.

"A car from here will cost you a fortune," Sal chimed in. "It's two and a half hours away."

"I'm driving you," Seth interrupted.

"No, no, it's fine." She scooped fruit salad onto her plate.

"I insist," he said firmly.

She tucked some hair behind her ear but didn't say a word. It seemed to me that Seth was trying to please her, and that Lex wanted nothing to do with the guy who'd been her sidekick all weekend.

With the clock ticking, I realized I wouldn't have time for the entirety of my surprise presentation. It was now or never. I clinked my juice glass to silence the room.

"I'd like to make an announcement," I said, standing at my seat. "I had hoped that we would all be able to watch *Becca Night Live* this morning—which I had transferred to DVD—but since some of you will need to leave shortly, I would like instead to present it as a gift to Becca to watch at home."

"That's awesome!" Becca exclaimed, inspecting the case I had just handed her.

"But wait, there's more," I said, and nodded to the rest. "Ready, guys?"

Seth, Lex, and Holly joined me at the head of the table.

"Well, Bec," I said, "we didn't have time to make a nine-ty-minute tape, but we wanted to do a little something in honor of the anniversary, as well as your upcoming fortieth birthday."

"So, naturally," Seth deadpanned, "we wrote a rap."

"A *rap?*" Becca asked in disbelief.

"We did it over email. It's pathetic. Keep your expectations very low," Holly warned. "Seriously, no one should record this. This is guaranteed blackmail material."

I surreptitiously tugged on my earlobe—the signal I had arranged with Sal to remind him to press PLAY on his phone's camera.

"Without further ado," I announced, "we'd like to present 'Becca's Rappin' Tribute.' One, two, three, go."

All:
Now here's a little ditty 'bout Becca Anne
Could she really be forty? I guess she can.
Then we got to show respect with a proper toast
To our bestie from way back, whom we love the most.

Lex:
Yes, I'm a girl from Queens, but I rap like a clown
Which you'll see in a minute when I break it down.
But for a dear friend, I'll gladly play the fool
'Cause I'm just so grateful for that day we met in school . . . school . . . school . . . school . . .

Seth:
On . . . the . . . playground of pre-K we did meet
Swingin' and a-slidin' and a-snackin' on treats.
I jumped in the sandbox, you did too,
Diggin' for treasures, gettin' sand in our shoes.

Jordana:

House went up for sale over there on your block
I moved right in, every day you did knock.
Just across the street from the time we were four
And it changed our lives forevermore.

Holly:

Chicken pox, driver's ed, sleepovers, and lice
We shared it all, even tonsillitis twice.
Then eighteen came—time to leave the 'hood
But with email and Greyhound, it was all good.

As an interlude, Seth stepped forward to perform a beatbox solo. Adam slapped his hands on the table to drum an accompanying beat.

Jordana:

Fast-forward a few and we're walkin' down the aisle
Bridesmaids with bouquets, toasts, and a smile.
Even at forty, we girls got game . . .

Seth:

And what about me?

All girls:

Good thing you don't look the same!

Lex:

Though I moved away, love you same as I did
In my mind, in my heart, just like when we were kids.

Holly:

No matter where we go or how old we grow
We all got your back, just sayin' so you know.

Seth:

Our skits still suck and our presentation's lackin'
But you're stuck with The Cast, can't ever send us packin'.

Jordana:
Congrats to Bec. We toast to you,
Our friend for life, and that is true.

Lex:
So put your hands in the air, get on your party suit . . .

Holly:
Keep on rockin' your life . . .

Seth:
Like this superdope tribute!

Becca, Nolan, Adam, and Sal erupted with applause as we stood there, frozen in position, our arms folded across our chests like we were Run DMC.

"Oh my God, that was *priceless!*" Becca panted. "My face hurts from laughing. *Please* tell me someone recorded that!"

Sal winked at her reassuringly. "I got it," he said.

I was thrilled. The weekend hadn't turned out as planned, but this was one of the moments I had really wanted to go smoothly, and it had.

Just as I was basking in my success, Nolan cleared his throat.

"So, um, *I* would like to make a presentation of my own to my wife, if you guys don't mind joining me over here." He got up from his seat and walked over to the iPad in the living room wall—a design element, like the one installed in the basement, that I had initially vetoed but ultimately conceded to my tech-savvy husband.

Oh no. Where is he going with this? A pit formed in my stomach, and I felt compelled to remind Nolan of his right to remain silent. Becca remained seated at the table, and the rest of the bunch slowly walked over behind her chair. Again, Nolan appeared to be one man against an army. Sal and I were the only ones to join him. He was, after all, a guest in our home. *Please prove me right, Nol. Please come through and be the man I know you are. Don't dig a deeper hole for yourself.*

"So, uh, last night, I had a hard time falling asleep," Nolan began. "I got to do a lot of thinking, and, uh, well, I made this."

He pointed to the iPad. "If you could all just gather around, I'd like to show it to you."

Slowly, everyone shuffled over. He tapped the tablet, and the movie began to play. At first, all we could see on the screen was Nolan holding a stack of papers in his hands and sitting on a kitchen counter barstool that he had clearly relocated in front of the iPad's camera. And then, like a blast, the volume kicked in.

"Good evening, and welcome to *Weekend Update*." His voiced boomed like a television news anchorman's in surround sound throughout every speaker in the house. I was impressed by his ability to navigate Sal's complicated audio system. "I'm your host, Mr. Subliminal, and here is today's top story."

I clenched my fists. *He's lost his mind.* I myself was no stranger to those 2:00 a.m. ideas that in the moment were brilliant pearls of wisdom but that after some sleep and caffeine always proved to be pure drivel. It took every ounce of restraint not to lurch myself past the group and bang a fist onto the screen to spare Nolan the humiliation. I had no idea why he was trying to mimic Mr. Subliminal—the *Saturday Night Live* character who mutters subliminal messages under his breath—but I did know that the weekend was nearly over and a peaceful farewell was so close I could nearly touch it.

"On Friday," Mr. Subliminal began, "Jordana and Sal *(check out his big zucchini)* graciously opened their lovely weekend retreat *(freakin' mansion)* to several guests in celebration of Becca *(totally hot)* Scardino."

"Ha." I giggled a bit too loudly. Silence was the only reaction from the rest of the group.

"Unfortunately, her husband *(selfish asshole)* was unable to attend the opening festivities due to work obligations *(ran home to his mommy)*. When he did arrive on Saturday *(looking like a cannoli on wheels)*, he managed to piss off several guests in a matter of hours. And now"—Mr. Subliminal put a finger to his ear—"breaking news from Nolan Scardino."

Nolan reached out of the camera's view, as if someone were handing him a report hot off the presses.

"It says here that Nolan *(repentant jackass)* would like to let his wife know how sorry he is for hurting her *(wishes he could take it all back)*."

I noticed Becca lower her head and look down at the floor. There was no doubt that publicizing a painful and private moment like this made her uncomfortable, even within her inner circle.

Mr. Subliminal continued: "Nolan wants Becca to know that he loves her unconditionally *(totally lost without her)*, and that no matter what she decides *(Dolly Parton or Kate Moss)*, she will always be a beauty. His beauty. Inside and out. Nothing has ever given him greater pride than being Becca's husband and Emma's dad *(true story)*."

My eyes welled, and I could hear someone else sniffle. I searched Becca's face for a reaction but found none. Her affect was flat, and her eyes remained fixed on the screen. If it had been possible to become invisible in that moment, I was sure she would have. I wondered if Nolan's mea culpa was too late.

"And that, America, is all the time we have tonight. On behalf of the entire team here at *Weekend Update*, this is Mr. Subliminal signing off: I. Am. Outta here!"

The screen faded to black. Just as I was about to applaud, a beautiful song I couldn't place—perhaps Coldplay or U2—began to play. For the next two minutes, we stood there at my dining table, watching a photo montage of Becca's life—pictures from their engagement, their wedding, birthday parties, vacations, Emma's birth, and just random everyday shots throughout the years that he must have downloaded onto the iPad. It was the type of thing you'd see at a bar mitzvah reception or at a fiftieth-anniversary party.

There was no hiding the tears streaming down my face. I grabbed a stack of napkins from the holder on the table and wiped my cheeks. As soon as I did, Holly and Lex held out their hands so I could pass one to each of them.

I looked over at Becca. She was biting her lip—a surefire sign she was suppressing a cry and trying to avoid a spectacle—and I saw her reach for Nolan's hand and their fingers interlace. *Oh, thank God!* Holly and I caught each other's eyes and smiled. She'd seen the hand-holding, too.

Becca pulled Nolan away into another room for several minutes, and when they returned, Holly raised a champagne flute of orange juice. "Everyone, I'd like to make a toast," she announced, dabbing the corner of her eye with the crumpled napkin in her free hand. We all grabbed our glasses from the table and held them in the air. "That was some audition tape, Nolan," she chuckled. "I'd like to officially congratulate and welcome you, the newest member of The Cast!"

"Hear, hear," I cheered.

"That was really great, Nolan," Sal said, patting his back.

"Yeah, really impressive work," Adam added.

Lex and Seth remained quiet.

"Oh, jeez, look at the time. I gotta go," Lex said, checking her watch.

A chorus of "aws" and "already?" soon followed.

"Actually, we're going to need to leave, too," Adam said. "I want to get her home to rest. I'm gonna take a quick shower and pack up."

As they went to their rooms, I thought this weekend may not have been the smoothest, but I hoped Becca could edit her memory to highlight the good and weed out the bad.

"Okay, Lex, car's all set," Seth said.

"You can't have her just yet," I said, reaching out to hug Lex goodbye. My comment was innocuous but intentional—a subtle dig and reminder to Seth that Lex was married.

As I stood in the doorway, watching Seth hold the passenger door open for her, Nolan jogged toward him and graciously stuck out his hand. I couldn't hear what was said, but the smiles and bro hug said enough.

I could feel someone approaching me from behind. Before I turned, I caught a whiff of orange scent, which instinctively released a small village of butterflies in my stomach. Only Adam could make hair gel that smelled like a Starburst candy seem sexy. *Wow, he's been using the same products for over two decades!* I thought.

"Hey," Adam said in his unique baritone. I spun around.

"Hey," I replied. I hadn't intended for it to sound as singsongy and flirtatious as it did.

"This weekend was great. Really cool. Thank you for having us. It meant a lot to Holly to be here. I actually had a way better time than I thought. That drum set is *sweet*! And I really appreciate your taking care of us this morning."

"Of course. Please. Don't even mention it."

"And by the way," he said, more hushed and breathy, "you look fantastic and, most important, very happy. Sal's a really good guy. You did okay, J."

I could feel my cheeks blush. "It was great to see you, too. I'm so glad you both came."

Adam smiled. "Well, thanks again," he said, and walked down the driveway to load the bakery truck with their bags, leaving Holly and me alone at the front door.

Holly laid her hand on my arm. "I hope we can see each other again soon. Maybe I'll call you for some parenting advice after the baby is born."

"I'm no expert, but I'm happy to talk. And I've got a ton of hand-me-downs in storage from my twins. If you'd like them, they're yours."

"Wow, I'd love that. Thank you!"

It wasn't lost on me that this was not the first time Holly would be taking my secondhand goods. However, the baby clothes were being passed along as a gift.

I waved from the porch until my guests were down the driveway and out of sight. When I returned inside, the house seemed quiet and cavernous. Becca was loading the dishwasher.

"Drop the knife, put your hands in the air, and step away from the sink!" I bellowed, in my best NYPD imitation.

Becca wiped her wet hands on her cargo shorts. "This weekend was incredible. I can't thank you enough for everything."

"It was totally my pleasure," I beamed.

She pulled out the elastic band from her hair, reset her ponytail, and twisted the band back in to secure it. "No, Jord. Really, *thank you*. I know this didn't turn out how you'd wanted, but I really do appreciate all the time and effort you put into this."

"How are you and Nolan?" I cut right to the chase.

She sighed. "The conversation isn't over. That video he made was charming, but it doesn't solve anything. It's a step, but you know as well as I do that ideas marinate in his head until the option to change a decision no longer exists. He gets these visions of how things are supposed to be and—" Becca stopped when her cell phone rang.

"Hello?" she answered. "Oh, hi, honey! Oh, sweetheart, I miss you, too. No, don't cry. Daddy and I will be home very soon. Just a few more hours!"

I could hear Emma's high-pitched voice on the other end: "Promise you'll never go away again!"

"Sweetheart, we'll be there soon. And I have a surprise for you when I get home!"

Becca ended the call and flashed the type of smile I knew would soon collapse into a frown and progress to tears. "I need to get home," she said. "I just want to be with her. I'm sorry. I have to go."

I wrapped her in a tight embrace. "It's just a blip," I whispered in her ear. "You're going to be fine."

My hands rose and fell on Becca's back with each heaving sob.

"How can I promise I won't ever go away," she said, "when I could die at any moment?"

"None of us can make that promise. We do the best we can to reassure our kids that they're safe and secure. But there are no guarantees. Not for anyone."

"I want a guarantee!" Becca wailed. She clutched her stomach and slowly slid down to the floor, pulling her knees to her chest. "Nolan would miss me, but he'd move on. But Emma? She doesn't have siblings. All she has is us. I hope one day she has friends like I have, but for now she's too little. Without me and Nolan and her grandparents, who does she really have?"

I understood the bond between an only child and her parents better than anybody, and the thought of losing my mother at a young age—or even now, as an adult—made my own chest tighten and my stomach turn. Other than the loss of a child or spouse, I could think of no greater nightmare than the death of my parents.

I slid down next to her and said, "Me. I love her like my own, Bec. As long as I'm around, she'll never be alone."

She shook her head and began to bawl again. "Goddammit, I worked too hard to get that child! I want to see her grow up. *I* want to be her guide. *I* want to teach her right from wrong and how to figure out what's important and what's bullshit. I don't want someone else having that privilege. *I* am her mom."

We sat there sniffling on the floor, squeezing each other tightly as if we were on the roof of a skyscraper with no guardrail.

"What if we learn after the surgery that my margins aren't clean and I end up needing chemo? That's going to completely undo Emma."

I pulled back. "Let's take things one step at a time. We're not there yet. But if that's where we end up, then maybe Nolan's job situation will be a blessing in disguise."

She wiped her runny nose with the back of her hand and looked at me, bewildered. "What are you talking about?"

"He'll have more time on his hands, you know?"

She stared at me. "No, I don't know. I haven't a clue."

An electric jolt ricocheted through me. *How could I have let that slip? I'm an idiot!* I need to save face but couldn't look her in the eye. "All I know is that he's questioning whether he wants to stay at the firm. That's all."

"'That's all'? What are you talking about? Why wouldn't . . ."

The door from the basement to the kitchen swung open. Nolan and Sal walked in, carrying large bowls of freshly picked vegetables from the garden.

"Why didn't either one of you tell me?" Becca asked, spite shooting back and forth between Nolan and me.

"Hey, what's going on?" he asked, stopping in his tracks.

"You had so much on your plate already, Bec," I blurted out, purposely beating Nolan to the punch and raising my palm in his direction. It was the same gesture I used during trials to discourage a client from potentially saying something he'd later regret.

"But he's my husband," she said, clearly miffed. "Shouldn't I know? Aren't we a *team*?"

I had to admit, I wasn't sure to whom that last sentiment was directed—Nolan or me.

"Bec," he began, "I'm sorry. I would have told you everything, but I didn't want to stress you out even more, given what's going on with the surgery stuff." He put down the bowl of cherry tomatoes and sugar snap peas he'd been cradling.

"But you told Jordana!" she fumed. Her eyes filled with a combination of frustration and fury, and her cheeks flushed. "I'm not a sick child, you know. I don't need to be coddled."

Nolan and I glanced at each other for guidance. He seemed frozen, his mouth agape. I decided to field this one. "We just thought we were helping—"

"*We?*" She pounced, her eyes bugging out from their sockets. "Are the two of you already in cahoots, deciding what I should and shouldn't be privy to? Determining what I can and cannot handle? Is this what it's gonna be like? Are you guys just rehearsing for when I'm gone?"

"Becca!" Nolan and I exclaimed at the same time.

"No!" he cried. "Not at all! Stop it!"

"Bite your tongue!" I blurted, and then found myself instinctively spitting on the floor, superstitiously shooing away the evil spirits, the way our mothers did when we were kids.

"Bec, I'll tell you everything," Nolan said. "I'll lay it all out right now. Gordon called me into—"

Becca straightened her posture, closed her eyes, and exhaled slowly. She seemed to have tuned him out. "Save it for the car. We need to leave now," she said with composure. "I just spoke with Emma. She's homesick." She paused a moment. "Well, actually, I think *I'm* homesick. I want to go get her."

I could see her lip quiver at the mere mention of Emma's name.

"Sure, okay." He nodded rapidly, like an obedient child wanting to please. "Gimme five minutes."

I got up and passed her a box of tissues. "Call me when you get home, okay?"

She nodded and blew her nose. "You don't need to protect me from everything, you know. I'm an adult. I appreciate where it's coming from, but it's okay to let me breathe."

I felt punched in the stomach. I would do anything for her, yet somehow I had become stifling, like an overbearing mother. She was rebelling against me and wanted her space. "You're right" was all I could say without either fighting back in my own defense or disintegrating into tears.

Nolan returned with their luggage, as well as the plastic bag of rice containing his cell phone. "I'm ready whenever you are," he said.

Becca walked over and sifted through her quilted duffel. "I got this shirt online, but it doesn't fit. If you want it, keep it; if not, bring it to yoga on Thursday and I'll return it."

Yoga! Thursday! My heart swelled. *She still wants to share clothes! She still wants to exercise together! She still loves me!*

"Thanks," I said, trying to play it cool. "Did you remember to pack the DVD?" *Shit. Was that too motherly?*

"I'd never forget it," she said, with a wink that I hoped meant, *Don't worry, we're all good* but feared meant, *Stop micromanaging me.* I couldn't tell.

Sal and I escorted them outside and watched from the front porch as Nolan held open the white Cadillac's passenger door. Becca sank into the beige leather seat and lowered her sunglasses over her face.

As the Caddy slowly descended the steep driveway and they waved goodbye, Sal wrapped an arm around my waist and I closed my eyes. I thought of Adam *daven*ing on the deck on Friday evening. I thought of my father, standing by his bedroom window with a prayer book in hand, twenty-five years earlier. And then, right there next to Sal, I began to whisper the Hebrew prayer for healing, along with Becca's name.

When I was finished and opened my eyes, Sal kissed my head. "Amen," he said softly. A lump formed in my throat. "Let's go home."

Part Two

Chapter 19: Holly

*A*dam claimed I was nesting. I disagreed. My sudden fixation with organizing the bakery's inventory was all about guilt. Our emergency room scare on July 4 made the baby's arrival seem imminent, and, as excited as I was to become a mother, I couldn't shake the fear that soon I'd be neglecting my first child. Adam laughed. He promised the store would be fine and that our staff would pitch in. He even vowed to maintain our mom-and-pop touch by continuing to make all the deliveries himself. "We're partners in everything, babe," he said reassuringly. "You're never flying solo."

For ten days after the reunion, Adam and I hung out in the back of our shop, counting wax paper rolls, checking the flour supply, and having all the *tachless* (Yiddish for *no-holds-barred*) talks about parenting and lifestyle we'd been too superstitious to explore prior to that point. Somehow, between reviewing Excel spreadsheets and signing paychecks, we resolved to accommodate my need to feel more modern without abandoning our religious observance. Then, on a Wednesday afternoon, just after I'd negotiated patronizing vegetarian restaurants in exchange for providing our offspring with a yeshiva education, my water broke on the floor of the stockroom.

Adam pulled the bakery truck up to the front of the store while our cashier escorted me outside. The rest of the staff crowded onto the sidewalk and waved goodbye as we turned away from the curb.

For most of the ride to Methodist Hospital, neither of us spoke. Car horns and the tinny melody of the Mister Softee truck were the only ambient sounds as we bobbed along Flatbush Avenue. But after the stars aligned and we found street parking a block from the hospital—which I told myself was a good omen—Adam shut off the engine and turned to me with a smile, his eyes wet and overflowing.

"I've made a lot of deliveries over the years," he sniffed, "but this is the one I'll remember for the rest of my life." We weren't even out of the truck, and already he'd dissolved into a sappy, nostalgic mush.

As a forty-year-old first-time mother who had difficulty getting pregnant, I just assumed giving birth would be hell. I'd heard countless war stories from trim twentysomethings about how painful it had been, so I figured it would be exponentially worse for a doughy geezer like me. Fortunately, I was wrong. My labor was so smooth and quick, Adam swore it was divine intervention. "I'm telling you, babe," he said, cradling our swaddled newborn in the recliner beside my hospital bed, "God's rewarding us for all those years of anguish."

Eight days later, at seven o'clock on a Thursday morning in the sanctuary of a synagogue in Crown Heights, our son was circumcised. I'd attended hundreds of brises over the years and had always been moved by witnessing our loved ones carry out a commandment and tradition that dated back to biblical times. But when our day arrived, I stood at the far end of the room with my spine pressed up against the emergency-exit door. The fact that a surgical procedure on a critical part of my son's anatomy was about to take place atop a pillow on my father's lap with a Manischewitz-soaked gauze pad to numb the pain was just too much to bear. Somehow, this whole scenario had been a perfectly acceptable and beautiful ritual when I was a guest; but now, as a parent, I thought it was absolutely barbaric.

Fortunately, the procedure was over in a matter of seconds and the sweet wine calmed the baby quickly. Adam made some passing remark about his boy being an alcoholic lightweight and then carefully lifted him from the pillow into the crook of his elbow.

Typically, this was the moment when the dad would introduce his son to the community and make a speech about the inspiration for the chosen name, but Adam fell silent. He stood at the microphone, staring down at our seven-pound, ten-ounce bundle, completely smitten and mesmerized, as if no one were watching and the two of them were alone on the living room couch. With his free index finger, Adam slowly traced the perimeter of the baby's face, starting at the top of his forehead, curving down around the outside of his cheek to the tip of his chin, and then up the other side. As I glanced around the room, I got the sense that everyone was as transfixed by my husband as he was by our son. Perhaps, had we been younger first-timers, or had this baby had been an addition to an existing gaggle of kids, someone in the crowd would have inelegantly cleared his throat, or sighed loudly, or made a show of pulling up his shirtsleeve to check the time. But the elephant in the room was alive and well, and no one dared interrupt the new dad who'd waited nearly twenty years to see this day.

Finally, Adam kissed our son's forehead and tilted his little face toward the crowd. *"Baruch Hashem,"* he said, his voice cracking as he leaned toward the mic and looked directly at me.

*"B'*Ezra*t Hashem,* with the help of God, this miraculous day has come. *B'*Ezra*t Hashem,* with the help of God, we have become parents to this beautiful baby. *B'*Ezra*t Hashem,* with the help of God, my incredible wife, the love of my life, my Holly, is healthy and had an uncomplicated delivery. *B'*Ezra*t Hashem,* with the help of God, may our son, Ezra, who is named in honor of my father, Edgar, always be watched over and blessed the way God has watched over and blessed us with Ezra to become a family."

Nose blowing ricocheted throughout the sanctuary. In all the years I had known Adam, never had I seen him so raw. He weathered our countless failed fertility attempts well, always maintaining his cool, rarely wallowing or growing frustrated. But that morning his elation was so evident that I couldn't help but wonder how much of his own suffering he had shielded in order to keep me afloat.

Later that night, after I put Ezra down in his bassinet, Becca called to check in and rehash the day. She mentioned how touching the ceremony had been and that the only thing that had kept her from completely losing it was the vision of my father, dressed in his blue-and-white seersucker suit, standing among a sea of men with prayer shawls over their heads.

"He looked like he'd come straight from a Martha's Vineyard cocktail party and arrived in a scene from *Fiddler on the Roof*," she chortled.

"Yep. That's my dad. He is who he is."

"So, uh, speaking of seersucker suits in Anatevka, where are you and Adam on that front? Is there a miniskirt in your future? Or are you going to keep things status quo?"

"Actually, we've made some headway," I said. "I've decided that wearing open-toed sandals and a denim skirt that ends just below my knee in no way changes my faith or desire to be an Orthodox Jew. I love keeping kosher. I love keeping Shabbos; it's twenty-five hours when I get to unplug and relax. I don't see that as restricting—it's a lifesaver. Could I change my mind and go back to wearing thick stockings and long sleeves in July, the way I have for the past twenty years? Sure. Could I take a Saturday afternoon trip to the mall like I did as a kid? Doubtful, but never say never. All I know is that right now, this is where my heart is and Adam is cool with it. I want to literally let my hair down. I need to feel that my son is entering a world steeped in culture and tradition but also progressive and tolerant of the way I was raised."

"So, what's the first step?"

"Realtor.com!"

My plan was simple: We'd find a home in the Five Towns area on Long Island's South Shore, because the community there had the exact religious-modern balance I was seeking and was an easy drive to the bakery in Brooklyn. We'd join one of the many local synagogues, and as soon as word spread of a new family in the 'hood, our social calendar would be filled with playdates, Shabbos dinners, and weekends lounging on neighbors' lawns. Then one day, maybe six months after our move, we'd be strolling along Central Avenue and notice an empty storefront for rent. Adam and I would instantly have the same thought—*next franchise location!*—and I'd call the broker on the spot. Our son and his friends (or perhaps our own future children, should we be so lucky) would grow up stealing cookies from the display case and then, as teenagers, work their first job as a cashier behind the counter. I had it all mapped out.

By mid-September, the dream was crystallizing. Our bid was accepted on a completely renovated splanch (split-level ranch) with a teak deck and a huge wooden swing, set on half an acre of flat land. We moved at the beginning of December, and on the first night of Hanukkah, just after we lit the candles in front of the dining room's bay window, I asked Adam to check on something in the basement. I followed behind as he descended the stairs, Ezra snoozing happily in my arms.

"You didn't!" Adam gasped, frozen at the base of the steps.

"I did!" I squealed, as softly as I could.

"No freakin' way!" He sat down on the cushioned stool, grabbed the sticks, and ran his finger over the cymbals.

"It's the same set Jordana has in her basement. I knew you loved it, so I asked for all the details, and she told me exactly what to order, including the champagne sparkle finish. A guy from the music store came over and set it up this morning when you were at work."

"But I thought we weren't doing gifts this year. Didn't we agree the house and all this new furniture was enough?"

I smiled and shrugged. "Oops."

He shook his head in mock disapproval and then ogled his shiny new toy.

"Well, I figured now that we have a basement of our own, it was time you got your drums. Maybe one day you'll teach Ezra. Maybe you'll even have your own band. The Fabulous Bakery Boys or something." I laughed, pleased by my own wit.

Adam rose from the stool and sauntered toward me, expertly twirling the sticks between his fingers like batons before gliding them into the back pockets of his pants, just as he did in high school. He looked just as cool as he did back then.

"How'd I get so lucky?" he whispered, just inches from my

face, and then kissed me softly on my mouth. I could feel my knees weaken as he lingered longer than expected.

We pulled apart and both looked down at our son.

"The Fabulous Bakery Boys," he said with a nod. "I like that."

Later that night, while checking email in bed, I noticed a message from Lex:

> *Hey, Hol! Hope your new place is fab and Adam loves your gift (Jordy told me about the surprise—awesome!). Did you give it to him yet? I'm sure it will rock his world (bad pun intended—couldn't resist). Wanted to let you know that I'll be in New York at the end of December and staying through New Year's. Jack's taking the kids to his parents' in Florida then, so I figured I'd come home for a visit. Any chance you're free? We'd love to see the baby (and, okay, maybe you guys too)! Let us know. XO*

We. Us. The use of plural pronouns to represent Seth and Lex's coupledom was still shocking to me. I prayed this relationship wouldn't be another failure for him, although in truth, Lex was the one with much more to lose.

Ever since she had returned from the reunion in the Berkshires and informed Jack that she was no longer in love with him, Lex's life had become headlining gossip of Chicago's North Shore. As a mother of three and *the* local source for personalized children's gifts, she was separated by far fewer than six degrees from the other youngish moms in the area who shopped at the Northbrook Court Mall, displayed an inordinate amount of oversize holiday paraphernalia on their front lawns, and stored their kids' ice hockey gear in the trunks of their luxury SUVs. Some women believed she dumped Jack for an East Coast lover she'd met online. Others swore she was having an affair with a beefcake physical therapist working across from the famed Beinlich's hamburger joint. The tales did possess a kernel of truth. Seth *was* from the East Coast, but, of course, he and Lex did *not* meet online. And he *did* explore a job prospect during one of his weekend visits, but his relationship with Lex was hardly an affair. According to both, it was love—genuine, unexpected, and unlike anything either had ever known.

Without question, it was her name and reputation that had been tarnished, not Jack's. She was deemed the ungrateful bitch, while he was the casualty of his wife's massive midlife crisis. Lex had seen the hot divorcees in their semi-sheer yoga outfits approach him at soccer games with those sympathetic, Botoxed eyes; one even pulled a lasagna out of the backseat of her convertible and told him she'd stop by later in the week for her "Le Cruise-it." Listening to a woman try to impress her husband with high-end French Le Creuset cookware incited laughter, not jealousy or regret. "Oh my God, Hol," she wrote in one of the lengthy emails I'd started receiving after her separation, "it was one of the funniest things I've ever seen. Jack doesn't know Tupperware from freakin' Teflon. I guarantee he thought this hussy wanted to take him on a cruise!"

To her credit, Lex never uttered a negative word in public about the father of her children. After all, she didn't hate him; she just didn't love him anymore. Other than her kids' well-being, the only thing she wanted was closure.

"I can't tell my kids that their father never felt like an equal partner," she told me when I called to thank her for the inordinate amount of personalized baby paraphernalia she sent for Ezra. "When I met Jack, he looked like what I thought I was supposed to marry. And for a long time, I assumed we were happy, and that this was how life was supposed to be. But then I spent time with Seth. He listened. We laughed. I realized that I'd forgotten what that felt like."

Looking at the *we* and *us* in Lex's email reminded me of that conversation. As weird and incestuous as their relationship felt to me, who was I to question?

Hi, Lex! Would love to see you guys! How about New Year's Day brunch at our house? I'll see if Bec and Jordana can come too. Love, H

Hosting this group as the first guests in my new home made me feel like I was starting the new year off on the right foot. Plus, if I needed to excuse myself for a short nap, they would certainly understand. They knew that Ezra's sleep schedule had been thrown by the move and how that translated to weeks of sleep deprivation for Adam and me. Jordana, who'd taken on a fairy godmother role and become my authority on all things Boy (she sent all of AJ and Matthew's hand-me-downs, which, in truth, was mutually beneficial because it provided her with the incomparable joy of de-cluttering her apartment), overnighted a costly essential-oil starter kit and insisted we diffuse lavender into the air to help Ezra sleep. She swore it worked on her boys, so I gave it a shot, but Adam abhorred the smell and immediately threw the whole contraption in the garbage.

By New Year's Eve, we were running on three weeks of erratic sleep and had become complete zombies. Like clockwork, Ezra cried out at 1:00 a.m., awakening Adam and me with his whimper on the baby monitor.

"Stay there," Adam said, reaching over from the other side of our bed, his fingertips gently grazing my arm.

"But you were on last night," I yawned. "That'll be two nights in a row, and you have a ton of deliveries in the morning."

"It's fine." He swung his legs over the side of the mattress and rubbed his eyes.

"Why don't you ask one of the guys at the store to cover for you? You know they'll do it for the boss. They won't say no to us."

"Absolutely not. It's a holiday. I can't ask them to work today." He yawned.

Seriously? Could I not have a better guy? I thought.

"Go back to sleep, babe. I've got to be at the store in a few hours anyway to load the truck. I'll be home before everyone gets here for brunch."

"You sure?" I reached over and put my hand on his back.

He nodded and adjusted his boxer shorts as he walked out of the room. I turned the monitor's volume down, and when I did, I could hear my aspiring-rock-star husband transform a famous Kansas tune into a lullaby and implore our son to rest his weary head and cry no more.

Ezra must have taken his father's musical plea to heart, because at seven thirty, the latest I had slept in weeks, I woke to the sound of the telephone, not the baby monitor.

"Hello?" I muttered into the landline's receiver on the fourth ring. My eyes were closed, still heavy from sleep.

I could hear some commotion in the background. "Hello?" a deep male voice said. "I'm looking for a Holly Marcus." I detected a hint of an Irish accent.

"This is Holly," I said, and when I did, sirens blared through the other end of the phone. My heart leaped. I shot out of bed and was down the hallway in Ezra's room a moment later to make sure he was in his crib. It wasn't that I expected my five-and-a-half-month-old to have pole-vaulted out, but still, I needed to make sure he was safe. He was, thank God, and sleeping soundly. I closed his door softly.

"Ma'am, this is Sargeant Carthy, of the Nineteenth Precinct in Manhattan. Your name is listed as an emergency contact on the cell phone of . . ."

Manhattan . . . Emergency contact . . . The only person who lives in Manhattan and with whom I'm close enough to be considered an emergency contact is Becca. Becca!

"Oh my God! Tell me Becca is okay, sir. Please, is she all right? What happened?"

"I'm sorry, ma'am, there's no Becca here. I'm with—"

"Rebecca! It's Rebecca! Her name is Rebecca Scardino! What happened?"

"Ma'am, please," the man said, sounding more stern. "I'm here with your husband. Adam." He paused. "There's been an accident. . . ."

And with that, I fell to my knees and lost control of my bladder on the newly carpeted hallway of our second floor.

Chapter 20: Jordana

*T*he call came in at a quarter to eight.

"Jordana, I'm sorry to wake you. I woke you, didn't I? Shoot . . ." Holly sounded flustered and winded. Ezra was wailing in the background.

"Hey," I said groggily, squinting to check the clock on my nightstand. While Holly and I had grown close, we still hadn't quite reached the intimacy of an early-morning phone conversation. "Everything all right?"

"I tried Becca, but she didn't pick up. Oy, please stop crying, Ezzie," she begged.

"Sounds like you've got your hands full over there."

"We're going to take a ride in the car, yes we are!" she said in a voice at least an octave higher than her normal one. "We're gonna go see Daddy! That's right. Can you get your arm in that sleeve, Ezzie? That's it. Good job! You're such a big boy!"

I heard the jingle of keys, a few footsteps, and then a mumbled "Dammit!"

"Hol, you okay?" I couldn't decipher whether this was an actual emergency or just an overwhelmed new mom trying to run an errand. Either way, it sounded like a shit show.

"You sure you don't want to call me back?" I glanced across the bed to see if Sal was still asleep. He was.

"Listen," she panted. "Adam was in an accident while making deliveries on the Upper East Side this morning."

"What?" I gasped, my torso rocketing up. "What happened?"

"I just got a call from the police. I don't have details. The cop didn't say anything other than that Adam was asking to see me and that he was at 72nd Street and Third Avenue and . . . Seriously? How am I supposed to get this infant seat belt over a puffy snow-suit? How do you loosen the strap on this thing? Ugh!"

I pulled my pajamas off, tossed them into the laundry basket, and headed over to my closet to get dressed. "Holly, what can I do to support you?" I'd recently picked up this phrase in my Medita-tion & Mindfulness class and had been trying to incorporate it into my daily lingo; I was pleased to see it roll off my tongue without conscious effort.

"Can you get over there and stay with Adam until I arrive?"

Now, there's *a request I've never gotten before.* "Of course I will."

I heard her start the car's ignition. "I don't know how long it will take me to get there; I can't imagine there's much traffic this early on New Year's Day, but still, it'll be at least a half-hour from my house . . . Shit!"

"Take a deep breath," I said calmly. "Try to relax and stay focused. You have precious cargo in that car. This will all be fine. I'm running out the door right now."

I scribbled a Post-It note for Sal and attached it to the cover of the toilet seat—his first stop every morning—and headed outside. It was a gray, gloomy morning with a slight drizzle of rain that would have turned to snow had it been a few degrees cooler. It was a perfect morning to read the paper in bed with a mug of warm tea nearby. Instead, I stretched my legs and began to jog the four long avenue blocks toward 72nd and Third. As I passed Madison and then Park, I willed myself to ignore the sirens in the distance. *It's just background noise, the daily soundtrack of the city.* But when the whirrs grew louder and closer, I quickened my pace. By the time I passed Lexington, I saw fire trucks, ambulances, police cars, and two cops rerouting traffic. Panic and adrenaline shot through me.

"Adam!" I screamed, my legs transitioning from a jog to an all-out sprint. As I neared the scene, the first thing I noticed was buttercream smeared across 72nd Street. Dented white cake boxes with squished New Year's–themed pastries littered the crosswalk, and shards of glass decorated the asphalt like large sprinkles. A crowd of coffee-toting, sweatpant-clad locals had already formed to gawk. Their gaping mouths turned my stomach.

"Adam!" I shouted again, elbowing my way through the mob. When I reached the yellow caution tape and took in the sight, I grew light-headed.

"Oh my God," I cried, instinctively shielding my eyes from what they had already seen. The bakery truck had plowed onto the sidewalk, flipped upside down, and missed the windows of the Citibank on the corner by about a foot. The van's roof was crushed, its windshield and windows shattered, and, as far as I could tell, there were no airbags to speak of. And yet, despite the horror, the sweet aroma of freshly baked cupcakes permeated the air, making the site smell like a celebration.

"Ma'am, you can't come back here," an officer said, one hand on his hip holster, the other in front of my face as I ducked beneath the yellow caution tape.

"Sir, that's my friend's truck. You must let me see him."

"Jaaaay?" I heard Adam moan. I turned and saw him lying on the ground, covered in blood, two paramedics by his side.

"Please," I begged the officer.

"Jaaaay?" Adam groaned again.

"All right, go ahead," the officer said, his tone softening.

I ran over and crouched down on the concrete near Adam's head—close enough to talk, but distant enough to give the EMTs space to work. Immediately, I could see that his nose was broken and one of his teeth was lying on the sidewalk beside my sneaker. I felt queasy.

"Oh my God, Adam. Are you okay?" I inched closer to hold his hand but then pulled away before he realized. I wasn't sure how he'd react to touching a woman other than Holly or a paramedic. "What happened?"

"I think I fell asleep," he said, his voice shaky. "One minute I was driving, and then, next thing I knew, I was upside down. Guess I shouldn't have thrown out that oil diffuser you sent us."

He managed a weak smile, which revealed he had lost more than just that one tooth.

"I'm gonna need you to move out of the way, ma'am," a paramedic said, wheeling over a stretcher.

I stood back and tightened my wool coat around me like a security blanket. Adam cringed as they lifted him off the ground. His face was scratched and bloodied, his white button-down shirt and black pants literally ripped to shreds. It was an absolute miracle he hadn't hit another car or a pedestrian.

"Are you in a lot of pain?" Surely an idiotic question, but I didn't know what else to say.

He closed his eyes and grimaced. "Not my best day. And I'm really cold."

I immediately unzipped my coat and threw it over him.

"Please remove your jacket, ma'am," one of the medics said.

I obeyed and walked beside the stretcher as they rolled him toward the back of the ambulance. Adam began to shiver, and I recalled Holly's request that I stay with him until she arrived. "Can I ride inside with him?" I asked one of the medics.

"That's up to the patient."

Adam nodded his permission.

The EMT motioned for me to climb aboard, and I slid in close to Adam's head. As we headed toward Mount Sinai Hospital, Adam looked paler. "I want to talk to Holly," he said, shaking.

"She's on her way to the city now. You'll see her soon."

"No," he chattered. "I want to talk to her *now*."

I glanced at the medics. "May I call his wife?"

They looked at Adam, then intently at each other, and then one of them said, "Sure, go ahead." I wasn't familiar with EMT protocol or the rules in the back of an ambulance, but I was grateful these two were so accommodating.

I whipped out my cell phone and pressed it to Adam's ear.

"Babe?" he said barely audibly. "You there?"

"She can hear you," I reassured him. "Just talk."

"Babe, I love you. And Ezra. I love you both so much. . . ." His lips turned downward into a severe frown; it seemed he either had tasted something awful or was stifling a cry.

I kept the phone against his ear in case he had more to say, but when blood suddenly spurted from his mouth and the shaking turned to convulsions, I pulled away and looked out the ambulance window as the medics came to his aid. I couldn't bear to watch. Hearing the sounds—the urgency in their voices, the banging of Adam's body against metal, the beeping of machines—was more than enough.

The bodegas, florists, and pharmacies that dotted the streets of the upper Nineties blended like a multicolor brushstroke of paint as we whizzed up Madison Avenue. Had it been possible to safely break out the ambulance doors, the way I leaped off the windowsill in Becca's hospital room when we were kids, I would have. But I was stuck—confined, once again, to a small space brimming with the noises, smells, and fluids of a loved one's medical trauma. I looked down at the phone, suddenly hefty in my hand, and I, too, began to tremble.

Chapter 21: Becca

When I arrived at the hospital, Jordana was sitting at a cafeteria table, staring blankly into the distance, her foot gently rocking Ezra's stroller back and forth.

"Where's Holly?" I asked, unwrapping my scarf and draping it over the back of a plastic chair. I sat down and peeked into the carriage, where Ezra was snoozing away.

"Upstairs with the doctors," Jordana replied flatly. She looked ashen; her coat was still zipped to her chin.

"How's Adam?"

She shrugged.

I wasn't sure Jordana had blinked since I'd arrived.

"I think we should sit with her, don't you? I'll call Lex and Seth and see if they can pick up the baby."

She snapped back to life. "Oh, no, no. First of all, I already texted them about the accident. And second, you know full well that you're the last person who should be hanging around a hospital in the dead of winter. It's flu season, and God knows what other germs are flying around. With your crap immune system and this six-month-old, the two of you should hightail it out of here."

Jordana was right, of course. I tended to pick up viruses as often as she picked up organic produce, yet my blood percolated the way it always did whenever she treated me like I was still a sick child. "I can make my own decisions," I said firmly. I could feel my face flush as I cleared my throat. "And I think I've got a pretty decent track record choosing what's right for my body."

"Oh, Bec! I'm so sorry! I wasn't trying to allude to . . . I didn't mean to bring up . . ." She covered her face with her hands like a little girl playing hide-and-seek and began to sob.

I sighed and slid my chair over to the other side of the table. "Shh, it's okay," I said softly, wrapping my arm around her back. *I was too harsh*, I thought. I knew the ferocity with which she protected me was rooted in love. And I also understood her well enough to know that this meltdown had to do with Adam's accident, not my health or decision-making ability. "Long morning, huh?"

She nodded. "And it's only nine fifteen." Jordana reached for a napkin from the small dispenser on the table and blew her nose. "It was awful," she whispered, dabbing her nostrils.

"I'm sure." I rubbed her back and waited for her to elaborate.

"Bec?" She looked at me, her eyes wide, wet, and filled with fright.

"Yes?"

"I fucked up," she said, barely audibly.

My brows furrowed in surprise. Jordana rarely cursed. "You? I sincerely doubt it."

"No, I'm serious."

"I'm sure whatever it is, it's not nearly as bad as you think. What happened?"

"If I tell you, you have to promise—I mean *really* promise—not to tell Holly," she implored.

Jordana was a master of concocting a good defense and never intentionally excluded anyone from anything, ever. The absence of the former and a plea for the latter concerned me. My imagination cartwheeled: *She kissed Adam in the ambulance. She professed her love to Adam. Adam professed his love to her.*

"I promise," I said, though pledging to withhold information from Holly pained me.

"I lied," she winced, her face creasing all over as if it physically hurt to say the words.

"What are you talking about?"

"In the ambulance. I lied. Adam asked to speak with Holly

when we were in the ambulance. I punched her number into my keypad and put the phone against his ear and I told him she was listening, but I didn't actually *make* the call. I think he thought he was dying and wanted to say goodbye or something. I mean, he was definitely beaten up and in pain, but just a few minutes earlier he was joking about the essential oils I'd sent to help Ezra sleep, so I figured, how bad could he be if he was kibitzing, you know?"

"You *lied* to him when he was in that condition? Why?"

"She was driving with the baby! If she heard how awful he sounded and knew how bad the accident was and that he was calling from the back of an ambulance, she would have flipped out. I didn't want her to be distracted on the road. But then . . ." Jordana welled up and reached for the napkin dispenser again. "Then he started projectile-vomiting blood and things got crazy. Had I known those might have been his last words . . ."

"I'm sure those weren't his last words. I mean, it sounds like it was a terrible accident, but he's strong. He'll pull through."

"Bec, promise you won't say anything."

"I won't, but how can you keep this from her? You're the most honest person I know!"

"It'll break her. I'd rather live with it and feel like crap than cause her any pain. Plus, she'll hate me all over again. I don't want to lose her a second time."

Before I had a chance to respond, Jordana's phone vibrated on the table and she grabbed it urgently with both hands. "Hello? Yes, of course. Vanilla yogurt and a bottle of water. Got it. I'll be right up. Becca's here. She'll take Ezra. Okay. See you in a sec."

Jordana stood and slipped the phone into her pocket. "Adam's in surgery," she said matter-of-factly. "Holly's in the waiting room. She hasn't eaten anything today, so I'm gonna grab her a bite and bring it upstairs. She wants the baby out of the hospital. You need to take him."

Clearly, the decision to leave the hospital had been made for me. I'd wanted to stay with Holly, but if this was the best way to lighten her load, so be it; I was there to help. I wheeled him out of the hospital, hailed a cab, and rolled him through the doorway of our apartment twenty minutes later.

"Hey! Easy E! What's up, my man?" Nolan beamed and bent over to tickle Ezra's belly. "It's about time we got some more testosterone around this place. Sheesh!" Ezra kicked his legs gleefully as Nolan extricated him from the carriage. "So, how bad was the fender-bender? You think they'll discharge him soon?"

"Actually, Adam's in surgery; turns out the accident was a bigger deal than Jordana let on in her text. I haven't even spoken with Holly. I can't believe I didn't pick up her call this morning. I feel terrible."

At 7:50 a.m., I'd heard the phone ring and seen Holly's number pop up on the caller ID but had been too tired to answer. *Too tired!* All those times I'd leaned on her for support, and there she was, reaching out in the midst of a crisis, and I'd let it go to voice mail. *Fucking voice mail!* I'd assumed she was calling about some trivial matter related to the brunch, like whether I thought anyone would be offended if she set the table with plastic plates, or if I could pick up some flowers en route to her house. *She can leave a message*, I told myself. But she left none. I learned of the accident an hour later via an all-caps text from Jordana telling me to meet her in Mount Sinai's cafeteria.

"Don't beat yourself up. It's New Year's Day; most people sleep in," Nolan said, nuzzling Ezra against the threadbare Columbia Law School T-shirt he'd slept in. They were looking out the living room window, watching the buses and taxis go by on the street below.

Though barely six months old, Ezra had already made his mark. Not only had he turned my dear friends into parents, but he'd mended Holly and Adam's relationship with Jordana, formed an inexplicable bond with my husband, and provided me with unexpected clarity in a time of need. If ever the perfect moniker had been bestowed upon a child, *Ezra* and *help* were an ideal match.

For me, that transformative moment came at Ezra's bris as I watched Holly's dad and noticed how out of place he seemed in his seersucker suit and large satin yarmulke sitting awkwardly high atop his bald spot. I wondered if, when he beheld the sea of black hats flooding the pews, he thought back to the day he decided to send his daughter on a teen tour of Israel, and how that single parenting choice shifted the entire course of her life, as well as the future of his family. I marveled at the interminable power of one decision.

Ezra's circumcision took place just days before my surgery, and I still hadn't reached a verdict on whether to cancel the reconstruction portion of the operation. After the Berkshires reunion, I read every study I could get my hands on. I spoke with any former patient willing to share her mastectomy experience. Nolan and I even met with a psychologist at the hospital who specialized in the long-term issues unique to pediatric-cancer survivors and their families. But standing in that crowded Brooklyn synagogue and witnessing the monumental impact one parental choice could have on the rest of a child's life, it all crystallized. I knew exactly what I needed to do.

My first memory postsurgery was in the recovery room. My parents and Nolan were there, and Mom held a cell phone to my ear so that Emma could hear directly from the source that her mother was okay. My father stood by the side of the stretcher, singing "You Are So Beautiful," and I knew even then, in my partially anesthetized state, that he was doing it more as a reminder to Nolan than as a message for me.

When the nurse came by the next day to see how I was healing, I told Nolan I'd understand if he wanted to take that time to grab a bite from the coffee shop in the lobby. The decision to opt out of reconstruction was not an easy one. And it was not a joint decision; it was mine alone. I had plenty of sounding boards, but no one wanted to sway me either way, because there was no correct answer. In the end, my mind, my gut and my heart all conveyed the same message: *Be you. Emma is watching. If you're proud and secure, she'll be proud and secure, and it will serve as a lesson for the rest of her life.*

Those were the words I repeated to myself when the plastic surgeon stopped by my curtained-off pre-op room minutes before the surgery. I was lying on a gurney in a hospital gown and cap, I had signed all the documents, my IV line had been inserted, and I was simply waiting to be wheeled down the hall. "It's not too late for me to scrub in," he said, and then asked if I felt confident with my decision. "I'm all set, thank you," I heard myself say between discordant heartbeats pounding in my ears. "Well, okay, then," he said with a shrug. "Good luck to you."

Less than twenty-four hours later, the nurse's slow and deliberate removal of every strip of gauze on my chest felt like a drum roll that went on for too long before a circus act. "I'm not leaving," Nolan said, and clenched my hand as I sat upright in the hospital bed.

When the last piece was lifted, I squeezed my eyes shut. I couldn't watch Nolan's reaction. I didn't want to see him instinctively cringe and then try to cover up the fact that he thought his wife was hideous, or that he should have fought harder to change my mind. I steeled myself. I would survive, with or without his desire for me.

"Bec, it looks awesome!" he said. He sounded genuine, but I was reluctant to peek. "Really, they did a great job! Take a look."

Slowly, I lifted my lids. The very first thing I saw was my husband's face. He looked utterly relieved. The nurse passed him a hand mirror to hold in front of me. There were two pencil-thin horizontal lines running from under each armpit, across my chest and stopping within an inch of each other at my breastbone. The whole thing looked clean and neat, not scary. As he held the mirror so I could examine my new appearance, he leaned down and kissed my head. "My beautiful wife," he said softly.

Through our health insurance plan, I was entitled to regular post-op home visits by a health aide. But, as it turned out, there was barely a need. Nolan insisted on being the one to clean my incision, change my gauze, and help me shower and dress. He even made an Excel spreadsheet to record everything from my temperature to what I ate to who sent which gifts. He was so on top of my care, the nurse half-jokingly asked if he'd consider working for her company.

I'm not sure exactly when it happened, but sometime between our heated Scrabble games and eating ice cream straight from the container in bed while binge-watching Netflix, I felt closer to Nolan than I ever had in our eleven years of marriage. We had certainly cleared other hurdles together, but there, with the tubes and his magic-marker charts measuring my fluid output and the stack of celebrity gossip magazines on the nightstand and the consecutive days of wearing only pajamas and not bothering to check his work messages even once, I felt he had truly become a part of me. He finally got it.

A week after the surgery, I received the all-clear from my doctor—clean margins, no sign of cancer, no need for chemo. I was done. I immediately called my parents and then sent a group text to the cast. Within a half-hour, I received four tear-filled telephone calls. Jordana's, naturally, was the first.

When I picked up Emma that afternoon from her bus stop, I debated whether to share the good news. I didn't want to harp on my health, but she had recently witnessed her mother undergo a drastic physical transformation. Hearing the positive outcome, I supposed, could provide some closure.

"Remember what I told you the night before my operation, honey, about the reason I needed to have it?" I asked, as we headed down the sidewalk to our building.

She nodded. "You said you did it so you could stay a healthy and strong mommy."

"That's exactly right. And guess what? Today the doctor told me I'm as strong as ever."

She smiled and slipped her delicate hand in mine. "Well, *I* could have told you *that*."

Nolan returned to work and said it felt as if he were starting from scratch. Colleagues were cordial but not warm, the new case assignments were unfamiliar, and Ilene Weston's watchful eyes made it seem even his trips to the bathroom were under scrutiny. Everyone from support staff to senior partners appeared to know about Nolan's gaffe and that the only reason he was still employed was because Gordon had a soft spot for him. Fortunately, Tennessee Morse's article got held up in the fact-checking stage, so it never ran, but the firm lost Thibault as a client. There were still rumblings about a lawsuit, but nothing had been filed and Nolan guessed it would ultimately fizzle out because Thibault wouldn't want the negative press that accompanied a suit. Despite the second chance, Nolan felt like a caged hamster and soured on firm life. The passion was gone. After a three-hour brainstorming lunch with an old law school professor, he was offered an adjunct position at Columbia—a bucket-list item he always thought he'd save for retirement but realized he was ready to tackle at forty instead. He resigned from Gordon, Michaelson & Stewart the next day.

In November, during the hiatus between his jobs, we went shopping for boobs. I had trouble saying the word *prosthetic*; it was too scientific, too cold, and, given that "artificial" was its official definition, I had no interest in using it to describe any part of my being. Jordana wanted to go and emailed a list of dates and times she was free, but I thought it might be more meaningful to share the experience with my husband.

"Hell yeah, I'm game," he said, rubbing his hands together when I proposed the idea. "Is there gonna be a runway? Will you get angel wings and stilettos?"

My, how far we've come, I thought, and called for an appointment.

When we arrived at the store a few days later, I knew even before entering that it had been a mistake to invite Nolan. The shop was microscopic (its address was 94 1/2, as if the space weren't quite deserving of a whole number) and behind the cloudy front window was a headless mannequin in an oversize, oxidized beige bra. On the floor beside the mannequin's amputated feet sat a floppy beach hat—the type I'd seen in photos of my grandmother on Coney Island circa 1962—and in the corner of the display, atop a lace-covered barstool, was a rusted watering can holding an arrangement of polyester flowers. This place screamed vintage thrift shop (but hardly in a hipster-cool way) and couldn't have been further from our baseless expectation of a candy-scented lingerie boutique.

I should have done a dry run before I schlepped him here, I thought, as I reached for the doorknob. A long string of bells dangling from the handle jingled as we entered.

"I'm sorry, dear, we're closed to the public right now; it's appointment-only," said a salt-and-pepper-haired woman behind a cluttered desk. The chain on her reading glasses swung beneath her chin.

"Actually, we're here for the one o'clock appointment," I said.

"Oh?" she asked dubiously, and slowly scanned her finger down a spiral ledger, where I saw my name neatly written in cursive. "Are you meeting Rebecca Scardino? Is she your mother?"

Nolan dug his hands into his pockets. I could feel the optimism hiss out of him like a punctured tire.

"*I'm* Rebecca," I smiled. "The appointment is for me."

The woman paused, as if her mind needed time to catch up to her ears, and quickly scanned my chest. "Oh, I'm sorry, dear; I was expecting . . ." She rose from her chair and came around the desk to extend her hand. "Oh, I don't know what I was expecting. Please pardon me. I'm Mary Catherine, but you can call me MC. It's lovely to meet you."

MC flipped the sign on the door so CLOSED faced out, and directed us to a narrow hallway. "Why don't you two get settled in there?" she said, pointing to a burgundy batik tapestry. Between the single metal folding chair and a stack of plastic storage boxes piled high on the floor, the dressing room could barely fit one person, let alone two. "I'll go grab some bras and breast forms for you to try. Size-wise, hmm, I'm guessing you're probably about a thirty-two around? Maybe thirty-three? Am I right?"

I nodded.

"And what did you have in mind for the cup, dear? Same as you were? Different?"

"Nothing crazy. Just natural. On the smaller side, I guess."

"Aw, come on Bec. Don't be boring." Nolan nudged me; a mischievous grin spread across his face, and he danced his eyebrows up and down. MC noticed. I blushed.

"I'll wait in the hall, and when you're ready, come out and show me what you've got. Okay?" He stepped outside the curtain and leaned his back against the wall. Above him was a shelf of wigged Styrofoam heads.

For the next two hours, I slid a smorgasbord of triangular-shaped silicone breast forms into the pockets of different bras. I tested large cups and small cups in strapless, demi, and full-coverage styles. I compared how each permutation looked beneath crew necks, V-necks, turtlenecks, tank tops, and halters. By the end, I was drained and Nolan appeared so turned-off and bored, I doubted if he would ever look at women the same way again.

"Okay, so, what'll it be?" MC asked, clipboard in hand. "Have you two made a decision? Remember, insurance covers some of this stuff, but not everything."

"I think we're ready. Right, Bec?" Nolan yawned.

"Yes. I'll take one set of the A forms and a few of those bras; I guess a couple of black, a neutral, and—"

"Wait, what about the C's?" Nolan interjected. "Didn't we like those?"

We? I thought. I saw MC look away. "No," I said softly. "I think I just want the A's. They were the most comfortable."

Nolan adjusted his posture and muttered, "Yeah, because they're practically nonexistent."

My stomach flipped. "It's more than I have now, and I thought you didn't care."

Nolan shook his head in disbelief.

"What?" I asked, pretzelling my arms across my chest.

"Nothing." He snickered.

"*What?*" I was getting annoyed.

"I'll just let you two chat for a moment," MC said, turning to walk away. "I'm gonna go check on something in the stock room." She couldn't disappear fast enough.

Nolan took a moment to gather himself. "You wanted me here for my opinion—as long as I agreed with you. You know, Bec, I thought you'd come through with this part. I got excited when you wanted me to come to this appointment because I assumed you were going to surprise me. I figured you'd give in on this because you won on the surgery."

Fire shot through me. "I *won?*" I whisper-screamed. "Are you *kidding?* The surgery wasn't a *negotiation.* It wasn't a *game.* This is my *body.* My *life.* Don't you *get* that?"

He raised his palms in the air like he was surrendering and forced a smile. "Okay, okay, it's fine. Calm down. I still love you. Get the stupid A cups. It doesn't matter."

Calm down? Fuck you. You started this. "It *does* matter, because you really *do* care."

"Forget it, Bec. I'm over it!" He sounded like a drug addict avowing cleanliness while a dime bag protruded visibly from his pocket.

I stared at him skeptically. Surely he was just a moment away from reaching out his arms, pulling me close, and offering some sort of heartfelt mea culpa. Instead, we stood beside that batik curtain in an unnaturally long John Wayne showdown, until finally, a tear busted loose out of the corner of my eye.

"You know," I said softly, wiping the tear and trying to control the lump that had formed in my throat, "last summer, after you were so amazing with my recovery, I decided to write off your initial freak-out as a case of referred pain. I told myself that your insensitivity was just masking your real fear that I would die. I gave you the benefit of the doubt. But now I see I was wrong. You really *do* give a shit how I look, don't you?"

Nolan opened his mouth to speak, but right then, MC returned and informed us that her next appointment would be arriving shortly. She was all smiles and feigned obliviousness, but there was no way she hadn't overheard us even in the farthest corner of that store. We left with the A cups and a handful of bras, and even though I believed I looked better than I ever had with my natural anatomy, I feared every time I wore those silicone forms I'd feel disappointment and resentment—my own toward Nolan, and his toward me. *Maybe the real prosthetic is Nolan*, I thought, *not the artificial boobs.*

In the days and weeks that followed, I lay in bed at night with a single phrase looping in my head: *First time, shame on him; second time, shame on me.* After his stint as Florence Nightingale, I thought we'd moved on to a stronger, better place, but apparently the tension had merely been lying dormant. Soon, I grew increasingly irritated by the most mundane things: his inability to correctly sort garbage into the proper recycling bins; buying moldy produce; I even threw an empty cardboard toilet paper tube at his head because he neglected to replenish the dispenser with a new roll. He thought I was being playful. I wasn't. He was bringing out the worst in me, and I hated it.

On New Year's Eve, Emma slept at my parents' so Nolan and I could have a date night, but neither of us had put any advance thought into the evening. So, since every restaurant was booked and the movie we wanted to see was sold out, we stayed home. I made grilled cheese sandwiches and heated up a can of tomato soup for dinner. He ate on a snack table beside his computer; I dined alone in the kitchen. Happy New Year!

By nine o'clock I was in bed, and by ten I was fast asleep. When I woke at 1:00 a.m. to pee, I found Nolan zonked on the couch beside a burgeoning laundry basket. I stood in the hallway for several minutes staring at my husband, his left limbs hanging off the cushions, *TIME* magazine's Person of the Year issue spread across his belly. I couldn't help but grin. I loved that he still mailed in the little postcard to renew his annual subscription.

The ebullient voices of drunken revelers carried up fourteen flights from the street, and I walked over to my bedroom window to watch. I loved New York at night—dark yet illuminated, anonymous but visible. There were couples holding hands, teenagers walking in packs, two guys making out on a bench, and a gaggle of twentysomething women smoking outside a corner bar. Life was moving. Time was passing.

Had it not been January 1, I wouldn't have cared that the night was a dud. I wouldn't have cared that he was working late, or that he'd fallen asleep without kissing me at midnight, or that a pile of his underwear was still sitting on the coffee table three days after he'd promised to put it away. But this was the holiday of resolutions—of forgiveness, new chapters, and clean slates. It had been a tough year, and if this was how we were going to start anew, the future didn't look promising.

I was willing to try, though. I was willing to convince myself, again, that there was a legitimate reason for our friction. Surely, it was a numbers game; two people who saw eye to eye 99 percent of the time were bound to go to war at some point in their relationship. But what do you do when that 1 percent issue is weighty enough to balance (or possibly tip) the scales? Marriages undoubtedly ebbed and flowed. Ours still had plenty of love, but the chemistry had been altered. Irrevocably damaged? I couldn't say for sure. All I knew was that we had reached a bifurcation; a crossroads we would one day point to as either the dissolution, or cementing, of our union. I stared out that window for hours, seeking inspiration and answers, until finally, around 5:00 a.m., I crawled back into bed and fell asleep.

"So, I'm assuming brunch at Holly's today is canceled, huh?" Nolan said, lying on the living room floor beside Ezra, who was attempting to eat his fist. "You think he's hungry?"

"Maybe. I'll check the diaper bag." I sifted through the various storage compartments and found plenty of toys and an empty bottle but no food. "I'm going to call Holly and ask if I should run to Duane Reade and pick up some formula."

I dialed Holly's number; Jordana picked up on the first ring. "Hey," she whispered.

"Hey. What's the latest?" I reflexively breathed back.

"Nothing yet. He's still in surgery."

"Okay. Listen, I think the baby's getting hungry. I'm happy to buy stuff, just don't know what brand of formula she uses." The truth was, I didn't even know if she used formula. I had been so determined not to whine about my marriage during the most joyous time in her life that I'd recently withdrawn and resorted to texts more than phone calls.

I heard Jordana repeat my question to Holly. "Can you bring him here? She'd prefer to breastfeed and doesn't want to leave the waiting room. Sorry to make you schlep back."

Another cab ride and twenty minutes later, Ezra was snacking comfortably beneath an ikat-patterned nursing shawl while Holly, Jordana, and I passed the time gossiping about Seth and Lex's relationship. We called it Slex Talk, and in that moment, our under-over predictions about the longevity of their relationship—all doubtful, all still repulsed, all fearful it was just a matter of time before Seth got crushed, but all in agreement to remain supportive—provided the perfect distraction.

Just as Holly transferred Ezra to her shoulder to pat out a burp, two men in green surgical scrubs entered the room, masks still covering their noses and mouths so that only their eyes were exposed. Jordana and Holly sat up, hopeful and eager, but I didn't. I knew. Right away, I knew. I could read the doctors' eyes as ably as I interpreted the eyes of every masked visitor who entered my hospital room when I was a kid. Pity, I learned early on, isn't tough to spot.

Chapter 22: Holly

So strong. So stoic. That's how everyone described me. "It's okay to cry" was a frequent refrain, and "you're allowed to be angry" was fairly popular, too. I knew I was supposed to feel something, anything, but I was numb. *Come on, people! He'll be back in a few hours,* I wanted to tell the throngs of relatives and friends crowding my new house. *He's just making a delivery! Why is everyone so sad?*

One of the few clear memories I have from the shiva week is all the whispering. Thanks to the acoustics of the open space in our unfurnished home, I spent seven days overhearing hushed comments about how "bizarrely" I was coping and what "tremendous shock" I must be in. I loved how everyone I knew had suddenly become an expert on grief.

Whatever I lacked in demonstrable sorrow, however, Jordana made up for tenfold. Her frequent disappearances during the shiva to cry in one of our empty bedrooms were perfectly understandable; other than medical personnel, she'd been the last to see Adam alive. But as the weeks passed and the mere mention of his name continued to break her, I grew annoyed. Our relationship had changed drastically for the better since the Berkshires, and she was now a cherished, central part of my life, but still, I was the widow here. This was my husband we'd buried, not hers.

A month after the funeral, when my official mourning period had ended, things quieted at home. The deli platter deliveries grew more sporadic, my parents and in-laws returned to their snow-bird routines, and my new neighbors settled back into life before we'd become *that* family on their block. The only two people who refused to loosen their grip were Becca and Jordana. They continued to be my wake-up call every morning and my good-night kiss on FaceTime each night.

At their suggestion, I made some promotions at the bakery to ease my responsibilities. There was no way I could juggle a store, a baby, and all the meshugas that come in the aftermath of burying your forty-year-old husband. But the more time I spent in the house, the more I felt Adam's absence. There were double sinks in the master bathroom, his-and-hers closets in our bedroom. Every time I looked at the things we had planned to share, the lonelier I became. I'd imagined so many birthday parties in the backyard, Passover seders in the dining room, Shabbos meals cooked in the kitchen. The loss of our unfulfilled dreams stung as deeply as if I were reminiscing about our past.

And then, exactly two months after Adam died, Ezra began to crawl. We were playing on the floor of the basement when, out of nowhere, he began to slither on his belly toward Adam's drum set. He worked those chubby little arms and legs until he reached the bass and then smacked his open palm against the face of the drum, starting this new chapter of our lives with a literal bang. As he repeated the motion and left saliva polka dots all over the membrane, an exuberant smile expanded across his face, exactly the way Adam's would have. Except for his auburn hair, this kid was his father's clone.

For a minute or two, I shared in his joy. I knew this milestone marked the beginning of his independence and, who knew, maybe even a genuine interest in music. But as he continued to pound, the repeated *thump-thump-thump* drowned out my sentimentality, and the deep, rhythmic sound reminded me of soil thudding against Adam's coffin. I closed my eyes and returned to that frigid afternoon at the cemetery, where a rotation of men with large metal shovels silently heaved piles of earth atop my husband. I shuddered each time dirt hit the wood, but I refused to look away until every inch of that six-foot ditch was filled, as if it were my job to ensure he was cozily packed in for eternity. And yet, despite everything my senses communicated—the feel of rending my garments, the sight of my husband being lowered into the ground, the sound of my voice reciting the mourner's Kaddish prayer beside his grave—the moment somehow lacked finality. Adam was gone and buried so quickly, it occurred to me that I'd missed him less at his funeral than I did every year when he went out of town to visit his brother.

But two months in, as I sat on the basement floor, beholding Ezra's development in Adam's absence, it hit. I began to hyperventilate. My hands grew clammy, my mouth parched; pins and needles prickled all over my face. I scanned the room for a phone to call for help, but both the cordless and the cell were upstairs.

Thwack. Thwack. Thwack. Ezra's cacophonous beats incited a torrent of emotion that twisted and whirled inside me until finally it emerged from my body in the form of a wail. I curled up on the carpet and cupped my hands over my mouth to muffle the cries. He was only eight months old, but I hated for him to see me this way.

These are the moments Adam should have experienced! These are the milestones we were supposed to share! Why him, God? Of all people, why a pious man like him, who wasn't born into observance but chose it? Snot and tears coated my fingers. I noticed the sticks Adam had left neatly on the drum stool and contemplated hurling them across the room but commanded myself to get a grip. *You're the only adult here. You have no backup.*

Drained and sleepy, I willed myself awake and watched as Ezra began to teethe on the shell on the drum. Something about him trying to lick the champagne sparkle finish made me smile.

"You like that, hmm?" I asked, lightly stroking his fuzzy scalp. "Guess you're your daddy's boy; he loved that, too." The past tense stung. I placed my hands a few inches from his back, poised and ready to swoop in with the save in case he lost his balance. And then I wondered, *Who would do the same for me?*

Becca and Jordana must have intuited a change in my tone, because they insisted on coming out the following Sunday. Both had visited regularly since the accident, but, given our decades of tension, Jordana's unyielding, martyr-like support had gone so above and beyond the call of duty that a cynical voice inside me wondered if she had something to hide. I hated myself for doubting her intentions, but I couldn't help it.

When they arrived, Ezra was napping and I was flipping channels in bed. They joined me upstairs and crawled under my covers, and the three of us lay beside one another like sardines. I turned off the TV, and we were all quiet for a moment.

"I was wondering when it would sink in," Becca said, breaking the silence.

"It's a process," Jordana added solemnly, staring at the ceiling, her fingers laced neatly over her abdomen. "You know, I was sort of thinking—and, Hol, if you're not ready for this, just say the word—but maybe we could help you get organized."

I could feel their peripheral vision on me. Clearly, this was not a spur-of-the-moment idea.

"You don't think I'm organized?"

"No, no, of course you are," Becca said. "What I think Jordy's trying to say is that maybe it's time to, you know, clean out some of his things or get your stuff in order."

"Oy, I don't know if I'm ready." I sighed, rubbing my temples.

Jordana rose from the bed and entered Adam's walk-in closet. "Let's just start and see how it goes. We'll do the work. You just relax. Don't move a muscle. Come on, Bec."

I pulled the duvet cover up over my nose so that only my eyes poked out.

"Okay, here we go," Becca said. Jordana grabbed a white button-down shirt off a closet rod and handed it to Becca to present to me.

"Keep, donate, or chuck?" Becca asked gently.

I waved her closer so I could sniff the collar. "Smells like his hair products. Keep."

"Okay. No problem at all. How 'bout this one?" Jordana handed Becca a black blazer. I had no sentimental attachment to the dry cleaner's chemical smell, but when I noticed a dark, paisley-shaped mark on the sleeve, I shook my head. "Can't. Sorry. That's the wine he spilled the night we learned I was pregnant. Keep."

Jordana stepped out of the closet and sat beside me on the bed. "I totally get it," she said, caressing my shoulder. "Maybe we should start with the sock drawer?"

It took four entire Sundays, but by the time April rolled around, his dresser was clear, the closet was bare, and all the miscellaneous items I wanted to keep were neatly organized and labeled in color-coded cartons from the Container Store, courtesy of Jordana. The empty spaces seemed cavernous, and I knew for certain that if this house could not be ours together, I didn't want it as mine alone.

On the final Sunday, as soon as our work was done, Jordana and her electronic label maker returned to the city while Becca and I ordered kosher Chinese takeout for dinner.

"So, I've been meaning to tell you," she started, as we sat at my kitchen table and spooned fried rice onto our plates, "I've been looking at rental apartments. I checked out a few open houses and wanted to show you the listings. We can pull them up online. Wanna look?" She held up her cell phone.

My heart sank. She'd occasionally alluded to tension in her marriage, but I truly didn't think it was separation-worthy.

"Hold on. Rewind." I put down my fork. "You're moving out?"

"What? Me? I'm talking about you! I've been looking at apartments for you and Ezra. I thought maybe you'd want to consider moving closer. To me. And Jord."

She was right. It completely made sense. They were my support, my family. I needed them nearby, and Manhattan was certainly commutable to the bakery.

"In fact, there's actually one that just came up in my parents' high-rise. Similar layout, two floors away. They could help you in a pinch, and I'd be a couple blocks away."

"That would be amazing. I can use all the hands I can get."

"I know . . . and that brings me to the other thing I want to discuss. You need to take care of yourself, not just for your own health and sanity, but for Ezra." She took a swig of water. "I'm not really sure how to say this . . ."

"What? Just say it. It's me."

"Do you have a will? Have you named guardians?"

"Guardians?" I asked, as if I'd never heard of such a thing.

"Yeah, like backup parents in case, God forbid, something happens to you."

Of course I knew what guardians were. I remembered when Becca and Nolan transferred the embryo that would ultimately become Emma into their surrogate. They called up their lawyer, even before Elizabeth had a positive pregnancy test, to draw up a will and name Becca's parents as the guardians in case something were to happen to Becca and Nolan before the birth. The lawyer, a trusts-and-estates hotshot at Nolan's firm, admitted it was his first time ever assigning guardians to an unborn child.

"No, I haven't really thought about it," I lied. "I guess I should."

"Maybe it's time. And, for the record"—she put her hand on mine and began to tear up—"I love you, and I love your son. I'm here for you and for him. Always."

I felt punched in the gut. The truth was, I had given it a lot of thought. Before Ezra was born, I would lie awake at night, dreaming about life as a parent. Since Adam died, those same wee hours had been consumed by fear about what life would be like for my child without parents.

Who would love Ezra the way I do? I'd ask myself. *Who would give him a solid family he could rely on and consider his own? Who would know Adam and me well enough to be able to say things like, "Oh, you got your sweet tooth from your mommy!" or, "Your dad loved the North American Mammals exhibit at the Museum of Natural History, too!" Whom could I trust to pass on our cherished Jewish traditions, to honor our choice of a yeshiva education, to explain to my son that, in spite of this devastating loss, my faith in God remained steadfast? And who could thoughtfully articulate that the religious decisions Adam and I made were not intended to be Ezra's life sentences—that one day, should our son find himself somewhere else on, or even off, the wide spectrum of Jewish observance, it's okay? He's allowed to question. He's permitted to challenge. He can think for himself. All we ask is that he be a mensch. Our love for him would be unconditional, eternally.*

The answer to each question was abundantly clear. It wasn't

a relative. It wasn't any of my Orthodox friends from Brooklyn. And it wasn't anyone at the bakery. It was Becca.

Just do it! I'd tell myself. *Call the stupid lawyer already and put her name in the will!* But each time I'd pick up the phone, I'd hang up. I felt like absolute shit for thinking it, but the facts were the facts: she was a two-time cancer survivor. How could I leave my baby in the care of someone with that track record? Yes, she'd beaten the odds twice, but what if, God forbid, there was a third time? Would she be as lucky? My son had already lost one parent. If he got passed off to a guardian, it would mean he'd lost both. Did I really want to set him up to lose his guardian, too?

And then there was the issue of Nolan. The guy loved my kid and was a wonderful dad. The trouble was, I didn't know where their marriage was headed. My money was on everything working out, but I couldn't predict the future. Knowingly putting my son in the hands of a rocky couple just didn't seem right. The thought of Ezra's becoming both an orphan and the child of divorced guardians broke me.

Ezra's best interest had to be my priority. But what constituted *best interest?* Living with a fantastic family that came with red flags, or someone with a lower statistical risk of illness and divorce but not nearly as dear to me? If I could be guaranteed Becca would never get sick and she and Nolan would remain happily married for the next fifty years, the papers would be signed. But that wasn't reality. Shit happens, as I knew all too well. The question became: Could I trust Becca's health and marriage to remain strong?

Though I lacked clarity on that issue, I did have a clear vision about our living situation. I put the house up for sale—it sold within days—and rented that two-bedroom on the Upper West Side near Becca's parents. Ezra and I moved in just as the trees in Central Park were beginning to bloom.

On our first Friday night, I decided to host dinner for all three families—Becca's, Jordana's, and mine. I needed to feel settled and knew that for me, there was no better way to create a sense of warmth and belonging than to cook, bake, and welcome the Sabbath with loved ones. Becca's mom graciously offered to take Ezra to the building's playroom while I prepared. When everyone arrived that evening, we lit the silver Sabbath candlesticks beside a framed photograph of Adam and then took turns squeezing onto my tiny balcony to watch the sun dip down over the Hudson. As the kids created spaceships out of empty cardboard moving boxes and the adults sipped wine around my table, I felt, for the first time in months, hopeful and alive. I was home.

At the end of the night, Jordana was the last to leave. Becca, Nolan, and Emma stopped by her parents' place to say hi, and Sal wanted to tucker out the twins before bedtime, so he made them run a relay race down the building's stairwell. As Jordana waited for the elevator to arrive, we stood in my doorway, where she asked me, for the quadrillionth time, if there was anything I needed.

"Actually, I think I'm doing okay," I said. It was the first occasion since the accident that I'd uttered those words aloud and meant them. "Thanks for supporting me, Jord. You've gone above and beyond. I don't think I'd be standing up without you."

Jordana's face fell, and her porcelain skin flushed so brightly that it matched her fuchsia skirt.

"You know," she said, her eyes fixed intensely on the marble saddle between my apartment and the hallway, "I've been meaning to tell you something." She fidgeted with the purse strap across her denim jacket. "Adam . . . He . . . um . . ." She pressed her fingers to her lips, forcing them shut like a dam. They lingered for several seconds, as if she were forcing herself to swallow a bitter pill. "He really loved you and Ezra," she finally said. "I feel like he's watching over you and would want you to know that."

I felt my eyes mist. "Thanks. I still can't believe this is my reality."

"*Our* reality," she corrected. And then her elevator arrived.

Part Three

Chapter 23: Becca

*A*fter a delightful Sunday morning touring the grounds of the Chicago Botanic Garden, Jordana and I walked a few blocks east into Highland Park and helped transform a suburban backyard into something resembling a Pier 1 window display. We hung colorful paper lanterns from tree branches, set out folding chairs, secured tiki torches in the ground, and turned a cloth-covered card table into a snack bar. It was a far cry from the last celebration we had attended in the Windy City—Lex and Jack's three-hundred-person, ten-piece band, black-tie wedding at a hotel on the Magnificent Mile—and the contrast with the way in which Lex chose to usher in this new chapter of her life was not lost on us.

"Think of it as a housewarming-slash-kickoff party," she'd said when pitching the idea of a celebration following Seth's June 30 move-in date. "Surprising him in his new backyard with you guys as the guests would be really fun. Don't you think?"

Though his online résumé submission had been the whimsical product of late-night tipsiness, Seth had received a job offer from a prominent physical therapy group in Chicago. He and Lex took it as a sign of fate, and one week later, he broke the lease on his New York apartment and rented a split-level ranch in Highland Park, Illinois, with three bedrooms and a playground on the corner. It was way more space than he needed, but only a ten-minute drive from Lex, and if his dream of being a cool step-dad one day were going to come to fruition, he'd do whatever was necessary to win their approval. Unfortunately, despite Seth's best efforts, her kids wanted absolutely nothing to do with him. From their perspective, their perfectly happy mother had gone away on a weekend vacation with her childhood friends and returned no longer in love with their father. To them, it was all Seth's fault. But Lex and Seth remained optimistic. They believed the kids would gradually come around and realize their mom was much happier.

Around noon on Sunday, after she managed to convince Seth that he was in dire need of a trip to Crate & Barrel for housewares, I received an "all clear" text from Lex. Jordana and I left the Botanic Garden and walked over to his new house on Pleasant Avenue.

By midafternoon, the ice buckets were filled, the music cued, and the citronella candles lit. Jordana and I made iced tea and walked around to peruse the framed photographs Lex had organized for us to display on scattered tray tables throughout the yard.

"Oh my God, did you see this one?" Jordana said, waving me over to a class picture of all of us from second grade. We were sitting cross-legged on the floor of our elementary-school library. Jordana and her perfect Cindy Brady braids were smack in the middle, holding the sign with the year and our teacher's name.

As I moved in for a closer look, my phone rang with a Face-Time request.

"Hey, Hol," Jordana and I said in unison when the connection came through. She was attempting to feed Ezra on her lap, but he kept grabbing the loose strands of her ponytail. "You're the first guest to arrive!"

"Give me a tour! Maybe if this little guy sees you on the iPad screen, he'll calm down and I'll get some of this sweet potato into him."

Jordana sighed. "Oh, Hol, don't get him hooked on using screens for self-control, especially at the table. They're ruining kids' social skills and ability to—"

"Hey, Miss Manners," Holly interrupted with a laugh, "I love you and I hear you, but right now I'm desperate."

Before Jordana could say any more, I channeled my best radio-announcer voice and began panning across Seth's backyard. "And here, ladies and gentleman, you'll find a single detached garage with a basketball hoop and slightly rusted chaise lounges stacked inside. To the left of the garage, you'll see a charcoal grill with gen-u-ine briquettes for all your barbecuing needs and a lovely garden of blue and white hydrangea . . ."

"It's working. He's eating. You've got the touch!" Holly smiled. "Sorry I can't be there in person, but I know you guys understand."

Ever since Adam had died, Holly had become highly risk-averse, particularly when it came to travel. Though she had named Jordana and me as Ezra's guardians in her will, she took every precaution to avoid leaving him in our permanent care. She refused to fly, ride the subway, or even cross a bridge without him by her side, which made overseeing her bakery's franchise locations a logistical nightmare. In fact, she'd started bouncing around the idea of selling Holly's Challahs altogether and opening a kosher café in Adam's name on the Upper West Side.

"Of course we understand," Jordana said, and blew a kiss.

"You know what," Holly said, attempting to transfer a whimpering, squirmy Ezra into his high chair. "I think I need to go. I'll call you later, when he's napping."

"Sounds good," I said, and noticed Seth's mom sauntering into the backyard in a sequined beige tank, white slacks, and a blinding amount of cubic zirconium. "The guests are starting to arrive anyway. I'm gonna go play hostess."

Walking behind Mrs. Gottlieb was Mr. Gottlieb, who looked just as cherubic and stout as he had when we were kids. His physique was, without question, exactly what Seth would look like if he forfeited daily exercise.

"Well, hellooo, ladies!" Mr. Gottlieb said, leaning in for a kiss. I smelled his generous application of Old Spice aftershave.

"Jaw-dy! Becca! Can you believe? The day has arrived!" Mrs. Gottlieb was positively exuberant. Other than Seth's birth and bar mitzvah, this was quite possibly the greatest moment of her life. His interstate relocation for a girlfriend had heightened the possibility that one day her son might actually get married.

"I still can't believe it! Lex and my Sethie! Who knew? I guess betta late than nevah, right?" she chuckled, before her smoker's cough acted up.

"Can I get you a drink?" Jordana asked.

"No, I'm fine, sweetheart," she said, clearing her throat. "Seventy ain't for sissies!" She looked at Jordana. "You know, I see the way you visit your parents all the time. It's a beautiful thing. They're very lucky to have a daughter like you."

"It really is my pleasure," said Jordana, though at times I wondered how she did it all. Even with round-the-clock help at home, balancing a full-time job, twins, and being the only child of aging parents was a hefty load. Amazingly, she never complained. In fact, she viewed the multiple visits to her parents each week not as cumbersome but as cherished time spent together. I wondered if Nolan and I would ever be a burden to Emma. If she grew up to be half the mensch Jordana was, we'd be incredibly lucky.

"Maybe I'll take that drink after all," Seth's mom said. "You think I could get a dirty martini around here? Those green olives are very tasty."

"I'll make one for you," I said. "I was just heading inside." As I walked past, she grabbed my arm and pulled me close.

"Honey, you look beautiful," she whispered into my ear. "We were such a wreck when we heard about you last summer. I see your mother every once in a while at the beauty parlor. She gives me updates. Thank God you're okay. We love you, darling. Only good health." She kissed my cheek in the same spot where her husband had left his cologne.

I smiled. "Thank you, Mrs. Gottlieb. I love you, too."

As I surreptitiously wiped off her lipstick on my way into the house, someone tapped my shoulder from behind.

"So, what's a girl like you doing in a place like this?" Nolan asked, sidling up beside me and wrapping his arm around my waist. "Come here often?"

I leaned my head onto his shoulder. "Did you pick up the food?"

"Done. The sandwiches are packaged, and the picnic baskets are all set. I even stopped to get the lay of the land and picked out a prime spot for us at the concert tonight."

As part of her surprise for Seth, Lex had purchased lawn tickets for our small party to attend Ravinia, the Midwest equivalent of Tanglewood, only a few short blocks from Seth's new house. The plan was to greet him in the backyard, schmooze for a bit, and then walk over to picnic on the lawn and listen to the Chicago Symphony Orchestra.

When Lex called to invite us, I wasn't sure Nolan would want to go. He and Seth had moved past their tension in the Berkshires, but the parameters of their friendship had been redrawn. Seth no longer straddled the line; he was unequivocally on Team Becca. While it was flattering, the knowledge that Seth thought I could do better saddened me. I wanted my friends to be Nolan's fans, for their love to affirm my love. If they could forgive him, maybe I could, too.

To his credit, Nolan was all in, not only for the Chicago trip but also in terms of working on our marriage. Adam's death hit hard. Seeing Holly widowed and Ezra lose a father uncorked something inside him. He arranged for my parents to babysit every Thursday so that he and I could have a dinner date to reconnect. In addition, and completely on his own volition, he reached out to the Long-Term Survivorship department at the hospital where I was treated and asked to meet a counselor specializing in spousal support. He had no interest in group sessions or regular therapy but found the reading material helpful and continued to check in whenever he felt the need for a tune-up.

Back in Highland Park, Jordana was once again in charge. "Quiet, everybody—they're coming!" she said, hushing the guests and corralling them to a corner of the yard.

"I really don't understand why buying new dish towels had to happen this morning," we could hear Seth remark to Lex as they made their way down the driveway. "I could have gone to the gym—"

"Surprise!" everyone yelled, as he reached the grass.

He dropped the shopping bag and looked at Lex, stunned. "Did you know about this?"

"I planned it," she said tenderly. "Welcome home. Everyone wanted to make sure you felt comfortable and settled. Especially me."

Seth greeted his parents, high-fived Sal and Nolan, enveloped me in a bear hug, and gave strong, prolonged handshakes to two Chicago couples who had come—the only people out of countless friends who'd sided with Lex, not Jack. Even then, the husbands looked as if they had been dragged into that backyard because their wives had told them they had no choice.

"Hors d'oeuvres, anyone?" Jordana asked, as she balanced a tray of pigs in a blanket on her palm like a waitress and descended the steps from the back door into the yard. Seth ran over, kissed her cheek, and popped a hot dog into his mouth.

"So, when are the kids coming?" he called out across the lawn to Lex.

As everyone turned to her for a response, her face fell. A second later, she forced a broad smile and sidled up to Seth, linking her arm with his. "Oh, they, um . . . they were all invited to parties for the holiday," she said.

He looked crestfallen. "Next time, I guess," he said, and wiped the crumbs from his mouth. I saw something dim in his eyes, and it hurt my heart.

There was no question he'd taken a tremendous risk by moving halfway across the country for a woman who was technically still married. The divorce was messier than Lex had anticipated. While she had expected the kids to live with her in the stately center-hall colonial they'd called home for fifteen years (and which she had recently spent six figures redecorating with a famed interior designer who'd appeared on HGTV), her oldest son wanted to move out and live with his father. He shouted this preference at her one afternoon while running out the door to hockey practice. Lex immediately vomited and then called me, sobbing. "Where's my happy ending?" she asked between cries.

The best advice I could come up with was generic and cliched: "Follow your heart; the rest will fall into place." What that would ultimately mean for Seth, however, I wasn't sure.

Unlike Tanglewood's pastoral vibe, Ravinia was a bit glossier. Both venues possessed a large amphitheater with sprawling grass for guests to picnic on, but as we stepped over people's legs and navigated around wicker baskets on our search for an open spot,

I noticed many more candelabras atop beverage coolers than I'd seen in Lenox, Massachusetts.

"Follow me," Nolan said, his hand in the air like a tour guide's. Somehow, he found a perfect setting beneath a tree. We plopped ourselves down among a sea of blankets, just as we had one year before.

As we unpacked and passed around the sandwiches, my phone rang with another video-chat request. This time, it was Emma and my parents calling.

"Hi, beautiful girl!" I said when her face appeared on my father's cell phone screen.

"Hi, Mommy! Guess where I am!"

"Where, munchkin?"

"I'm on the roof of Aunt JoJo's apartment building, watching fireworks! See?" She pointed the phone's camera at my parents, who were waving and blowing kisses but not speaking, as if it were a silent film from the 1920s.

"Wow! You *are*?" I asked with mock surprise. I knew Jordana had made the arrangements for them. Given that her parents were watching AJ and Matthew, my parents had Emma, and Holly was home with Ezra, she had given her doorman permission to let them up to the building's roof to take in the spectacular views of the East River show.

"Look at that!" Emma said, and turned the camera around so I could witness the exploding colors in the night sky. She zoomed in closer, over to the Queensboro Bridge and the surrounding buildings that made the skyline twinkle. When she did, I caught a glimpse of the distinct brick facade of the hospital that helped save my life—twice. It was right there, a quiet, enigmatic bystander on the bottom edge of the screen, as if it were an extra in a movie. It hadn't snagged the lead role, but it played a memorable part.

The Chicago Symphony Orchestra walked onto Ravinia's stage, and the audience erupted.

Emma caught another gorgeous burst of color, this time directly over the hospital, and then handed the phone to my parents.

"Happy Independence Day, sweetheart," Mom said, positioning the camera so that their three faces smushed together in an Emma sandwich. Mom winked at me—an unspoken acknowledgment of the significance of the day.

"So, what do you think? Some view, eh, kiddo?" Dad said, and shot my mother a knowing glance, before clearing his throat. "We just couldn't let you miss it."

As the music of *Swan Lake* filled the air, Nolan inched closer on the blanket and wrapped his arm around my shoulders. I glanced at my friends on the lawn, and then over at my parents and daughter on the phone's screen. "Thanks, Dad," I said, marveling at my life's script. "The fireworks are great, but the view I've got right now is pretty remarkable."

Acknowledgments

When you spend several years working on a book, there are many people to thank.

First, I would like to acknowledge the inspiration for this novel: the ten families from Hollis Hills who comprised the cast and crew of the original *Saturday Night Live*-style videotape. Their generosity, humor, and compassion left an indelible mark on me and set the standard for true friendship.

I would also like to acknowledge the late David Klatell, a phenomenal teacher and gem of a man, for suggesting I turn my master's project into a book. I don't think either one of us expected it to become a novel, but he planted the seed that ultimately blossomed into this work.

I am enormously grateful to Jennie Nash for her insight, sharp eye, and hand-holding throughout the early phases of this manuscript. A writer could not ask for a better sounding board or cheerleader.

I am deeply appreciative of the lovely Lisa Grubka for her passion, confidence, editorial finesse, and steadfast commitment.

Thank you to the team at SparkPress—Brooke Warner, Lauren Wise, Crystal Patriarche, Rebecca Lown, and Annie Tucker— for making this dream a reality and for connecting me with the phenomenal Ann-Marie Nieves whose tireless publicity efforts have helped shine a spotlight on this book.

I am extremely thankful for the those who graciously read, reread, critiqued, and rooted for this book throughout its various stages of development: Michelle Witman, Rebecca Raphael Feuerstein, Kira Bartlett, Rebecca Schwartz, Molly Morse Rothstein, Stephanie S. Goldstein, Yvette Sharret, Andrea Lieberman, Kelly Mamaysky, Jackie Friedland, Melinda Goldman, Leslie Levin, Diane Pallone, Ericka Schnitzer-Reese, Amanda Bergen, Vivi Septimus, and especially Beth Erdos and Debbie Zucker, who analyzed the lives of each character and adopted my imaginary friends as their own.

Without a doubt, I hit the jackpot in the parents and sibling department. I am proud and blessed beyond all measure to be Vicki and Joel Blumenfeld's daughter and Josh Blumenfeld's sister. They are the gold standard of human beings; the ultimate examples of how to live life as a mensch. "Follow your bliss" and "just be yourself" were credos Josh and I were taught growing up in our parents' home. The existence of this book, and its underlying message about the importance of authenticity, are proof that their advice was heeded.

I owe a tremendous debt of gratitude to my husband, Dan. I am so very lucky to have a partner whose love and devotion I never question. He has championed this book, and the greater cause, from day one, and I am grateful for his unyielding support and dedication to our dreams, values, and family. Judy and Marvin Kamensky, thank you for raising "such a good boychick."

And finally, to Mia Natalie. You are my prize. My heart. It was worth it all to get to you.

About the Author

*A*my Blumenfeld's articles and essays have appeared in various publications, including the *New York Times*, the *Huffington Post*, *O, The Oprah Magazine*, *George*, and *Moment*, as well as on the cover of *People*. She is a graduate of Barnard College and the Columbia University Graduate School of Journalism, where she was the recipient of the James A. Wechsler Award for National Reporting. She has been interviewed on the CBS Evening News, FOX News, MSNBC, and NY1 and has contributed to two nonfiction books. She lives in New York with her husband and daughter. This is her first novel.

Author photo © Diana Berrent Photography

Selected Titles From SparkPress

SparkPress is an independent boutique publisher delivering high-quality, entertaining, and engaging content that enhances readers' lives, with a special focus on female-driven work. Visit us at www.gosparkpress.com

Just Like February, Deborah Batterman, $16.95, 978-1-943006-48-9. Rachel Cohen loves her Uncle Jake more than anything. When she learns he's gay, she keeps it under wraps, and when he gets sick, she doesn't even tell her best friends—until she realizes that secrecy does more harm than good.

Love Reconsidered, Phyllis Piano, $16.95, 978-1-943006-20-5. A page-turning contemporary tale of how three memorable characters seek to rebuild their lives after betrayal and tragedy with the help of new relationships, loyal corgi dogs, home-cooked meals, and the ritual of football Sundays.

Elly in Bloom, Colleen Oakes. $15, 978-1-94071-609-1. Elly Jordan has carved out a sweet life for herself as a boutique florist in St. Louis. Not bad for a woman who left her life two years earlier when she found her husband entwined with a redheaded artist. Just when she feels she is finally moving on from her past, she discovers a wedding contract, one that could change her financial future, is more than she bargained for.

Gridley Girls, Meredith First. $17, 978-1-940716-97-8. From the moment Meg Monahan became a peer counselor in high school, she has been keeping her friend's secrets. Flash forward to adulthood when Meg is a recruiter for the world's hippest, most paranoid high-tech company, and now she is paid to keep secrets. When sudden tragedy strikes just before Meg hosts the wedding of her childhood BFF, the women are forced to face their past—and their secrets—in order to move on to their future.

On Grace, Susie Orman Schnall. $15, 978-1-94071-613-8. Grace is actually excited to turn 40 in a few months—that is until her job, marriage, and personal life take a dizzying downhill spiral. Can she recover from the most devastating time in her life, right before it's supposed to be one of the best?

About SparkPress

SparkPress is an independent, hybrid imprint focused on merging the best of the traditional publishing model with new and innovative strategies. We deliver high-quality, entertaining, and engaging content that enhances readers' lives. We are proud to bring to market a list of *New York Times* best-selling, award-winning, and debut authors who represent a wide array of genres, as well as our established, industry-wide reputation for creative, results-driven success in working with authors. SparkPress, a BookSparks imprint, is a division of SparkPoint Studio LLC.

Learn more at GoSparkPress.com